MISCONCEPTION

D1520616

MISCONCEPTION

Avner Hershlag

iUniverse, Inc.
New York   Bloomington

MISCONCEPTION

Copyright © 2010 Avner Hershlag

iUniverse books may be ordered through booksellers or by contacting:

iUniverse
1663 Liberty Drive
Bloomington, IN 47403
www.iuniverse.com
1-800-Authors (1-800-288-4677)

ISBN: 978-1-4401-8387-4 (pbk)
ISBN: 978-1-4401-8389-8 (cloth)
ISBN: 978-1-4401-8388-1 (ebk)

Printed in the United States of America

iUniverse rev. date: 3/1/2010

In loving memory of my parents,

My mother, Mania Hershlag

And my father, Professor Zvi Yehudah Hershlag

And God created man

in his own image,

in the image of God

created He him ...

Genesis 1:28

In a country where the right to bear arms is a constitutional amendment, I propose a new amendment, the first for this century: The right for every woman to bear a child.

Dr. Anya Krim, in testimony before the Senate Subcommittee on Reproductive Rights

Prologue

Bethesda, Maryland

This time I won't let the doctor pull down my underwear. No way will this man feel my balls again and measure my penis with a yardstick. I hate him. I hate the clinic.

For six months, Mom's been dragging me every week to this nightmare of a place, to see the awful doctor. The freezing stethoscope and his cold hands give me the creeps. Why would the bastard think his white coat gives him the right to embarrass me in front of the nurse, telling her with his smart-ass attitude to look at my private parts, pulling my elastic without permission?

I look awful in the mirror, with just my boxers on. Like Mom always says, I'm all skin and bones. And my arms are so skinny and long—down to my knees, like a monkey. If they have kids strip here in the middle of winter, can't the government pay for a little heat? Whatever. I think the president's keeping all the money to himself.

Yessss. The blond nurse is back. Her hands are warm. Sure, take my blood pressure. You want the other arm, too? She smells good. I wish she'd keep leaning over like that. Haven't seen a better pair of legs—not ever. I wish this part of the visit would last forever.

"So let's see how much progress we've made," the doctor says. Short and ugly in his white coat, the sleeves stained with some brown stuff, he stands there like a rock star waiting for applause. He makes me spread my arms apart. He takes the stupid magnifying glass out of his dirty coat and goes searching for gold in my armpit. Hope he chokes from the stink.

"No hair follicles," the doctor dictates to the nurse with not a touch of emotion, like a mechanic checking under the hood. Duh. I could've told him that without the magnifying glass.

Now comes the part I really hate. "Could you please pull down your underpants for me, young man?"

I wish the animal wouldn't see me like this, drenched in sweat. He makes me feel like a lab rat.

I can still hear them laugh. Boys and girls. I imagine that jerk standing in front of the entire class, giving an anatomy lesson on my private parts as I walk in late one day. They all stop cold, short of some giggles in the back, but I still catch a glimpse of the "model" of my privates that he had made from two olives and a toothpick. That's how Mom finds out I'm different than the other boys in class, when I start coming home on lunch-break to use the john. Next thing she does is drag me here. Every Wednesday afternoon I have to visit the NIH clinic for odd-looking kids.

"Young man, we don't have all day."

The little toad is scolding me now. Doctors have no feelings. To him, I'm one more experiment. Nothing else. Now he comes closer and tries to pull down on my elastic.

"No!" I push the doctor. Takes him by complete surprise. His face's bright red from his puffy cheeks through his wide forehead to what's left of his hairline. An overripe tomato.

"Mom, could you come in for a moment?" He calls my mother, "Mom." Creep.

Mom steps in. The small room feels crowded.

"Honey, let them finish the exam. We have reservations at O'Donnell's for lunch."

Big fuckin' deal. Mom is sweet. But it's this grown-up thing again. Bribe your kid and make him do something he really hates doing. Besides, the only thing I really like at O'Donnell's is sneaking into the kitchen and watching them take one of the live crabs out of the tank and dump it in the boiling water.

The doctor comes near me. No. Not again, mister. This time I push him so hard the scumbag has zero chance of touching my underpants again. The doctor takes a step back and hits the wall behind him. He's shaking with anger. Great.

Mom says, "Let me talk to him alone." The doctor and the nurse leave.

"Honey—"

"I know, Mom. It's for my sake. You've told me a million times this doctor was going to help. But he's done zilch. I'm just good for some f—" I swallow the rest of it. My way of avoiding soap in my mouth tonight.

"This doctor doesn't give two hoots about me. The other day I heard him tell his nurse that I'm part of a study he has to do for the NIH. He's like that Dr. Mengele we learned about in sch—"

"Shush. Don't you ever mention that Nazi again. What a horrible thing to say. Now, you've got to let him finish this."

"Tell you what," I decide to compromise, "I'll let him do it if he doesn't call the nurse in."

Mom promises the doctor I'll behave. I love it. The ugly duckling is scared shitless of a twelve-year-old.

Round three. The little doc and me. Alone. The nurse behind the screen, Mom outside the door. This could be the knockout. Maybe I could bite his ear ... I smile. No more taking advantage of a little boy. I'm in charge now.

"I'll do it myself," I say. I pull down my Calvins. It's still embarrassing, but I feel better.

The doctor approaches me. Still a bit shaky. Again the stupid magnifying glass.

"No pubic hair," he dictates to the nurse behind the curtain. Now he takes his "oddballs"—this ridiculous-looking string of different-size plastic balls. He measures them against my balls.

"Size one."

Guess it didn't get much lower than that. Thank God he isn't asking the nurse if they grew from last time. His cold hands mash my balls. Gross. "Soft," he adds.

Now for the yardstick. "Penis one and a half inches. Any change?"

Asshole.

"No, doctor," says the nurse. I guess from her tone she also hates his guts.

Mom and I walk into his office to hear the verdict. The little judge sits there behind his desk, indifferent, avoiding eye contact, pretending he's too busy going through my chart.

"I'm afraid we haven't made much progress, Mom."

Mom asks, "Have you found out what's wrong with my boy?" She squeezes my hand. Mom is the only person in the whole world who cares about me. Even Dad totally freaked out on our first visit. Couldn't deal.

"The boy has Fragile Y Syndrome," the doctor leans back in his chair. For the first time, his lips thin out, attempting a smile.

"What exactly is Frail Y—?"

"Fragile Y," Frankenstein corrects my mom. "It's a genetic problem he was born with. And nothing can be done to change it. His Y chromosome is weak. You know. The X, the kind that girls have, is okay."

Mom tightens her grip on my hand. She feels me making a fist. Ready when you are Mister I-don't-give-a-damn-how-my-patient-feels. Maybe this time I'll bite your ear off. Then you'd really see chromosomes.

Fuckin' jerk. Winner of the gold medal for zero compassion. He tells me I have some horrible disease—and all of a sudden, he's all smiles. My misery makes him happy!

Mom feels me getting ready to jump to my feet and beat the hell out of the shmuck. She pulls me back.

"He is *a boy, right?"*

"Of course." He tries to please her. Maybe he's sensing danger. Then he strikes again. "He's a little boy with a weak Y chromosome. His penis and testicles will always be small."

Thanks for making me feel so good. So special. I wish I'd never met you.

"What will he be like as an adult?" Mom's voice sounds shaky.

"Tall and skinny. With a micropenis and two microtesticles."

Why don't you rub it in, mister? I think you should show me yours.

"He'll most probably have no sperm. So, he'll most probably be, hmmm. sterile."

You think I didn't get it, right? You just told my mother I'll never be able to have children.

"Oh, and one more thing. These kids are frequently low achievers in school. They sometimes have to attend special classes. Usually they don't make it to college. But they can do menial work. Society has been pretty good—"

"Bastard!"

Yeah, Mom. Give it to him. Give it to him good.

Mom stands up now, tall and angry, leaning over the desk, looking down at the ugly dwarf.

He raises his hands, as if she's pulling a gun on him. "Sorry, but noth—"

"Nothing can be done to change it. I heard you the first time. Now you listen to me. Listen to me good. You may be a big fucking professor at the NIH, but I've got news for you. You know nothing about the human beings that you try to tack these fancy diagnoses on. Fragile Y or not, my boy is not a low achiever. He's the best student in his entire class. You hear me? The best."

Finally, we're out of that awful place. It feels good to know we're never coming back here again. Never. I clutch Mom's hand and stay real close to her, as my feet crunch the fall leaves that carpet the NIH grounds.

Mom is the only one who ever stood up for me. Always. I love her so much my heart hurts.

Reprotech Inc., West Virginia, twenty-eight years later

What made this dog different from any other dog they'd been working on?

Dr. Jeremy Coddington, known as Cody, gripped the legs of the anti-vibration worktable with both hands, praying his fine tremor, the kind he always developed under pressure, would escape the eyes of his boss, Hugh Nicholson. While Cody remained seated, Nicholson's gaunt, hunched-over body paced the small room, eyeing the computer screen every few seconds. The voltage in the room ran high.

A little excitement couldn't hurt, Cody thought. *Keeps my coronaries open.* This wasn't remotely close to the stress in obstetrics.

When Nicholson had offered him the job two years ago and told him he wanted him to clone dogs, Cody thought the idea was ludicrous. Why would anyone waste all these resources—the time, the money, the emotions—on such an effort? There were so many other worthy causes.

It seemed like ages ago, when after a sleepless night on the labor floor trying to fend off the next disaster, Cody would wait bleary-eyed with a twenty-four-hour-old beard in front of the OB board for his fellow residents' daily lynching. They'd gang up on him—an easy target, progressively more reclusive, and never "one of the guys." He was shorter than everybody, even the female residents. And when they surrounded him, he'd shrink even further into his bloody scrubs, ready for the guillotine. "Why didn't you use 'spoons' on the baby's head … or vacuum … and fucking pull this nine-pound baby out?" the female chief resident, his nemesis, would yell in front of his peers. The others were buddies, shedding their obstetrical anxieties at the First Amendment bar every Friday night. He never went with them. He didn't think doctors should drink.

"This baby was born blue, thanks to you. And he's seizing now." He'd hear the chief resident's words in his sleep. Night after night, his obstetrical disasters would come back as nightmares. Babies he'd delivered would show up as deformed adults, screaming to his face, "What have you done to us?"

So, he'd taken the job with Nicholson and now woke up in the bowels of the old WW II shelter Nicholson had chosen for his cloning operation, where no one would ever think of looking for him. He felt safe.

Okay. He cloned dogs. Beats OB. Or anything else where he'd be held accountable for human lives. Not that cloning was an easy feat. But in two years, Cody was back to himself, realizing it was only his anxiety that had made him a klutz on the OB floor. That he really didn't have two left hands. He'd actually succumbed to what everyone else was saying—that he was *dangerous.* Any mishap could mean another life put in jeopardy, another baby born compromised … defective … handicapped … dead! Here at the shelter, he worked with molecules, not living, breathing humans whose lives were in immediate peril, abandoned in Cody's unskilled hands.

Working alone for hours on his tiny clones would normally put him in a Zen mode, feeling more relaxed than on a therapist's sofa. He'd mastered the technique, operated with low anxiety. His self-esteem had made a comeback. His hands were now rock stable. Here they had transformed into *two right hands!*

The boss's pacing made him uneasy. Nicholson rarely came to the lab. Surrounded by a million dollars-worth of equipment, with twelve incubators stacked up two at a time, his workstation, the place where he operated on dot-of-dust size embryos under the microscope, already felt claustrophobic.

Cody had no idea what made today's job so special. By now, they'd successfully cloned over a dozen dogs. All different breeds. So what's the big fuss over the Cavalier King Charles spaniel? Was it the money? The boss had a habit of blending business with science. The customer had brought Cookie, his nine-year-old dog, to be cloned—Cookie, who was dying of mitral valve disease. The customer had also brought a print of the van Dyck painting of King Charles flanked by two spaniels to use as a prototype.

Nicholson stopped pacing and pointed at the painting that rested against the wall next to Cody's station. "These spaniels clearly have a longer nose than sick mom here."

"I can't make the nose any longer," Cody said.

"I didn't ask you to. How about checking for mitral valve disease in the clone?"

"Done. And I've screened for all the other diseases that shorten these dogs' lives."

"Such as?"

"Problems with heart, hips, knees, and eyes. We're screening each embryo for all four systems and will identify the healthiest one."

"What about syringomyelia?"

Cody wasn't sure he heard right. True, Nicholson had gotten a bachelor's in Biology from Penn before starting Wharton Business School, but Cody had never heard a layperson mention this rare condition before. Even the enunciation was impeccable.

"It's that condition where water replaces part of the spinal cord. The dog gets weak in the knees, sometimes can't walk at all," Cody's boss explained.

"Honestly, Mr. Nicholson, I have no clue how to screen for it. There's currently no DNA test available."

"Let's hope we'll get lucky and the dog won't develop it."

Cody sighed. He knew not to expect a pat on the shoulder. Nicholson was not one to praise him for what he *was* able to do. Genetic screening would likely give the newly cloned King Charles a healthier, longer life. But Nicholson's talent was to find that one thing Cody was *unable* to do. The boss demanded perfection from himself, as well as from anyone who worked for him.

Cody remembered Anya. How he missed her! After another rough night on Labor and Delivery, she'd come into the tiny call room in her blue scrubs, her hair still wet from the shower, and sit on the edge of the bed across from him, her hands smelling of lavender soap. In the intimacy of the call room, Anya would go over each case they'd overseen that night, pointing out his errors, making sure not to deflate any confidence left in him. Anya was quick to praise his intellect, his scientific advantage over the rest of the residents, reminding him of their Harvard Medical School days, where Cody was king. Down in the obstetric trenches, Anya Krim would find the right words. She'd reassure him that mistakes in patient care were allowed in residency, that they were part of the learning curve. But Cody knew she was just being kind. He had watched her in action.

The thought of the two of them alone, sitting on the bed in the call room, inhaling her scent, Anya's scrubs revealing but a hint of her shapely figure … time and again he'd play it out in his dreams, in his fantasies. Dreaming of her, of them, was his escape from the daily horrors reality had presented him. Yet, he was never as acutely aware of how much he'd desired her until one day, over lunch, she'd told him she started dating this guy, Dario. The sharp pang came with no warning. The hatred toward the man he hadn't met for snatching "his" Anya. The anger toward her for betraying him. And later, alone again, his self-esteem dropped to a new low. He was a fool to think he'd ever had a chance with Anya. She'd only seen him in one crisis. And then another. And another. Pitiful? Yes. Attractive? No.

Now he missed having his closest friend and ally beside him. As far as Cody was concerned, it was Anya Krim who provided the crutches for him to hop on from one year to the next until he graduated Lincoln Hospital's OB/Gyn residency.

No use looking back. Cody was grateful to Nicholson for taking him in, for recognizing his scientific talent. He knew how much Nicholson detested doctors, and that it was an unusual move for him to hire a physician.

"Do you realize the revolution that cloning is about to bring?" Nicholson now cracked what Cody considered a smile. "Breeding is for the birds, a bad genetic experiment. You start out mating two award-winning animals, and if you're lucky, what do you get? An offspring like Cookie, as pretty as Mom and Dad or prettier. But then what? Its life span is bound to be shortened, because no one checked for the disease genes that are rampant in the breed."

Nicholson is a man of vision, Cody pondered. Always thinks big.

"We *should* be able to get them back to their normal life span," Nicholson countered. "It's why cloning is superior to breeding. Leaving things to nature is too risky. Cloning's going to replace all breeding. The reason why the suicide rate is so high among breeders—"

"It is?"

"Don't interrupt me. Is that they could never satisfy the sophisticated customer, who can easily detect the most subtle differences between puppies. And why are they different? It's called biology. Look at you and your brother: you, a world-class scientist; your brother, a school janitor. Obviously, you got the bigger piece of the apple pie a la mode. And your poor brother got the crumbs. You came from the same parents, right?"

Nasty. Cody loved his brother. So what if he was a janitor? This wasn't the first time Nicholson used the example of Cody and his brother to prove cloning was superior to sexual reproduction. And Cody knew where the attitude came from: Nicholson—an only child—was jealous. Recently, in a rare moment of candor, Nicholson told him how, as a child, he had eavesdropped on his parents in their bedroom. He heard his mom whisper, "I think I'm ovulating, honey," and his father respond, "Then we're better off not doing it tonight. God forbid we'll have another child like Hugh. Another Fragile Y. Another eunuch!"

"What do you think?" Nicholson tossed a magazine onto his table. *Thoroughbred International.*

Horses? Was Nicholson kidding? This was first time in two years Cody heard the boss suggest another animal to clone. Horses were more complex animals than dogs. The headache would be as huge as the animal.

"So, we're on to racehorses?"

"It all depends on you."

"On me?"

"Yes! Our client is crazy about racehorses. You give him a perfect dog, and we'll get him begging us to clone his horse, Hercules."

Cody had to talk Nicholson out of it. But how?

"Is he a gelding?"

"Gelding?"

"It's a polite way to say the horse had been castrated," Cody said, immediately regretting the word. Nicholson frowned. "A horse is a complex animal. Not an easy task."

"Who said this was going to be easy?" Nicholson clapped Cody on the back. "Cloning has a high failure rate; we know that. But you and I will ace it! There's big business in horseracing. We're talking six, even seven figures."

Cody got up from his seat and turned to face Nicholson, who was still towering over him. "You can clone, but they won't let a cloned horse run."

Nicholson eyes sparkled with excitement. "Oh yes they will. Just wait till we make a new Hercules."

"I doubt it. Over seventy countries signed an agreement barring any horse not naturally created from running. Even plain artificial insemination is forbidden. A cloned horse isn't eligible to run, nor is it eligible to be registered in the stud book."

"Then we'll start our own book of cloned studs."

"Ambitious. Next, you'll be cloning humans."

"Exactly." Nicholson's eyes brightened. "Now that the human genome has been mapped, we should be able to clone a human being and run it through a checklist, making sure it doesn't have any genetic disease."

Just like the spaniel, Cody thought, horrified and excited by Nicholson's plans. A human clone! How he'd love to work on that.

He watched his boss leave the room.

"He's here." The secretary buzzed the intercom. "The boss is bringing him to the GIS room."

"Thanks for the warning." Cody got up at his workstation. Taking extra caution, he placed the petri dishes with the King Charles embryos he'd been working on aboard a single tray. He crossed the corridor, tray in hand, and entered the GIS room. He'd never seen Nicholson so anxious over a client's visit. Nicholson had rehearsed with his staff every detail of the visit, down to the timing of the coffee and the kind of china to be used.

Cody had just finished placing the embryo dish in the incubator when Nicholson and the client walked in. He turned around and took a step toward the two men. The client's handshake was firm. He was about Cody's height, fit, wearing an Armani pinstriped three-piece suit.

"Is the puppy ready?" he asked. Cody couldn't place the accent, but each word was meticulously pronounced.

"Not quite," Nicholson jumped in before Cody had a chance to respond. "Here we work differently from other cloning operations. For us, it's not simply trial and error. We check and recheck each of our embryos through the GIS—the Gene Imaging System—which Doctor Cody will demonstrate in a minute. Only after we select the healthiest embryos, do we implant them into a surrogate dog. With us, you get 100 percent accountability."

Cody fought to suppress a smile. Accountability! Huh! By the time the dog developed a disease that would shorten its life, it would be years later, and tracing the problem back to Reprotech was close to impossible.

OB was different. If you had a problem during labor, the impact of what you'd done was apparent as soon as the baby came out depressed and blue. And if the baby was doomed to lifelong handicap, he—Cody—couldn't undo it.

With cloned dogs, if the puppy came out defective, you simply went back to your bench, changed some things, and made another one. Clients didn't have to know how many puppies you'd gone through before you had a presentable one.

"Dr. Cody, why don't you take it from here?" Nicholson said.

Cody obliged. "I'd transferred Cookie's genes from the piece of skin we removed from her belly into eggs taken from Proxy, our surrogate dog. This is what we've got at this point." He picked up a remote control and turned on four monitors at the end of the room. Each of the four monitors displayed an image of five embryos.

Cody turned off three of the monitors. He walked over to the only screen that was still lit and pointed to an eight-cell embryo he had zoomed in on. "This embryo is an identical reproduction of Cookie's DNA. I'll show you how we know that."

He touched another button. A fluorescent sign, GENOTYPE, shone over the panel of three more monitors in the center of the room. Two monitors lit up simultaneously, each showing an expressionistic combination of dots.

"What you see is a genetic map of a dog's cell—the genetic code for an entire canine being," Cody said. "The genetic fingerprint on monitor 5 is from an eight-cell embryo we created. Monitor 6 shows Cookie's fingerprint. To the naked eye, both 5 and 6 look identical. Our computer compares them gene by gene, one gene at a time. Thousands of genes are checked for each embryo."

Cody turned on four monitors on the right. The fluorescent sign above them read PHENOTYPE.

"We've developed this decoder, capable of translating the genetic map into a precise photographic image of what the cloned dog should look like. In other words, the phenotype."

The client stared at the panel of screens, the rapidity of his breathing the only sign of his excitement.

"This is what your new dog will look like should we choose to use the embryo we've just seen. Here she is a puppy," Cody shone his laser pointer at the first screen, "and this is what she'd look like a year old, then as a three-year-old, and finally, as a nine-year-old."

"Show us the comparison images, please," Nicholson said.

All the screens went dark except the one displaying the nine-year-old phenotype picture of the clone. A recent photo of Cookie came up on the next screen over. Cookie was lying on her stomach, her head buried between her paws.

"I can't see her face," the client exclaimed.

"Unfortunately, your dog was too sick to pose for us. So, we decided to go back to the original image of the King Charles spaniels as seen in this van Dyck painting." Cody flashed the painting on another screen and zoomed in on one of the two spaniels. "Here you can clearly tell the most important features of the breed: the flat skull, round eyes, the long nose, and high-set ears. What do you think, sir?"

The client spent several minutes studying the two images. There was silence in the room. Cody held his breath.

"Everything looks the same," the guest finally said as Cody let the air out of his lungs. "All—except for the nose."

"We're aware of this, sir. Cookie's nose is shorter, and we can't lengthen it."

"I know. I just wish we could have the classic look back."

"Thank you, Cody." Nicholson got up. "Sir, we can return to my office."

Now for the good part, Nicholson thought as he and his client entered his office, leaving Cody behind in the GIS room.

This was the best time to squeeze out the dough, when the dog was ill, very ill, but not dead yet. "I expect to have your new dog ready in nine weeks." He indicated a chair for his guest and went around the desk to sit in his own.

"As long as it's not longer than that." The client's voice quivered. "The vet gave Cookie no more than six months to live, but she's not doing well now. She's been admitted to the best vet hospital and hooked up to two IVs. She's on oxygen." The man's façade had crumpled. He looked as though he were about to cry.

"I'm sure you got her the best care." *He's not even going to flinch when I give him the figures.*

"How much do I owe you?" The client's voice was hardly audible. He reached inside his jacket and took out a checkbook.

Nicholson decided to double the price. "It's fifty thousand today and another fifty thousand when you get the puppy."

The client leaned over Nicholson's desk and wrote out the check.

"Pleasure to do business with you," Nicholson said, suppressing his jubilation. This was a good point to get up and escort his guest out. But the client took his time, remaining seated, in deep thoughts. *Things have gone really smoothly so far. Don't spoil it now with a list of conditions.* Sometimes clients were difficult like that, holding him hostage until they got to see the cloned dog and made sure it looked exactly like their old pet.

"I was impressed by this GIS system," the man finally said.

Nicholson exhaled the air he'd involuntarily held. "Yes!" No reason to be humble. "First of its kind." He leaned backward in his chair, stretching his arms behind his head. "Ours is the only system in the world that can scan the genes and create a realistic image of what your dog's going to look like."

"I realize it. Cloning could work on species far more complex than dogs, right?" The client cocked his head.

"Absolutely." Nicholson sat up straight. He shouldn't let this opportunity slip away. "We feel more than ready to move on."

"Then you're the man for the job. But *this* job has got to be 100 percent perfect."

Nicholson thought he knew exactly what his client was talking about. From what Cody had told him, they had to make the horse look like it was naturally conceived or else it wouldn't be allowed to race. "We've always planned on racehorses as the next step."

"Racehorses?" The client's hand went to his mouth. He let out a little chuckle. "Oh no. There's absolutely no need for another Hercules. I can replace a racehorse."

So, he wasn't attached to his horse the way he was attached to his dog, Nicholson surmised. Cookie was a close family member. Hercules, on the other hand, was just another employee.

"It's human beings you can't replace," the client said.

"You mean—"

"A human being. I'm talking about human cloning." His own face blank, the client studied Nicholson's face for response.

Nicholson felt like a captain of a ship caught in a bad storm. He felt the blood drain from his face. The man meant it! There was no sign he was joking. This man wanted him to make the leap from cloning a dog to cloning a human. Now!

"Who, exactly, did you have in mind?" he asked. His voice came out faint. His confidence was gone. He wasn't due yet for his weekly injection, but he could surely use one now. His spine did a poor job holding his body straight. He arched over his desk.

"Myself, of course. I've only managed to father girls. If I don't have a male heir soon, I lose everything I own."

"We can help you select the sex of your child," offered Nicholson.

"Why would I want to do that? Are you feeling all right, Mr. Nicholson? You look like you've seen a ghost."

Nicholson feigned a smile. "I'm fine. Just a bit surprised."

"As I was saying, why would I want to use science just to select the sex? Look how much I've invested to get an exact replica of my dog. I'd rather have a child who's my perfect clone, without contamination of a woman's genes. To my knowledge, human cloning hasn't been outlawed in the United States."

He was right. But Nicholson knew the prevailing sentiments in America were strongly against it. What the client was asking him to do wasn't considered legitimate. He'd have to do it in secret.

"No one's been able to clone a human yet," he pointed out. *Cody's going to freak out when I tell him this is our next project. Accountability was his biggest fear. That's why he ran away from OB. The tiniest mistake in cloning this man, and both he and I might as well slash our own wrists.*

The client got up. "I'm wasting my time," he said and turned around to face the door.

Nicholson stood and circled his desk in a hurry.

"It's okay." The client touched his arm. "I understand. You're not ready. I just wanted to check with you first before I went elsewhere."

"Elsewhere? Who do you know who'd clone a human being?"

"I have a call in to Doctor Anya Krim at Lincoln."

Nicholson froze. Anya Krim, the doctor Cody didn't stop talking about. Everything he—Nicholson—did was perpetually compared to Anya. And Nicholson, who since childhood hated doctors, had absolutely detested the woman he'd never met. Not only was she a *doctor*, she also stood to win any competition between them for Cody's allegiance. Now this. Now she stood a chance to win the race to human cloning!

"Anya Krim? How did you hear about her?"

"Google. She's successfully cloned a human heart in a pig."

Cody had bragged about her feat. He'd said she was the only one who was a better cloner than he was. Nicholson panicked. He *had* to talk the client out of going to her.

"Oh, I know who she is. A *doctor.* You'd have to have a major illness before she'd take you on for her research."

"She's gotten private funding to continue her work."

"But she won't clone a human. She claims all she'd do is therapeutic cloning—produce new organs for transplant. She's stated to the media and to Congress there's absolutely no reason whatsoever to clone a human being. But you and I know better, don't we? So, as far as reproductive cloning goes, we're the only show in town. And I mean in the country."

"Are you telling me you're ready to do it?"

Nicholson met the client's stare. "Absolutely. We'll proceed with preparations right away. I'll send you an estimate in a week, to be followed by a contract once we agree on my fees."

"Don't you need to check with Doctor Cody first? After all, this *will* be the first cloning of a human being."

"Trust me. Cloning a human is any cloning scientist's dream. And Cody *is* the only man for the job."

"Very well." The man beamed. "This is more like it, Nicholson. I expect my clone to look like me, behave like me, think like me. I expect him to be identical to me in all respects."

"And it will be, Your Highness."

CHAPTER 1

▼

Washington D.C., sixteen months later

Something's wrong with this baby, thought Doctor Anya Krim.

Twenty hours in labor and the baby wasn't coming. What could be wrong? Was it the womb? She eyed the monitor. No. Contractions were regular, forceful. The baby was getting excited with each contraction, his heart rate accelerating. The muscle pouch that held the unborn child was working full force.

Was the canal too narrow? She felt the pelvic bones framing the head. There was plenty of room; this mother had big bones. Anya remembered her residency lingo: the kind of pelvis you could drive a truck through.

It had to be the baby, then. But why? She felt the sutures on the skull: presentation was perfect. And the baby was tiny, especially in relationship to mom. Bonnie Marshall should have been able to sneeze the little peanut out a long time ago.

Maybe the baby wasn't done nesting in the womb, holding on for dear life to its cradle, while the cradle continued its incessant, rhythmic attempts to eject it. The canal that lay ahead was wide open.

Maybe it's me. Maybe I'm out of practice.

She hadn't delivered a baby in eight years. And now what used to be routine for her seemed impossibly difficult. *What was I thinking when I agreed to deliver this baby? I should've known better. How many patients I'd helped conceive had begged me to deliver them? It had to be hundreds. She'd told each of them the truth: they were better off in the hands of an obstetrician who'd been in the trenches day and night. How stupid was I to break my rule for Cody? What was I thinking, that I'd walk in, catch the baby, and walk out—end of story?*

The cervix had been open for over two hours. Anya continued to stretch it to make more room for the baby's head.

She sat on a stool between the stirrups that supported Bonnie Marshall's long legs. Dysfunctional labor. Liz, the delivery room nurse, looked at the mother. "Something is wrong with this delivery."

1

Anya attempted a smile. "Brilliant. You must've been sick during bedside manners week in nursing school."

Bonnie's emotionless face gave no indication of whether she cared if the baby came out.

How unfair, Anya thought. For so many women, pregnancy was no more than an accident. A mishap.

"Maybe we should let the epidural wear off," Liz suggested.

"Maybe it's time for you to go on break," Anya offered. "This has been a long stretch."

"Thanks, Doctor Krim. But I'll stay. I wish you'd deliver babies all the time."

I wish, Anya thought. She wondered if Liz could read her mind. Did she sense that Anya felt out of place, an alien who had landed unexpectedly in the labor and delivery microcosm?

"Push, Bonnie, push," the delivery room choir recited. Liz, a large woman herself, was practically lying over Bonnie's upper belly.

Violent contractions were coming less than a minute apart. But Bonnie hardly flinched. Her face was lime-white, as if all the blood had gone up to her flaming red hair.

"Don't you worry, Bonnie, all babies come out in the end," Anya said. Her blue scrubs were drenched in a mix of sweat and the amniotic fluid that had broken more than three hours earlier. The nursing assistant wiped Anya's forehead with a wet sponge, removed Anya's foggy goggles, cleaned them with wet gauze, and fitted them back over her ears.

Anya had been up for over twenty-four hours. Now, with the repetitive gallop of the fetal monitor, the "push-push-push" from Liz, and that delivery room stench—a mix of Betadine, the patient's secretions, blood, and the sweat under her double layer of scrubs—assailing her, Anya's mind drifted.

It wasn't the stench that had driven her away from obstetrics. Not the bad hours. It wasn't even the *bad* babies she was terrified to deliver. It was *any* baby, *every* baby. She couldn't stand the thought that she'd never have her own.

Professor Feinberg thundered into the delivery room. "Doctor Krim, I've been looking for you."

Not him, Anya thought. *Not here. And not now.*

"Doctor Feinberg?" Anya said

"I wanted to congratulate you—"

The stout professor wore a small, blue, scrub top, his mammoth belly barely covered by green, extra-large bottoms.

"You've outperformed yourself. I thought you'd reached your peak when you cloned a human heart in a pig. But you keep coming up with new surprises. A *human* pancreas in the mouse! By God, this may be the first step to rid the world of diabetes. Are you ready for your testimony in the Senate?"

She kept her eyes fixed on Bonnie. "I haven't had time yet to prepare. But I'll be ready. Don't worry."

"Doctor Krim's going to testify as an expert witness in front of a Senate committee on the Embryonic Stem-Cell Bill. You know why?" he asked an audience of two nurses, a nursing assistant, an anesthesiologist, and a woman in labor. "She was able to grow a piece of human pancreas in a mouse. Now the little mouse makes insulin every day. Can you imagine? This woman is a genius. Once we transplant diabetics with a new pancreas, they'll never need to take insulin again."

Claustrophobia overwhelmed Anya. The professor had invaded her space.

"Professor, I'm busy. Push, Bonnie, push." Anya stretched the vagina. "I need some fundal pressure."

"My pleasure," said Feinberg. Anya heard the nurses gasp at this breach of protocol. "A double step stool," he ordered the nursing assistant, who hurried to stack one step stool on top of another, bowing for the king of the OB/Gyn to climb up to his throne. "I see a good one coming," he said, cheerfully leaning his stomach across Bonnie's.

"It's too much pressure, Professor, the baby doesn't like it," Anya said sharply. "Why don't you make an appointment if you want to talk to me? I'm really pretty busy—"

"Why are you here at all, Doctor Krim?" Feinberg's graying eyebrows tented upward. His right eye seemed narrow and mean, while his glass eye, painted dark brown, stayed wide open. With his cap and his face mask, he looked like a pirate who had just captured Bonnie's pregnant mound and declared it his.

"I don't understand," Anya said.

His good eye turned icy. "You know damn well what I mean. How long has it been since you've delivered a baby?"

"Push, Bonnie."

"I asked you a question."

"Eight years," Anya said faintly.

"Eight whole years," Feinberg enunciated slowly. "Eight years is like a lifetime in obstetrics. What on earth made you decide to do a delivery all of a sudden? Some kind of a divine inspiration?" He threw his arms in the air.

Feinberg was right. But there no way she'd tell him that. "This patient was sent by Cody. He was a resident here. Doctor Jeremy Coddington."

"Oh, I remember Cody! How can I forget? The first time I met him was right here, on the labor floor. He was struggling to pull a ten-pound baby from below on a five-foot even mom."

"Five-four."

"Size doesn't matter," he said. "By the time you sectioned the mom, the baby came out in severe distress, with two broken clavicles. And the rest of his residency got worse. Thank God he's not practicing OB anymore."

"This patient is from out of state, Professor. Cody asked that I deliver her."

"So Cody's deciding who should be delivering babies in *my* department? Well I'm still the chairman. And I say there will be no more babies for you after this one."

No more babies for me.

"Your place is in the lab."

"We'll finish this conversation later," Anya said. The baby's heartbeat had started to dip after each contraction.

"Hold it." He raised his hand. "Coddington never took initiative when he trained with me. Do you seriously think that he'd choose to send a patient to Lincoln Hospital on his own volition? Someone told him to do it. Someone who wanted *you*, and only you, to deliver this baby."

Feinberg was right again. Anya, too, had wondered about Cody's motive. He knew she wasn't practicing OB anymore. Since he was a follower, not a leader, whose orders did he take? Who told him Anya should deliver the baby? And why? She'd have to revisit this later. Right now, she had a job to finish.

"She's having 'lates.' Turn her to her side, Liz, and give her oxygen," Anya said. Her face white with rage, she whirled on Feinberg.

"You're getting in the way of this delivery. Please leave."

Feinberg stepped down from the double stool and crowded her again. "You were hired to work on stem-cell research and organ cloning. Instead, you've become the fertility guru to Capitol Hill and the White House. Don't think you've become untouchable just because the First Lady hired you as her fertility doctor. We'll finish this discussion later." He thundered out as he had thundered in.

The late decelerations of the baby's heartbeat did not recover with the change in position and oxygen. "We need to crash her," Anya said. "Open a c-section tray and call a resident to scrub in. Also, call the NICU."

"Doctor Gordon and the NICU team are on their way."

Anya sighed in relief. Having Alex Gordon around was reassuring. But she couldn't wait for him to arrive. The baby wasn't getting enough oxygen and needed to come out.

Within seconds, the delivery room transformed into an operating room. Liz handed Anya a fresh gown and a new set of gloves and then painted Bonnie's stomach with yellow Betadine solution. The resident stepped in, her hands dripping water; a nurse gowned and gloved her. Together they opened a large sterile paper drape and stretched it across Bonnie's body, leaving only a square window to expose the surgical site.

"Have you re-dosed the epidural?" Anya asked the anesthesiologist.

"She's ready."

"Incision time's ten past 5 AM," Anya said. She took the scalpel and made a straight incision from the belly button down to the pubic bone. Skin, fascia, peritoneum—and the smooth purple uterus was exposed. She could feel the baby's head through the thin wall of the lower segment.

You're not out of practice. You'll never be.

She cut through the uterus, taking care not to cut the baby. Black curly hair, shampooed with a mix of blood and meconium—the baby's bowel movements during distress—emerged through the uterine incision.

Liz grabbed Anya's arm with her soaked gloved hand. "Free at last, free at last."

The ache at the pit of Anya's stomach was a reflex she'd always had at the sight of a new baby entering the world. *In a matter of minutes, another woman will turn into a new mother.* Pain shot from front to back, like an ulcer punching a hole in her stomach.

Bonnie remained expressionless. *This baby would be better off in another home,* Anya thought.

Alex Gordon stood behind her, looking at the baby. For a second, they made eye contact. She could tell his smile from under the face mask. A blanket was draped open over the arms of the NICU nurse Alex had brought with him, as if she expected the baby to parachute from the ceiling.

"Is there something wrong with this baby," Liz whispered, "or am I just beyond tired?"

"You might be right." Anya noted each facial feature as she drew the baby's head through the incision: each one seemed deformed: the eyes—slanted and drawn upwards, the ears—low-set, the nose—beaked, the palate—high-arched.

Ignoring her beeper's new vibe, Anya pulled the baby's head backward, allowing the front shoulder to come through the incision. She suppressed a sigh. Now the other shoulder. She kept a firm grip on the head with her left hand, while her right slid along the spine to grab the baby's feet.

Anya could see a huge hole in the baby's abdomen. The baby's gut protruded through the hole.

"Oh jeez," Liz cried softly. The neonatal team began barking orders.

Anya heard Feinberg's clogs behind her. *He's back. I'm going to kill him. I'm going to kill him now!*

"You can thank your friend for this mess. Special delivery of a monster baby. Someone knew this baby would turn out this way, and they wanted you, and only you, to deliver it. I want to know *why* they chose you."

Don't you call this little baby a monster! Right there, right above that big stomach that I'm so dying to punch, there's a big hole. When did you lose your heart, Feinberg? Was callousness in your job description? "Professor, you've got to stop," she managed.

"I'm out of here," he turned toward the door. "But come see me in my office after the case. You've got some explaining to do."

Anya sighed with temporary relief. But not even a sigh came out of the newborn. Anya wiped its face. Mechanically, she completed the delivery. Cradling the baby securely in her left arm, she double-clamped the umbilical cord.

"Can you tell the sex?" she asked Alex.

"Absolutely not," he whispered. With a gloved hand, his fingers spread the two skin folds between the thighs, exposing an ill-defined bulge. "This could be either an underdeveloped penis or an overdeveloped clitoris."

"Ambiguous genitalia," she said. He nodded in agreement. They both knew what that meant. There was no way to tell Bonnie Marshall whether she'd just given birth to a boy or a girl. Indeed, they wouldn't know for days.

Anya handed the baby to the NICU nurse, who took it to an open warmer. Using a tiny preemie laryngoscope, Alex slipped a plastic tube into the baby's windpipe. The nurse started to pump oxygen-rich air while he worked on the IV.

Anya came over to Alex's side. "What can I tell the mom?"

"Not much, I'm afraid. I don't even know if the baby will live."

Anya approached the head of the delivery table, where Bonnie lay quietly. She squeezed Bonnie's shoulder. "They're taking care of the baby now."

"Thank you." The words were barely audible.

Anya saw a nurse take a footprint of the baby before the neonatal team wheeled it to the NICU. The nurse took the birth certificate to Bonnie for her signature.

"Jesus Christ!"

Anya rushed to her side. "Bonnie, what's wrong?"

"Look, Doctor, look!" Bonnie held the birth certificate out to Anya. "The baby has six toes. It has six—" She began sobbing.

"It's easy to fix" Anya said. "I know it's a shock, but we can remove the extra digits in a few days, and no one will ever know. Calm down." She stroked Bonnie's arm and sat with her. "Can you tell us if there's any way to contact the baby's father?"

"That's a problem," Bonnie whispered. "There *is* no father."

CHAPTER 2

▼

In the locker room, Anya tried to imagine the look on the face of the midwife who had delivered her in St. Petersburg. In her case, too, there was no father. He had disappeared before he had a chance to find out his wife had died giving birth. Before he even knew whether he had a boy or a girl.

Fatherless *and* motherless. That's how she grew up. Babushka, her maternal grandma, had given her all the love and warmth she could've wished for. She had filled all of Anya's childhood needs. Her street wisdom had always guided Anya as life became increasingly more complex. It made sense to her that Babushka had picked up where mom left, since her mother sacrificed her own life to have her.

But her dad was a different story. She never forgave him for running away. For not caring. He could've been the one to come home to with her report card during her first year in the United States, the only foreigner in middle school. He could've been there to hear her speech at her Harvard College commencement, the dean's praise on Harvard Medical School graduation, the good things Feinberg had to say about her when she finished her OB/Gyn residency at Lincoln.

The wound had never healed. She'd learned how to grow up without a father. Or had she? She'd never envied friends for their material possessions. Anya was never the jealous kind. But from childhood playdates and sleepovers, through parents' weekends in college, to Christmas breaks forever, that thin crust that had bridged over the hollow would always break open. The hurt was visceral. And now, in her adult life, trying to forge a meaningful relation with a man was like building a house in the air. The foundation wasn't there.

She spoke briefly to Sonia, the social worker on the floor. "It's going to be a nightmare to place this child in a home. We have a hard enough time with perfect babies that are 'hit and run' victims."

"You mean the mother isn't going to keep the baby?"

"She's already signed the papers. We'll give the father forty-eight hours to show up. And then it becomes a dispo problem. If this baby makes it."

"Dispo," was hospital slang for "disposition." At both ends, the just-born and the not-dead-yet, there were many lives no one wanted any part of. Baby Marshall was one of them.

She thought of the e-mail Cody had sent her:

Anya,

You have to help me. I'm sending Bonnie Marshall to Lincoln in labor. I know you don't do deliveries. But you've got to do this one for me.

Cody

Cody, once again calling for help. And what a surprise—the case turned out disastrous. A Cody special. Only this time he was no longer a resident, nor a practicing OB/Gyn. She had lost track of his career after she turned down his request to work in her lab on reproductive cloning.

Did Cody know the contents of the package he'd sent her? A simple ultrasound could have detected most, if not all, of the anomalies. Maybe he sent her the case *because* he knew it was complicated.

What was his connection to Bonnie Marshall? Did Cody know who the father was? Could *he* be the father?

Anya scrubbed her forearms and hands, trying to rid her skin of any remnants of the delivery. She stuck her head under the faucet. The warm water soaked her long black hair.

She stood up. Someone was staring at her. A man.

A sharp pain shot through her temples.

He grabbed her from behind, a large and rough hand covering her mouth, the other arm clasping her waist. He smelled like sewage. His long body clutched her, enclosing her entirely from behind. She felt his head lean against her shoulder. "Not a sound, darling, not one word, or I'll kill you."

She leaped toward the door.

"Where are you running? It's me, Dario."

She stopped. There, the smell of his cologne. *Passion* for men. She turned around to face him.

"Dario! You scared me to death."

"I needed to talk with you privately."

"In the women's locker room?"

Doctor Dar-rio DaCosta. They were first introduced at the Twenty-First Amendment, when a friend dragged her to happy hour one Friday afternoon. From the first syllable drawn to the rolling r, his name registered like a musical note.

Dario was over six feet tall, thin but muscular, with thick black hair that required no conditioning to fall into place. His brown eyes were kind and wise, his nose, classic Greek. Dario was one of those rare human beings God had put together on a good day.

Dario was dressed in a tux. *Omigod! The fund-raiser.* She had forgotten all about it. Her evening dress hung on the locker behind him.

"I guess we've missed it," she said.

"We can still make it. So what if we don't get a cocktail?"

"I can't go. I've just had one of my worst experiences ever."

"I'm so so-*rr*-y. But it's even more of a reason for us to go. You can tell me about it on the way. They're honoring Victor Sachs." Dario rolled his r in the Spanish-accented English she found hard to resist. His night-dark eyes gazed at her warmly.

"I've asked Caroline, my lab director, to be there. She could say a few words on my behalf."

"But Victor started the Foundation for Stem-Cell Research because he feels indebted to you. Bill and Hillary will be there. Michael J. Fox's giving a speech."

"The last thing I feel like right now is working the room," she groaned.

"It'll be good for your career."

"Maybe. But my head's not there at all. I'm not very good at handling obstetrical disasters. I can't just hit delete, erase what I've just been through on the labor floor, and go out for the night."

He wrapped his arms around her. "Sounds like this was a rough one. A couple of drinks may be just what you need."

We don't seem real, she thought, watching the two of them in the mirror. She was so tiny next to him, almost nonexistent. Her eyelids were half closed. Her nose stuck out over her sunken cheeks, hollowed from exhaustion. What did he find attractive in her? She looked like death on vacation, as her grandma would say.

"Look at us," she pointed at the mirror. "Eliza Doolittle and Henry Higgins. Me, all sweaty and messy in scrubs; you, all decked out in a tux."

"You should come to the fund-raiser just like this. A doctor straight from the trenches will make a big hit," he said. Her beeper went off. She didn't notice her own sigh of relief.

"If you want, we can skip the party. I'd love some time with you alone."

"I don't think I'd be very good company tonight."

"Tomorrow?"

"We'll see. Maybe I'll be less cranky. But now I really have to go. They just paged me again." She yanked the beeper out of her pants and read the message on the screen: "Megan Tanner is bleeding vaginally. Her father wants you to see her now."

CHAPTER 3

▼

Chief Resident Nina Russo's voice was apologetic. "The senator said it was urgent."

Megan had been in coma for two years. Her father was the senior senator from Wyoming. "What's so urgent about a comatose girl bleeding vaginally? Jesus, Nina. I haven't slept in thirty-six hours."

"The senator insisted," Nina said. "He knows you only see fertility patients. Or at least you used to, until tonight. He says the First Lady swears by you, that he'd have no one else but you take care of his daughter."

Anya took the stairs from the second floor to Megan's room on the eighth. The residents called it the "stairway to heaven."

"Tanner's obsession with his daughter is driving us all nuts," said Nina, when she met Anya in front of Megan's room. The word in the OB/Gyn department was that Nina only slept during lectures and surgical procedures.

"The senator pulled me out of a crash c-section to call you. I don't think the man's used to waiting for anything."

"Set up the pelvic tray," Anya said. She watched her resident move sluggishly toward Megan's room.

Anya recalled Megan's story. It was two years ago, on a foggy night after a school prom, that the then seventeen-year-old girl was injured when the car, driven by her boyfriend, hit a tree. Following multiple surgeries and two months in the intensive care unit, her condition stabilized, but Megan had slipped into a coma and hadn't woken. Her father, Senator Tanner, endowed ten million dollars to the hospital, divided over ten years. The hospital CEO had agreed, in return, to give Megan a private room in the hospital instead of transferring her to a chronic-care facility.

A uniformed guard sat at a small desk in front of Megan's door. He let Nina go in but stood to block Anya's way. He was big. Thick. And he stared at her with dark, piercing eyes.

"Sorry," he said, "but I can't let you in there."

"I'm Doctor Krim. The senator asked me to come up and examine his daughter." She leaned forward. "Now!"

He was unnerved. "ID, please."

She reached into her pocket. "Here you go."

"Okay, Doctor."

He handed her a pen. She glanced at the other names on the visitors' list, thinking that Tanner had gone over the deep end. What kind of peril did he think his daughter was in?

"The only name I recognized besides yours was Dario DaCosta," Anya said to Nina as she entered Megan's room.

"On Megan's visitors' list? Yeah, you didn't know?"

"I knew he was the senator's bereavement therapist, not that he was cleared to see Megan." Anya remembered how coldly she had just treated Dario and winced. "Let's take a look at our patient."

Megan was dressed in a pastel pink nightgown. Her face, surrounded by auburn curls, looked peaceful. A tattered brown teddy bear and a well-hugged Raggedy Ann doll rested against her shoulders.

"Pathetic, isn't it?" Nina asked. "She hasn't changed much in two years."

"She looks like Sleeping Beauty," said Anya. "It's a melancholy, this effort to make it seem as if she's just been tucked in for the night."

"The senator acts as if she's going to wake up any minute. Notice how he re-created the décor from her bedroom at home."

The walls were covered with posters of Antonio Banderas, Antonio Sabato Jr., Sarah Chang, Tara Lipinski, and Maroon 5.

"I've heard she was a violin prodigy," Anya stroked one of Megan's hands. "She'd be the new Sarah Chang," the senator had said in an interview after the accident..

A metal stand at the foot of the bed held the sterile pelvic examination tray. Anya walked over to it, glancing up at the clock.

"Have you ever examined a woman in coma? I mean from below?"

Nina didn't respond. Was she falling asleep on her? "Nina?"

"I'm sorry, Doctor Krim."

"Have you ever done a pelvic on a comatose woman?"

"This will be a first."

"And only my second. It's much harder than you imagine. The speculum wasn't designed for the unconscious *and* virginal patient." Anya stretched number 7 latex gloves over her hands.

"Her legs are like white sticks," said Nina. "Two years in bed will do anyone's muscles in, no matter how much physical therapy they get."

Anya effortlessly spread apart Megan's knees, with the soles of the feet touching in a frog-leg position. "Hold the flashlight, please."

She spread the speculum blades, exposing the cervix.

"Cervix is clean. There's a single spot of blood and no discharge. So far looks quite normal, right, Doctor Krim?" Nina asked.

"Except—it has a slightly blue tinge."

Anya removed the speculum. Nina squirted K-Y Jelly on two fingers of Anya's gloved right hand. Anya's left hand pushed down on the lower abdomen. "Is something wrong?" Nina asked.

"Can't feel the top of her uterus."

Anya withdrew her hand, disposed of her gloves, and rinsed the powder from her hands. When she returned to Megan, she covered the girl's pubic hair with a clean sheet, then pushed Megan's gown up to her breasts, exposing her abdomen.

"That's her bladder drain." Nina indicated the catheter, which exited from above the pubic triangle into the bag hanging on the bed rails. "And this is the feeding tube." A rubber tube emerged through a 1cm hole in the skin of Megan's upper stomach.

"She was in the OR for over ten hours straight the night of the accident," Nina said. "Five surgeons. The urologist repaired her bladder, the general surgeon placed the tube in her stomach, the neurosurgeon drilled burr-holes in Megan's skull to drain the blood; the orthopod pinned and plated the multiple fractures in her arms and legs; and the chest surgeon put in the tubes between her broken ribs to drain the blood and air. All that effort for nothing. By the time they found her, the brain was long gone."

Anya focused on Megan's skin and the prominent veins, a blue network that stretched over the lower half of her belly.

"You think her belly's distended?" Nina asked, watching Anya's hands palpate a small mound that extended from the pubic hair to Megan's belly button.

"It feels like a firm, globular, symmetrical mass," Anya said.

"Is the reason why you couldn't feel the top of the uterus, because it rises totally out of the pelvis?"

"Right. And your differential diagnosis, Doctor Russo?"

"Could be just a huge fibroid."

"Benign would be nice. And what else?"

"Could be a malignancy. A virulent sarcoma."

"With a tumor this size, she should've had massive bleeding," Anya said. "One thing I can already tell you: this case is sure as hell not routine. Why didn't the residents call when the uterus started to grow?"

Nina flipped through the medical chart. "I ... I don't see a recent Gyn exam. But the last note says that she's had irregular periods for the first few months after the accident. Nothing in the chart about any recent bleed. I don't think she's had a period for over eighteen months."

"All we've seen was light spotting. To me, that pretty much rules out a tumor, benign or malignant."

"What else could it be, Doctor Krim?" Nina asked.

"Remember the cardinal signs you were taught as a med student? Blue cervix, abdominal swelling, no periods?"

"But—"

"Don't resist it, Nina."

Nina still fought the inevitable diagnosis. "It can't be, Doctor Krim. Not in her condition."

"Why don't you bring ultrasound machine, and we'll see if the cardinal signs work the same way when the patient's in coma?"

Nina left to get the machine.

Anya knew only one diagnosis was possible, as bizarre as it seemed. Watching the clock above Megan's head, she used her stethoscope to count Megan's heartbeats. Barely fifty-six beats per minute, a typical slow pulse for a brain-damaged patient. Now Anya slid the stethoscope over Megan's lower belly. Again, she looked up at the clock. There was an unmistakable rhythmic pulse faster than Megan's heartbeat.

"Who else knows about this?" she asked Megan as she had asked many pregnant teenagers in years past. Megan didn't know she was pregnant, nor would she ever find out. Did Tanner know when he summoned Anya to see his daughter so urgently? Was the bleeding an excuse to get her involved? And if he didn't know, was she, Anya, the first one, the only one, to find out? What should she do next?

"Sorry it took such a long time." Nina pushed the door open and wheeled in ultrasound machine. "No machine was available on the labor floor. I had to get it from 3 North. Are you Okay, Doctor Krim?"

"I'm fine," Anya said. She felt her face get warm. Careful to avoid the feeding tube above and the bladder drain below, she squirted sonographic jelly on Megan's abdomen and placed the square transducer over it.

"I think we have our answer, don't we?" she asked, staring in wonder at the settings on the ultrasound control panel.

"Omigod," Nina shrieked, "she *is* pregnant!"

"Let's try to date the pregnancy," Anya strained to sound matter-of-fact. How far pregnant Megan was could determine the ultimate management of her case. But Anya already knew the pregnancy was advanced. "The distance between the baby's temples is 4.5 centimeters. What does your dating table say? Should be right about mid-pregnancy."

"Sorry, Doctor Krim," Nina emerged from a trance and fished out her plastic reference table from her coat pocket.

"Abdominal circumference is 15 centimeters. Nina?"

"Nineteen-point five weeks."

"And the femur length is 3.5 centimeters."

"Twenty weeks to the dot."

"The baby has two arms, two legs, two kidneys, a four-chambered heart. Brain's intact. GI. Everything seems normal."

"Can you call the sex?" asked Nina.

Anya moved her scanner. As if on cue, the baby stopped moving for a moment, posing for an underwater photo op. Anya examined the groin carefully for what was present, and more important, what was not. "Clearly a girl. Did you bring the vaginal probe?"

"Sure. You really think it's necessary?"

Anya recoiled. What a dumb question. *Control, maximum control,* Madam Tartakova would yell at the Kirov school, hitting Anya on the calf muscle with that awful stick just as she was about to attempt the Tournes Fuentes.

"I don't do unnecessary exams at 10 PM," she said. Could she bring herself to have the same level of compassion toward her resident as she had for every patient, even the most annoying? "The vaginal ultrasound is the closest you can get to the pelvic organs and, therefore, always complements the abdominal sono," she explained.

Nina shrugged. She opened a box of condoms and handed Anya one.

With Megan in the frog-leg position, Anya squirted jelly on the tip of the probe, slid the condom over it, applied more jelly, and gently inserted it into Megan's birth canal.

The bastard, she thought. *A deviant. Only the sickest pervert could have done this. He'd been where the ultrasound probe is now. He would've had to spread these thin, contracted legs apart, climb up the air mattress, lie on top of her, not caring about her feeding tube or the bladder drain. Ugly! A necrophiliac with a subspecialty in comatose sex.*

The familiar pain shot straight through her temples. She felt cold and clammy.

"Could you at least use a condom, pleaaase?" She tried to reach for her purse.

"I don't like wearing a rubber raincoat." Her assailant kicked the purse with his foot. "Feels unnatural."

Soft music emerged from two Bose speakers standing at the corners of the room.

Close your eyes, give me your hand, darling
Do you feel my heart beating?

"What's that?" Nina asked.

"'Eternal Flame.' By the Bangles." Anya must've listened to this song a hundred times.

"Never heard it before."

"Megan must've liked it." Anya didn't tell Nina it was *her* all-time favorite. *How odd*, she thought, of all places, to hear this song in the hospital room of an unconscious patient she'd just met for the first time.

"Doctor Krim, I just got beeped to the DR."

"Go. I'll keep you posted."

No more babies for you, Anya Krim.

No more, Professor Feinberg had said. He'd probably already told the medical staff office to suspend her OB privileges. Anya stared achingly at the tiny living human on the ultrasound screen. There was no way on earth she would be allowed to touch Megan. Feinberg would make sure of that. No OB care. And absolutely no deliveries.

Anya glanced at the clock above Megan's bed: 10 PM. She covered Megan's lower half with the blanket, pulled the probe from under the sheet, replaced it on the sonogram machine, and took off her gloves. Only then did she push Megan's knees back to supine position. "Eternal Flame" went on, bringing back memories…

She used to curl up in bed, lights off, listen to the song, and think of her mom.

A strong whiff of alcohol told her she was no longer alone.

She turned around. The man staring at her made sure the right side of his neck was in full view, exposing a scar. Anya knew it was a bullet hole from Vietnam. Nelson Tanner III used his scar in place of a business card. He didn't introduce himself. Instead, he just stood there, letting intimidation sink in. Anya didn't flinch. She surveyed the marine crew cut, the square and deeply furrowed face, the straight shoulders and the serious set of pecs that filled his business suit. She knew he expected her to quail.

"You must be Doctor Anya Krim," he finally said. There was alcohol on his breath.

"Senator. I don't know why you decided to call *me* to see your daughter."

"Actually, I couldn't tell one Gyn from another. My secretary told me you're supposed to be the best."

"Your secretary?"

"Yes. She said you took care of the First Lady. That everyone on Capitol Hill, from senators to secretaries, calls you for everything on earth, from yeast infections to morning-after pills."

"Your secretary has her information wrong. My practice is limited to infertility."

Tanner limped over to Megan's night table, his prosthetic leg stomping loudly. He lifted the flowers from a vase and threw them into the waste can. They couldn't have been more than a day old, Anya thought. "Are you telling me that you refuse to take care of my daughter?"

"Not at all, Senator. I'd love to take care of Megan."

"You know this was her favorite song."

"Sorry?"

"'Eternal Flame.' Her absolute favorite."

"As I was saying, Senator, not that I don't *want* to care for your daughter. I'm not *allowed* to—"

"What do you mean not allowed to? You work for Lincoln Hospital, don't you?"

"Please sit down," she said. Instead, he filled the vase with the new bouquet he had brought.

"I don't need to sit down. What's this all about?"

"Senator, please." Anya didn't take her eyes from him. "I have something difficult to tell you."

Reluctantly, he sank into the club chair beside Megan's bed.

"You know that Megan's been bleeding vaginally," she said.

"Indeed. That's why I had you called."

"I've just completed a full exam, including a sonogram."

"And? How's she doing?"

Anya rotated the screen so he could see it. The picture she'd frozen on it showed the profile of the fetus sucking its thumb.

"This is the sonar image of Megan's uterus, Senator. As you can clearly see, there is a live fetus in there. Your daughter's pregnant."

She saw his face turn pale. His hands went for his temples. With his elbows leaning on his knees, he stared at the ground.

"I'm terribly sorry," she said. "I can only imagine how you must feel. This is … well, I'm so sorry."

He said nothing.

"Sir, your daughter is pregnant."

Now his eyebrows rose. "Impossible. My daughter hasn't left this room in two years."

"I'm aware of the circumstances."

"Someone's trying to get back at me … someone is setting me up."

"This is not some tragic prank, believe me. You asked me to check your daughter. I found her to be pregnant."

"How sure are you, Doctor?"

"One hundred percent."

"Holy shit! How far along is she?"

"About mid-pregnancy. Megan has another twenty weeks to go to carry the baby to term."

"In other words, you're telling me that my daughter has been raped!"

Instinctively, Anya closed her eyes.

He stamped his good foot. "This is my baby. Do you understand? My baby. And you're telling me that some animal jumped—"

"I didn't tell you *how* she got pregnant."

The leg hit the floor again. "Have some respect, for God's sake. What do you mean, 'you didn't tell me how she got pregnant'? How else? She woke up from her coma one night and snuck out for a quickie in the parking garage?"

Shaking with tension, Anya turned off the ultrasound machine. The baby's image disappeared.

She turned to face him. "Unfortunately, since your daughter is pregnant, I won't be able to take care of her."

"Doctor, you're the best, and I'll have only the best take care of my daughter."

"You'll have to take it up with my chairman. I—"

"Bullshit. Feinberg, like anyone else in this fucking hospital, knows which side his endowment's buttered on."

"It's illegal for me to—"

"I sit on the Board of Trustees, Doctor. Feinberg's up for reappointment this year. Mark my words. He'll beg you to take Megan on."

"I hope so," Anya said. "But now that I've finished the examination, it's time for me to go home." She stood and went to the door. He limped after her. When she turned around, they were practically nose-to-nose.

"Shut the door," he said.

She realized the security guard was just outside. She closed the door.

"Someone in this hospital took advantage of my unconscious daughter and r—"

Her hands went up to cover her ears. "Please, Senator. We both have the same suspicion, and I'm sure the police will investigate this thoroughly."

"It's more complicated, Doctor. Sit down for a minute." Anya sat. He stood next to her.

His expression softened. "I'm sure you realize I can't call the police. The media loves scandals involving public figures. Remember the fiasco when

Megan had the accident? How I was publicly lynched for letting this boy drive her under the influence with no drivers' license? They didn't allow us to grieve in private. Not for a second." He sighed. "When it comes to my child, I won't let anyone damage her reputation. Do you have any idea how much I love this girl? I'd give everything I have, I mean e-v-e-rything, if she could wake up—" his voice cracked.

Now he was just a daddy, Anya thought. And with all the power and influence he had, there was no one he could turn to. Anya looked back at the child lying on the bed. "Senator, I'll take Megan on as a patient. But you'll have to clear it with Doctor Feinberg."

He lifted his head. "Thank you." His smile was sad.

"I still don't know how that'll help you find out the father's identity," she added.

"And I thought you were an expert in genetic fingerprinting."

"What made you—?"

"Hold it," he raised his hand. "You *are* the Anya Krim who's dabbling in stem cells, right?"

"I'm not sure what you mean by 'dabbling,' Sen—"

"Whatever," he waved his hand. "You and I will have a chance to dig into it at my committee hearing—"

His committee hearing? She had forgotten Tanner chaired the committee taking her testimony. She was starting to get a sense of what she was up against.

"The reason I mentioned it is because, reading your résumé, I noticed you've had extensive training in genetics."

So, you didn't just pick a random "gyno," Senator. My name didn't just come up casually. You'd taken the pain to review résumés, lots of them, I assume, before you determined I was to become your daughter's obstetrician. And you chose me because you knew I could fingerprint the baby. You must have known your daughter was pregnant before you called me to see her!

"I've never had to use genetics to prove paternity," she said. What she didn't tell Tanner was that this was the second case of a missing father that she'd been dealing with in fewer than two hours.

"Does that mean that you'll help me find out who did this to my daughter?"

"I'll do what I can." She shook his hand, then left.

CHAPTER 4

▼

"We're closing. You have to leave now."

Anya eyed the clock. It was midnight. She was the only one left in the library. The librarian with the purple hair, who always seemed to enjoy torturing her for staying late, glared at her.

She collected the pile of articles she'd gathered. Had the old witch been more helpful, she wouldn't have had to stay so late. But this woman had turned giving medical students a hard time into an art.

"You have to be more specific, young lady. There are volumes on top of volumes written on the Y chromosome," she'd announced.

So Anya had to find the volumes herself and then Xerox what she needed. Professor Collins's extended deadline was the day after tomorrow and she still hadn't found a single paper on Fragile Y Syndrome. Not only was she dealing with the smallest chromosome in the body, it was also the only one women didn't have. Collins had assigned her this most bizarre disorder. Was it some sexist statement of the professor's, teasing his female student? Whatever it was, the professor had picked a subject on which there seemed to be no literature. Just great.

Outside, a rainstorm caught her by surprise. Within seconds, her T-shirt was drenched. She ran across 23rd Street, her sneakers hitting every puddle with a splash. Fog engulfed her, but it was just one more block to her dorm. Thank God. She'd shower, sit at the fireplace in her soft, velvet bathrobe, sip hot chocolate, and listen to Rod Stewart.

For a brief moment, she would actually forget the Y chromosome. Forget Collins. Enjoy life.

She arrived at her building. Fumbling for the keys, she thought she heard a rustle in the bushes that flanked the entrance. She turned around. There was zero visibility. No one was there. It was all her prolific, sick imagination. Medical students were notorious for seeing cadavers come back as ghosts at night. The night was spooky, and she was alone on the street at half past midnight.

She opened the door. Her room was on the third floor. It was her first year in a single. She didn't have to worry about waking a roommate up or interrupting someone else's studies. No one drank in her room. No one made love on her bed.

Inside her room, wrapped in a fluffy towel, she turned on the gas-operated fireplace and put on the Rod Stewart CD, loud enough so she could hear it from the shower.

She turned the water on full volume. She liked it hot enough to turn the miniature bathroom into a steam room. She let the towel fall on the floor and stepped under the water, leaving the door open.

"If I listen long enough to you—" Rod Stewart sang. No more sex chromosomes tonight. The shower massaged her fatigued shoulders. For a minute or two, she stood in bliss. "Knowing that you lie, straight face, while I cry."

The song was over. Three minutes and thirty-three seconds, her shower "budget." Long ago she'd decided to direct what a psychologist had called a mild case of obsessive compulsive disorder to constructive channels. She was more compulsive than obsessive, anyway. And that played well into her life. There was no time wasted. Every minute was planned. Even the music.

She dried herself and put on her bathrobe. In a few minutes, she'd boil some hot chocolate, curl up in front of the fireplace, and read Anna Karenina. She was allowed ten minutes. She smiled. At least she recognized how ridiculous she was. Insight was key to mental healing.

She thought she heard a sound coming from the bedroom. She paused a minute and then realized it was just the wind against the building.

The bathroom mirror was steamed up. She wiped it with her hand, enough to see her face.

As she opened the drawer to find a hairbrush, a terrible odor violated the room. A dead mouse? In the drawer?

She looked back at the mirror, and her mind exploded with terror.

"Let go of me, you son of a bitch." She broke his hold, writhing.

"You've got to wake up. It's me, honey."

Her sheet was drenched. She shivered. "I'm going to scream—"

"No one's trying to kill you, honey. You're safe and sound in your bedroom." Anya opened her eyes and half-sat up in her bed, catching her breath. Dario tried again to touch her shoulders, but she shrank from him.

"What are *you* doing here?"

"I got worried when you didn't answer the phone, so I came in to see if you were all right."

She felt exposed and pulled her nightgown high over her breasts. Her gown was wet, and she felt her nipples showing. He smelled good. He wore a blue fitted sweater that flattered his physique.

"I gave you my house keys to water my plants when I was out of town, not to barge in on me like this," she said, regretting her words before she was finished. *He must think I'm a freaking iceberg. He's going to run away, which he totally should. He's going to get up and walk through this door, and I'll never see his face again.*

But Dario didn't move. Instead, he leaned over to the side of the bed and collected the duvet off the floor, wrapping its soft fringe around her long neck. Her shivers lessened. She felt warmer. And safer.

Dario picked up two pillows from the floor and arranged them behind her back. Again he sat on her bed, his thigh touching her feet.

This time she didn't move. She hoped he'd touch her again, collect her in his arms. She needed to be hugged. But she said nothing.

Maybe he was afraid the iceberg would melt if he squeezed too tight, and water would flood the apartment. Why would he even want to stick around? The hot dude of Lincoln Hospital, who could go out with anyone, why would he stick with *her*, who'd just yelled at him for checking on her after a six-month platonic relationship. Who did she take him for, some kind of celibate priest who'd used religion to suppress his libido? Too bad she was Jewish. A priest would've been perfect for her. Second best—an impotent man. That wasn't Dario. Many a times she'd noticed his flag rise to full mast in her honor. But that was when they'd first met. When she still played the role of the shy, virginal girl out on a first date. And then the second. And then the third. It was sort of fun back then. And it felt kind of safe. For a while, Dario seemed ideal for her, the perfect gentlemen, only the bulge in his groin giving away his muted desire. But by now they were getting into a tedious routine of good-bye kissing at the door, the door that led nowhere.

"I know what you'd been through." His big brown eyes fixed on hers.

"I don't know what you're talking about—" *I'm better off shutting up. I need to set myself free of the insensitive bitch armor. It doesn't take the pain away.*

Dario gently took her chin with his index finger and turned it toward him. "Anya. We've waited way too long. We need to talk."

"Not now. I'm tired."

"I understand."

No you don't. "I wish you weren't so nice. I don't deserve it."

"I think I can help, honey, if you'd only let m—"

"You don't—"

"I do. I know about the … incident."

Thank God he didn't say the word. She took a deep breath and met him at eye level. "How did you figure that one out?"

"I've become an expert in sleuthing emotional traumas. I've been trying to piece things together—"

"Good luck!"

"We don't have to talk about it now."

"Thank you, Doctor."

"Please, Anya. No cheap shots. At least let me say that the way you've been handling everything is totally acceptable and normal."

"Normal? You're kidding me, right? Eight years. Eight long years after the beast attacked me. And I still can't have sex with a man. You call that normal?"

"I don't like labels, but this is—"

"Classic posttraumatic stress disorder. Bullshit. I know you're trying to make me feel better about myself. But I'm way overqualified to be a good patient. I studied PTSD in Psych. And I know exactly the kind *I* have. A most protracted, chronic condition. What I suffer from is not just shell shock. It's more like the whole building had been destroyed, down to the foundations. My PTSD is incurable. My sexuality is forever decimated." *Nice thing to say to a boyfriend. If that wouldn't make him run away, then I've definitely lost my touch.*

"You're brilliant, honey. But not when it comes to yourself." He pulled her to him. *Finally*, she thought, regretting everything she'd said. Better to leave things where they are. She rested her head against his chest. *At least we can cozy up. At least I have that left. For now.*

"We'll work through things." He caressed her hair. "Slowly. We need time."

CHAPTER 5

▼

R eprotech, West Virginia

This is my chance to hang up, thought Cody as the recording repeated the news that Lincoln Hospital had been chosen the best hospital in the nation by *USA Today.* He had no idea what he was going to tell Bonnie once she got on the phone. Congratulate her? Convey his sympathy? Apologize?

"The patient was already discharged from the hospital, sir," the operator was back on the line.

He sighed. "But she'd just given birth this morning. I thought—"

"Usually they stay forty-eight hours after delivery. I don't know. Maybe she checked out AMA."

Why would Bonnie sign out against medical advice? Cody wondered. *And where did she go?* He doubted she'd asked Nicholson to send someone to pick her up. Did Bonnie decide to run away and hide from Nicholson after she'd realized they had her carry a deformed baby?

Cody stared at his computer screen, dumbfounded. He'd read and reread the e-mail that Anya had sent him. But even so, he refused to process the information. It felt surreal. The barrage of information he'd been fed, the faulty inventory "Baby Marshall" had been born with, were all channeled to a dead fuse. A total disconnect in his brain didn't allow the siren to go off announcing the birth of a cloning disaster, custom-made by Cody. His brain, traumatized and reconditioned by his obstetrical mishaps, had been remodeled to zero accountability. According to the way his neurons now functioned, there'd never be consequences, regardless of how badly he'd performed. He was a cloner now. Nicholson acted as a shock absorber when it came to minor screwups. Now his brain couldn't process a major calamity. He refused to make the connection between Baby Marshall and the embryo he'd carefully cloned, which had passed the most rigorous genetic testing. This way, he could face Nicholson with the news without the visceral reaction that would surely have consumed him.

Nicholson met him in his office. Past his bedtime, he wore a checkered houserobe and slippers and looked relaxed in his chair.

Cody closed the door behind him. "Mind if I sit?"

Nicholson leaned forward. "Something's wrong."

Maybe it wasn't such a good idea to get him out of bed to hear this news. He could have one of his temper tantrums. "Things," Cody cleared his throat, "things didn't go as well as we had anticipated."

Nicholson's eyebrows angled upward. "So, what've we got? A stillbirth?"

I wish. Wouldn't that be a blessing? "No," Cody let out an involuntary sigh. "The baby was born alive, with several anomalies." *Several. Huh. Could he have understated the situation more?*

"Now hold it." Nicholson raised his hand. "First human cloning in the world, and only a *few* anomalies. Not too bad for a start."

Maybe it was a mistake to give Nicholson less than the full picture. "Some of them are pretty major," he managed.

"But fixable, right?"

"Well—" Cody hesitated.

"Well what?"

"By the time they finish fixing, there would hardly be any semblance to the client."

"Not funny." Nicholson's posture was taut. He squeezed one hand in the other.

"I didn't—"

Nicholson didn't let him finish. "Did you just call the baby 'it'? The baby's a boy, right?"

There was no way to massage this one. "They're not sure yet."

"Fuck!" Nicholson's fist hit his desk so hard his mother's picture fell flat. "Fuck them! A bunch of *doctors,* that's who they are. A bunch of ignorant doctors! You tell them to take the diaper off and look!"

"I wish it were that simple," Cody said quietly. He felt his stomach churning. "They're sending a blood test."

"Now this is really fucked up, when they have to do that." Nicholson's forehead furrowed. "His Highness is going to be very upset."

Thank you for keeping me in the dark. The client was some kind of royalty, and you chose to hide it from me. "His Highness?"

"I promised him full confidentiality." *Of course. To you, I'm no more than a technician. When things go well, you take the glory. Now we're facing disaster, you'll find a way to pin it on me.* "The only reason he wanted a clone was he needed a male heir. Sounds like we can't even present him with this ... less than a trophy, right?"

"Right." Cody's reply was barely audible. At least the boss was finally grasping the extent of the disaster.

Nicholson's back arched. Cody knew this was a preamble to a second wave of attack. The testosterone patches Nicholson wore on his skin had hardly replaced the natural hormone. So at times of crises, he had to call on other hormones, like adrenalin, to help him cope. His autonomic nervous system would dispatch waves of adrenalin, yet their effect would be short acting and insufficient to stave off the crisis.

For a fraction of a minute, Nicholson's foot shaking was the only sound Cody heard, like the beat of the drums in the background of a muted movie score. Nicholson's back straightened. The second tier militias must've arrived. "So, your fancy system didn't predict this disaster. Apparently it's not half as good as I'd bragged to our customers."

I never told you the GIS would work on humans. And you never asked me. In fact, you never asked anything: not if I could clone a man, *not if I wanted to clone a man. You didn't ask how I felt about it. If I felt it was ethical? If I thought it was, perhaps, sacrilegious? A* technician *has no position; doesn't think independently; has no moral code. What about you, Nicholson? As the brains behind this—how do you feel about cloning? Or shouldn't I ask?*

"I'm waiting, Coddington." Nicholson's voice jerked Cody out of his contemplation.

"For what?"

"The GIS. The GIS, damn it!"

"I guess in a sm—"

"I'm not paying you to guess."

"In a small animal, the chance for an error is much lower."

Nicholson got up and walked around his desk. Now he was very close to Cody, generating a thundering voice from his scarecrow body. "Explain how that works, exactly. I thought genes were genes. In animals *and* in humans."

Now Cody was back to his most dreaded nightmare. Accountability. Except, instead of the delivery end, he was now expected to assume responsibility at the production end, where life begins.

"Our system probably screws up all the time," he said, "except, on a small animal, it's hard to tell. Even Dolly was considered a perfect clone until she got sick, prematurely aged, and died. In a human being, gene-copying imperfections are bound to show up earlier."

"Like at birth!"

"Like at birth."

"This should be an important learning experience for all of us." Cody didn't trust Nicholson's sudden burst of "understanding." "So why do you think this happened?"

Cody took a deep breath. This was his chance to divert the attack. "Most likely, these anomalies are the results of abnormal genetic imprinting," he ventured.

"Imprinting?" Nicholson asked suspiciously. "You never mentioned that before."

You didn't ask. "I never believed the scientists who predicted that human cloning will result in the creation of a 'freak collection.' I thought we could prove them wrong."

As usual, Nicholson was a quick study. "So now you believe cloning could cause an imprinting disorder?"

"I do. Baby Marshall may be the live demonstration. When conception occurs naturally, an embryo is created from the sperm and the egg. Mom and Dad each contribute about 30,000 genes. There are two copies of every gene, and together, they form a master program to build an embryo cell by cell."

Nicholson leaned forward. "But sometimes genes from Dad have to be turned off to let the mother's genes dominate, while at other times, the mother's genes stay dormant and the father's genes take over, right?"

"Exactly."

"I just didn't know it was called imprinting. It sounds like in cloning we don't have to worry about this, since there's no Mom and no Dad."

"Actually, that's not true. Take Baby Marshall, for example. The DNA we took from His Highness's skin cells and injected into an empty egg already had the grandparents' DNA—*His Highness's father and mother!* We're hitting the cell all at once with a barrage of ready-made DNA mix. Instead of old-fashioned DNA from Mom and Dad taking turns dictating outcome, things get more haphazard, with messages from Grandma and Grandpa overriding at times, creating anomalies."

Nicholson frowned. *He's thinking this is bad for business,* Cody realized. "We really need to work out these glitches."

"I'll do my best."

"Two weeks ago, I asked you to go to the morgue to get a DNA sample from that girl who was recently murdered. Her father called me yesterday. Bet you he'd pay just about anything to have his daughter cloned. If you thought there was lots of money in replacement pets, I have news for you: the real money's in replacement children. We just have to work out the science."

"But we have to proceed with great caution," Cody said.

"I know, I know."

"Seriously, Mr. Nicholson. What you've just told me only makes me want to push harder on the brake. If the parents of that little girl get their wish anytime soon, I expect the nightmare to recur: a baby with multiple deformities. The medical costs will be huge. And you'll be hit with a lawsuit no insurer will cover."

"Okay, Okay. I got the picture. I'm going to leave it up to you to tell me when you *are* ready." *I wish I could believe that.* "But something else bugs me. Anya Krim—"

Every part of Cody's body, at standstill throughout this exchange of words, awoke. His visual cortex flashed a snapshot of Anya's small body lost in oversized scrubs, struggling to deliver Baby Marshall. Cody imagined her face at the sight of the deformities. He felt ill. How could he have done this to her? "She's the only one I could trust—"

"I know. She's also our competition. Do you think she could know that this baby was cloned?"

"Not in a million years. They see major anomalies every day on the labor floor."

"I hope you're right," Nicholson said. "How do you intend to figure out what went wrong with Baby Marshall?"

"Rescan the embryo's DNA. But what I'd really need is to get my hands on the baby's DNA. I need a blood sample."

"Why don't you ask Doctor Krim? You two are buddies, no?"

He must be kidding. "Bad idea. You don't want her to think that I was involved in the creation of this baby. If I ask her to provide me with a blood sample, she'd either suspect that it was a clone, or she might think that I'm the baby's father!"

"You might be right. Let me see what I can do," Nicholson said.

What *could* he do? The baby was tucked away at Lincoln's NICU, which was guarded like a fortress. And Nicholson knew it. Cody had never seen Nicholson engage in a criminal act. Yet, he didn't like the confidence he had sensed in Nicholson that he could get a blood sample from the baby. "I beg you," Cody said. "Nothing illegal."

CHAPTER 6

▼

Nothing illegal!
Cody was a wuss. A crybaby. What was he, Hugh Nicholson, supposed to do? Have the court order Lincoln Hospital to give Reprotech a few drops of the baby's blood? Cody was useless when it came to creative problem solving. He was no more than a *technician.*

It took Nicholson time to calm down and consider his options. He straightened his mother's picture on his desk. With Mom gone, there wasn't a single person left in the world who really knew him. Who knew how tough life has been. Not a single person who understood the energy and determination it took to wake up every morning with only one thought in mind: how do I prove myself today?

Without the baby's blood they were stuck. They had to figure out what went wrong before Nicholson's other cloned pregnancy, one so secret he had warned Cody he'd kill him if Cody revealed it, was due to deliver. And there was only one person who could get the blood for him.

Maybe it wasn't such a great idea to rush Destiny to Reprotech this late at night, Nicholson thought after he hung up the phone with her. The drive from D.C. took a good two hours, and by the time he'd called her, she must have already had a couple of drinks. Yet Nicholson saw no other way.

"I could barely hear you on the phone," she said when she came in. The familiar scent of perfume took over his office. Neither the late hour nor the long drive had muted her energy. Her brown eyes stared straight at him. Her prominent lips were stained with maroon lipstick, highlighted with a darker shade. Her brunette hair was combed down to her shoulders. She wore a skimpy green blouse tied above the naval, unbuttoned at the top to expose half her breasts. Her white pants flattered her small, flat bottom and long, thin legs. "You got me at a bar on Capitol Hill. I was working," she said.

"Work? As in?"

She ignored his sarcasm. "I was having drinks with Senator Spears from the Senate Appropriations Subcommittee. Takes a lot of work to soften up these people on the Hill. Spears will require much more before I get a rise out of him."

She didn't get a rise out of me either, he thought. He was already on the testosterone patch when they went out on a date a couple of years back. He had hired her to work full time at Reprotech fresh out of a bad marriage. Watching her walk around the office awakened his dormant senses. Smelling her perfume as she neared him, hearing her sing along with the iPod while she wiggled her tight jeans to the music—he decided he had to have her.

Of course she agreed to go out on a date with him. His first date. Ever. And she was very sweet about it, too. He thought the date went very well. Throughout the evening, he felt a huge buildup. He even forgot for a while that the date had a purpose: he was out to prove he could really be with a woman. Maybe that was the reason why he'd failed so miserably later that night. Lying naked on her bed, limp and frustrated, he watched his tiny, flaccid penis and knew that in his case, body and mind were forever disengaged. Destiny was his road test—and he'd crashed.

That night Nicholson was determined not to let this humiliation recur. Through his own research he found out that the testosterone maintenance patch was insufficient for sexual function in a Fragile Y. He needed a booster injection anytime he wanted sex. Cody agreed to write him the requisite prescriptions. But with Destiny, it was all over. Except, each time he saw her he got a jolt of pain in his groin.

Valentine's day fell shortly after their "date." Destiny's office looked like a high-end nursery, with at least a dozen bouquets. After-hours that day, checking on the cards that came with them, Nicholson realized how many admirers she had, men *and* women. Hmmm! Of course. How could he, the virgin of all virgins, have recognized "it"?

Realizing he couldn't concentrate on work with Destiny walking around the office, he created a position for her to lobby Congress as the vote on the Embryonic Stem-Cells Bill neared. And since her lobbying was mainly after hours, he found her a daytime job as well.

She owed him much. And he knew he could call on her for help, day or night.

"I heard about Baby Marshall."

"How? Who told you?"

"This loud nurse, Liz, from labor and delivery, was in front of me in the cafeteria, telling another nurse about a baby born with grotesque anomalies. As she was describing the case, I had this strange premonition I knew who she was talking about. And then when she mentioned there was no father, I just knew it had to be Bonnie."

"You're right."

"How terrible. I'm so sorry," Destiny said, sinking into the chair in front of his desk.

"I appreciate your sympathy." He needed it. He caught a whiff of her perfume and took comfort in its familiarity.

"Is there anything I can do to help?" Destiny never said anything she didn't mean. And never offered to do anything she wasn't planning on following through. There was something special about this woman.

"That's why I called. We're trying to figure out what went wrong. We thought we had an airtight system of checks and balances, and we failed."

"You shouldn't be so hard on yourself, Hugh." She reached over his desk and took his hand. He found her touch soothing. "There's nothing more complicated than cloning a human being. And no one's managed to do it so far."

What a pleasure to be able to vent to a woman with such high intellect. "The client doesn't care. All he's looking for is results. If he finds out Baby Marshall is his clone, he'll demand his down payment back. I could go bankrupt from this. And if I don't come up with the money, my life may be in danger!"

She cupped both his hands with hers. "Look at me," she said. He lifted his head, fighting back tears. She smiled at him. "Remember, you're not the one who'd cloned this baby. You relied on Cody. It was Cody who'd led you to believe—"

"Yes. Cody is a convenient scapegoat. But he'd warned me we might not be ready."

"Yet he *was* ready. Didn't he use this GIS thing he'd invented to test the embryo's DNA? Didn't he predict the baby was going to be a perfect replica of the dad? And all the ultrasounds in pregnancy. Normal. Normal. Normal. This is what you get from your in-house *doctor.* An *obstetrician,* mind you. It's time this man assumed responsibility. It's Cody who failed. And Cody should pay for it!"

Strong words coming from the woman with the softest hands. "I never trusted doctors. And I'm not about to start now," he said, relating obliquely to what she said. Blaming Cody for this mess was not only too easy, it also solved nothing. "The problem now is how to prevent another catastrophe. And in order to do that, we need to test the DNA."

"You mean you need blood from Baby Marshall?"

"Unless they kept the cord blood."

"I doubt it. Bonnie was hardly in the state of mind to sign the consent."

He admired her quick wit. "Which leaves us—"

"With drawing blood from the baby." She sat back in her chair, contemplating.

"Problem?" he asked.

"Yes, problem. In fact, big problems. And I don't know which is worse: camouflaging myself as one of the nurses in a unit where people work intimately with each other or dealing with the tight security in the NICU."

"Do you think you can do it?"

I'll do my best was not going to be enough. "It will get done. I promise."

CHAPTER 7

▼

Even in jeans and a T-shirt, her hair still wet from the shower, Janet Cartwright still looked the First Lady, Anya thought as she walked into the East Wing office.

"You've got your direct conduit to the president. Now is the time to use it," Dario had said. She knew Dario wasn't trying to corrupt her. He just cared about her, worried that if the president vetoed the Embryonic Stem-Cell Bill, it would not only kill any financial support she so desperately needed to continue her research, it would make her work illegal!

But now, as Janet held out her hand, Anya knew she couldn't take advantage of their relationship. It wasn't fair. Janet should be treated like any other patient. Still, Anya hadn't felt this awkward and uneasy since the day she'd taken on the First Lady as a patient.

Janet sat down on the sofa, signaling to Anya to sit next to her. "Maybe it would make you feel better knowing that every time you see me here, you're making the life of the Special Service guys much easier. And mine." The First Lady grinned.

Anya felt the pit of her stomach go into spasm. What was going to be routine pre-op consultation was not routine at all. Nothing was routine when the patient was the First Lady of the United States.

"Your egg retrieval is scheduled for 9 AM tomorrow," she started.

"I can't wait," Janet said.

"We're going to put you in a twilight sleep using three drugs. Then I'll use the vaginal ultrasound probe to scan the ovaries to look for eggs. Under the guidance of the ultrasound, I'll pass the needle through the wall of the vagina and into the ovary."

"Ouch. I'm asleep through all of that, right?"

"Yes. You'll feel no pain. In fact, the drugs give you amnesia."

"Just for the procedure, right?"

"I promise you. I've asked my lab director, Caroline, to be with me. She's going to sift through the fluid I get out of the ovary and look for eggs. She has the best pair of hands and the most precise vision in the business. She'll personally handle your entire case, from eggs to embryos."

"Good. How long did you say it would take?"

"Ten, fifteen minutes. The procedure's very safe. But there's always the remote chance of a complication."

"Such as?"

"Such as puncture of the bowel, bladder, blood vessel, infection, bleeding, the risks of transfusions."

"Just like riding on the Beltway, or aboard *Air Force One*. I know I can trust you. I know I picked a winner."

A winner. She wondered if Janet knew that her doctor had just been stripped of her OB privileges.

"You have to start the progesterone shots right after the egg retrieval," Anya said. The other day she had taught the president how to inject his wife in the butt with the hormone considered essential to create optimal conditions for embryos to grow in the womb.

"Boy, do I remember! I still have your green iodine marks on my ass. Robert's target. He can't wait to get me. To him, this is all a game." Janet got serious again. "Now tell me the truth, Anya. What are my chances?"

"With Caroline handling your eggs and your embryos, it could be as high as 20 percent."

"Did you say twenty?"

"My grandma used to say, 'You can't make the bride look prettier than she is,'" Anya smiled.

"Your grandma had something to say about everything. Even about my fertility."

"That's why I love her so much. There was never any holding back."

"But is 20 percent specific to my case?"

"You mean—as a First Lady?" Anya smiled.

"No. As a cancer survivor."

She never forgot to mention the cancer. Every time they met. Anya, on the other hand, tried to store Janet's history as remotely as her brain allowed. She needed to stay on target, upbeat, inspiring confidence in her patient. "No," she said. "Not really."

"Be honest with me, Anya. After my chemotherapy, I went into menopause for almost a year." Janet fought back tears.

"I know. But your periods have been back for over a year. And you're regular now. Right?"

"Yes. But are you sure my hormones—"

"Your hormone levels are fine." They weren't in court. Hippocrates didn't include *the whole truth* in his oath. There was no sense in being scientifically correct here. Keeping Janet's spirits high was far more important. "And you've been responding very well to the fertility drugs for—"

"An old maid."

"You're forty-two. That's not old. You're at the prime of your life."

"Only my ovaries don't know it." Right she was. There was a disconnect between the ovaries and the rest of the body. A major error in women's reproductive design. "What about genetic anomalies in my eggs? Aren't they more common after chemo?"

Right again. "At your age, we plan to check the baby's genetics anyway. You worry too much."

Janet knitted her eyebrows. "You can't check for everything, right?"

Right a third time. If an egg had an abnormal gene, there was currently no test to detect it. But there was no reason to make Janet panic. "We can check for chromosomes."

"I'm scared, Anya. I've never felt like this before. Not when I almost bled to death when my tubal pregnancy ruptured, not when they diagnosed my breast cancer, not with my mastectomy."

Anya placed her hand on Janet's. It felt cold and clammy. "The egg retrieval is safe. We rarely have complications."

"That's not what's scaring me. I'm afraid of failure."

You and I. You should only know how much I dread not getting you this baby. "You mean of not achieving a pregnancy? That's not a failure."

"Yes it is. You don't have to humor me."

How do I explain to her that if the chances are, at best, four-to-one to get pregnant, not getting pregnant is an expected outcome rather than a failure? "I'm not trying to humor you. But I wouldn't consider it a failure." She chose to leave out the explanation.

"To me, it *is* a failure. That's the point. When I married Rob, we planned on a big family. I was worried his career might get in the way. Little did I know it would be me!"

"Be kind to yourself," Anya said. "You're doing everything in your power to have a child. You're a fighter. You're *my* beacon." Was this the right thing to say, or was she putting even more pressure on Janet?

"That's sweet of you. Sorry. You caught me at a bad moment."

"Remember, there're always other alternatives."

"What, adoption? We've been through that. When I lost my periods after the chemotherapy, Rob and I talked about adopting. But he wouldn't agree to a private adoption for fear we'd be criticized for taking advantage of our status. So, we went to an agency, begged them to keep it out of the media. They did. But we were flooded with requests. Dozens of couples were ready to give up their babies for the opportunity of being adopted by the president and raised in the White House. Rob and I were disgusted with the whole thing and called it off."

Baby Marshall, Anya thought. She wondered how he was doing. She yearned to pick him up from his lonely crib and pull him close to her chest. *I've come to take you home baby.* She glanced at Janet. Oddly, they shared much more than the sofa.

"Have you considered donor eggs? There's more privacy there. The baby will get genes from your husband, and you'll have the experience of carrying and delivering the baby."

"Rob's already told me he'd rather stay childless than have another woman's DNA mixed with his."

Anya stopped short of going on to the next option. Given the president's strong religious convictions, it would hardly be appropriate. Not that she'd decided if she'd consider getting herself cloned—if all else failed.

"Do you see where I am right now?" Janet's voice started to crack. "If I don't get pregnant this cycle, I'll never be a mom. Never!"

There was a knock on the door.

"Come in," Janet said, regal once more.

An aide entered, leaving the door open. Anya got up, recognizing the code. Their meeting was over.

"I'll do my best to make it work." She smiled at Janet and hugged her.

"I know you will. You're the best. Thank you for being my doctor."

CHAPTER 8

▼

Anya stood in front of the double doors that separated the hallway from the NICU. Finally, she'd managed to free up a few minutes to see Baby Marshall for the first time since she'd delivered him. *Him,* she caught herself thinking. She was aware that the sex had yet to be determined, but she couldn't bring herself to think of the baby as "it." Alex Gordon had updated her several times since the baby's birth. Every time he called he was able to report additional improvement. Now she couldn't wait to see for herself.

Up to the time she'd pulled the baby out of the birth canal, she'd been resolved to remain childless. What was it in Baby Marshall that incited such a drastic change? What was it in this poor, deformed baby that had awakened her maternal instincts? Was it simply the fact, that she had not laid her hands on a baby for eight years? *Any baby?* Was it that she felt responsible *because* she was the one who'd delivered him and *because* he was in such poor shape? Anya knew that obstetricians should never take possession of the babies they deliver. Never! But in this case, she didn't feel guilty.

Dario, even Feinberg, had suggested there was a reason why she'd been asked to deliver this particular baby after being retired from OB for so long. She had argued a conspiracy was ludicrous. Yet, the more she thought of Baby Marshall, of how, of all the thousands of babies who got delivered at Lincoln every year, she got to deliver *him,* she was starting to think that maybe the selection wasn't random. But not in a conspiratorial way. Cody, the Cody she knew, would've never wanted her to deliver a baby he knew was deformed. Cody was the instrument of fate. It was meant to be! She wasn't a religious person. Nor was she superstitious. Yet, as a scientist, she was certain that there was order in the world.

She swiped her ID across the wall-mounted unit. The doors didn't budge. She tried again. Still no click.

Anya buzzed the intercom.

"Yes, please?" a Latino male voice asked. Probably the NICU secretary.

"This is Doctor Krim. I'm trying to get in to see a baby."

"Just swipe your ID on the wall, Doctor."

"I did. Twice. It's not working. Could you buzz me in?"

"Sorry, Doctor. But there are new regulations as of today. We're not allowed to buzz anyone in."

Today! All of a sudden! I wonder if this has anything to do with me. "Is there anyone I can talk to?"

"Sure. I'll get you the supervisor."

The NICU head nurse had a reputation of running the place like a prison warden. Anya prayed for one of the babyies' parents to come by so she could follow them, but there was no parent in sight. She felt as if they were all looking at her on the screen at the nursing station. How humiliating! "How can I help you, Doctor Krim?" She recognized the alto voice.

"I'm trying to get in to see a baby."

"That won't be possible."

She didn't even ask which baby I was here to see. Bitch! "Could I ask you why, please?"

"Your name has been flagged by specific instructions from Doctor Feinberg. Security had been instructed not to allow you entry. Not to the NICU and not to the labor floor. Is there anything else I can help you with?" The voice was cold and metallic.

I should've guessed it was Feinberg. He's using his authority to punish me, as if I'm still his resident. "You've helped me plenty," Anya said.

She'd have to find another way to get in. They had no right to stop her.

She had already turned her back to the door when the head nurse's voice came on again, "One moment, Doctor Krim."

Maybe she changed her mind. "Yes?"

"The social worker would like a word with you. She'll be out in a moment."

The social worker. Why would she be looking for me? Don't tell me they'd found the father. Bonnie said there was no father. My father was never found. And this one, the one Bonnie said didn't exist—this one would just show up? Anya wished it weren't true. Absent fathers like this didn't deserve the title. Nor the baby.

The door flipped open. Sonia, the social worker Anya had spoken to after the delivery, emerged. Her face was grim.

Did Feinberg instruct her to tell me the NICU is off limits? That would be like him, part of the intimidation strategy he's made into an art. "I have some news I need to share with you, Doctor. Why don't we step into this room?"

They walked into a small, empty waiting room. Anya felt a sharp cramp in her womb. "Is the baby okay?" She tried not to sound too frantic.

"The baby's fine. It's doing better, in fact. It's ... it's the mother."

Anya let out an inaudible sigh of relief. "Have you found the mother?"

"Yes, we did. But … not in a state we were hoping for."

"What happened to Bonnie?"

"They found her earlier this morning in a motel room. She was dead."

CHAPTER 9

▼
————————————————————————

R eprotech, West Virginia

"I need the injection," Nicholson said on the phone. There was urgency to his voice.

Cody had just received Anya's e-mail that Bonnie was found dead. Dead. The birth mother of his anomalous clone. The drought in his tear ducts reminded him how he'd changed, how unable he was to have deep feelings. Bonnie was a woman he'd worked with, seen almost every day for the last two years. And now that she was mysteriously dead, killed perhaps, he couldn't as much as shed a tear! Did Nicholson know she was dead? Did he have anything to do with her death?

Goddammit, Cody thought. The man had his priorities screwed up. *I'm still trying to figure out what went wrong with Baby Marshall.* He was about to start scanning the DNA from the embryo against the entire human genome he had stored on his hard drive. It could take all night, if not longer.

"How soon do you need it?"

"Now."

Sighing, Cody got the medicine out of the fridge and walked over to Nicholson's office.

"I'm ready if you are," Cody said, closing the door behind him.

"Finally," Nicholson said. He leaned over his desk and unbuckled his belt. His left hand caught his pants in midair, holding them right below his genitals.

Hardly the right time to bring up Bonnie up, Cody considered. He took out a fine-gauge needle and withdrew the fluid from the vial he'd brought with him. The drug was a mix of three different medicines, which together eased muscle relaxation and increased blood flow to create an erection. Wearing non-latex gloves, he swabbed the penis with alcohol and injected the medicine right into the shaft.

Why the urgency? Cody wondered.

Who was the woman?

CHAPTER 10

▼

"Baby Marshall?" A skinny man in scrubs and a white coat approached the evening charge nurse who was seated at the NICU's nursing station. It was 9 PM, a relative downtime in this hectic unit.

"Have you been here before?" the nurse asked. The man wore a face mask, mandatory for anyone who'd stepped foot in this unit. Immature babies lacked any immune system to deal with the most trivial infections. Not only a sneeze, even breathing over their cribs could kill them.

"Many times. I'm from ultrasound," the man said, his voice husky.

A small rectangular radiation counter was attached to his white coat lapel, the hallmark of anyone who worked in radiology. Right next to it, his hospital photo ID declared:

TODD BURNS
ULTRASOUND TECHNICIAN

"He's there," the nurse said unexcitedly, pointing in the direction of a heated open crib, oversized for the tiny baby, "the one with the colorless card. Haven't had one minute to change it to blue. We only got the sex assignment today."

"I came to scan the baby's head," the technician said.

"Again?" She gave him a piercing glance. "He was just scanned yesterday. There hasn't been any sign of bleeding in his brain since the day he was born. Doctor Gordon just changed the orders the other day to reduce the head scanning to once a week."

"I know, ma'am. But the radiology attending had reviewed yesterday's studies. They're technically poor. Must be a lot of interference from all the machines in the unit. The doctor asked me to repeat the study. This time in radiology."

"Take a preemie out of the unit? Over my dead body." The nurse stood, both hands at her waist, ready to fight it out.

"Are either of the parents around?" Burns asked. "They have to sign the consent form."

"You must've just landed from another planet, Your Technical Highness. You couldn't have scanned this baby before. Don't you know this little baby

41

has no claimers?" She neared his face to his. "For all practical purposes, I'm this baby's mother. And he isn't going anywhere."

"Look, the baby's only on oxygen. We'll transport him with a tank."

"What about the IV?" she said. "He's getting medicine that's keeping his blood pressure stable. Without it, he's dead."

Destiny tried to stay calm as she processed the news. She had spent the greater part of the day planning the safest way to get the baby's blood. Masquerading as one of the nurses was too risky. NICU nurses spent long hours working together. Showing up as the phlebotomist wouldn't work, since blood drawing at the NICU was done exclusively by nurses and doctors of the units. The only other idea she had come up with was an ultrasound technician. There was a high level of personnel turnover in radiology.

Destiny had no idea Baby Marshall was still on life support. Her sources within the hospital reported the baby to be doing well and on his way to the "step-down" unit. She realized now the job Nicholson had assigned her involved significant risk to the baby's life. But it was too late to back out now. "Don't worry," she told the nurse, maintaining a low, husky voice. "We'll keep the IV running. I'll take good care of him. I promise. Before you know it, we'll be back. Fifteen minutes tops."

"Let me check with Doctor Gordon first," the nurse said reluctantly. "Remember, his decision is final. No more bargaining." She lifted her right index finger in a threatening way.

"Now don't you move, Burns, until I come back."

Destiny surveyed the unit. She counted five nurses, all of whom were busy with timed feedings, medications, blood drawings, and IVs. Just as the charge nurse left the unit, a new admission arrived from Labor and Delivery. Two of the nurses rushed over to "get report" from the pediatric team.

Destiny turned the heating dial of Baby Marshall's crib to battery mode, thus avoiding the alarm going off when she unplugged the unit. Using manicure scissors, she cut the wristband, where an electronic sensor was attached, designed to sound off an alarm whenever the baby was taken past the NICU's doorstep.

The baby didn't flinch. Destiny made sure the oxygen nasal prong was in place, the tubing firmly connected to the oxygen tank attached to the crib, and that the IV was secure. She rolled the crib through the double doors and found herself in the corridor outside the unit. Not one staff person had even bothered to look in her direction.

There was no one else in the service elevator, but Destiny kept her mask on, just in case. She got out on the third floor and with a master key, opened the blood-drawing room. "Piece of cake," she told Baby Marshall. "This will take me seconds and then I'll bring you right back." The baby's chest was making its usual, rhythmic excursions, his color—excellent. He was fine.

Destiny had worked as a phlebotomist for one year. She picked the skinniest needle, a twenty-four-gauge "butterfly," and a vacuum connection to a red-top test tube. Gently, she tightened a tourniquet on the baby's left arm, but the arm was riddled with needle sticks, most of them failed IVs and blood draws, she guessed.

She should've known better ... Difficult access to veins could become *the* major problem in managing a preemie. She shouldn't have overestimated her capabilities.

The baby had a prominent jugular, but she didn't dare go there.

So all she had was the IV. That was it! She'd get the blood directly from the IV needle through a vacuum connection.

She turned off the IV for a minute and connected the vacuum connection to one end, a test tube to the other. No blood came back. The vein must have collapsed. Damn!

She placed gauze under the IV connection and disengaged the vacuum. No blood. She placed the tourniquet above the IV and massaged the arm to increase the flow. A drop of blood stained the gauze. She reconnected the vacuum and the test tube. Blood started dripping into the test tube. Her forehead was sweating, but her hands remained steady. Three cc, Nicholson told her at Reprotech. He needed 3 cc to screen the DNA.

She eyed the baby. Had his color changed, or was it the light in the room? Back to the test tube: 1 cc, she estimated. She looked at the baby's chest. The excursions seemed more labored. Shallow. Back to his face. It was ashen.

"He's getting medicine that's keeping his blood pressure stable. Without it, he's dead!"

She remembered the charge nurse's words. In order to draw blood directly from the IV needle, she had had to stop the IV from running. *How long had it been that his medicine wasn't going in?* she wondered. Two minutes, maybe. There were 2 cc in the test tube. The baby's body went limp; 2 cc would have to do. With shaking hands, she disconnected the vacuum tubing, reconnected the IV, and gently pressed on the baby's chest.

Come back. Pleaaase. Come back, Baby Marshall.

She massaged the chest bone gently and then let go for a minute. But his chest didn't move. The baby didn't gain his color back. She placed two fingers on his neck. No pulse. She tried the other carotid artery—no pulse. Both groins—nothing. Destiny gasped.

The baby was dead.

CHAPTER 11

▼

"You did good," Lori smiled and turned over to face Nicholson. They were lying in her single bed. This time he managed to last longer, prolonging the foreplay. The injection worked. "You really mean it?"

"Of course, silly," she stroked his chest. "You took your time. Didn't it feel so much better?"

"It did," he said. "Was it better for you?" He thought he noticed pink splotches on her Irish-white skin. This was their fifth time together. Would he recognize her orgasm if she had one?

"It was really nice," she said. He wished he knew what girls meant when they said that. "You get an A." She stroked his head gently, like a proud teacher.

Lori's sensitivity more than made up for any missing IQ points. Nicholson knew she had enough experience to know—watching his tiny penis and underdeveloped testes—that he was different down there. *Very* different. Yet she made him feel good.

He was lucky to have her. She was the only one of the five surrogates who worked for him that he'd dared flirt with. Actually, there were only four surrogates left. Thank God Lori didn't ask any questions about Bonnie. Funny how shy he became around the girls. He was their employer. And they were all on estrogen pills that prepared their wombs for a pregnancy with a cloned embryo, forbidden by contract to have sex. Once Lori started to show that she might be willing to reciprocate his clumsy scouting, he decided to make her the last surrogate to have an embryo transfer. And once they started to see each other, it was an outspoken understanding that her contractual vow to celibacy didn't include him.

He studied his watch. "I better scoot." He got up and started to get dressed.

She put on her bathrobe and hugged him. "Soon again."

"You bet." He kissed her, hoping he hadn't already morphed back into an ugly frog.

CHAPTER 12

▼

Anya's 10 PM meeting with Doctor Alex Gordon at his office next to the NICU was a routine check on the baby she'd delivered. By this time, all visitors were gone and the staff was at a minimum.

Gordon's eyes glistened. "Wait till you see the baby. You'd never recognize him. He's healthy!" He pointed to a series of Polaroid pictures arranged chronologically on his desk, monitoring the baby's progress.

So that's what they called healthy, Anya thought as she studied the photos. She could barely discern the baby's features. All she could see were bandages, tubing, and monitor wires.

"I don't know how you do it," she said. Alex was her favorite newborn doctor. When they were residents together, he'd had a huge crush on her. Of all the men she'd turned down since, Alex was the only one who didn't tell her she had a problem with relationships. What would Alex tell Dario if they met? Anya wondered. She hurried back to the Polaroids on his desk. "Is he off the respirator now?"

"Absolutely. We've weaned him off the machine two days ago. Today, he's just on a little bit of oxygen. By tomorrow he should be on room air."

"And the jaundice?"

"Much better. He's spent two days under the Bili-Lite. His extra toes are almost ready to fall off. Soon he'll be ready for a night at the opera."

"What about his gut?" Anya indicated a photo showing the baby's abdominal wall wide open, bowels hanging out of it.

"I know it looks gross," he said. "Normally, the bowel's all wrapped in a moist towel. Now that it looks like the baby's going to make it, the pedi-surgeons are back in the picture. They say they'll be able to return the bowel into the belly and close the skin defect in the belly with a graft. All they're waiting for is the consent."

"And—"

"Even though Bonnie told us that there was no father, now that she's dead, the hospital social services are following protocol. They're advertising. If the father doesn't show up by tomorrow, and chances are he won't, the baby'd be left with no mother and no father. By the way," he added, "I never quite understood that 'no father' business. Do you think this case is any different from the usual missing in action FOB?"

FOB was father of the baby in resident lingo. Back in their residency days, it was the rule, rather than the exception, to see a teenage mother walk in to the labor floor ready to deliver accompanied by her mother, who'd become the baby's caretaker. The male partner, the phantom FOB, would be absent, his identity and in many cases his race—unknown. "My gut feeling," she said, "is that it *is* different here. Bonnie didn't seem like the typical unwed teenager."

"So your theory is what, that there isn't an FOB at all? What are we talking about, then? Immaculate conception?"

Was he making fun of her? "I didn't say I knew, Alex. I just said it feels different from a hit-and-run."

"Do we have any clue *how* she died?"

"Not at the moment," Anya shook her head. "Her body's at the medical examiner's office. She could've been on drugs, but the drug screen when she showed up in labor was negative."

"Now that we've verified the mother is dead and the father—if any—is at large, the court will have to appoint a guardian," Alex said.

We're going in circles. I better hit him with it soon. "So it's a dispo problem then." Anya tried to sound matter-of-fact.

"Sure. No one wants this baby." *How far off can highly intelligent people like Alex be sometimes?* "I may have a solution," she said. "How difficult would it be to adopt this baby?"

"Depends on how much the court would insist on looking for the father. In the typical missing FOB cases, with a live underage mother, the court's been very helpful."

"And you could help, too, right?" She studied his face. Was he reading her?

"I can expedite the process. It would require tons of paperwork from the hospital. You mean to tell me that since this morning you've identified an adoptive family?"

So he didn't get it. "Not exactly."

"Then you must've had one of your infertility patients in mind."

"No."

"Who, then?"

Go now! "Me. I'd like you to help me adopt the baby." She said it. Anya felt her shoulders relax.

Alex's jaw dropped. "Maybe I didn't hear right," he said. "Did you just say you want to adopt this baby?"

Now *he* sounded nervous. The anxiety that had just left her must've flown across the room and infected him. "I did," she said.

"Are you out of your mind? Why would you adopt a homeless newborn with multiple deformities and ambiguous genitalia?"

"Because ... he's a homeless baby with multiple deformities and ambiguous genitalia."

He stared at her. "You're serious."

"Damn right. I could give this child a loving home."

He stood and walked around his desk. His face was close enough for her to smell the soap on his face. His warm eyes sought Anya's. "Look at me. Why would a thirty-something, highly successful doctor, the most attractive woman I've ever met, why would she—you—adopt at all? I don't understand. Why don't you concentrate on a relationship that might result in the creation of an amazing human being like yourself, your very own genetic offspring? I could see lots of men, your humble servant included, who'd love to be given the chance to audition for the role."

Alex's reaction only saddened her. "My grandma used to say '*The cobbler goes barefoot.*'"

"Isn't the saying, 'the cobbler's children go barefoot'?"

"No. At least not in my case. You don't understand. I'll never be able to have a child of my own. Never. Here I am, making all these babies for other people, my patients, while— I want Baby Marshall, Alex. Will you help me?"

He scratched his thinning hair. *He doesn't know how to say no to me. It wasn't fair to put him in this predicament.* Suddenly, her inner peace was broken. She'd have been better off asking a stranger. "This is the most beautiful, generous, and selfless act I could ever imagine anyone doing," he said. "But it's bound to ruin your life."

"Let *me* worry about that. I've thought it through. Will you help me?"

He didn't try to escape her eyes. Nor did he hesitate. "Of course I will. But I need to discuss it more with you."

"It's a deal." She could hardly wait any longer to see the baby. She stood. "Shall we?"

They exited his office.

As they neared the NICU door, she felt like a Mexican drug smuggler approaching the U.S. border. Instinctively, her eyes went for the security camera on the ceiling. She imagined the security officer calling his supervisor, "It's that crazy doctor again. She's back!" Even if someone weren't watching at this moment, her trespassing had already been documented. But she didn't care! Feinberg was unreasonable. There was no way she would let anyone stop her from visiting a baby she had delivered.

Alex swiped his card in front of the NICU. The doors swung open.

They stopped at the scrub station, washed then dried their hands, and put on sterile gowns.

"I wish we could scrub all day together," Alex said, smiling. "You know, save water. Shower with a friend …"

She smiled back at him. "Let's not get carried away."

He took a deep breath. "Okay. Off to Baby Marshall."

They walked into the NICU, Alex navigating between the islands of open cribs.

Anya's heart was doing flips. The babies' last names were written in pink for girls, blue for boys, at the head of each crib. She wondered if Baby Marshall's tag was still yellow. Crib by crib she studied the names.

A nurse rushed toward them. "Doctor Gordon, I've been looking all over for you. You didn't respond to my page."

"I'm sorry. I must've left my beeper off."

"It was about Baby Marshall—"

Anya felt her heart sink. "What happened?"

"This … X-ray technician came. Said he had to take the baby to the ultrasound unit—"

"I never ordered it!" Alex's voice escalated.

"I told him not to move until I found you. I thought you might still be in your office. And then I paged you and waited in your office for your callback. When I came back to the unit, the ultrasound tech was gone, with the baby. I called down to Radiology. No one had seen the baby. And they've never heard this tech's name before!"

CHAPTER 13

▼

"Destiny called while you were gone. She sounded distraught," Cody said.

"Distraught? Did she get the blood?" Nicholson went to his closet to pick out a business suit, a fresh white shirt, and a tie.

"She did. But she was anxious to talk to you. She … she was angry I couldn't get you on the phone right away."

"I'll call her after I've finished talking with our guest," Nicholson said. He seemed unusually chipper, considering that they were expecting the client any moment. Could it be a lingering effect of the medicine he had injected him with an hour and a half ago?

"I have Mrs. Wilson for you, sir," the secretary buzzed in.

"Put her through," he said.

Mrs. Brenda Wilson's snarl sounded so loud on the speakerphone, it was as if she were calling locally and not from Texas. Nicholson knew there was nothing to fear. Just another rich, lonely old lady who thought that money could buy her love. Puppy love. He had at least half a dozen customers like Mrs. Wilson. There was always a dog. When these ladies grew older, they worried that they'd outlive their canine companions. That was when Nicholson's sales rep would jump in, suck up to the old ladies over a cup of tea, and promise to have their pooch cloned.

"I know what you're going through, Mrs. Wilson," Nicholson said. "When my dog died last year, I was distraught. Believe me. Lorna was my best friend. Yes, I named her after my mother." The lady ate it up. "It was after Lorna died that I decided to dedicate the rest of my career to cloning dogs for dog lovers." He used one of his old marketing slogans: "The future is in cloning, not breeding."

Mrs. Wilson hung up happy. Nicholson leaned back in his chair, content. Not a bad way to make a living, making old ladies happy.

Cody hadn't gotten much sleep since he'd found out about Baby Marshall's deformities. As Baby Marshall's cloner, he felt responsible. The emotion-free anonymity of working with his building blocks—bits and pieces of DNA—had become a live baby. Natural parents are also guilty when their child develops an anomaly or comes down with a genetic disease. But their responsibility is inadvertent. Their lovemaking had set free a sperm and an egg to go on a mating dance. Random DNA strands from Mom and Dad wrap around each other, and after days of coupling, uncoupling, and reshuffling, a whole new person is formed. If anything goes wrong with this baby, it clearly reflects no wrongdoing on the parents' part.

But Baby Marshall was single-handedly crafted in Cody's lab. Each building block was inspected before it completed its course in the production process. Cody felt personally responsible for everything that went wrong. This was a failure of the worst kind. Why? To have a live baby—the very first human clone in the world—and for that baby to have so many spelling mistakes, was not only sad for the client but could set off a chain reaction, with criticism of his actions from scientists, ethicists, and politicians.

Cody resisted the temptation to call Anya. Yes, he could find out more about the baby. But he mostly wanted just to hear her voice. As it was, he felt guilty about her. If he did call, it should be to apologize. How did he come up with this stupid idea that only Anya should deliver this baby?

He knew how upset Nicholson had been about the results. And how much he stood to lose. Yet since the delivery, Nicholson had put no pressure on him to find an answer. The two men enjoyed a trusting relationship. Cody knew Nicholson recognized the pressure on him, and so he didn't add any. He trusted Cody to find out what went wrong—and fix it.

In advance of the meeting, Cody and Nicholson hadn't discussed how much the boss would tell the client.

"He's here," the secretary said through the intercom.

"Your Royal Highness," Nicholson welcomed the man at the door with a bow and a handshake.

His Royal Highness! He'd unknowingly cloned some kind of royalty, Cody realized. Nicholson must've not told him to keep him focused on his work. But knowing it now made the impact of Baby Marshall's deformities graver.

"How's your King Charles doing?" Nicholson asked.

"Cookie's fine. Except she's developed diabetes."

"I'm sorry to hear that. Is she on insulin?"

"Injections three times a day. Plus a diabetic diet and hourly finger sticks."

Cody's stomach lurched. While he had labored to rid the new dog of diseases that frequently affected the breed, he had missed a diabetes gene and stuck the dog and her owner with a lifelong disabling condition.

"But otherwise she's doing well, right?"

What a con artist, Cody thought. They were a good team. He could've never been so slick. Nicholson could sell anything.

"I've come to get a progress report," the client said. "It's been over a year since you've committed to produce my clone. You keep sending me meaningless updates. So, I decided to come and see for myself where you are."

Moment of truth ... or maybe not.

"Your Royal Highness, in our original conversation, I told you that experience from animal cloning has taught us that out of hundreds of embryos, only few make it to a pregnancy and that the miscarriage rate is very high. Cody's been working day and night on your case. Twenty embryos cloned from your genes passed the most stringent GIS testing. So far, we've transferred four of my surrogates, each with four embryos. Two of them didn't get pregnant, while the other two conceived but miscarried. We still have four embryos left, and we can make more—"

"Are you telling me everything?"

Cody felt sick to his stomach. What did the client know?

"Of course, Your Highness."

"There's been no foul play, right?"

Foul play? Cody started to sweat profusely. Did the client know?

"Foul play?" he heard Nicholson ask. "I beg your pardon, sir, but I'm not sure I—"

"Like selling my cloned embryos to couples with *no* sperm and *no* eggs."

Cody dabbed his forehead with a tissue. They were safe, for now at least.

"Please, sir," Nicholson said, his hand on his chest, as if his integrity had just suffered the most unfair insult, "you're dealing with scientists."

"Are you sure your operation is ready for this undertaking? How certain are you of a successful clone?"

"One hundred percent."

"Cookie has diabetes. What guarantee do I have that my clone will be healthy? Why should I trust that you'd make good on your word with human cloning if you made an error on a dog?

The client left, giving them a three-month extension on the contract. Cody broke the silence. "What happens in three months?"

"We lose the contract. He'll go elsewhere. For all I know, he's probably already looking for another venue. New cloner-wannabes are popping up every day. Last I heard, cloners from Italy and Israel claim they have the first pregnancy."

"What about the money?"

"We'll lose it. A 10 million dollar contract! And he's going to want his advance back. That's going to hemorrhage us."

"What if he finds out about Baby Marshall?"

"I've just been thinking about that," Nicholson said. "Wouldn't be good, would it?"

CHAPTER 14

▼

Senator Nelson Tanner III lit his Cuban cigar, inhaled, kept the smoke in for a moment, and then released a gray cloud into the foggy night. From his hotel window he could see the headlights of the cars exiting the Kennedy Center garage. Another concert had ended.

Since Megan's accident two years ago, he hadn't gone to any event at the Center. *The night of the accident the weather must have been just like tonight,* he thought. Zero visibility. What had she been doing with that jerk? The most popular girl in the entire class. And a senator's daughter. And whom did she end up with for a prom date but this nobody, this pothead. They found alcohol in her. Of course. The guy couldn't wait until they got to Virginia Beach to get her drunk. What a shame his "disappearance" had been arranged so fast, that he, Tanner, didn't get a chance for revenge. God, would he have loved to get his hands on his neck, see him choke, the asshole, watch his face turn purple, watch him take his last gasps.

"You've got to relax, Senator." He heard the woman's voice, felt her knead his back. He still had on his Armani suit. Her hand reached over and loosened his tie. "Too much tension in your life. Here, take this." She handed him a glass of merlot. He took the glass, sniffed it. It was St. Emilion for sure. How did she know it was his favorite? Was she one of these research girls at the Senate who picked her nighttime targets based on information she'd discovered? No, it couldn't be. He didn't remember ever seeing her there, nor anyone even half as attractive as she was.

"Thank you, but not now. Keep it for later." He granted her a smile and handed the glass back to her.

Tanner wasn't sure how they had gotten here or why. True, it was the Presidential Suite where Richard Nixon had spent many nights, but he hadn't booked it. Had she?

He had met her earlier at the Fairfax Bar of the Ritz Carlton, where he'd gone alone to have a drink.

"So you're now in charge of the Embryonic Stem-Cell Bill, Senator?" she'd asked, sitting on the bar stool next to him.

"I'm sorry?" He turned to her.

"It's Destiny," she took out a cigarette.

"What do you mean?" his hand shook slightly as she held her cigarette to his lighter.

"My name. My name is Destiny."

So he bought her a drink. And she quizzed him on the Stem-Cell Bill.

"Are you a stem-cell expert?" he asked.

"Oh no. How boring. I get paid too well to change careers. But I have a lot of free time during the day, so I read. This cloning business is fascinating. I'd love to be cloned. Can you imagine having two of me the same night?"

"So it's Destiny, hmmm … Are you a graduate student?"

"You're cute, Senator. Do you always ask girls you're gonna sleep with for their diplomas?"

She undressed. Her fingers released the knot in his tie like a trained Girl Scout. She unbuttoned the top three buttons of his dress shirt, exposing his gray and white chest hair.

Tanner sat on the bed, unhooked the below-knee prosthesis, placed it against the wall, and got under the covers. Her fingers traveled south.

He started to breathe heavily. She laughed.

"You've got to untense, Nelson. There are no Democrats in this room. Just you and me. I really think you need a drink."

She took the glass of merlot and held it to his lips. "Come on, Senator, drink it."

An alarm sounded in his brain.

He took the drink from her and flung it on the floor.

"What are you doing?" she asked. "We were just starting to get to know each other."

"Get dressed and evaporate," he ordered her.

Destiny sprung out of bed, put on her top and jeans, and tossed her lingerie in her carry bag.

"Your loss," she said.

"Hold it," he held onto her bag, "I need to see your driver's license."

"Why, you want to give me a ticket?"

He grabbed her arm. "Who sent you here?"

"You're paranoid, Senator. Way too uptight for me." She released herself from his grasp.

"Why were you asking about stem cells?" He attached the prosthesis onto his stump.

"Good-bye, Senator," she said, dressing quickly and running out the door.

He sat, staring after her. No doubt, someone was trying to set him up. But who? More than a handful of lobbyists had marched into his office, or had wined and dined him, trying to sweet-talk him into a changing his vote to fit their agenda. But there wasn't an immediate suspect he could pick from the crowd.

Tanner got dressed and scanned the room for cameras. He saw none. With his pants on and his shirt still unbuttoned, he checked the phones for taps. Four paintings hung in the living room and two in the bedroom. He removed each and checked front and back. There was no trace of anything suspicious. If there was a surveillance device in the room, it was expertly hidden.

He took his BlackBerry out of his coat jacket and dialed a number.

"Detective Relman, please."

CHAPTER 15

▼

"Come in, come in," Feinberg called. But when Anya opened his door, she couldn't see him.

A toilet flushed. Mystery solved.

"So you're trying to avoid me, huh?" She heard him through the open door to the bathroom.

He had paged her incessantly all morning, while she was working the phones, trying to deal with the Baby Marshall situation. She finally gave in. "Sorry, Professor Feinberg. I've been extremely busy."

"Yes. I know all about *that*," he said, emerging from the bathroom door. His solitary eye stared at Anya, measuring her response.

She'd dreaded seeing him one-on-one since the delivery. Once again, the man was getting intimately involved in her business, something he used to do daily when she trained under him. Since residency, she'd managed to distance herself, marking the boundaries he wasn't allowed to cross. Now, not only was he intruding, he'd confiscated any independence she'd labored so hard to gain. The man had turned power flexing into a science.

Feinberg wiped his wet hands on his white coat. Anya caught a strong whiff of hot dog. He must've wolfed one before he'd gone to the bathroom.

Anya knew he expected her to feel smothered by the giant ego residing in his short body. But as arrogant and narcissistic as he appeared, Feinberg was actually highly insecure with himself, always looking for approval. Not one, not two, but *three* ego walls were required to boost his self-image. No one had ever heard of more than half of the professional societies honoring him.

Around the window were the photos of the chairman with patients and other D.C. dignitaries. *No common theme except for gender*, she thought, scouting the photos. Hillary Clinton. Condoleezza Rice. Carly Fiorina.

He circled his desk and almost disappeared in his giant chair. "You entered the NICU despite my instructions," he said. "You're playing with fire, Anya Krim."

Don't let him intimidate you. "You have no right to keep me from checking on a baby I delivered."

"I told you at the delivery of this freak of nature—"

She clenched her fists. Were it not for the desk between them, she would've punched him. *Bastard. How dare he desecrate ... no, no! The baby's not dead.* She tried to control the pain in her face as her womb cramped. "That freak of nature is someone's child."

He kept on staring at her blankly. "Anyway, I've blocked your entry into the NICU. My duty is to protect the hospital." He took a cigar out of the box and sniffed it.

"Protect the hospital against *me*?" Her voice went up an octave.

He smirked, residue of hot dog between his teeth. "Even the most talented people can be slaves to their obsessions."

Obsession. She knew he'd go there. "Which obsession?"

"Your obsession with babies." Asshole. Her anger fueled the blood in her veins. "Why else would you trespass the Labor and Delivery floor *and* the NICU?"

Don't let him shake you out of balance. "I've done nothing to be ashamed of." She folded her arms. What else did he have to say?

"You came to this hospital with some heavy baggage. So since you and I both know what's in that Pandora's box you've been carrying around—"

That night in the call room, forty-eight hours without sleep. She should've never confided in him, knowing he was the kind of person who'd archive her bio only to unsheathe it against her at a convenient moment. Back then, the pendulum of their relationship would still swing between friendship and hate. Now the friendship was gone. "Go ahead, say it."

"Your obsession with babies has driven you over the edge. That legendary brain of yours turns into mush when you think of motherhood. Otherwise, how can you explain your recent behavior?"

"If you mean the delivery—"

"I know. It was a referral from the infamous Doctor Coddington. You know damn well that's not what we're talking about. It's your actions *following* the delivery. You broke into the NICU."

"I'm the obstetrician on record for Bon—"

"Record shmecord. You were told to stay out. And you didn't!"

"You were the one who'd taught me," she raised her voice, "that a good obstetrician always has two patients: the mother *and* the baby."

"You've let your past creep up on you, mar your good judgment, and corrupt your professional conduct."

Her temples throbbed. "My professional conduct?" she screamed. "How far would you go to blemish my reputation, Professor?"

He wasn't shaken by her screaming. If anything, he seemed pleased that he had elicited so much anger in her. He leaned forward. "How far would *you* go to have a baby?" His glass eye seemed warm compared to its icy counterpart.

Anya reeled, speechless. She heard her blood thundering in her ears.

No. He wasn't going to make her cry, she willed herself. "You were my mentor, Doctor Feinberg." The words came out unevenly. "I cherished the earth you walked on. You were the closest any mortal could be to God!" Her voice broke once more. She stopped and regrouped. The rest of it got easier to say. "Now that I've grown up, you feel threatened enough to want to destroy me."

"I trained you to check on babies you've delivered. I didn't train you to get emotionally tangled in your patients' lives. And I definitely didn't educate you to resolve your quest for motherhood by adopting a baby you deliver."

"I didn't—"

"I know what you've done."

Big Brother's watching. She knew it! "It was a thought expressed to a colleague privately."

"There's no privacy here." *You're not kidding, Professor.* "Doctors are public figures. Your so-called 'thought' is on record now. And we're going to Be watching you much more closely from now on. The Marshall baby has been missing from the NICU as of last night."

"I know." *God! Where's this all leading?*

"I know you know. In fact, the FBI is going to question you tomorrow. You're a suspect in this baby's kidnapping."

CHAPTER 16

▼

A *suspect in the baby's kidnapping!*
As Anya's Saab cut through the fog that obscured the Tanner estate, she rubbed both her temples with her free hand.

I can't be distracted. I have to be strong. God only knows what he's summoned me for in this shitty weather. The property was enormous. It took her fifteen minutes to reach the end of the road. The Spanish-style two-story villa was like a mismatched transplant in this Alexandria, northern Virginia neighborhood.

She rang the bell. The white cloud of air she exhaled made her realize she'd held her breath too long.

A formal smile on the butler was as cold as the weather. He hung up her coat, which stuck out like a rag in a closet stuffed with furs. The butler signaled her to follow him.

"Ah, Doctor Krim." Nelson Tanner got up from the sofa as she entered the living room. Limping, he made his way to her. His handshake was firm and brief. Megan's headshot smiled at her from the white baby-grand piano behind him.

"Ready for the Senate hearing tomorrow?"

"I haven't had much time to prepare."

"I'm sure you'll do fine. Why don't I give you a tour until Mrs. Tanner joins us for tea." His smile seemed more like a nervous tic.

He didn't bring me here for a tour.

Tanner started up the winding, wood-paneled staircase, Anya in tow. At the top of the stairway, they crossed the landing and entered a room on the other side.

"Organization's not one of my daughter's fortes," he said.

A chill crept up the back of Anya's neck. The pillow was on the floor, the comforter half off the bed, as if Megan had awakened in a panic, realizing she was late for school. Her backpack lay open on the floor. Next to it was a pile of books and notebooks. In front of the open door of her closet, jeans, T-shirts, underpants, bra, and a pair of sneakers were piled up on the carpet. *Why hadn't they straightened up?* Anya wondered.

59

Tanner said nothing.

A cough startled her. She wheeled.

"You must be Doctor Krim. I'm Gladys Tanner." The woman who entered wore a purple bathrobe and white slippers. She used both hands to cradle a martini. Anya credited her lateness to her labor-intensive hairdo and the heavy makeup. Her eyes were bloodshot.

"Has he shown you the baby's room yet?"

"Gladys, please!"

"Why, Nelson?" The tremor in her hands increased. "There's no reason to hide—"

"We were just passing time until you came. Now we can go down and have tea."

"It's right here, next door to Megan's room," Gladys Tanner insisted. "You *have* to see it, Doctor Krim."

Gladys took a sip from her glass. Her tremor ceased for a moment. "You should see what Nelson has prepared for the baby."

Anya took in the smell of fresh paint at the door of the nursery and looked around in amazement. An artist had painted a large image of Snow White on the wall across from the crib, the seven dwarfs playfully scattered along the other walls. A new crib stood in the middle of the room, a small Calder mobile swirling above it. A wooden, carved, rocking chair sat next to the crib. On the changing table were a box of Pampers, a bottle of baby lotion, Wipies, and baby powder.

"Nelson's thought of everything," said Gladys. "Everything is ready for the baby to—"

"Let's go, girls. Tea time," the Senator interrupted and steered Anya toward the staircase.

"So, how's my daughter doing?" Tanner asked.

The Tanners sat on each end of the sofa, across from Anya. Gladys was busy nursing her glass, gazing forward aimlessly. Husband and wife were obviously disengaged from each other. Did these people ever have a conversation?

"I saw Megan yesterday afternoon," Anya said, trying to capture Gladys's attention. "She's doing as well as can be expected. The baby's doing fine."

"Good," was all that Nelson Tanner managed to say.

Let's get to the point, Senator.

There was still no expression on Gladys's face, no emotion.

Tanner glared at Anya from under his bushy eyebrows. "I need you to help me determine who raped my daughter."

Raped. Anya shuddered. Tanner hadn't learned yet not to use the word with her. Or else he didn't care.

He studied her intensely. "Doctor, are you with me?"

Anya took hold of herself. "Yes, Senator. Please continue."

She knew what was to come next. Her spine stiffened. She knew he'd pick up exactly where they'd last left off. "I asked the FBI to determine paternity. They said you were the only one, as Megan's doctor, who could do it."

So, now he had her trapped in his living room, pressuring her to do something she'd already told him she wouldn't do. "I appreciate the trust," she said, crossing her legs. "But it's a bit of a stretch. I'm not trained in forensics. Once the baby's delivered, there shouldn't be a problem fingerprinting his or her blood."

But she knew that was not what he was looking for. "That would be too late," he said. "I need you to determine paternity *now*, while the baby's still in the womb."

"Close to impossible, Senator, unless—"

"Unless?" He arched his eyebrows.

"Unless I performed PUBS on the fetus," she said.

"PUBS?"

She'd expected him to pretend this was the first time he'd ever heard the word. Who was he kidding? He'd assigned several of his staffers to research it all. Maybe her answer was intended for Gladys's ears. "Percutaneous umbilical blood sampling," she sighed, turning halfway to face Gladys. "This procedure would involve drawing blood from the baby's umbilical cord."

Tanner barely waited for her to finish. "Do it," he said, as if she was one of his underlings.

Gladys broke her silence. "This sounds risky. Isn't it?" Her voice was raspy and low.

"Gladys, let the doctor finish."

So, the couple does communicate after all, Anya thought, her eyes wandering from one end of the sofa to the other like a spectator at a Ping-Pong game. "I'm not going to let you shut me down, Nelson. Not when it concerns my baby."

"This is important, Senator," Anya said. "Mrs. Tanner is right. It's a procedure that carries serious complications."

"Such as?" Gladys interjected.

"Such as bleeding from the umbilical cord," Anya said, examining the couple's reaction. Tanner's face remained blank; Gladys's tremor grew.

"Doctor, tell me the truth," she said, her voice loud and sober, "can the baby die from it?"

Anya hesitated. "Rarely ... but there've been cases."

Ignoring her husband's disapproving stare, Gladys Tanner made eye contact with Anya. "This is my baby you're talking about, Doctor. And my baby's baby. I won't let you do it."

"I'm afraid my wife's not in the right state of mind to make this decision," Tanner said.

"Doctor Krim," Gladys leaned forward, "if you're going to do this test—and most likely you will, since Nelson always gets his way—when you check for paternity, make sure they check *every* man who's come in contact with my daughter."

Anya remembered the sign-in clipboard at the security desk outside Megan's room. Was Gladys referring to anyone in particular?

Tanner ignored his wife's comment. "Some nerve James Earl Knox has got. As CEO of Lincoln Hospital, he should've started a rape investigation immediately. The man's afraid that the findings of the investigation might stop me from donating money. He doesn't realize that as long as Megan is a patient at Lincoln Hospital, the place is like—"

"A shrine" Gladys said, letting out a short, husky laugh.

"My second home."

Gladys lit a cigarette.

"Put that out cigarette, please," Tanner snapped.

But Gladys didn't seem to bother. "Sorry I can't be as sweet as Megan, honey. Isn't that why you find it so charming, so great, to spend every evening with her?" She held the cigarette between two long, arthritic fingers. For a moment, the tremor halted. Her voice came out strong. "See, Doctor, my husband has practically given away our entire estate to the hospital for this privilege. Did you know that he spends every night having intimate conversations with my daughter?"

The smoke she had deliberately exhaled into the room started to encompass them. Anya could swear she was smelling gunpowder. She had to get out before she became one of the casualties.

But Gladys went on. She finally had an audience. "And guess what? Megan doesn't talk back. She doesn't disagree. Just like *he likes.*"

"Gladys!" Tanner yelled.

"You don't have to worry, honey. I'll excuse myself." Gladys took one last puff and left the cigarette to burn in the ashtray; she got up and moved slowly toward the staircase. On her way, she stopped at Anya's chair. "Take good care of her, Doctor ... my baby."

Anya's eyes followed Gladys as she left. The butler reappeared to support his mistress's body as she slowly made her way to the stairs.

"Why is it so urgent that we identify the father now?" Anya asked once she and Tanner were alone.

The smoke had cleared.

"I need to know," he said simply.

He'd rather not waste words on what he considers a done deal already. "That would hardly justify performing an invasive procedure on the fetus."

"This maniac could be anyone … for all I know, he could be black, could be Hispanic, Chinese."

If the baby came out colored, your standing among your conservative friends would be seriously threatened. Any objection I might have that has anything to do with Megan's welfare and her baby's welfare is dwarfed against your political future!

"I'm not a bigot," he said as if he read her mind, "but the Tanner legacy hasn't been tainted for generations. I'd prefer it stayed that way."

The Tanner legacy! What a farce! "You realize both you *and* your wife have to sign the informed consent? You're both considered guardians."

He shrugged. "I'll talk to Gladys."

Was he really going to discuss it with Gladys? Did Tanner care about his wife's feelings, or was he simply going to intimidate her into signing?

"Along with his semen, the rapist might've introduced an infection into Megan, right?" the senator asked.

"Unfortunately yes."

Professor Robertson's STD PowerPoint presentation flashed through Anya's mind. Gonorrhea and chlamydia; he called them the Siamese twins of sexually transmitted diseases. A rip-roaring pelvic inflammatory disease was a given. Infertility—if she survived this attack—was likely. Syphilis was making a comeback. It would spread through Megan's entire body, infecting every system, including her brain. The bastard had literally fucked her brain. And once syphilis got to the brain, it would turn her into a lunatic. Flash—slide change. Genital herpes. He almost definitely had that to offer.

The senator leaned forward, frowning. "What you really want to say is that she could've been assaulted by one of those AIDS victims who're getting their revenge by infecting others, right?"

Cindy from 7-tower. Cindy was all Anya could see now. HIV-infected from rape. Enough to turn a young, beautiful, and smart student into a semblance of a human being hooked up to IVs, heading toward lifelong misery and eventual death.

It was as if he were asking her to beat him harder, so he would feel more pain. But she couldn't lie to him. "That's one possibility, Mr. Tanner."

She could hear Robertson's roar: "No one considers hepatitis an STD. But it is. People get it from sex. And they will go on to liver cancer or liver failure by the time they're forty."

"Hepatitis C is the other major assassin, correct?" Tanner continued his self-torture. "And then the baby could be infected … and die."

"Rarely," she hesitated, "but yes. That could happen."

"The tests are almost 100 percent accurate, aren't they? Surely you *have* tested Megan for AIDS and hepatitis C."

Anya remembered *her* anxiety while she had to wait for the same tests to come back. And even when they turned out to be negative, she'd had nightmares about the retesting in three months coming back positive for HIV. "We have, but it takes several days for the results," she told the senator. At least in Megan's case retesting wasn't necessary, since it had been twenty weeks since the assault.

"Damn it! Tell them to hurry."

Enough said about that, Anya thought. "I'll need to get a tube of blood from you and your wife," she said.

The senator was mute for a moment. "That's the most ridiculous thing I've heard in a long time. What are you trying to prove, that I'm Megan's father? I see," his eyes brightened as if he's seen the light. "First you have to prove we're the real parents. Only then will you let us decide about testing the baby's blood. Good delay tactics, Doctor. Too bad I'm not going to go for it."

She was tired of fighting with him. But it wasn't like Anya not to put up a fight. "You know as well as I do that in any paternity investigation, establishing the genetic lineage is essential."

Now she expected him to ask, "So now that you're telling me you need blood from both of us, does that mean that you're going to test the baby too?" Surprisingly, he didn't choose to go there. "Hold it," he said, raising his hand, "how on earth would blood from me and my wife be helpful in solving who the baby's father is?"

Maybe he's not just bullying me. Maybe he has something hide. A deep secret only his DNA would reveal! This thought, though not yet fully processed, made Anya even more determined to get the Tanners' blood.

"We could take a buccal smear," she said, referring to a smudge taken from the inner cheek, "but blood is the gold standard!"

"You're not getting the point, Doctor. I'm not a sissy. This isn't about getting stuck. I simply don't see the need for it."

"But—"

"I said *no*, Doctor. No!" he said calmly and got up, signaling that her visit was over.

Anya stood. "I don't think we're getting anywhere. I'm not convinced you want to help the investigation. You're telling me to stick the baby's umbilical cord, but you won't let us draw *your* blood."

Tanner didn't react. He walked her to the door and showed her the way out without another word.

Anya couldn't figure Tanner out. The domineering husband, the racist Capitol Hill power broker didn't jibe with the loving, grieving father. As the fog that engulfed her Saab grew thicker and the night darker, her thoughts got more sinister. *Why was Tanner so resistant to having his blood tested? What secret did his DNA hold? When Gladys told Anya she should check* every *man who'd come in contact with Megan, did she mean her husband?*

CHAPTER 17

▼

The sample that Destiny brought Cody of Baby Marshall's blood kept him awake all night. He was anxious to discover what went wrong so that he could put the boss's mind, as well as his, at ease. This way he might be able to correct the error so it didn't happen the next time. And next time was around the corner. With every week, the other ongoing pregnancy they had of a surrogate with a clone felt like a ticking time bomb. He had nightmares about another malformed baby born. Another monster he'd created. He *had* to figure out what went wrong with Baby Marshall before clone number 2 was due to deliver.

Nicholson walked in at 7 AM. Cody was pleased; he could use the company.

"How's it going?" Nicholson asked, giving him a light pat on the back.

"I'm checking the DNA."

"Do you think there's a chance you'll find something? With 30,000 genes, who knows what we're looking for?"

"It's a bit of a crapshoot," Cody admitted. "I'm going to concentrate on genes responsible for some of the anomalies the baby was born with."

"But there may not be a specific gene for, say, a defect in the abdominal wall, right?"

"Absolutely. It may not be a problem at the DNA level. It could be a translation error, from DNA to RNA, or it may not be either of them, in which case the protein analysis may provide some answers. I just want to find a lead, any lead."

"Agreed." The boss sounded satisfied. "We've got to come up with something before we try to clone the royal client again. I know you're working hard on that. In the meantime, I'll try to stall him as much as I can." Nicholson pointed to a journal on Cody's desk. "What's this?"

"Anya Krim's article in *Nature*. She and her coworkers are reporting success in producing stem cells that were exact matches for seven out of ten patients, including two young adults with spinal cord injury, two patients with Alzheimer's disease, one with Parkinson's, and two children with diabetes."

Nicholson's anemic face reddened. He stared at the journal as if willing it to vanish.

"Goddammit! While we're futzing around with troubleshooting, Krim is galloping ahead of us!"

"But Doctor Krim is strictly working on stem-cell research," Cody said. "She's not trying to clone a human being." Cody was still toying with the idea of asking for Anya's advice regarding Baby Marshall's DNA testing, without telling her it was the baby he had sent her and that she had delivered. Now, he realized, he'd have to go behind Nicholson's back if he wanted to contact her. And there was no way he'd betray the boss.

Nicholson was relentless. "Just watch what'll happen next," he said, pacing across the lab. "Krim's getting attention by cloning stem cells to cure illnesses. She's the new messiah all these disease-stricken families, from Alzheimer's to Parkinson's, have been praying for. And this wave of gratitude is sure to sweep Congress. Even Republicans are showing signs they might vote against the president to give embryonic stem-cell research federal funding."

"The president will veto. The majority of the Council on Bioethics has called for a moratorium on cloning of any kind. He's accepted the church position that embryos in the dish are 'little persons.'"

"Unless Doctor Krim's enthusiasts managed to gather two-thirds of the votes in both the House and the Senate necessary to override his veto."

The boss's jealously had drowned any rational judgment he might've had. "But wait a minute, isn't that what we want?" Cody swiveled his chair around to face Nicholson.

"Do you really think that Krim will stop there? Do you really think she'd stop short of reaching Mount Everest?"

"I'm not following you," Cody said. But the truth was he was starting to understand his boss's thought process. Nicholson had spent a fortune lobbying for the Embryonic Stem-Cell Bill. Yet, he was so competitive, he couldn't stand the thought that Anya stood the best chance to make an impact on the vote in Congress. And what made it worse was that she was a *doctor.*

"Everyone knows stem cells are just foreplay," Nicholson went on. "Cloning cells, organs—that's all amazing. But the real thing—the climax we aim at—is cloning a human being! Listen to the pro-lifers. They're telling the truth: one thing *will* lead to another. Guaranteed! And I bet you Anya Krim's driven to do just that. Trust me. She's devious."

Cody knew the way Anya's mind worked. And her values. Anya would never consider cloning a human being. "That's one thing I can tell you she's not," he said.

"You're the last one to be objective. You've been in love with this woman since medical school. Probably still are." Nicholson paused, contemplating. Cody could tell the turbines of his mind were revving up. *What was he going to concoct now?*

"How about you call her up and set up a visit to her lab?" Nicholson's eyes shone with excitement. "We could use a little 'industrial espionage.' Have her show you her setup. Everything: her equipment, her protocols, tools, solutions she uses. And then you bring her protocols and we try them here. What do you say?"

CHAPTER 18

▼

Anya approached the witness table facing the committee members who sat on the dais. She felt tense and unsettled. Was she internalizing a general atmosphere that pervaded in the room, or was it her own personal distress?

As she sat down in front of a sea of microphones, her anxiety grew. Room 192 at the Dirksen Senate Office Building, where the special hearing on embryonic stem-cell research of the Senate Appropriations Subcommittee on Labor, Health, and Human Services, Education, and Related Agencies took place, was packed with Senate staffers and reporters.

This was her one chance to change the balance in the committee enough to get it to vote in favor of the bill. The task was formidable. In order for her to win, Anya thought, sizing up her stern-looking audience, she had to accomplish three things: first, to separate stem cells from cloning. *Say "yes" to stem cells, "no" to cloning,* said the signs her fellow scientists held on the Capitol steps this morning. Second, to divorce stem cells from the abortion issue. Her only chance of winning her argument was to convince pro-lifers they could go on objecting to Roe v. Wade and support stem cells. Not an easy feat. The last task, perhaps the most difficult one, was to separate the brains from the hearts of the committee members. There was little chance to change the way each senator *thought.* So, she would speak to their emotions, make them *feel* why it was an absolute necessity to support the research.

The press knew she was the First Lady's doctor, but no reporter had a clue of her connection to the committee chairman. The blackout on the Megan Tanner case still held fast.

Anya looked at Nelson Tanner, but he avoided eye contact. He gaveled for silence.

"Doctor Anya Krim," he said, "is director of the Center for Human Reproduction at the Lincoln University Hospital. I believe you had some questions, Senator Godfrey."

"Yes." Senator Rebecca Godfrey, Democrat from Nevada, straightened the papers in front of her. "Doctor Krim, could you please tell us what treatment is available to women who have nothing wrong with them but whose husbands are sterile?"

This was obviously a warm-up, starting with soft questions from a friendly Democrat. Anya leaned toward the microphone. "If there's absolutely no sperm to be found, not even by surgical exploration of the testicles, then the only viable option is using donor sperm."

"Correct me if I'm wrong, Doctor," the senator grinned at her, "if the husband has no sperm, it's not unusual to take sperm from an *anonymous* donor, someone the couple has never met, and inject it into the wife, right?"

C'mon, Senator, this is all public knowledge. "That is correct, Senator."

"So, is it accurate to state that half of the genes that the child resulting from such a procedure will have will be from an unrelated, unknown *stranger*?"

"Correct." Anya wished she had a cue to derail Godfrey from this line of questioning. *Ask me about stem cells, Senator. That's the only dish we're serving today. The single item on the menu. Stem cells!*

But their minds didn't connect. "And what fertility solution do you have for *single* women seeking motherhood?"

"Same. Donor insemination."

"And in that case, again, they would end up carrying and delivering a child with half of his genes donated by a nonfamiliar stranger's seed. Right?"

"That's correct."

"Now, Doctor, what if we have the reverse situation? The husband has millions of vigorous sperm, but the wife has no eggs. You've treated such cases, haven't you?"

I don't know where this is all going, but it better be good! "Yes," Anya said. "Many women, sometimes very young, are found to be in premature menopause."

"Exactly. And what do you have to offer such an unfortunate woman?"

You're treating me like a child in class, Senator. "Egg donation."

Godfrey remained oblivious to Anya's body language. "Eggs from a *stranger!*" she practically screamed through the microphone. "So even though half the genes will come from her husband, this woman will carry in her womb for nine months, deliver, and then rear as her own child, the product of her husband's sperm and some young woman's eggs?"

Anya chose not to answer this rhetorical question.

"Now, Doctor Krim, let's look at the last scenario. What do you offer a woman seeking fertility who is not attached to a man and, unfortunately, has no eggs?"

If this was going where Anya thought it was, it wasn't going to be good. Still, she had no choice but to answer. "She could have donor sperm and donor eggs. Alternatively, we have a program called Adopt an Embryo. Such women could have a transfer of embryos from another couple that has completed their family and had extra embryos frozen."

"These 'extra embryos' will then result in a child whose DNA would be entirely foreign, paternal *and* maternal, isn't it so?"

"Correct."

Now she's going to lay it on the committee, Anya thought. Godfrey paused for a second and then leaned into the microphone. "Then, don't you think that in those cases, where the conventional fertility treatment has only DNA from total strangers to offer, cloning one's own genetic makeup presents a preferable way to reproduce?"

If she is thinking she's being helpful, she's wrong. Dead wrong! The senator wasn't there to support Anya in a tough struggle; in fact, she probably didn't care about stem cells. Rebecca Godfrey was out to attract media attention with her super-liberal views: stem cells sounded scientific and dry; cloning—human cloning—was sexy!

The first goal Anya had set for herself had failed. Her drive to separate stem cells from human cloning had faltered in the hands of a so-called ally.

"Now, wait a minute," exploded Senator Joseph Spears, Republican of Utah. "Mr. Chairman, allow me to protest the line of questioning by my distinguished Democratic colleague. Some men and women are not meant to procreate. This is God's will. Humans have to be humble before the Lord. How dare they conspire to go against the divine providence

The pendulum swung from unwanted liberal tie-ins to deep Christian conservative convictions. Anya knew she had no chance of persuading them with rational arguments.

"Doctor Krim," Tanner said, "before Senator Spears expressed his views, you didn't get a chance to answer Senator Godfrey's question. Let me rephrase it. Do you support human cloning?" Now he was looking straight at her, enjoying his power.

"*Reproductive cloning* of humans," she corrected him. He was trying to put words in her mouth, and she was determined not to let him. Tanner was full of himself, as were most of the other senators flanking him, Republicans on the right and Democrats on the left. Many of them came from families where legacy meant everything. Nelson Tanner himself was the III: every firstborn male in the Tanner clan was given the name Nelson and was subsequently catalogued. Had Megan been a boy, she would have been Nelson Tanner IV.

Why did these families use the same name when their offspring were supposedly reared to be individuals? Anya guessed that the name represented the common core from which they'd drawn their life. And that common core was based on their blood relation—*partial sharing* of the same gene pool.

Cloning would provide such families with *total sharing* of their genetic legacy, with little room for individual deviation. It was actually the ultimate biologic expression of *conservatism.*

Clone me! Clone me! Anya imagined everyone of them yelling out loud if and when cloning ever became legal. Spears, Chase, Palermo, Kraft, Erhardt, and Bailey: surely they wouldn't miss the opportunity of having their very own "Mini Me."

"First of all, the road to cloning a human being is filled with land mines," Anya said. "Even animal cloning is extremely inefficient. It took about 400 failures before Dolly was cloned. In pigs, of 1,400 embryos cloned, only 5 babies were born. In mice, of 1,500 embryos cloned, only 8 babies were born. And of those babies, two-thirds died during the first week of life."

"Why is it that clones die so readily?" asked Senator Chase, clearly pleased that science was on his side.

She wished she knew the answer herself. "Maybe we haven't discovered the gene for sustaining life."

"Right. And isn't it true that even if they survive, cloned animals are expected to die young?"

You were smart enough to be elected U.S. senator. Can't you see that I'm trying to make a distinction here? "Because we clone a baby from adult cells, many scientists are indeed concerned that the clone would have a shortened life span," Anya said. "Doctor Wilmut, the man who cloned Dolly from her mother's breast cell, had to put Dolly to sleep because she was getting old and sick prematurely."

"This just goes to show that human cloning is unsafe," Senator Spears jumped in as if he'd just waited for her to confess. "Up to 98 percent of mammalian cloning results in miscarriages, stillbirths, and life-threatening anomalies."

"Any other questions from committee members?" Tanner asked.

"The emotional risks to cloned children are enormous," Senator Spears went on, ignoring the chairman. "Imagine this: a child grows up knowing her mother is her sister, her grandmother is her mother, and her father is her brother-in-law. How's that for a family structure?"

Tanner gaveled. "Would anyone *other* than Senator Spears care to make a comment?"

"I agree with Senator Spears," said Senator Erhardt, Republican from Georgia. "These 'production lines,' making Xerox copies of ourselves, threaten the uniqueness of our individuality. What's your answer?"

They were being ridiculous, yet she had to be politically correct. What a farce!

"Senators," Anya said with the little patience she had left in her, "I've already stated that I'm *against* reproductive cloning. But, for the record, it's absurd to suggest that cloning Michael Jordan would produce another basketball megastar. If Michael Jordan hadn't been coached so well, he'd never become who he is, no matter what genes he was endowed with."

"Mr. Chairman," Senator Spears again didn't wait for permission to speak. "Human cloning would encourage the perception of children as objects designed to have certain characteristics. Advancing biology and fighting disease does not mean tampering with the code of life against the Lord."

"Thank you for this most valuable testimony, Doctor Krim," Tanner said.

You're not going to wrap up like this, not before you hear me out. "Excuse me, Mr. Chairman, but you haven't given me a chance to discuss the other type of cloning. The *therapeutic* kind. I've just finished an experiment making stem cells from fat cells removed by liposuction. These stem cells can be used to make new organs."

"Hold it," Senator Spears held up his hand. Eager to battle, he leaned forward, raising his voice. "Doctor, I think that *I* know the answer, already. But help me out here, for the sake of some of my colleagues who haven't had a chance to look into this issue as closely. In order to produce a stem-cell line, you have to sacrifice *live* human embryos, embryos that could go on and become human beings like ... hmmm, me and you, right?" Spears looked to his peers on the right and the left as if he had just been handed a trophy.

Wrong, Senator! You're dead wrong! And you know it, too. You know we'd never destroy normal embryos to do this. You know abnormal embryos are tossed every single day around the world. What's wrong with getting the DNA from cells usually disposed of—to save a life? But Anya knew whatever she'd say couldn't change the association in conservatives' minds between stem cells and the pro-life issues. Spears had just tightened the last screw.

Anya felt her entire body clench. She was defeated the second time around. Not only did she fail to separate stem cells from cloning, she hadn't succeeded in pulling stem cells away from the abortion controversy. Spears knew exactly what he was doing. Once he conditioned senators to think *abortion* every time stem cells were mentioned, conservative constituents would steer them away from supporting the bill, or they could kiss their Senate seat good-bye.

This time, Anya didn't wait for permission to speak. Political correctness has gotten her nowhere. She let the words fly out of her mouth. "Listen to me!" her voice cracked. "Open your ears, your minds! Most important: open your hearts! Yes, this is the future we're talking about! It is in your hands, yes in your hands, to see into the future 'beyond your own noses' as my grandma would say. Have *a vision* for God's sake! Didn't the people elect you to this office so you could look out for them, bring them to a better place than where they are now? A group of distinguished doctors and scientists is telling you that right now, medicine doesn't have the answers to many conditions; medicine can't cure Alzheimer's, Parkinson's, spinal cord paralysis, most cancers. We sit there, we watch these people suffer and die." Her eyes blurred. She thought of Christopher Reeve. And Dana Reeve. They had given research a huge boost, but now they were gone, and only their name remained: the Christopher Reeve Foundation.

"This is not a Democratic issue," she went on, "not a Republican issue! This is about humanity—preserving human life and making their quality of life and their loved ones better. Chris Reeve and Ronald Reagan both died before they could see a cure. Michael J. Fox is very much alive. You've heard him testify. What an amazing young man. But if you insist on blocking this bill, on calling it bad names, be it cloning or, God forbid, *abortion*, Michael J. Fox's Parkinson's will continue to devastate his body unabated!"

"Wow, Doctor. Please don't hold back!" Tanner said, a smirk on his face. Anya could hear muted giggles from his fellow Republicans.

"As Christopher Reeve said in this taped message," she waved the DVD she had brought with her, "stem cells have been called the body's self-repair kit."

"I'm sorry, Doctor," Tanner checked his watch, "but we're running out of time. You can leave the DVD with me, if you may."

Anya was getting irate. The committee had no interest in hearing her out. She was wasting her time.

"How come no one's mentioned sex?" Senator Lauren Barrington, a California Democrat, asked.

"Excuse me, Senator," asked Tanner. He flashed a tired smile.

"Yes, Mr. Chairman. As usual, the most important issue, human sexuality, has been suppressed. And you know why? Men dominate the world—all because they have sperm. Pay attention: I didn't say penises. Men may have the illusion that their penises are the reason that they're in command, but they're wrong. Penises are the *vehicles* to deliver men's most precious treasure: sperm."

Anya could see the reporters around her respond. Lauren Barrington was a media favorite.

"Excuse me, Senator, but it's getting late. Please stay focused," Tanner said.

"You'll be surprised, Mr. Chairman, how focused I am. Just give me a chance." She gave him a rowdy smile. "Women have forever labored at the child-making production line by themselves—from nine months of pregnancy, through a painful delivery—and then, living at home, raising the child, waiting at night for the man of the house to bless them with his presence. The only obligatory role left for a man is to provide sperm. How many times have women dragged their husbands to bed because they were ovulating?"

Not my problem, Anya thought, wincing.

"How many times have you heard married people complain that sex is no longer enjoyable? What they don't tell you is that the reason they don't enjoy it—men and women—is because it becomes a chore, like homework. Now, ladies and gentlemen, the key to women's freedom is at hand. For the first time, we've encountered a reproductive method that does away with sperm. In fact, men are no longer necessary to partner with women in the procreative process. Human cloning will make sexual intercourse purely recreational—if not obsolete," Barrington said. "Indeed, human cloning will eliminate the need for men."

Barrington had to pause to allow the laughs to peak and trough. "Mr. Chairman," Anya screamed into the microphone, "why isn't anyone listening? I'm here to ask you to help hundreds of thousands of people with incurable diseases." *And instead, you've chosen to talk about everything else but saving lives, because all you care about is your political career and who'd get today's headlines. It's all about you, you, you!*

"We have to close," Tanner said, his face blank. Anya collected her briefcase, heavy from all the scientific papers she'd spent weeks preparing and never got a chance to present. The Republican majority was going to vote en bloc against the Stem-Cells Bill. Her strategy has failed.

A strong wind blew in her face as she made her way out of the Dirksen Senate Office Building down Constitution Avenue. The U.S. Capitol stood to her left. The image of the Washington Monument in the Tidal Basin swayed with the wind. The building she had just left, which for years had epitomized democracy in her mind, now seemed much less glamorous, filled with short-sighted self-serving politicians.

The voice of the people was left unheard.

CHAPTER 19

▼

Professor Feinberg didn't wait for Anya to sit down. "Termination," he said instead of hello. "Aborting the pregnancy is the only solution to the Megan Tanner mess." At least with Feinberg, you always knew where you stood. The short man sat tall at his desk, like King Solomon after he'd made a verdict of biblical dimensions.

Anya hadn't sought Feinberg's opinion regarding Megan's care. Yet she wasn't shocked at his words. Back in her training days, Feinberg had preached to his residents that abortion was a legitimate solution for troubled pregnancies.

"I disagree," she said.

He frowned. "Okay, let's see now. Have you given any thought as to why Senator Tanner hired *you* to be Megan's obstetrician?"

He's being a pest again. "I don't know. I can't read into my referring physicians' minds."

"This is the second time you're asked to be the OB. This time, on a comatose mom and by no else than Senator Tanner himself."

"Why would that upset you?" she asked, knowing the answer.

"Senators' obstetrical cases go to the chairman of the department." Of course. This was all about him. In the big picture, Feinberg was a little person, whose ego survived on outside boosters. If she wanted to play the political game right, she should've asked Tanner, "Did you run it by Doctor Feinberg?" But she never did. She hated hospital politics. "And guess how I found out about it?" *Tell me, Professor. I'm as curious to hear about it as much as I'd like to discuss last year's snowstorm.* "From James Earl Knox himself." *Now why am I not impressed?* "So, of course, he had asked me why *I* wasn't taking care of the senator's daughter."

She knew why Knox would have wanted Feinberg to be Megan's OB. The only way for the hospital to avoid a media scandal and a state and possibly federal probe was for Megan to be *un*pregnant ASAP. And Feinberg had performed thousands of abortions in his lifetime; Megan was an ideal candidate. "Doesn't the CEO have issues of greater priority than Megan's pregnancy?" she asked.

"This is his priority now. In fact, he now has *two* disasters to deal with. And both are your cases, my dear."

"Oh really?"

"Oh really," the fat man mimicked her.

A Lincoln Hospital fable from before Anya's time: Feinberg had acquired his glass prosthesis when an angry resident who couldn't tolerate his mockery had stabbed his left eye with a scalpel.

She hated him for bringing out the worst in her.

Feinberg lit his cigar. Smoking was prohibited in the hospital, but no one dared touch Feinberg. "Do you remember when you interviewed with me for residency? You said you wouldn't do any abortions. I still ranked you first as a candidate for our residency program."

And he'd never missed an opportunity to present her with the bill. They both knew it wasn't legal to discriminate against resident applicants because of their abortion stance.

Feinberg blew smoke in her face. "Can't you see this baby has no future?" he asked. "Her mother is brain dead, the father, a God knows what."

Compassion was not in his lexicon. "I've done the ultrasound. This baby is *full* of life. I'm in the business of creating life. A new person who'll enjoy living. A human being who'll contribute to this world. I make my impact through the little people who'll grow up to become big people—an Einstein, a Lincoln, a Martin Luther King—they are my emissaries, my extensions. I can't be a part of this destruction of a human life."

He snorted. "Save me the fluff. This baby won't make it to first grade. It's okay by me, Doctor, if you want to continue to play out your righteous ideology. Just stay off of my turf."

He leaned back in his chair as if he were getting ready for a spa treatment. "The problem is that the senator insists that only you care for Megan. He knows you'd never abort her, which goes to show how obsessed he is with his daughter. And now with this pregnancy. "

"No one can force me to abort my patient! Not even you!"

The man thrived on conflict. "Then you've disregarded good medical judgment. There've been very few cases of live births to comatose mothers. Fact or fiction?"

Anya ignored his rhetorical question.

He sat up. "Doctor, look me in the eye. What do *you* know about the effect of a mother's dead brain on her fetus?"

"Not much," she admitted, "but she's over twenty weeks pregnant. How do you propose we terminate her, exactly? Not a D and E for Christ sake."

Anya detested this procedure. During residency, she'd dread scrubbing on a dilation and evacuation, which involved aborting a second-trimester fetus. The procedure would be deemed complete only after all four limbs had been counted and the fetal skull reassembled on the surgery tray like puzzle pieces—evidence that nothing was left in the uterus.

"In this case, I don't think a D and E is appropriate," Feinberg agreed.

"So what procedure were you planning? Saline abortion?"

A saline abortion involved injecting saline, often with another drug. Several hours later, the uterus would expel the fetus.

The professor shook his head. "Under the circumstances, I think the procedure of choice is cesarean—"

He's ready to cut her open. Plain and simple. He'd never do it on another patient. But in Megan's case, he's treating her as no more than a corpse. "At this stage of pregnancy, you'd call it hysterotomy, wouldn't you?" She leaned against the window sill, trying to keep calm.

"Don't you get technical with me. I don't give a hoot what name you call it. You open up the top of the uterus and remove the baby. No need for anesthesia in Megan's case. Should take you fifteen minutes if you're slow."

It was turbo-engine Feinberg again. Everything had to be done as if he were late for a train. But Anya wasn't looking to do the fastest procedure. In fact, she wasn't going to do any procedure.

"Since the mother is in a coma, there's no one to sign the informed consent for surgery," Anya said, fully aware this was the last thing he cared about. Still, she might as well try, since she knew there was no better argument.

"Oh," he waved his hand, "the senator will sign. *And* his wife."

"I wouldn't bet on it. Let me ask you this." She took a deep breath. "Had *Megan* awakened and been asked to consent, would she have agreed to have her uterus cut open and her live fetus removed? And *the baby*, if *she* had a mind of her own, would she have agreed to capital punishment before she had had a chance of any wrongdoing?"

Anya had to stop and exhale.

Feinberg's expression didn't reflect any effect that Anya's arguments might have had. "This sounds just like pro-life rhetoric."

"I'm not ashamed. I can see this little girl grow up, take ballet lessons, maybe even get really good, a prodigy of sorts."

"Twinkle, twinkle, little star, how I wonder what you are." Megan's baby was lying on her back, staring at the Calder mobile swirling above the crib, her arms and legs moving with the music. Snow White and the seven dwarfs were keeping her company. The nursery that Grandpa had built her smelled like fresh paint mixed with baby lotion.

Feinberg jerked her from her thoughts. "So, we're planning dancing lessons already," he said, the familiar mockery in his voice.

By now, she was oblivious to his indifference. The image of the little baby stayed with her. "I will do whatever it takes to keep this baby alive. And please don't tell me this is some personal, egotistic crusade. It's not my baby. I'm not doing it for me. This little girl is Megan Tanner's "Eternal Flame," and I will keep it burning."

His smirk vanished. He used both elbows to thrust himself forward. "It's mighty dangerous for an OB/Gyn to be a pyromaniac. Remember what happened to Nero Caesar? He set his own palace on fire."

Anya stood. "What are you saying?"

"Exactly what are you *thinking*, Doctor? If you insist on keeping this baby alive, Megan Tanner may very well be the last patient you're allowed to see at Lincoln."

Last patient! "Are you threatening me?"

"If I am, so what?" he asked. "Are you going to report me?"

Jerk. He knows he can't fire me on the grounds of refusal to abort. Yet he'll find something else. "I will not abort this patient!"

"Terminate, Anya. Terminate —or be terminated."

CHAPTER 20

▼

The refuge her office offered Anya, for now, was most likely not going to last long if the circle of adversity continued to close in on her.

She opened the door. Dario got up from the sofa. She gave him a hug, her head sinking into a comfortable crevice in his chest.

He must be thinking something's happened, she thought. *He must be wondering what was it that had finally melted his iceberg.*

But Dario said nothing. He just reciprocated her hug.

"I'm glad you're here," she said and shut the door behind her. "I wanted to show you this e-mail I got this morning." She sat at her desk and clicked her mouse. Dario stood next to her, his hand caressing her shoulders.

"Here we go."

Dear Doctor Krim,

We really missed you at the Stem-Cell Foundation Dinner. But everyone understood that your priority was patient care, as always. How else would my wife and I have gotten our miracle twins had you not been there for us during our most desperate moments? We were truly blessed to have you in our life, not only as our doctor, but also as our friend.

I thought you'd be happy to know that in one evening we managed to raise over 5 million dollars, plus pledges from at least a dozen senators and representatives to move legislation forward.

I know how important this is to you. And I hope this letter will make you smile. Ever since the day you called to tell us we were pregnant, the smile never left our faces.

You are always in our thoughts, Doctor Krim.

Yours truly,
Victor Sachs

Dario squeezed the back of her neck. "See? You didn't have to be there physically. You were there in spirit. This could be a huge boon to your research."

"I wish I was as confident as you are," Anya sighed. "All the money in the world won't help if there's no support in Congress. Right now, anything I say on Capitol Hill is worthless. It's funny they call it a hearing. I wish you were there. They turned it into a showcase for the politicians. All the preparation I'd done was a total waste. Nobody cared about stem-cell research. And of course the conservative majority dominates. As far as they're concerned, anything that smacks of cloning should be banned. End of story. So I don't think Victor's 5 million dollars are going to go very far. We might as well send it to Africa to fight AIDS."

Dario walked over to the sofa and sat down. "How can we make the old farts change their minds?"

She liked hearing him say "we." "Terminal illness, maybe."

He giggled. "You mean the senators'?"

She shrugged. "I just don't think anyone cares that much until it touches them personally. Look at the Reagans. Once she saw her husband starting to decline with Alzheimer's, Nancy and his children understood stem cells may be the only hope to make new brain cells."

"Too bad he didn't live to see it happen."

She sat on the sofa next to him. Their knees touched. She felt warmth throughout her body, the comfort of having a friend. She eyed the clock on the wall. "By the way, don't you have office hours?"

"I moved all my patients to the afternoon. How did your meeting with Feinberg go?"

"Awful. Plain awful." His arms cuddled her gently. She felt sweaty and dirty against his freshness and that familiar sensual scent.

"Was it about Baby Marshall?"

"No. This time it was the *other* baby he wanted to discuss." Anya freed herself gently from his embrace.

Dario's smile disappeared. "What gives him the right to interfere in every case you take care of?"

He was cute, being protective of her like that. "Unfortunately, he's still the chairman," she said. "And this case is unusual, to say the least. *And* high profile."

"I see." Dario thought for a moment. "So, he doesn't agree with your management of the case?"

"He," she hesitated, "he wants me to *abort* the baby."

Dario must have noticed the chill that went through her body. Abortion. Just having to enunciate it gave her the willies.

"But you don't do abortions!" Dario cried

"Believe me, he knows that." She sighed. "Honestly, he doesn't care. Or if he does, he's making a huge effort to conceal it."

Dario buried his face in his hands.

Anya shook his arm. "What?"

He lifted his face, found her eyes, and said, slowly, "I'm worried this isn't just a string of bad coincidences."

"Stop it. You're going to make me paranoid."

"I'm not trying to. I love your naiveté. But you shouldn't ignore the warning signs. Feinberg's set you up with Megan's pregnancy."

Warning signs? "He was complaining *he* should've been Megan's obstetrician," Anya said. "He was pissed Tanner didn't ask *him* to manage the case, since he's the chairman of the department."

"He told you that? Then he's a con artist. The truth is Tanner *did* call him first about Megan."

Anya wiped her palms against her the sofa. If Dario was right, she was even less in control of the situation than she thought. "How do you know that?"

"Tanner told me." Was this a breach of patient-therapist confidentiality? Anya knew Dario wouldn't disclose anything he'd heard in a therapy session, except these were unusual circumstances. And no other person she dealt with had her interest in mind. "He was surprised Feinberg didn't want to take on the case," Dario continued. "Apparently Tanner said he was too busy with administrative work to give Megan the attention she deserved. So he recommended you."

If Dario was right, then both Tanner and Feinberg managed to fool her. "Tanner made it sound like *he* handpicked me."

Dario shrugged. "He's a politician."

Anya stared at the floor. "Okay," she said after a short pause, "even if that's true, where's the warning? I was Feinberg's chief resident. It would've been natural for him to mention my name." Was that entirely true? Yes, she was his chief resident, but they hadn't stopped arguing for four years. She never knew where she stood with him. And, for the first time, it was critically important for her to know!

"Except now he's giving you a hard time for doing OB. My guess is that when Tanner wanted someone to take a look at his daughter because she was bleeding, Feinberg already knew that Megan was pregnant. So he jumped at the opportunity to get you involved, knowing he'd get you in trouble with the hospital administration, since you'd do whatever you could to block an abortion."

Her instinct told her he was right. Both hands fisted on her knees, her heart quickened.

"Now wait a minute. Are you saying the string of coincidences was premeditated? Bonnie Marshall was referred to me by Cody, remember?"

"I know. And I admit I haven't found a connection to Feinberg. But don't you think it's odd that the first delivery you do since residency is this bizarre case? And that the baby disappears from the NICU? Has that ever happened before?"

"I don't know," she said. "Anyway, where does Feinberg come in?"

"He's trying to pin the disappearance on you. Feinberg's already gotten you one foot in the swamp with Megan. Now, he figures, he gets you implicated in Baby Marshall's disappearance and you sink. The man's trying to get rid of you."

Anya felt as if a nasty chambermaid were tightening her corset one notch at a time. "Why?"

"Because he finds you threatening."

"Me?" She let out a tired giggle. "I've always admired your imagination."

"Feinberg's nervous about his reappointment as chairman. His contract runs out the end of the year. The OB/Gyn Department has been losing money under his leadership. Knox wants him out!"

That was common knowledge in the hospital. But there was no guarantee it would actually happen. Firing a chairman wasn't easy, not even for the president and CEO of the hospital. Notoriously, most chairmen left their post in a coffin. "I know. But what does it have to do with me?"

"You're administration's alternative."

"You're not serious! Judging by the last two days, my name spells disaster to the administration."

"Nonsense! You've got to realize who you are. Your work is groundbreaking, nationally *and* internationally. On top of it, you're the First Lady's doctor. You give them the exposure they're so desperate for. Administration loves you." He took her hands. "Haven't you noticed how Feinberg keeps hiring mediocre doctors? These are the people he likes to have around: quiet, nonambitious, no one who's trying to outshine him. And then there's you. Double boarded in OB/Gyn and Reproductive Endocrinology. More than 100 papers in peer-review journals. You're young, ambitious, successful—and a woman! You're every hospital CEO's dream of a chairman."

She wished she could believe that. "So, in this testosterone-fueled cosmos, you're saying that being a woman is an advantage?"

"In OB/Gyn, yes! Around the country, whenever there's a chair position open, they look for a woman. 'Women taking care of women' is the slogan."

He was right. But she'd never considered herself one of these sought-after leaders. She didn't have the political savvy required to move up the ranks. Nor did she have any desire to fit into the mold. "Back to Feinberg," she said.

"He knows you from training. He's aware how desperate you are to have a child … and that you've been looking for a child to adopt."

She was hoping he wouldn't go there. "So—"

"He'd set you up as the suspect to have kidnapped Baby Marshall."

She sat back, crossing her knees. "Now, let's see if I follow you. Feinberg wants to get rid of me. He's just found the perfect opportunity … so first, I get a request to deliver Bonnie out of the blue from Cody, whom I haven't been in contact with for two years. Was *that* orchestrated by Feinberg?"

"I don't know," he said. "Continue."

"The baby's delivered, goes to the nursery, and when I sneak in to visit, after Feinberg takes away my OB privileges, the baby's missing. You're suggesting what, that Feinberg *arranged* the kidnapping? And that he's so ruthless in his pursuit of reappointment he'd risk doing something so awful?"

"Precisely."

She remained skeptical. "Even if you're right, so what? I've already had the dubious pleasure of being investigated by the FBI. It must have set the record for the shortest investigation ever. I had absolutely nothing to tell the two detectives. They seemed embarrassed with these ridiculous allegations."

But Dario insisted. "Feinberg knows you had nothing to do with the baby's disappearance. Yet, he stands to lose little if he continues plowing into you. He figures you'll ultimately be worn out and resign. And that's all he wants."

The scientist in her couldn't accept any thesis without solid evidence. "You have nothing to prove this, right? Are you suggesting I base what I do next on your intuition?"

"I knew you'd have a hard time buying it. I don't blame you. But sometimes I worry that you may not be as street-smart as you need to be in that complicated world of yours. All I'm asking you, *begging* you, to do is to keep your eyes open.

"And be careful. Be *very* careful."

Dario's warning continued to resonate with her the rest of the day. She had to give it serious thought. She trusted him. With not too much encouragement from her, he continued to be committed to their relationship. Dario had dropped everything this morning and sat waiting in her office—just so he could tell her of his suspicions. Something was happening to her from within, something new, something she couldn't quite control. Just thinking of Dario, his smile, his embrace, filled her heart.

Things will unfold eventually, she decided. Time will tell if everything that's happened in the last days was part of a plot or just a string of coincidences. In the meantime, she'd watch her step.

CHAPTER 21

▼

"Menus, gentlemen?"

"Any specials, Harry?" Tanner asked the waiter.

Human cloning. Nicholson stopped short of saying out loud. Of course here, at the Senate Dining Room, you were measured more by what you managed *not* to say than what actually came out of your mouth. In fact, it wouldn't be such a bad idea, Nicholson considered, staring at the menu in front of him, if they had political items listed on the menu, along with the price. After all, this *was* where much of the wheeling and dealing was done on Capitol Hill.

"I'll have the usual, Harry," Tanner said and closed the menu.

"Meatloaf?"

"Of course. We'll do dessert with my next meeting."

The stopwatch is on, Nicholson thought.

"And you, sir?"

Tanner's assistant had warned him the meeting was going to be short. He could talk until Tanner stopped him. And without food in his mouth.

"Crab Louis, please."

"Bloody Mary, Senator?"

"Yes," Tanner said. "You can bring it with the food. I have a long afternoon ahead of me. Better not let anyone take advantage." He winked at the waiter.

"Diet Coke," Nicholson said.

"See what I mean?" Tanner addressed the waiter. "Whenever they want something from me, they never order alcohol."

The waiter smiled, collected the menus, and left.

Nicholson scanned the room, relishing the scene. The Senate Dining Room was abuzz, Washington's political elite discussing matters at the top of the nation's agenda, he imagined. Mom always said he'd reach far. Now he was seated for lunch with the most powerful man in the Senate. And whatever the result of their meeting was going to be, just being here meant he'd already achieved greatness.

Measure every word. Don't just shove it down his throat, or he'll spit it back in your face. "Senator." Nicholson wished his voice didn't sound so squeaky compared to Tanner's bass. "I won't take up much of your time. I know what kind of responsibility lies on your shoulders with regards to the Embryonic Stem-Cell Bill. And I very much respect your moral and religious convictions. But I've come to implore you to see some of the positive benefits of stem cells."

Tanner studied the business card Nicholson had placed in front of him. "So you're with—"

"Reprotech, Senator."

"Catchy name. What does your company do?"

Careful. Watch every word that comes out of your mouth. "We clone animals. Mostly house pets."

"Nice," the Senator said. Nicholson couldn't tell if he was referring to animal cloning or the drink he'd taken a sip of now that the meatloaf had arrived. Nicholson took a bite of the Crab Louis: tasteless dish with a fancy name.

"I'm always intrigued by what people do to make a living," Tanner said. "You're the first animal cloner I've met. I bet your job is exciting, taking someone's old pooch and making a younger version. At Harvard, I took a fascinating course in genetics. I wanted to be Mendel." Tanner had an interest in science. Maybe there was hope. "So, my friend, I'm jealous that you can play with genes all day, with all these new technologies. And I'm sure you make a lot of people happy."

He's being friendlier than expected. Continue to play it safe. "That's right. Pet owners are forever grateful."

Tanner took another bite of his meatloaf. "And your plan is to switch from cloning animals to cloning humans? That would be quite a leap, wouldn't it?"

Nicholson felt a sudden drop in energy, the kind he'd get when he'd miss one of his testosterone patches. Shit! His plan was to gradually build up his case, inject some emotional fuel, and only when he felt Tanner was ready for it, hit him with the real reason he was here. But Tanner, a seasoned politician and a war veteran, knew to steer clear of land mines.

"Senator, back to stem cells—"

"Science hasn't caught up with the fantasy," Tanner leaned back in his chair, smiling. "Hollywood's obsessed with cloning. *Jurassic Park*, *The Lost World*, *Multiplicity*, *Gattaca*, even *Star Wars*." He took another sip of his drink. "You didn't expect me to be such a movie buff, huh? I watch a lot of movies when I visit my daughter at night …" His speech trailed off; the smile was gone. His mind was elsewhere.

Megan, Nicholson remembered. Tanner had changed the script. But he got to his daughter after all.

"How *is* your daughter, Senator?" Tanner must've heard this question hundreds of times in the last two years. Did it still elicit much in him in the way of emotions?

"Thank you for asking. No major change in her condition." The senator kept an even tone.

That's if you don't consider pregnancy a major change. Handle with care. He's not only a powerful senator, he's also a bereaved father who thinks his comatose daughter was raped. Show him compassion, and he'll melt.

"I'm praying for your daughter's recovery, Senator. There *have* been cases." He ventured.

"Let's change the subject," Tanner said, businesslike.

"Senator. With your permission, I'd like to explain—"

Tanner held up his hand. "The other day I'd presided over extensive hearings. We heard testimony from Doctor Anya Krim." *And she failed miserably,* Nicholson mused. "Do you know her?"

"I've heard of her."

"You should meet her. Smart woman. And quite a looker, if I may say so," Tanner grinned. "You're not married, right?"

The back of Nicholson's neck broke out in a sweat. "No."

"The two of you could enjoy each other's company. You should have a lot in common." Tanner finished his meatloaf and wiped his mouth with the napkin.

Forget Anya Krim for a minute and listen to me, goddammit! "Senator. The United States is getting involved deeper and deeper in conflicts abroad. As someone who stands behind the president's tough policy, you should give cloning a second thought."

The senator frowned. "I'm sorry, but I fail to see the connection."

"There are Iraqi war veterans who can't father a child."

"You mean those who've been shot in their private parts? You have to be pretty unlucky, don't you, to be shot in both testicles?"

Nicholson pushed ahead. "That's what happened in some cases," he said. "But you don't have to be shot. You could be exposed to biological warfare, maybe part of this mysterious Gulf War Syndrome."

Tanner looked at his watch. "What do you have to offer them?"

"Cloning our war heroes," Nicholson looked for a trace of emotion in Tanner's face, but found none. "Instead of their partners having to use some stranger's sperm, cloning will sustain these men's genetic legacy."

Genetic legacy. He hoped Tanner would think about his own legacy, and how there wasn't going to be a Tanner IV, unless Tanner III was cloned. But Tanner said, "Forget the rhetoric. What you're suggesting, if I understand you, is for these individuals' DNA to get duplicated, without adding their female partner's DNA to the mix. Nice touch."

"The partner still gets to carry the pregnancy and deliver."

"That's still not a fair deal to the woman, is it? I'll tell you something about us war veterans: we're all lucky to be alive. The losers are those who've died from war, disease, and famine. Sometimes God has given men a sweeter deal. I'm under contract with Him. I will never let anyone act against the divine providence."

Divine providence. Nicholson felt the crab salad come up his throat. Once religion stepped in, everything was lost. This was useless. The man was unmovable.

Tanner focused on a woman in a business suit who'd entered the dining room. "Thank you for your time." He stood. "My advice to you is, don't give up your day job," Tanner shook Nicholson's hand. "Stick to cloning old ladies' pets."

CHAPTER 22

▼

T he fluorescent arms of the alarm clock showed it was 6 AM.

The president sat up in a panic. In the darkness of their bedroom, he got out of bed, taking care not to wake Janet.

If this were the egg retrieval day, now would be his time to produce sperm. Now.

"Don't leave home without it," he remembered Doctor Krim saying jovially.

"Don't forget to bring us your husband's specimen," Anya had reminded Janet on the phone.

"'Specimen.' Doctors have their way with words," he'd said. "The fluid that comes out of me at the peak of emotional and physical excitement, this physical expression of desire and hopes for procreation, is reduced to a mere '*specimen.*' Once our fertility voyage's over, I wonder if we'll ever be able to enjoy sex again."

"Once we have kids, we'll have a new code around them," Janet replied. "Anytime I get the urge, I'll ask if you're in the mood to give me a 'specimen.' What do you think?"

He chose an empty room in the East Wing.

Nightmares that he wouldn't be able to perform on demand had marred his sleep. This was the first time, after the initial consult they had with Anya, that he had to be involved. Before that he was an outsider, allowing Janet to do the work. Now, he felt the responsibility, guilty that he hadn't been more involved. He let her go through this ordeal alone, just like the breast cancer, when he couldn't make it to her chemotherapy—always on the campaign trail. He should've been more attentive, cared more. He was the president now, and he could make time for his wife.

He tried to relax, erase any bad thoughts. It'd been years since he'd fantasized. The place, the time, the circumstances—nothing made him feel desire.

Janet's face and figure, her loving touch, came back to him. A warm feeling replaced the angst that had been fermenting in him all night. He and Janet were on their way to success. After ten years of marriage, meeting every possible obstacle, they finally had a chance, a real chance, to have a baby.

He viewed with pride the product of his labor: the jar was almost half full.

89

CHAPTER 23

▼

The heavy snowstorm that paralyzed Washington simplified the logistics of the First Lady's egg retrieval, dubbed "Operation Easter." With official Washington shut down, the Secret Service still had to close traffic between Union Station and the White House. The snowstorm had nullified the previous plan to airlift the First Lady by helicopter to the roof of the Abraham Lincoln University Hospital. Instead, the limousine made its way along Pennsylvania Avenue, with a snowplow leading the way.

The Center for Human Reproduction was located on the third floor. Large color photos of newborn babies, its proud products, smiled at Janet Cartwright, mitigating the anxiety brewing within her.

It was five to nine. The procedure would start in five minutes. Everything had been orchestrated and rehearsed at least half-a-dozen times. Anya was already in the changing area, ready to receive the First Lady.

"Are you sure you got enough sleep last night?" Janet asked, noting Anya's pallor.

"I feel great. Can't wait to harvest those eggs." These were God-laundered lies. How many times in her career had Anya told patients she felt well rested, when the truth was just the opposite?

Anya led the First Lady to the dressing room. "Please change into the hospital gown. Tie's in the back."

"Bra and panties, too?"

"Everything."

For a moment, the First Lady of the United States stood before her totally naked. *Pretty good body for a woman of forty-two,* Anya thought.

She tried to avoid staring at the scar that traversed Janet's right breast and made a full circle around the nipple. Whoever had performed the operation, Anya considered, did a good job.

"I insisted on coming here, despite the logistical nightmare," Janet said.

"I know. And I appreciate your confidence in me."

"Now you have to make it work."

"Janet, remember, I'm a physician not a magician. You know the stats for your age."

"If I had to go by statistics alone, we wouldn't have made it past the New Hampshire primaries, and I'd have been dead and gone. But look, I've managed to survive Stage III breast cancer—and we won the election. This is my third and last frontier, and I don't intend to lose this one either."

The heart monitor indicated sixty-four beats per minute. If there was any anxiety in Janet at all, Anya thought, it didn't show.

Lying flat against the mattress that covered the OR table, Janet Cartwright struggled to control the shivers.

"The IV is the last thing you'll feel before I send you off to the island of your choice," the anesthesiologist said. She inserted the IV needle into the already numbed skin and got immediate blood return. The saline solution started to drip.

"Here's the deal, Doctor Krim," Janet said, "you make me a mommy, and I make you rich and famous."

"Now the piña colada," the anesthesiologist said, piggy-backing a milky-white solution through a pump into the main IV line. "Think of your next vacation. Imagine yourself on the beach in Jamaica, far away from cold and dreary D.C."

The First Lady fought the anesthetics. "If you don't succeed, Doctor Krim, if—if I don't h-a-ve a ba-by, I—"

"If I don't have a baby, I—"

Alone at the scrub station, Anya tried to complete the First Lady's last sentence. She remembered an anesthesiologist telling her that he'd uncovered people's deepest secrets as they were going under.

Whatever it was that the First Lady intended to do to her, it wasn't good. Some of Anya's competitors in other fertility clinics had recently offered a money back guarantee if there was no baby at the end of the production line. But Anya had never heard of a fertility specialist getting *punished* by the patient. That would be a first.

In a moment, I'll be sticking a needle in the vagina of the First Lady of the United States. Nothing is routine about this case. And everything is at stake!

Janet's Secret Service guard, looking silly in scrubs, added to the drama. He had placed himself closer to the head of the OR table so that the exposed bottom of his boss was blocked from view.

Anya dried her hands with a sterile towel, donned the OR gown, and put on number 7, powder-free non-latex gloves. She noticed the security officer's eyes wander from the First Lady to the door, toward a tall, olive-skinned woman who pushed an isolette, the baby incubator turned egg incubator, through the door. Caroline, Anya's chief embryologist, looked as sensual in the OR as she did in her street clothes. The light blue scrubs, cap, and mask added to her attraction.

Caroline positioned the embryo incubator close to Anya and whispered, "Takes a lot of courage to do this. I give you a lot of credit."

"How so?"

"For racing against her biological clock. I just hope that if we fail to get her pregnant, you won't feel defeated."

"Don't you worry about me."

"But I do. The last few days, you've been through the ringer."

"Let's proceed. We're the A team, remember?" Anya's eyes twinkled above her face mask.

"I'll do my best."

"Let's get to it."

Once Janet's legs were covered with sterile towels, Anya signaled to the nurse to turn the music dial up: Barber's *Adagio for Strings.*

"Kill the lights," Caroline ordered the nurse. She believed eggs didn't like light.

Anya inserted the ultrasound probe into Janet's vagina. She scanned Janet's pelvis, looking for follicles—fluid pockets. Each of them harbored one egg, Anya hoped. The nurse handed her the long, skinny needle.

God, please watch over me while I do this. Don't let me have any major complication now.

"She's been under anesthesia for ten minutes," Caroline said from her command post at the incubator.

Anya steadied the slight tremor in her hand and drove the sharp needle through the vaginal wall and into the left ovary. On the monitor, she could see the tip of the needle enter a follicle, which immediately collapsed, the fluid escaping into a test tube held by the nurse, who handed it to Caroline. A moment of silence prevailed. Anya kept her needle tip in place, awaiting Caroline's announcement.

"We've got egg number 1. It's brown," Caroline said. She rolled her Rs, Anya noticed for the first time.

Anya continued the procedure. Her needle rapidly advanced between the follicles, watching them collapse one at a time.

"We have six eggs from the left ovary," Caroline said. "All brown. The eggs are probably too old."

She'd heard Caroline give these gloomy reports before. Generally, Anya wouldn't take her comments too seriously. They were more an alibi to avoid criticism in case the eggs didn't fertilize or in the event there was no pregnancy. But in the First Lady's case, she took Caroline's words at face value. It made sense that at Janet's age, the eggs might be "old." Add the insult of aggressive chemotherapy, and what do you get?

With half the retrieval done, Anya felt her body spasm. *Please, God, one good egg. That's all I ask for.* Anya switched to the right ovary, repeating the maneuvers.

"This side is better." Caroline said.

Thank God. Anya removed the vaginal probe from the vagina.

Janet Cartwright's legs were taken off the stirrups, and her body was straightened out and covered, Caroline closed the two windows of the egg incubator and removed a tray loaded with petri dishes containing the entire egg yield from the case. She pulled her mask off, letting a broad smile spread from cheek to cheek.

"Thirteen eggs," she told Anya. "Baker's dozen."

CHAPTER 24

▼

N elson Tanner's back stiffened while he watched Professor Rogers leaning over Megan's bed. As if this was the first neurologist he'd ever brought to her bedside, Tanner felt a flutter within his ribcage. When the reflex hammer got ready to hit the patellar tendon below the kneecap, his heart galloped. *Maybe ... maybe he'll get that knee to jerk.* But Megan's knee, bent over Rogers's hand, didn't flinch. Rogers tried the other knee. Nothing. The doctor uncovered Megan's skinny feet, her toes freshly pedicured. Rogers used the end of the hammer to stroke Megan's right sole. Tanner watched her toes fan out in response and her big toe flex toward the top of her foot. He elicited the same response from the left foot. Tanner's heart no longer raced. *Positive Babinski reflex on both sides.* Nothing changed in two years.

Right after the accident, the young resident who'd examined her explained this was a sign of brain injury, a primitive reflex normal only for children under two years. "I wouldn't worry about it," the resident offered back then. "They all have it when they first come in and then it goes away when the brain wakes up." But Megan never woke up. And the damn reflex was still there. Tanner knew what the rest of the neurological exam would be like. Rogers touched the tuning fork and let it vibrate at Megan's ear. His perfect-pitched child, his violinist, lay still, impervious to the sound. Rogers used the ophthalmoscope light to test the pupils. Out of habit, Tanner peeked over the doctor's shoulder. The pupils stayed wide, not reacting to light.

What can he tell me that I don't already know? Why did I bother flying him from England? It had been over six months since he'd brought an expert to see Megan. "It would take a miracle ... a miracle ... miracles do happen." He didn't need an expert to tell him that. He'd come to hate them. Couldn't stand the academic arrogance when, straight-faced, they'd all come up with the same verdict: Megan was in deep coma—that her beautiful, unique, smart brain—was still asleep. No one dared say "dead." But Tanner knew they meant it. He could tell from their body language they considered her a lost case ... a goner ... a vegetable. Why didn't they go ahead and say it rather than shrug and talk about miracles? Since when did doctors believe in miracles? Did they hold back because he was the father? Because he'd paid them to come? Because he was a senator?

"Why don't we sit down and talk," Professor Rogers, gray-haired, bespectacled, wearing a brown tweed suit, said. Tanner found his British accent soothing. Professor Kenneth Rogers was the director of the International Center for Brain Injury in London.

"Would you like something hot to drink? Tea? Coffee?" Tanner asked the man who'd come straight from the airport.

"Water will do just fine," Rogers said, motioning to the bottle of Poland Spring water on the table between the two chairs they sat on. "I've reviewed Megan's entire file," Rogers started. "I'm afraid—"

"You don't have to be so careful, Professor," Tanner waved his hand. "It's been two years. All I've been hearing is bad news."

Rogers sat up to the challenge. "Prognosis is—"

"Poor. I know. And you don't think the pregnancy—"

"Will wake the brain up? I doubt it. I'm not aware of any cases. I just want to say, Mr. Tanner, that I'm sorry you're going through this."

No doctor had ever said that before.

"But I don't want you to lose hope. The human brain can rebuild its nerve cells. Remember the Terry Wallis case?"

All the other doctors told him to *forget* Terry Wallis. That the Arkansas man who woke up from a coma nineteen years after he'd fallen twenty-five feet onto the roof of a pickup was the exception. He should not spend the rest of his life waiting for Megan to do the same. He should move on.

"Conventional medicine hasn't much to offer."

"You mean nothing, right?" Tanner buried his head in his hands, facing the floor.

"Except—"

Tanner cocked his head. "Except for what?"

"We could put her on the embryonic stem-cell brain injury study."

Tanner felt a jolt as if he was hit by a lightning. Whoa! Someone had actually dared talk about stem cells to him not at a lobbying lunch but here, at the Holy of Holies, Megan's room.

"Can you elaborate, please?"

"Stem cells in the fetus can put all organs together. The brain's one of them. When we inject stem cells, we try to fool the injured body into believing that it's a developing fetus."

"Sounds like a good theory. But—"

"Stem-cell injection into rats with spinal cord injury makes them walk again!"

"You want my daughter to be one of your lab rats, right?" Tanner regretted the words just as they came out of his mouth.

But Rogers was unfazed. "Our preliminary results are promising. By now, we've injected stem cells into the spinal fluid of about three dozen patients with severe brain injuries. Most of them showed improvement, and many regained consciousness. We were able to show reversal of brain atrophy on MRI. We have two youngsters, about Megan's age, who woke up from a coma and are both attending university now."

Tanner took a few minutes to process what he'd just heard. The anti-Stem-Cell Bill antibodies dispatched earlier, returned back to his bone marrow like stray bullets. He wanted to fight the idea. But here, in this room, there was no Senate subcommittee. There was no bill to kill. Here, he was a full-time father. And a distinguished professor of neurology, a doctor he liked, was telling him this could save his daughter!

"Could this be done with other kind of stem cells? Say, from the umbilical cord?"

"We've tried. And the results are far less promising. See, using embryonic stem cells makes sense. Every cell in an embryo is capable of developing into various cell types – skin, bone, muscle, liver, pancreas, and brain. As long as we get to the embryo before it starts specializing, we can redirect it to make new brain cells exclusively. I'm not trying to give you any false hopes, Mr. Tanner, but this is the most promising treatment for brain injury since I started practicing neurology over thirty years ago."

Rogers got up. Tanner stood, too, and escorted him to the door. Rogers put his hand on Tanner's shoulder, his expression compassionate. "I know this isn't an easy decision. I can treat your daughter right here. There's no need to transport her to London. But first, treatment with embryonic stem cells has to be legal."

CHAPTER 25

▼

"Screwdriver, Senator?"

From the wet bar corner of the 1 Washington Square Hotel suite, Destiny watched Senator Joseph Spears undress. The tremor in his arthritic hands made obstacles of the buttons on his shirt. She knew he wouldn't accept her help if she offered. Finally, the shirt came off, exposing an emaciated chest wall densely inhabited with white hair. His arms were atrophic with no muscle definition, she noted. For sure he wasn't taking advantage of the Senate gym. He struggled to unbuckle his belt and unzip his pants. Swollen knees crowned his bony calves.

Destiny watched the man in his white underpants, moving slowly to the ottoman at the end of the bed, where he neatly placed his clothes, as if someone were going to check for wrinkles. She couldn't detect an erection. Maybe the Viagra hasn't kicked in yet.

His birth date had been omitted from the official bio she found on his Web site, yet when she watched him on C-SPAN during the Senate committee hearing, she didn't guess more than sixty. Destiny was mad at herself. Her instincts had betrayed her. The man who just slipped under the covers had to be in his mid-seventies. Would she have turned down the job had Nicholson told her Spears's real age? Could she afford to? Was Spears too old and fragile to handle the excitement?

She squeezed half an orange into vodka. "Homemade aphrodisiac," she said, handing him the drink. He took a swallow.

Destiny watched her shadow on the wall, cast by the roving candle flame. In a sheer robe, accentuating her breasts, there wasn't much more she had to do.

"When was the last time you had sex?" she asked.

"Oh, I ... I can't recall right now."

"More than a year?"

"It's more ... more like ten years," he said quietly. "My wife has been dead for over six. And before that, she was sick for a long time."

A sad widower. He'd caught her off guard. She'd never been fully immune to people's vulnerabilities. She sighed. One day, when she wasn't on a job, she'd be able to show her good side, her giving side. But tonight there was no time for compassion.

He chuckled. "For me, getting some action means a heated debate with the 'Washington Boys.'"

Destiny knew all about the Washington Boys, the men-only conservative club that for years was the power that ran the nation, long before Cartwright. *But these days, the pendulum was swinging our way*, she thought. *Finally, the world was coming to realize that women are in control of the critical crossroads: food, conception, family rearing, and, of course, sex.*

She saw a hint of his arousal under the covers. "Why don't you get into bed? I'll let you be in full control," he said.

She studied his small frame. "Hold your horses, Senator. You need to give Viagra time for full effect."

"It's been an hour already."

"So what happened?" she asked. "This lobbyist who introduced us at the bar—"

"Richardson."

"Which lobby does he work for?"

"Christians for Life. We've known each other a long time."

"Excuse me for eavesdropping, Senator. I couldn't help hearing you mention Anya Krim to Mr. Richardson."

"Oh, the doctor? Yes. I've never seen Richardson so agitated. He was worried her testimony at the Senate subcommittee hearing would change my vote on the cloning bill. I told him no chance. Good ol' Richardson. He had this killer look on him when he spoke about the doctor. Why did you ask? You know her?"

"Your buddy from Christians for Life," she said, ignoring his question. "Did *he* give you the Viagra?"

"He didn't have to. It's now the hottest pill on Capitol Hill."

"Then let it work. A little bit of patience will pay off in a big way, trust me."

She neared the bed.

"Senator."

"Call me Joe."

"Joe, about the Embryonic Stem-Cells Bill."

"Yes," he laughed, "why don't you get in bed so we can discuss it?"

"You and I are going to have a lot of fun tonight. But you have to promise me one thing."

"Anything you want."

She dropped her robe on the floor and stood naked in front of him. He was ready.

She leaned toward him. "I want you to vote in favor of embryonic stem cells."

"For you, I will. Now come to bed, darling." He closed his eyes for a second.

Whatever he said now meant little. Tomorrow he'd remember nothing. She shouldn't have given him the drink. How stupid of Nicholson not to have modified the protocol for this antique.

But it was too late to reverse anything now. She got under the covers and hugged his small frame.

He raised his face from between her breasts. "The bed is starting to spin."

"You've had just a little too much to drink."

"Maybe we can open a window."

"In a minute," she said. "Try to relax, honey."

His body felt de-energized and limp. He was gasping for air. "The window—"

"Holy shit!" she yelled. She ran to open the window. His breathing grew more labored.

She sat on the bed and shook him gently. "Joe, wake up. Please wake up." She knew he couldn't hear her. His breathing got shallower and shallower. Covered in sweat, Destiny grabbed her robe, her eyes fixed on Spears. Who could she call for help? His face turned ashen.

His chest stopped moving. She leaned over his nostrils. No air was coming out. She felt for his carotid artery.

The senator was dead.

CHAPTER 26

▼

Anya awoke to the ringing of her phone. Since her residency days, calls in the night almost always meant disaster. Several potential horrors crossed her mind: the First Lady's bleeding from the egg retrieval; Megan's hemorrhaging; Baby Marshall found dead; they've found evidence that she, Anya, had kidnapped the baby … She picked the receiver.

"I'm afraid I don't have good news," she heard Caroline say.

It's the First Lady, shit. She's bleeding. It's been years since I had a patient with a major bleed from egg retrieval. Of course it would happen now. She should've had one of her young associates—well slept and worry-free—do the procedure.

"None of the First Lady's eggs have fertilized," Caroline said.

No fertilization! This was a calamity Anya simply didn't expect. Was it because the president's sperm had always tested normal or because she was too preoccupied with other things that could go wrong? She sighed. Thank God Janet was fine.

"Please repeat what you said. I just woke up."

"Yesterday I inseminated each egg with 100,000 sperm. The president's sperm was vigorous. A short time ago, I looked at each of the thirteen eggs under the highest magnification. I still see active sperm knocking against the walls. But as far as I can tell, not a single sperm gained entry. Not one. "

"I'm coming over." Anya, wide awake now, barely noticed the clothes she put on.

That there was no fertilization meant there would be no embryos to transfer. And the couple's hope to have a child would be shattered.

Could it be that the president was infertile? Anya envisioned Robert's sperm, by the millions, bouncing back and forth against the wall that surrounded each egg. Normally, it took a single sperm per egg to start a process that could end up in a baby. But for some reason, not one of the millions had succeeded in entering. Robert was forty-five; men didn't lose their fertility this early. Indeed, they never lost it.

I pray it's him, Anya thought as she left her apartment. *If it's the sperm, maybe we can still succeed. But if the eggs are the problem, nothing can be done.*

The recognition that the First Lady's cycle might fail hit her hard, shook her from within. Yes, she could pretend she was touched because of the patient's age and the fact that Janet was a cancer survivor. But Anya had treated countless women over forty before, many of whom failed. And quite a few were cancer survivors. No. It was the fact that Janet Cartwright was the First Lady that made the difference here. Anya had been assigned to beat the biological clock. And if she failed, her chances to get support for her stem-cell research would surely plummet. She was upset she felt self-serving. But she knew this was the truth.

"Good morning." Caroline looked up from her working station as Anya entered the embryology lab. "You didn't have to come here. I'd told you everything on the phone."

"I know," Anya said, "but I wanted to see with my own eyes. This case is kind of ... special." The truth was, she didn't need an excuse to be here. She was the director of the center. And the embryos she came to see were her patient's. So why did Caroline try to make her feel as if she was trespassing?

"Of course," Caroline said. "It's just that you got so little sleep the last few days, and an overdose of stress."

"As have you," Anya said. Caroline nodded. She seemed tired and strained. She wore no makeup. Her usually tight skin gave way to bags under her eyes. Her hair was unkempt, collected in a hurry by a bobby pin.

"Do you want to see the eggs?" Caroline started to cross the lab from where she sat.

"Yes, please."

"No problem," Caroline unlocked the incubator, took out the tray with the petri dishes, and gently carried it to the hood housing her microscope. She sat down at her microscope and placed the petri dish beneath it, adjusting the focus at high magnification. "Here you go. I just finished cleaning them."

Anya peered into the monitor attached to Caroline's microscope. She could see the glass needle, or "pipette," that Caroline had to use to move around the eggs. Caroline's hands were shaking, she realized.

"The eggs all look mature," Caroline said.

Eggs that don't fertilize are for Caroline what for me a patient who doesn't conceive with treatment is. I could have the hardest case, where pregnancy rates are notoriously dismal, and I'd still feel guilty! Caroline knows Janet is on the brink of losing fertility, that she stands no more than a 10 percent chance. But she's still being defensive. "There could still be a problem with the egg, though," Anya said.

"Of course. The First Lady isn't exactly a spring chicken."

"Could I see the sperm, please?"

"I've just looked at it. Still very active after twenty-four hours in the lab."

She's being territorial again. "Could I see it?"

"You're serious, aren't you?" Caroline asked. She frowned, "This would be a first."

True. When it came to sperm, Anya'd always relied on Caroline. But given the sensitivity of this case, she'd expected Caroline to go along with her request. Maybe Anya had touched a nerve. Caroline had always seemed a frustrated embryologist. Sensitive to Caroline's emotions, Anya would always mention the embryologist's role when patients thanked her for a pregnancy. But was that enough? When a patient would come back after she gave birth, it was her fertility doctor she wanted to thank and show the baby to. The embryo lab, where her baby started his or her life, was forgotten.

Caroline moved over to the next microscope station, where a petri dish filled with fluid stood on a heated stage. "Here. It's all yours now."

Anya turned on the microscope. The screen reminded her of rush hour at Piazza Del Popolo in Rome: it was swarming with thousands of active sperm, vigorously traveling in different directions.

She remembered Janet's press secretary's words: "You got one chance, Doctor Krim. One chance only. Because after this, Janet Cartwright is going back to being full-time First Lady."

"You're thinking, I got one chance and I blew it, right?" Caroline fast-forwarded Anya to now. "I put 100,000 of these guys over each egg. How could I know that not a single one would break through the wall?"

Here we go again. "You shouldn't feel guilty."

"Same goes for you," the embryologist said.

Was Caroline being nice, or was that her way of telling her that she, Anya, was captain of the ship? "Why don't we do ICSI rescue on all the eggs."

ICSI was direct injection of sperm into the egg. Caroline was a master at it.

"ICSI doesn't work that well at this stage," Caroline said. "After the eggs have stayed up all night resisting hoards of sperm, they'd hardly appreciate my poking them with a needle the morning after."

She's right. Many centers wouldn't even try ICSI after the egg has been exposed to sperm. But what had they got to lose? "It's a last resort. We've done it before."

Caroline set up her Narashigi micromanipulation equipment, a sophisticated system of hydraulically operated glass needles hooked up to a powerful Olympus microscope. She turned up the volume of her CD player, her agile body under the blue scrubs moving to the beat of the Gipsy Kings. She placed the petri dish holding the First Lady's eggs on the heated stage and peered through the microscope, stabilizing her elbows on the padded edge of the anti-vibration table especially designed for this super-delicate procedure. In a quick, decisive movement, she focused on a single egg, using the microscope to magnify it four-hundredfold. The image projected on the TV monitor. The egg took up almost the entire screen. A halo—the "polar body,"a condensation of DNA—crowned the large, empty egg. The egg was mature, yet barren. For two days, it had been waiting for sperm to come in, to no avail.

"Now, let's see which one of you guys is going to get lucky today," Caroline said, her voice bright.

Anya knew that Caroline cherished the dominance her work gave her. She had full custody of the sperm, a man's lifeblood, far removed from his scrutiny.

"How do you know which one to inject?" Anya asked.

Caroline picked a single sperm and pulled it through her tiny needle.

"I see some serious male bonding going on." Anya watched the other sperm that tried to tag along. Injection of more than one sperm into the egg would result in an abnormal embryo. And that was the last thing they needed.

Caroline used the sharp end of her needle to break away the excess sperm. "Go back to the bachelor's pond, little tadpoles," she told her subordinates.

She stabilized the egg with the glass pipette in her left hand, while her right hand pierced the egg with a needle, releasing the sperm into it. She withdrew the needle. The sperm sailed slowly into the oversized, unfilled egg, cherishing its new surrounding, like a guppy thrust from a plastic bag into a fish tank.

"One down," Caroline said, and moved to the next egg. She worked rapidly, injecting a single sperm into each egg with not the slightest tremor.

"All done," she announced. "Now we'll let them spend the night together. It's going to get hot and humid when the lights go off." She replaced the petri dish in the incubator and locked it.

"By the way, what's up with the rape investigation?" she asked.

Rape investigation. Anya's heart made flips within her ribcage. *It's been eight years, and they've never found him. They probably stopped looking a long time ago. Wait a minute: how did she know?* Anya had never told her. Then she realized what Caroline meant.

"Megan's? Not much. I don't think the FBI will come up with a suspect."

"How come?"

"Because I don't think that's how she got pregnant."

"You're kidding me. Then what happened? She wasn't one of our patients, right?"

"I wasn't hired by the senator to inseminate his comatose daughter, if that's what you mean."

"Then she had to have been ra—"

Reflexively, Anya's hands went for her ears. "Stop! Please."

"No, seriously. How else could she've gotten pregnant?"

Anya hesitated. "There's one more possibility."

"What?"

She swiveled the stool she was seated on to face Caroline. Their eyes met. "Cloning."

Caroline looked at her in disbelief. "You need to go on vacation. You're under way too much stress for anyone to handle."

"This has nothing to do with stress. It's my intuition."

Caroline's body coiled. Anya felt she was getting ready to jump on her and grab her throat. "You have to base such a proposition on more than intuition," Caroline said. "Hundreds of people are at work around the world, trying to clone a human. And not one of them has been successful. You know why? There are 3 billion letters in the DNA code in every one of the 100 trillion cells in the human body, meaning you have 3 billion chances of a misprint, a typo, that wouldn't only preclude the production of an identical copy, but most likely result in a child with major anomalies. God, this gives me the willies. This isn't science fiction. It's science terror."

Anya didn't appreciate the lecture. "Chill out. I simply like to examine all options."

Caroline picked up her backpack. "I'm off."

"Where are you off to now?"

"The gym," Caroline said.

"I wish I could detach myself like you," Anya said.

"That's one advantage of being just the technician. I do sperm and eggs. You do the people part."

"You'll check fertilization in the morning?"

"Bright and early."

"What if we get no results?"

"Then you'll have to tell the president and the First Lady it's all over," Caroline flew through the door.

Anya sat for a few minutes, thinking. Why did Caroline want to talk about Megan's pregnancy? Caroline detested small talk. What was her specific reason here? Did she know something that had to do with Megan's pregnancy and was trying to find out if Anya was aware of it? Was it her imagination, or did the dynamic in the room change after she told Caroline her theory on how Megan was impregnated?

Chapter 27

▼
_____

"Senator Spears passed away last night," Senator Tanner said as he walked into the First Lady's East Wing office.

"So I've heard," Janet said They both sat down, her desk between them. "What's prompted you to deliver this sad news in person?" She hoped she didn't sound rude, but her reserves of patience were low this morning. Still sore from the egg retrieval and sleepy from the anesthesia, it took willpower to get up, put on some decent clothes, and make her way from the bedroom to her office before the senator showed up.

"It's the circumstances of his death that trouble me," Tanner said.

What circumstances? An aging politician getting the kiss of death in a hotel room? "He died of a heart attack having sex, right?"

"So I'm not the first to t—"

"Don't you worry, Senator." She smiled. "You hold the copyright. This was just an educated guess. He was a widower for many years. Robert and I have tried to find a wife for him a couple of times."

Tanner seemed surprised. "I didn't know that. I came here because I thought you should hear about it from me before the rumors start hitting the Hill."

"I appreciate it." *A white lie never hurts.* "Where did it happen?"

"One Washington Square. The Richard Nixon Suite."

"Of all places. Men can be so stupid sometimes." Janet paused. "Tell me something. The senator must have been in his mid-seventies. This *had* to be another Viagra OD, right?"

Tanner sat down on a chair next to Janet's desk. "Viagra OD *is* the circulating rumor."

"Was the woman a call girl?"

Tanner kept his all-business demeanor. "The FBI's investigating. They don't know."

Janet sighed. "I'm not a prude, but this self-inflicted tragedy irks me. Spears was a brilliant politician who succumbed to the most primal of instincts. I often wonder if and when men will stop thinking with their penises."

Tanner coughed. "Politicians have always shown this unique capability of brain-penis dissociation. Think of Bill Clinton. And it's never interfered with their ability to govern."

Was he endorsing this behavior? "Let's move on. Let me guess why you came to *me* and not my husband with the Spears announcement: the Embryonic Stem-Cells Bill. Right?"

She'd caught him off guard but watched him bounce back promptly. "Spears *was* the ranking Republican member."

As if she didn't know. "Great loss. A good soldier. So who's the next in line?"

"Jeff May," he said.

This was marginally interesting. "Really? He could infuse the subcommittee with new blood." Oops. She hoped she didn't insult him. She didn't mean to, but Tanner *was* an old fart.

Tanner continued, his face emotion-free. "We've been in a deadlock."

"Tell me about it. Has May said anything in public on stem cells?"

"No, but he's pro-life."

"Of course. Another young politician who knows which side his bread is buttered on." This was getting tedious. She pressed against her lower belly as a wave of discomfort jolted her. *Let's wrap it up, Senator. I need to go back to bed.*

"I wanted to give you heads up on the upcoming vote. I think the subcommittee is going to vote *for* the Embryonic Stem-Cell Bill."

Did I hear right? "Hold it," she raised her hand. "Didn't you just tell me this Jeff May is a pro-lifer?"

A pause. "It's not him," he cleared his throat. "It is *I* who decided to change my position."

His voice was colored by emotion. The only time she had seen him so emotional was after Megan's accident. Spears's death was an excuse for Tanner to come talk to her. And he preferred to relay his change of heart to her and not directly to the president. "My husband's going to be upset. He's been counting on you not to let the bill get to the full Senate. What made you change your mind?"

Tanner hesitated for a moment. "I finally understood embryonic stem cells may be the only hope to cure many diseases, even regenerate brains."

"By any chance—"

She didn't have to finish the sentence. "Of course," he said. "Megan's condition brought Doctor Krim's message home. Where medicine is now, there's nothing the best doctors can do to wake Megan up. This was what I was told by every expert I'd flown in to see Megan. That *conventional* medicine had nothing to offer her. Nothing. It's been two years since

Megan's accident, and there hasn't been a single progress in medicine to offer any hope. Zero!"

"And then what happened?"

"I had her seen by Professor Rogers, a head injury expert from England. And the only thing he'd suggested that might get her out of a comatose state is using embryonic stem-cell injection directly into the spinal fluid. He's already had a few successes."

"Sounds like we have a conflict of interest, no?" she asked. Janet was surprised at herself, for the words that had just come out of her mouth. She sounded like Robert.

"There's no conflict of interest," Tanner made eye contact. "None whatsoever! My personal stake and the public interest are one and the same. The conservative position *sounds* pro-life, but it's not. Thousands of human embryos are thrown away in clinics around the nation. They serve no purpose at all. If instead of being tossed they'd be used to make new cells—hearts, kidneys, livers, brain,—many lives could be saved. And my daughter, yes, my daughter, who's one of many thousands of young people who'd barely started their lives when accident hit them and are now lying in a vegetative state, may one day wake up—open her eyes, get up, walk, talk," his voice cracked, "go to college. Don't you see, Janet? This is the true *conservative* position, for it conserves life. *This* is pro-life!"

It was hard for her to imagine what it was like for Tanner to watch his daughter lie in a vegetative state. She wanted to hug this man, the broken person sitting in front of her, after he'd removed the mantle of omnipotence. She started to rise, but her buttocks stuck to her chair. As much as she *felt* for him, she was the First Lady. Her job was to support the president. "I understand how you feel, Senator. Robert will be disappointed. But he'd told me already that if the bill passed, he'd veto it."

"You think? After all the criticism he got when he vetoed the first stem-cell bill?" Tanner asked.

"My husband is fully prepared to veto. He'll use it if he has to. He feels human embryos should not be used as commodities, spare parts. He's convinced that if this bill passes, cloning will be next. He's determined to stop this reckless science. Forever."

Back in her bedroom, Janet thought about her meeting with Tanner. Her words had sounded so cold. So not hers. Nelson Tanner had moved her. Undisciplined emotions ran through her brain. The fertility hormones managed to make a mess of her usually well-organized mind. And the new injection she started last night—the progesterone, designed to mimic pregnancy—was no help either. She fought hard to resist a strange maternal feeling, as if the baby were already there.

She *had* to get pregnant. There was no choice. There *would* be a child running in the corridors of the White House. *Her* child. And *Robert's.* How could the president have a legacy if there were no child to leave it to?

Her mind drifted. What if the stem-cell bill was vetoed by Robert, and she was still without a child?

The moral arguments she and her husband had used against human cloning suddenly seemed spurious. Indeed, she realized, with all her support of her husband's efforts to ban human cloning, she'd secretly wished for the bill to pass.

This was how far *she* would go to have a child!

CHAPTER 28

▼

Reprotech, West Virginia

Hugh Nicholson sat at his desk, trying to determine which limb of his mutated fruit fly to disarticulate. Playing with fruit flies was a nervous habit he'd developed as a teenager. Cody knew to keep up the stock if he wanted the boss to stay calm.

Nicholson waited for Destiny with trepidation. He hated confrontations. He especially dreaded confronting her. Yet, he couldn't treat Spears's death as if it never happened. After all, she was working for him.

Destiny walked in without knocking. "Still playing with your live toys, Hugh? Nothing more interesting to do?" She planted a kiss on his cheek and sat down on the sofa.

Nicholson breathed in her perfume. "This isn't just a run-of-the-mill fruit fly. We changed the limb code. Look." He lifted the fly. "No limbs coming out of the chest. Instead, there's one growing out of its head. Genetic engineering at its best. Right here at Reprotech."

She crossed her legs. "You'll never grow up. But I assume you had other reasons to call me, besides the demo."

I better get it over with, he thought, wiping his sweaty hands on his pants. "Yes." He let the fly fidget. "We need to talk about Spears."

Destiny made the sign of the cross. "Poor man."

A devout Christian all of a sudden? Give me a break! "Poor man?" he asked. "Someone in this room had something to do with his departure."

She didn't appreciate his sarcasm. "Suit yourself. You were as responsible for his death as I was."

No more sweet-talking from Destiny. "How so?"

"You sent me to have sex."

"Have sex, yes. Not to kill the poor guy!"

She sat, her back taut. "Before we started doing anything, this man looked like he was ready to check out."

Nicholson kept the pressure on. "Did you give him anything?"

Destiny walked over to his desk.

110

Reflexively, Nicholson tilted back his head. "I didn't kill the man, Nicholson. You wanted me to sleep with him so he'd change his vote. Which I did."

"That doesn't do us much good now!"

"His death was an *accident*. Accident! And I wasn't even the one who'd given him the Viagra, if it makes any difference to you."

He grimaced. "Could you please sit down?" He paused. "I believe you."

She returned to the sofa, annoyed. "What I'd expected of you, instead of this cross-examination, was encouragement. Do you have *any* idea how freaky that whole thing was, having to seduce Grandpa, who then goes stiff, gasping for air, me and him alone in a hotel room?"

"Who did you end up calling?"

"Tanner. Don't worry. He has no idea the call came from the same woman who'd tried to seduce him."

Nicholson broke another limb off the fruit fly. His face burned with rage. "You called *Tanner*? What the hell was that all about? Were you trying to tease the devil himself?"

Destiny's annoyance with him increased. "Try to put yourself in my place. What would've been *your* choice? I expected he'd have the highest stakes in this and would do anything to keep it quiet."

"And did he?"

"You bet he did!" She almost jumped off the sofa. "You haven't seen the obituary, I gather. The cause of death is heart attack. Period. Funeral's tomorrow. No FBI. No investigation."

He'd never give her the pleasure admitting she was right. What Nicholson wanted, above all, was to see Spears buried and gone before anyone had a chance to question the cause of death. And that was precisely what he was going to get. Nicholson stretched in his chair. "I assume you've looked into his replacement already."

She crossed her legs. "Of course. Jeff May of Illinois. Another conservative."

Even if she's not in the right mood, I should plant the seed now. "He should be an easy target, no?"

There was a short pause. He studied her face. She was enraged. "You want me to f—"

"Should be an easy job. And from what I've seen on TV, way more pleasant."

Her neck veins grew huge. "You're disgusting. I don't want to hear any more." She got up. "I'm out of here."

"Before you leave, what about Baby Marshall?"

She turned. "What *about* Baby Marshall?"

"I told you I wanted just needed a few cc of blood, not the body."

She placed both hands on her waist. "I didn't want the poor baby to die. It was," she sighed, "an accident."

Maybe it was time to be generous, he considered. "Okay. I accept that. So now that you've exposed yourself—"

A tired smile appeared on her face. "Sure. They've been looking for a man wearing a face mask."

"You mean you've left no tracks?"

"None whatsoever." She thought for a moment. "Let me ask you something. It's been bothering me since the baby died. What were your plans for this baby should Cody find DNA spelling errors in his blood?"

Nicholson shrugged.

She leaned across the desk again. "Com'on, Nicholson. You make plans for everything. Don't tell me you had no agenda here! Admit it. You were going to order the baby's execution to remove the incriminating evidence, no?" Her face was so close he could feel her breath.

"Sit down," he said. "Have you noticed any signs of an FBI investigation at the hospital?"

"No. I don't think there's a lot of public interest in this baby. There's only one person who *wouldn't* let the baby rest in peace."

"Who?"

"Anya Krim."

"Why?"

"She'd approached the hospital social services about adopting him."

"What? That's the most idiotic thing I've ever heard. Why would she want to adopt a genetic accident?"

Destiny shrugged. "Beats me. The woman's missing a few screws in her head. All I know is that she's been obsessed with this baby since the day she'd delivered him."

"Well, she's going to find out the baby's dead."

"Right. Plus, she has her own problems to deal with. Like Tanner's daughter."

Nicholson rubbed his eyes as if he'd just woken from a bad dream. "Let's go over this again. What you're telling me is that Anya Krim—the doctor who delivered Baby Marshall, who'd just testified at Tanner's committee to allow stem-cell research and *ban* reproductive human cloning—you're telling me that the same woman is taking care of Tanner's daughter's pregnancy?"

"What a coincidence, right?"

"A bad one. She's got Tanner's ear. Her testimony in front of his committee hurt our cause. I'd rather have a conservative Congress ban all cloning. It would be easier to reverse. But if they buy her distinction between stem-cell research and reproductive cloning and move on to legislate against cloning alone, we might as well move our business to the Cayman Islands."

"That wouldn't be so bad, would it?" She winked. "Sounds like you've just enrolled in the Anya Krim fan club."

He sighed. "Hardly."

"Do you want me to do something about her?"

"Watch her. Report any unusual development. You're allowed to scare her. But don't hurt her. Are we clear on that?"

She raised her hand. "Scout's honor."

CHAPTER 29

▼

"Habanos?" Feinberg flipped open the cigar box and offered it one to his visitor.

"Thank you, Professor, but I'll pass," Anya said. "I assume you didn't bring me here for a smoke."

The professor lit his cigar. "Fidel was right. He gave me this box last year when I headed the physicians' delegation to Cuba."

I wish he'd get to the point. "I have patients waiting."

He parked his cigar in the ashtray. "No idle talk with Doctor Krim," he said. "No no no. Doctor Krim is all about business. No pleasure."

She'd have to delay rubbing her temple, where a pounding headache, aggravated by the smoke, made it feel like it was going to pop.

"Okay, then. Your choice," Feinberg leaned back. "The FBI's telling me that you're resistant to go ahead with the PUBS."

"Megan's mom told me there was no way she'd allow me to stick the baby's umbilical cord."

"You know better than that. Patients can be manipul—"

"I didn't manipulate her."

"I didn't say you did. Only she must've heard somewhere that the baby could die from PUBS."

"Which is true."

He raised his hand. "When was the last time a baby died from PUBS in this hospital?"

She knew he was right. With experience, the procedure has gotten safer since her residency.

"You didn't answer."

"I haven't been following the stats since I stopped doing OB."

"Except you've gotten back into OB twice the same week. Or, should I say, the same day!"

Unfair! Feinberg knew damn well that she got trapped into Megan's case. That Megan was pregnant when they had called her to see the patient for a consult.

"Senator Tanner wants PUBS done for paternity."

"Not only Tanner. James Earl Knox as well."

"The voice is Knox's voice, but the hands are the hands of Tanner," she said.

"Anya," Feinberg leaned on his elbows, "maybe you haven't heard, since we haven't made it public. The FBI is looking for a serial rapist. All hospital employees are getting fingerprinted. They're being told it is for their new ID card. But we've yet to get the r—" He saw her pain. "Sorry."

He knew. She knew he knew. And she appreciated his consideration. The man wasn't all monster. Somewhere within that hyperinflated chest there was a heart.

"This investigation can't wait until after the baby's born?" she asked.

"And put more helpless patients at risk?"

"What if Megan wasn't—"

"Come on Anya. We both know how a comatose patient gets pregnant, even if we don't annunciate the word. Immaculate conception happened only once in history. Where there's a pregnancy, there's been sperm."

"I really have to go now," she said. "I understand the forensic need to identify the father ASAP. But as the baby's advocate, I have to say no. There would be no benefit to the baby and a potential threat to her life."

"It's not really your choice, Anya. I'm *telling* you to do it. Here." He pushed a hospital form across his desk. "Have the Tanners sign this consent form. The matter's closed."

CHAPTER 30

▼

"Have they searched for him all over the hospital? The step-down unit? The well-baby nursery? What—a baby in the NICU disappears just like that?" Anya screamed into her cell phone. "The baby's been missing for over twenty-four hours, and there's not a clue as to what happened to him. Security's barring *me* from entering the unit, but a little newborn in a crib can be whisked away from the NICU unnoticed? Someone in this hospital must be held accountable!"

"Calm down, please," Dario said at her side. "I'm having a hard time as it is driving us safely to the OB/Gyn Ball in this downpour."

"I know you're trying to help," Anya said into the phone. "But I'm begging you to try harder. You know how important this baby is to me. Call me if you hear anything. Day or night."

"Who was that?" Dario asked when she hung up.

"Alex Gordon, the doctor who's been taking care of Baby Marshall. They haven't found the baby yet."

"I'm sorry, honey." He freed one hand from the steering wheel and caressed the nape of her neck.

"Thank you." From the passenger seat, she watched his sculpted silhouette illuminated intermittently by the streetlights. "Do you really mean it? I thought you'd be relieved the baby's gone."

"I know how much you cared. After all, you're the one who brought him into this world. And you must feel even more responsible because his mother's dead."

"You said 'cared.' Past tense. You think the baby's dead, right? Do you know something you're afraid to tell me?"

"I wouldn't keep anything from you," he said. "I don't know what happened to him. But honestly, what kind of life was waiting for him?"

"He was an excellent candidate for surgical correction," she said stiffly, before she realized that she, too, was talking about the baby in past tense.

The rain was coming down so hard the windshield wipers barely made a difference. They were heading north on Rockville Pike. White Flint Mall was to their right, and Dario turned his car into the parking lot. *By now, the shoppers have gone,* Anya thought. Were she and Dario the only people still on the road? At this rate, they might have to swim to Half Hollow Country Club, where the OB/Gyn end-of-the-year party was taking place. She wondered if she'd be the only attending physician to show up.

"I don't want to hurt your feelings, honey. But don't you think the baby's better off—"

"Dead?" she burst out. "No one's better off dead. There's *hope* for him."

Dario shut off the motor. He touched her shoulders. She could barely see his face. "You got yourself too emotionally involved," he said. "You should try to step back."

She freed herself from his grip. "You want me to be cold and indifferent?"

"You couldn't be." His voice was soft. "You're the most compassionate woman I've ever met. And I don't want you to change. Not ever. But in this baby's case, you're letting your feelings cloud your judgment."

"There's nothing wrong with that. I'm done being a doctor on this case. This child is an orphan, and I want to adopt him."

"Why?"

Pain rose in her chest. "Why?"

"Yes, why? I need to understand something. What made you choose *this* baby?"

"Because," she choked on the words, "because he's helpless. Alone in the world. He's in the hands of strangers, none of whom care about him."

He hugged her. "I need to prepare you for the possibility that he won't be found alive."

What does he know that he's not telling me? "Be straight with me, Dario. I'm not as fragile as I may seem."

"Honest to God, I don't know where the baby is. But I have bad vibes. A baby in his condition taken out of intensive care may not survive."

He's right. I've been denying the inevitable. "I pray you're wrong," she said.

The rain slowed.

"I really don't understand why you insist on adopting," Dario said. "I mean any baby! You're young. You're smart. Successful. Gorgeous! You have extraordinary genes to give your child. Don't you want to have your own baby, conceived with a man you share your life with?"

She burst into tears.

"You look smashing." Dario said.

Anya wished she *felt* pretty.

"I mean it," he insisted. "Without a drop of makeup or jewelry, you're stunning."

They were in the valet line in front of the country club. Anya watched her young residents as they emerged from their cars with their significant others, all decked out, ready to party. When she was a resident, she'd never bring a date to these affairs, knowing "dates" had expectations.

There was just one car left in front of them.

"Remember what I do for a living." Dario turned to face her. "I understand what's going with you much better than you think. And I'm ready to wait."

A psychologist, yes, but a mind reader? She looked up at him, working on a smile. "Let's just try to have fun tonight," she said.

CHAPTER 31

▼
————————————————————————

Anya was back at the hospital. Ignoring Dario's protest, she decided she had to personally check the First Lady's canister. Caroline didn't argue when Anya told her at the party what she intended to do. Nevertheless, Anya sensed a subtle resentment.

"It's a great idea," Caroline said. "Sorry I didn't think of checking it before. But you don't have to do it, Anya. You have enough stuff to deal with right now. I'll check and report back to you."

"I want to look into the canister myself, make sure not a single embryo's been left, and that it's filled to the rim with liquid nitrogen."

Human embryos could stay alive—potentially forever—as long as they were submerged in liquid nitrogen, the deep-freezing substance that kept the temperature at 196 degrees below 0 centigrade. Anya hadn't opened one of these tanks in years. Yet, the memory of the cool, white, odorless vapor rushing in her face was still fresh in her mind.

"I filled up all the tanks and signed off on the frozen embryo inventory," Caroline told her. "The tank we've designated for the First Lady has no embryos in it, as per the inventory, and should be filled to the rim. As I've said, I'll gladly check one more time if you want me to."

She's being territorial again. "Thanks, Caroline. You know how much I trust you. The First Lady was pleased to hear you'd be handling her eggs and embryos. But for my own peace of mind, I need to look myself. As far as the First Lady's IVF cycle goes, the responsibility's mine."

This was the next thing that could go wrong. She tried to imagine who would be torturing her this time? Professor Feinberg? James Earl Knox? Nelson Tanner III? All three of them together in an investigative committee from hell?

When was the frozen embryo canister checked last, Doctor?

I think—

You think, Doctor, or you know?

I told Caroline to check it the night before.

You told Caroline? Did it occur to you that you should've checked it yourself? That had you spared a minute or two of your precious time and examined the

119

tank before the First Lady's embryos were plunged into it, you'd have realized that it was three-quarters empty? Now, all the First Lady's embryos are dead.

And you've got blood on your hands.

"Suit yourself," Caroline shrugged. "Here's the key to the cryo room. Just make sure you shut the lid tight, or it'll set off the alarm."

The cryo room was located on the ground floor. Anya closed the door behind her. An eerie feeling took over her as she stood facing three stainless steel tanks, each two feet tall and two feet in diameter. Liquid nitrogen was piped into each tank through the wall from the manifold room. *I'm here on my own, but in a strange way, I'm not alone at all.* Keeping her company were thousands of viable embryos whose lives were suspended in a pause mode.

Anya spotted the tank Caroline had designated for the First Lady's embryos. She had to climb up a double step stool to reach the lid.

With considerable effort, she jerked it open. A strong, odor of rotting fruit or camphor assailed her nostrils. Her eyes became watery, her nose started dripping, her temples pounded mercilessly; warm sweat covered her from head to toe. Still, she had the presence of mind to put the lid back on before she jumped off the double stool. She could barely see anything through the thick vapor that filled the room.

This isn't normal liquid nitrogen vapor. This is some kind of noxious gas. Dangerous! Lethal! Any embryo exposed to it will die immediately. Someone's trying to sabotage the First Lady's fertility treatment!

Anya ran to the door. Her chest was tight, and she struggled for breath. She shut the cryo room door behind her and rushed back to the lab, panicking. The tightness in her chest got worse.

The lab was empty. There was no one to call for help. Close to fainting, Anya dragged herself to the elevator outside the lab. The buttons inside the elevator were blurry. She felt for the bottom one and pushed it, praying it was 2.

What was it that just happened? She tried to focus in the elevator. *Why would anyone do this?*

Seconds later, the elevator door opened to the Emergency Room.

"Omigod, what happened to you?" an intern yelled.

"I've been exposed to a poison gas in the embryo cryo room."

"It must be liquid nitrogen. Let me get you a stretcher."

"No. Not liquid nitrogen. And don't put me on a stretcher yet. I need water to rinse my eyes. And a pair of scissors."

She was rinsing her eyes above the sink when he brought the scissors, together with other ER doctors.

"Now, cut off my clothes," she told him. Her head was pounding.

"Excuse me?"

"You heard me. Get two large plastic bags and cut off all my clothing. Seal them in one bag and then put one bag inside the other."

"Doctor Krim, I'm Jeff Roberts, the chief resident down here," a young doctor said. "What are you complaining of?"

"I think it's nerve gas. Tell your intern to cut my clothes off. And get me some atropine."

"Do it, Greg," the chief ordered. Anya leaned over the sink, continuing to rinse her eyes. She felt the scissors cut her scrubs. In a matter of seconds, she was stripped to her bra and underpants.

"This is the decontamination shower, Anya. Tell me if it's hot enough." A familiar voice. A blessed voice. Thank God.

"Dario, how did you get here?" Her eyes were still closed.

"The chief resident called me. I'm on the hospital's bio-chem rescue team. You'll be okay. Here, hold my hand."

One more thing she didn't know about Dario. She let him lead her to the shower, feeling strong streams of warm water from all directions. "Take off your underwear," Dario said, "and hand them to me. I'll throw them in the contaminated bag." She felt for his hand and handed him her soaked bra and underpants.

"Keep rinsing your eyes," he ordered. "Are you sure it was nerve gas?"

"No, but I have the symptoms."

"You're probably right. We have a more specific nerve agent antidote kit Mark I injector." Dario jabbed a needle into her thigh. "Works against soman. I'll repeat the injection in fifteen to twenty minutes."

"You should dispatch a team to the cryo room," she told Dario. "We need to decontaminate it and make sure the other storage tanks are kept shut or else all the embryos will die."

"A special ATF unit is already there. They're investigating the possibility of terrorism."

Terrorism? As she felt her body cleansing, she began to refocus on what just happened. If this was indeed nerve gas, it would threaten the life of any person who'd open the lid. Yes, the poison could kill embryos. Yet the tank had no embryos in it. Someone had planned a nerve gas attack on the person who was going to open it first. Normally, that would be Caroline. Why would anyone try to kill Caroline?

Could *she, Anya,* be the target? Could anyone manage to sneak into the cryo room and put the poisonous gas in the freezing tank during the hour or so that had elapsed from when she told Caroline she was going there?

Who wanted her dead?

CHAPTER 32

▼

"I just needed some TLC. I guess I'm as needy as any patient," the First Lady told Anya when she showed up.

That's a bit of an understatement, Anya thought. Janet's call came in at 7 AM, only two hours after Anya had finally managed to fall asleep in the resident call room. Dario's presence was big help. The magic of his hands massaging her sore body had finally calmed her. Now, the only physical reminder of last night's nerve gas attack was the burning in her eyes.

Janet Cartwright was still in her nightgown, seated on the blue suede lounger in her bedroom, reading the *Wall Street Journal. Perhaps she really believes she is no needier than any other patient,* Anya thought, *but that isn't the case.* Two days following egg retrieval, most patients were up and about. Many would go back to work. And almost no one would demand—and get—a house call.

"How's your belly?" Anya asked.

"Achy."

"Let's take a look."

It occurred to Anya that setting up a gynecologic table and an ultrasound machine in the First Couple's bedroom had been a bad idea. The mini hospital setup must have made Janet remember what she'd been going through, perpetuating her need to be seen by her doctor. But it was too late to change it now. It was by trial and error that Anya wrote the manual of "how to treat the president's wife for infertility" as they went along.

Janet got up on the exam table and lay flat on her back.

"Show me where you're hurting most."

"All over," Janet said, her hand barely touching her pelvis.

"Here?" Anya palpated gently with both hands. Through Janet's thin abdomen, she could feel the ovaries. "Here?"

"It's about the same wherever you touch. It's more like a nagging pain. You know—like Larry Shafer, my former press secretary."

Anya smiled. "Assume the position." She used the remote to drop the foot of the table while guiding Janet's legs onto the stirrups.

Anya put on non-latex gloves and squirted K-Y Jelly on her fingers.

122

"Does it hurt here?" she asked, gently feeling Janet's ovaries, which, as she expected, were enlarged from the fertility drugs and sore from being needled during the egg retrieval.

"A little tender," Janet gasped.

"Everything feels normal," Anya reassured her.

Janet sat up. "How are my embryos?"

"Doing everything they're supposed to do."

"I don't hear your infamous infectious enthusiasm."

Janet could see right through her, Anya thought. The record with ICSI-rescue at Lincoln, sperm injection after eggs have already failed to fertilize, like anywhere else in the world, was bad. Pregnancies were rare.

"Everything depends on what the embryos will do in the lab over the next two days," Anya said.

"In other words, my chances are lousy."

Anya reached for Janet's hands. Their eyes met. Janet fought back tears. She was a strong woman, Anya thought. Any woman who starts a treatment cycle knowing at the outset she's more likely to fail was a heroine in Anya's eyes. But Janet's courage was further compounded by going through the ordeal from the White House, keeping it out of the public eye, aware of having added one more stress factor to the president's life. Janet's womanhood was challenged twice: once with her mastectomy, twice with infertility. Was she worried about Robert staying with her should she fail to conceive?

"I hope everything will still be okay at Lincoln when I need to have the embryos transferred," Janet said, her voice quivering slightly. "Two more days can be a very, very long time."

"I'm not sure what you mean by that," Anya said. Did the First Lady know already of what had happened to her last night? "Why wouldn't everything go as planned?" she asked.

"I've been losing sleep over this Megan Tanner mess. I'm told that the FBI is launching a probe."

So Janet didn't know about the gas attack in the cryo room. Thank God for small favors. "Says who?"

"Peggy Wheeler. My new press secretary. Haven't you read the papers?"

"Not for the last three days."

"Lincoln Hospital's been on the front page of the *Washington Post* every day. CNN has played it up with news alerts and expert panels. And they're not done milking it to death."

Anya let go of Janet's hand. "What does this have to do with us?"

"The first item I put on Peggy's agenda was to keep the media in the dark regarding my IVF cycle. But now, with an army of reporters at Lincoln, a leak is just a matter of time."

"Are you upset that I'm taking care of Megan?"

"Well, that's part of it."

Anya realized the tremendous pressure the First Lady was under. Yet, this didn't give her license to dictate who she should see as a patient.

"Okay. I'm involved in another high-profile case. But I promise you, it has absolutely nothing to do with you."

"I thought you didn't do any OB."

You won't let go, will you? "I don't ordinarily. Senator Tanner told me it was you who'd recommended me."

"I told him that you were a good doctor, that's all. Not in a million years did I think he'd approach you for Megan. And besides, I thought you'd have the common sense to say no."

This is crazy. She got me to make a house call so she could yell at me for taking care of Megan. "If you really want to know, I was appointed to be Megan's doctor against my will. And I'm keeping your treatment completely separate from Megan's. It's not even in the same area in the hospital."

Janet moved on to a new concern. "I'm worried about having my embryo transfer at Lincoln Hospital, with all of the media around."

"What's, uhh, Peggy suggesting you do? You've got to complete your cycle."

"This morning she tried to talk me into having the embryo transfer done here at the White House."

Peggy's telling her boss to get another doctor in the middle of a cycle, Anya translated. The First Lady just modified Peggy's advice, taking out the personal part. It was much easier to say she wanted to move out of Lincoln than to say she wanted to switch to another doctor. But Anya decided to respond to what she heard, not what she *thought* she did. She removed her gloves, shot them into the wastebasket, and sat down on the stool across from Janet. "I promise you that Megan Tanner's case will have no bearing on you. It's in the hands of the FBI, and I'm sure they'll resolve it quickly. And your embryos are better off getting transferred right next door to the lab. Transporting them elsewhere is too risky."

"Doctor Krim, could I have a word with you?"

Peggy Wheeler ambushed Anya as soon as she closed the door to the First Lady's suite. "Please come into my office. This shouldn't take more than a couple of minutes."

"I have patients waiting," Anya said.

"Let them wait," Wheeler waved her hand. She didn't bother to introduce herself. They both remained standing. Janet's new press secretary was a head taller than Anya, in an all-purple business suit that disguised any hint of femininity.

"After last night's nerve gas attack in the cryo room, we no longer consider your facility safe," Wheeler said.

I should've guessed that was the reason she'd advised Janet to change doctors. "I—"

"You seem surprised that I've found out so quickly, right? This is the White House. Nothing escapes us."

Normally, Anya would've figured out herself that the White House had to be notified as soon as it happened. Whether it was the effect of the gas, her chronic sleep deprivation, or the two combined, she wasn't thinking straight. "Does the First Lady know?"

"We didn't want her to freak out. So no, she doesn't know."

Anya sighed. "The cryo room's completely separate from the embryo lab. It's on a different floor," Anya said.

"I know. It still doesn't put anyone's mind at ease here at the White House. While the FBI and the ATF investigate, we have no intention of sitting idle to see whether a more direct attack will be launched. I want you to move the First Lady's embryos to another facility."

Anya sat on the nearest chair available. "Out of Lincoln? Where to?"

"The Bowie IVF Center."

Bowie? Either Peggy didn't know Lincoln was the best center for infertility treatment or she didn't care. "You're not serious?" Anya's voice was higher pitched than she'd intended. "You mean as in Bowie, Maryland? How did you come up with that?"

"We've done extensive location scouting these last few days, looking outside the Beltway, away from the public eye."

These people are out of their mind. "They barely do fifty cases a year there. Their pregnancy rate is dismal."

"Actually, I couldn't give a hoot about the results of the First Lady's embryo transfer. Let her play. Every First Lady needs a hobby. I've looked up the statistics on the Internet. At her age, chances for a live birth are less than 10 percent. Plus, I keep having these dreadful nightmares of the First Lady calling the president out of an emergent National Security Council meeting because the baby's got an earache."

"So, you'd rather she didn't conceive?" Anya asked. "And I thought that once a woman took over as press secretary, motherhood would no longer be viewed as a curse at the White House."

Wheeler took a sip of water. "My concerns about getting Operation Easter out of Lincoln have broader implications. I need to get the First Lady—and Lincoln Hospital—out of the limelight. Lincoln is our 'field hospital,' first in line to absorb casualties in case of a terrorist attack on the White House. We can't afford to lose it as the presidential trauma center. We have to keep it open *and* accredited. And anyone, I repeat, *anyone* who presents an obstacle to this end will be history."

Anya wondered what Janet would think if she knew her closest assistant didn't want her to get pregnant. That there was little room left for her pursuit of motherhood in the grand scheme of national security. "Then you might as well get me fired," she said, "because I'm not letting you or anyone else transfer the First Lady's embryos to Bowie."

She left, slamming the door behind her, aware that the press secretary's mouth was open, though no words emerged.

CHAPTER 33

▼

The visit to the White House left Anya unsettled. She wasn't sure how serious Peggy Wheeler was about moving the embryos, but she dreaded that scenario. Yet, she had to admit that Janet's eggs hadn't done well at the Lincoln embryo lab she had so passionately praised. If the First Lady decided not to move the embryos and ended up with no pregnancy, Anya would be held responsible. There'd be no reason to think results would've been better in Bowie, but that would be a hard sell to the White House in the face of failure.

Maybe Caroline could help.

Anya could never figure out how Caroline managed to pay for a Watergate apartment. True, Anya had doubled her salary to $150,000, recognizing how indispensable she had become. But even so, Caroline didn't come close to the income of other Watergate dwellers. How little she knew about her embryologist's background. Did she come from money? She wasn't even quite sure of Caroline's ethnic origin.

Anya practically Leaned on the doorbell. After another moment, she heard a rustle behind the door. Then a pause.

Finally the door opened.

"Oh hi," Caroline said, her face averted.

"May I come in?"

"I guess so." Without much enthusiasm Caroline led Anya into the living room without offering to take her coat. Even before Anya sat down, Caroline went to the kitchen. "I have to finish up here," she said. "Do you still feel a bit woozy?"

Anya's tone was flat, devoid of animation. "I feel fine, thank you. Dario's antidote did the job."

"I bet you he could've injected a placebo and you would've been fine. Just having him there must've cured you instantly. I tell you, he's one hot hunk." For a moment, it was old Caroline again. "He's a keeper."

"I know," Anya said.

"The minute I'd heard of the attack," Caroline still spoke from the kitchen, "I called Labair, the lab air-testing service, to comb the entire lab.

They went through the procedure room, the recovery room, and the entire embryo lab. While they were working, ATF agents closed off the cryo room and the adjacent manifold room, where we store the liquid nitrogen. Labair worked all night. By dawn, they declared the center ready to operate."

"You've done a terrific job."

Caroline didn't respond. Anya heard her washing dishes. "Would you like some tea?"

"Thanks, no. I just need to talk to you for a few minutes."

"I'm listening."

Caroline stood tentatively at the far end of the room. Barefoot, she wore a T-shirt, no bra, and a pair of blue jeans that were only zipped up halfway.

It was unlike Caroline not to be ready to leave the house by midmorning, Anya thought. And her face was smeared with mascara.

"Are you all right?" Anya approached her embryologist. Caroline wore layers of makeup. That was new. She usually wore none on her naturally olive-colored skin.

Large black-and-blue marks circled around both eyes. Her right cheek was bruised and swollen. Her Modigliani neck showed scratch marks, and her T-shirt was ripped.

Anya took a step back. "God, what happened to you?"

"You wouldn't believe it. I was just robbed at the ATM machine around the corner. In broad daylight." Caroline limped to the sofa and sank in it, wincing.

A lie, Anya thought. Someone beat the hell out of her. "We have to call the police."

"No. Don't."

"I'll take you to the ER. They'll take care of you, document your injuries—"

"I'm fine. Really. Just a few bruises. I've already reported the attack to the police. You know what they said? ATM robberies are common. And they never catch the perp."

More lies, Anya knew. And it was a strange coincidence that her embryologist had been attacked the day after the gas attack at the cryo lab. "You need to be checked," she insisted.

"Don't doctor me. I'm too embarrassed to go to the ER like this. I'll be the topic du jour at the 21st Amendment."

Anya's mind raced, trying to connect the loose ends. Even though she hadn't consciously considered it, a suspicion must have nested within her that Caroline was involved in the gas attack. Was this assault on Caroline proof she *wasn't* a culprit, or was it in fact evidence that someone was trying to silence her? Anya took a deep breath. "Are you sure someone wasn't roughing you up because you work with me?"

"Now you're getting ridiculous. When you rang the doorbell, I was getting ready to fill up the bathtub and soak in it. Do you mind if I call you later?"

There was no sense in staying, Anya thought. She left Caroline with more unanswered questions than she came in with.

CHAPTER 34

▼

One last-ditch effort, Anya thought as she arrived at the Senate dining room and let the maître d' show her to Tanner's table. Tanner got up. "Nice to see you again, Doctor Krim."

Anya shook Nelson Tanner's hand and sat down across from him. The chair was still warm from the person who sat there before. She tried to avoid the stares from the other tables. Maybe they were curious because of *him*.

Tanner didn't wait for her to open the menu. "May I suggest the bean soup? It's one of the signature dishes here."

Bean soup was just about the last thing she'd order. But she didn't care about the food. "Thank you. I could use something warm."

"Two soups, Harry," he told the waiter.

Anya has been told that Tanner would kick people out of his office as soon as a three-minute hourglass was empty. She got to business as soon as the waiter left. "Senator, I came here to discuss something very important." A misleading opening, she thought. It's not like they haven't discussed it before.

Tanner blanched. "I hope you don't have bad news."

"Your daughter and her baby are both doing fine."

But was "fine" the appropriate word to describe Megan's disconnect from the world? And Megan's baby: was she "fine," growing in the womb of a brain-dead mom, with no father to care for her when she came out?

He sighed. "That's a relief."

The soup was placed in front of Anya. "I'm glad," she said.

"I hope you're not going to do 'the coffin' on me."

"The coffin?" Was he being morbid?

"Inside joke," Tanner said. "A journalist named Tristram Coffin once wrote that a Capitol Hill portrait photographer 'teased and smiled' Tennessee senator McKellar into posing for her. The photographer was livid. When she saw Coffin sitting in the Senate dining room, she dumped a bowl of bean soup over his head."

Anya smiled. "I promise not to use the soup for anything other than for a culinary purpose." The senator managed to keep his sense of humor, she thought. But his smile soon disappeared. Very few people, probably none in this room, knew Tanner's soft spot the way she did. Even here, in the epicenter of the Senate, the man sitting across from her was saddened by his daughter's condition, apprehensive about what the future must hold for her, feeling at a loss. All the power in the world wasn't going to bring Megan back to consciousness. And now—her baby.

"Senator, the FBI investigation has reached a dead end. The way things stand now, it's unlikely we'll know the identity of the father before the baby's born."

Tanner frowned. "I know. FBI Chief Relman called me with the news. You know what I told him? I told him whatever they were trying to do was no more than an exercise in futility. What did they expect, for God's sake?" He leaned over the table. "Megan got pregnant five months ago. Any evidence is long gone. At least now you finally understand why it is absolutely crucial to get blood from the baby."

This was going the wrong way. Anya tasted the soup. It was as bad as she thought it would be. The waiter brought a refill of Tanner's Bloody Mary and he started to sip it, his eyes locked on Anya's for reaction.

Here we go again. I have little to lose. "Still, Senator, we *could* wait until the delivery to do paternity testing?"

The senator put his drink down. His head was so close to hers she could smell the vodka.

"Please don't challenge my hospitality *or* my intelligence," he said. "I know exactly what you're trying to do."

"Senator, I'm not *trying* to do anything. I have no ulterior motive. The only interest I represent is your daughter's and her baby's."

The dining room got quiet, as if everyone were eavesdropping. "Doctor Krim," he put his hand on hers, "I don't question your motivation here. It's pure. It's noble. It's all of that. But you're still dealing with a patient—"

"Patients."

"Thank you. Patients who're not capable of making their own decisions—and I'm their proxy."

"You and your wife. And you're not the baby's proxy."

"My lawyer's taking care of the papers," he said. "It's a formality. Of course I'll be the baby's proxy. Who else? The father in abstentia?" His voice rose.

We're going nowhere. Better get to the substance before my time's up. "I want to discuss PUBS."

Were those tears in the corners of his eyes? Anya reached over and touched his hand. "Senator?"

He snapped back. "I'm sorry. Yes. You said PUBS. Remind me. It stands for—"

"Percutaneous umbilical blood sampling. I'm reluctant to do this procedure on your granddaughter. If we get a bleed, we could lose her."

"Professor Feinberg told me it was safe," he said.

"There's no procedure without the chance for complications," she said. "The only lesson I recall from first year medical school is, '*Primum non nocere.*'"

"I know. I know, 'First do no harm.'"

"Please explain why we can't wait to ID the father after the delivery and thus not risk the baby?"

She hoped Tanner didn't detect the intense emotion she was feeling. But who said that to be effective, doctors had to be emotionless? Weren't doctors in the healing business to begin with *because* they cared?

He checked his watch. *The hourglass is empty,* she thought. "You've asked me 'why' in a previous conversation, and I gave you my reasons. I'm not about to repeat what I've said. We're running out of time, Doctor. If you keep resisting me, I'll have little choice but to take legal action!"

Legal action! If she didn't agree to do the PUBS, Tanner wouldn't hesitate to go that far.

Tanner broke the silence. "We have a lot in common, Doctor Krim. We're both dedicated to my daughter and her baby and want the best for them. We only differ in what we think is best. I think that had my daughter been conscious now, she would've wanted to know who the father of her baby was. You're a great doctor and a wonderful human being. I plead with you: perform the PUBS. If only for the sake of a grieving man."

CHAPTER 35

▼

Moment of truth, Cody knew when Nicholson told him of the royal visit. There would be no further extensions. Their grace period was over.

Nicholson was on the brink of losing his mind, Cody decided. He seemed more hunched over than usual, eyes puffy and hair disheveled. Today of all days, Nicholson could have used a testosterone boost. Yet, there was only that much testosterone Cody could safely give him without causing bone loss. If the hair follicles made light of the amount of testosterone they've seen coming from the patches, what did the brain think?

Nicholson must have put his suit on in a hurry, paying little attention to the stain on the sleeve. His white shirt was unevenly stretched under the jacket, the top unbuttoned, and the collar sticking out. The knot on his tie was lopsided. Hardly the garb for a visit from a royal client.

Only good news will cheer him up. "This is the first embryo." Cody pointed at the screen. "And this is the DNA." He turned on the GENOME monitor. It took less than ten seconds for the DNA to turn up on the screen.

"Let's move on to the next embryo," Cody said the minute he saw the DNA pattern.

"Why? What's wrong with this one?" Nicholson asked.

"No good," said Cody. The boss was in a foul mood.

"Hold it right there," Nicholson stopped pacing for a minute. "You didn't show me the PHENOTYPE."

This was what Cody was trying to avoid. "I don't need to see what it will look like. I can tell by the DNA already."

But Nicholson insisted. "Show me."

Cody eyed the clock. The royal client was due in fifteen minutes. "I thought you wanted me to rush. This is slowing me d—"

"Do it. Now."

Cody's heart thumped like a tom-tom. He had to wipe his hands on his scrubs before he touched the keyboard. "Okay," he said in a low voice, "but don't freak out when you see it." Cody turned on the PHENOTYPE monitor. Within seconds, four facial images appeared on the screen.

Nicholson sank into the only chair available. "Looks like a Down's Syndrome to me."

Cody sighed. "Now do you believe me?"

Cody felt he and Nicholson worked in an ultra-slow pressure cooker. But now the pressure cooker was about to reach its boiling point. The client's visit could hurt their operation. The contract was for 10 million dollars. Lose that and they couldn't go on. No wonder the boss looked like he'd been run over by a truck. And Cody knew the responsibility lay with him.

Cody got up from his computer and neared the monitor, examined the DNA of the third-to-the last embryo, and shook his head. "No good. Only two left. I need to prepare you for a failure this time around."

"Anya Krim and her team reported the creation of the first human pancreas from stem cells," Nicholson said. The news of a five-year-old child, cured of his diabetes and requiring no more insulin after the transplant of Anya's made-from-stem cells pancreas, made headlines. Cody knew what was coming next.

"Have you visited her lab yet?"

So he didn't forget. Cody should've known better. Nicholson rarely forgot anything. But Cody had chanced it. Whatever the consequences, he would not betray his friendship with Anya. He'd always detested scientific espionage. A scientist's intellectual property was frequently the only real asset he owned. And Nicholson had the gall to tell him to spy on Anya, his mentor, his friend ... his love.

"No, I haven't."

"I wish you'd listened to me. If you'd gone there, you might have been able to figure out some of the reasons we keep getting defective embryos."

"You know we're a thousand times more complex than animals. I'm not sure that you'd get a call from our Japanese customer that her cloned poodle is screwing up on the Nikkei Exchange."

"There's no time for jokes," Nicholson said. He approached the monitors. "Is this number 9?"

"It looks much better, doesn't it?" Cody magnified the image maximally.

"It sure does. All eight cells are about the same size, round and clear, with no fragments. But let's see the phenotype," Nicholson stopped in front of the third monitor.

Cody turned on the PHENOTYPE control panel. A passport-type photo appeared on the screen.

"I have a hard time recognizing the prince without his suit," said Nicholson.

"No problem, boss." Nothing could faze Cody now. His body jittered with ecstasy—a scientific orgasm. Even if the *other* cloning didn't come out right, or if there was a premature obstetrical death, this one, the client's, might very well become the first successful human cloning. *The first in the world.* And he, Cody, the loser OB/Gyn, would be glorified as the scientist who had achieved it.

Cody had never seen Nicholson so happy.

"I told you we had ourselves a winner," he said. "This embryo will produce a perfect clone—a non-faded carbon copy of the client."

Neither of them mentioned they had felt the same way about the embryo they had implanted in Bonnie Marshall.

One normal embryo was a lot, Nicholson surmised. Only people in the cloning business could appreciate how hard it was to get it right. How, even in animals, you were much more likely to get it wrong. And how, given the complexity of human genetics, coming up with a complete set of normal human genes with not a single spelling mistake was already a remarkable achievement. His heart filled with hope. It would take exactly thirty-eight weeks, or nine months minus two weeks, from the day Cody would transfer the client's embryo into a surrogate, thirty-eight weeks till they'd find out for sure this embryo translated into a normal baby. Normal!

Yes, it was Cody who'd done the actual work. But it was he, Nicholson, who'd orchestrated it, fought the devil, and persevered. He'd be world famous; the wealthiest men and women from all over the world would be desperate to get an appointment. And then ... and then, once he was certain Cody'd got the technique under control, he'd be ready for the ultimate cloning: himself, after getting rid of the Fragile Y.

"Nice to see you again, sir," Nicholson said, beaming. He held out his hand.

Fruits and nuts were set out on the coffee table. The client didn't notice them. Nicholson gestured toward the sofa, but the client didn't move.

"Mr. Nicholson, I'm ready to hear your progress report."

Nicholson felt his euphoria vanish. The client came with an agenda. He cleared his throat. "We have an embryo that has passed all the genetic testing. It checks out perfectly."

But His Highness didn't soften his military stance, nor did his expression change. "How many?"

He must be kidding. He knows damn well I said "an embryo." "Excuse me?"

"How *many* embryos check out perfect?"

Nicholson swallowed a ball of saliva. "One."

"Only one? It has taken you this long to produce a single embryo?"

Nicholson feared his knees would buckle. "We've been working long and hard, sir. We've produced multiple embryos. But I'm sure you're aware this isn't an efficient process."

"I'm aware that your operation isn't efficient at all," the client interrupted. "For the amount of money you're getting paid, you have very little to show for. How far is the surrogate?"

Nicholson held onto the sides of his desk. "What do you mean, sir?"

"The surrogate carrying my embryo. How far is she in her pregnancy?"

Adrenaline was back, dispatched to all stations at once. God! Did His Highness somehow find out about Bonnie Marshall? "This embryo will be ready for a transfer into a surrogate in two days."

"You mean all this time you haven't transferred a single embryo?"

Nicholson sighed. It didn't seem like the client knew that his defective clone had been delivered. "We've had several that didn't take," Nicholson lied.

The client's face remained emotionless. "I remember you warned me this process had 'low efficiency,' as you put it. So what's my realistic chance of getting a live baby from a single embryo?"

There's no number that would appease him. "When I said low efficiency, Your Highness, I didn't mean in *achieving* a pregnancy. I meant it's rare to get an embryo that's a perfect genetic match of the client, with no misprints. In fact, it's phenomenal that we have an embryo that's tested perfect."

The client checked his watch. "You don't even give me the courtesy of coming up with a straight answer. Wrap it up and get it ready to go."

A sharp pain crossed Nicholson's chest. *What does he want me to do, gift wrap the embryo?* "I'm not sure I understand—"

"I'm terminating our contract. I'd like to check my embryo out. Have Cody freeze the embryo for me and put it in a liquid nitrogen container."

The guillotine was hoisted. *Terminate the agreement. A goddamn disaster.*

"Freezing takes about an hour," Nicholson managed, as if it made any difference.

"I know," the client said calmly. Nothing was new to him. "I'll wait here until he's done. In the meantime, you and I can discuss the repayment of your advance."

Two copies of a contract waited for Nicholson on the coffee table when he returned from the lab after instructing Cody to freeze the embryos.

Seated at the sofa, His Royal Highness was all business. "Before our meeting, I asked my lawyer to draft a termination of agreement."

"But—"

The client raised his hand. "For what I've hired you to do, I've given you as much time as I care to give. Your stuttered barrages of excuses have all been heard. It's time you acknowledge the inevitable: our relationship is over. You're fired!"

Fired. Nicholson felt he'd just plunged from the top of Mount Olympus to the bottom of an abyss. He sank into the chair next to the sofa.

"For the work you've done so far, even though it was far from satisfactory, I'm ready to waive half the advance." *Half the advance? I'm broke. Bankrupt. Finished.* "I hope you realize I'm being generous. This contract makes our previous agreement null and void, and you agree that you have no more financial claims to the remainder of the money, and that our business relationship is terminated."

With shaking hands, Nicholson lifted the contract and pretended to study it. But his eyes were too blurry to focus. "I'm sorry to see our relationship end," he managed.

"So am I." The client handed him the pen.

"I'm not sure I can make payroll," Nicholson told Cody. He had called him to his office after the client left.

Nicholson was seated in the chair, bent over like a pretzel, his hand on his chest, his face grimaced in pain.

"Are you feeling all right?" Cody asked. "Should I call an ambulance?"

"No." His voice was faint. "Don't worry. I'm not dying. Our operation *is*, though. We might as well pack up."

"Let's not forget we still have a live pregnancy with a cloned embryo." Cody sat down in front of Nicholson's desk. "This could be your big breakthrough. The very first normal human clone! You'd be world famous! And rich!"

Nicholson didn't seem cheered. "We already have a 'first.' The *first abnormal* human clone. What guarantee do I have that this one won't be the *second abnormal* human clone? That would surely establish our reputation."

So far, Cody had managed to bring the boss's mood from bad to worse. "But all the tests are perfect so far. The level two ultrasound shows that all the organs are intact."

"Déjà vu. You called Baby Marshall's ultrasounds normal all the way to the end of the pregnancy."

"This time it's different."

Nicholson's voice got louder. "You know damn well you can't guarantee a normal baby. Tell me you can guarantee this baby will be normal." Nicholson paused.

"I—"

"Here we go again. More stammering. I want a scientific answer, *Doctor*. Doctor *and chief scientist*. You tell me how you can guarantee, this time around, that this baby's not going to come out a monster. That's all I want you to tell me. Plain and simple. I'm not asking you to predict if the child will win the Nobel Prize. I just want to know that this time, this baby will pass inspection."

"There's only one way to be sure."

"What way?"

Cody cleared his throat. "Screen the baby's entire DNA."

"Where do you get the baby's DNA from?"

"We have to stick a needle through the surrogate mother's uterus and get blood from the umbilical cord."

"Then do it," Nicholson shrugged.

Beads of perspiration sprouted all at once. *He knows I can't just go ahead and do it. He knows damn well I'm not the surrogate's obstetrician.*

Cody hesitated. "And what if I find some problem with the baby's DNA?" He dreaded playing out that scenario.

Nicholson's face went blank. "In that case there *shouldn't be* a delivery, right?"

Cody's hands, covered with cold sweat, held onto his chair. The room started to spin. His speech was lost.

Nicholson got up. "Make sure we get the blood drawn immediately."

Cody got up, still feeling faint. "This is not going to be so simple."

"Why?"

"You know why. Because the surrogate is Megan Tanner."

CHAPTER 36

▼

The summons was hand delivered to Anya's office. She ripped open the PERSONAL AND CONFIDENTIAL envelope and removed its contents.

His Honorable Nelson Tanner III
v. Anya Krim MD and Lincoln Hospital.

Doctors shouldn't be dragged into a courthouse to be told how to practice medicine, Anya thought as she entered the district court at 333 Constitution Avenue. Her patience grew thinner as a hefty policewoman with rough hands searched her body. She followed the signs to Judge Miriam Thomas's office. Still, she wasn't intimidated. There was something else, something she couldn't quite decipher, that caused her distress.

Anya was surprised to find Tanner alone in the judge's chambers. When she called Dario, he was adamant she should bring a lawyer with her. But she'd decided against it. She knew how she felt about the PUBS, and no lawyer could change it. She was ready to fight Tanner on behalf of his daughter and granddaughter. She was the only advocate they had. She was *their* lawyer!

Anya nodded to the senator, ignoring the hand he'd held out. The *Honorable* Nelson Tanner III. What a farce. She watched him sit down. Anya took the other chair facing the judge's desk.

I'm right and he's wrong, Anya told herself. *Don't let him intimidate you.*

"I'm sorry I had to drag you here," Tanner said.

"I wish I could believe that, Senator. After all, you had a choice, didn't you?"

"Not really."

They both stood as the judge walked in. "Please sit down. This is an informal hearing." Judge Miriam Thomas, a fiftyish, bespectacled, African-American judge, read from the papers in front of her. She gave Anya an intense look above her reading glasses.

"What do you have to say, Doctor Krim? Why won't you agree to perform the procedure?"

"Your Honor," Anya said, "I appreciate Senator Tanner's desire to know with certainty who the baby's father is. But this procedure carries with it a substantial risk."

"They do it every day in the hospital, Your Honor," Tanner broke in.

The judge wore a faint smile. "Is that accurate, Doctor?"

"PUBS is frequently done, Your Honor, as a life-saving procedure for the fetus. We choose to do it only if we're absolutely certain the results of testing the baby's blood will make a difference in how we manage the baby before it's born. We don't make such decisions lightly. And if we're convinced that the results won't contribute anything to the pre-delivery management, we choose not to do it at all."

"Are you aware of any instances of forensic use for PUBS?"

"No. To the best of my knowledge, this procedure has never been used to establish paternity."

"Your Honor," Tanner tried to break in.

The judge gave him a stern look. "I'll let you know when you can speak." She glanced at her notes. "You mentioned the procedure was not without risk. Is that your main objection to performing it?"

"Yes, Your Honor. This procedure may end up killing the baby before he or she gets her chance to come out of the womb. I'm not ready to put the baby at such risk just to satisfy the senator's curiosity."

"Senator," the Judge turned to Tanner, "so far it makes perfect sense to me that Doctor Krim is reluctant to perform an invasive procedure on your daughter's baby while it's still in the womb. Why the rush to stick the umbilical cord now?"

If I told the judge Tanner wanted to make sure the father was white, this hearing would be over, Anya thought. *And I would win.*

"Your Honor, there's public urgency here," Tanner said. "There've been cases in other hospitals of serial rapes of comatose patients. If a DNA sample isn't obtained immediately, the doctor and the hospital are putting all comatose females at risk of being raped. As long as he's still at large, he could strike again, and someone else will fall victim, long before my daughter is ready to give birth."

A sharp pain ripped through Anya's pelvis. With both hands she held onto the arms of her chair.

"Are you all right?" The judge went over to the water cooler. "Here, have some water."

"Thank you," Anya said and sipped from the plastic cup. "I'll be fine. "Sorry for the little interruption. Please proceed."

So this was it. Anya realized what it was that had so deeply disturbed her about this hearing. All along, she'd anticipated these words: *The rapist was still at large.*

"Any further comments, Doctor Krim?"

"Yes, Your Honor. Perhaps the senator could tell us what he intends to do if the paternity testing turns out not to his liking. Is he going to take me back to court and try to force me to terminate the pregnancy?"

"I will never have this pregnancy terminated," Tanner raged. "This is my grandchild, Your Honor."

The judge turned to Anya. "What *is* the chance of losing the baby as a result of this procedure?"

"About 1 to 2 percent," Anya said. "Had Megan been conscious, I'm convinced she wouldn't have wanted to take this risk."

Was that true? After she was attacked, Anya went on a painful search to find her assailant. Back then, she would've given anything to look him in the face, see him go behind bars. Punished. Yes, she admitted to herself, the motivation to *punish* him was ten times stronger than the desire to protect other potential victims.

"Senator, any last comments before we adjourn?"

"No, Your Honor. I want to thank you for recognizing the urgency in this matter."

Judge Thomas stood. "You'll have my decision this evening."

It was ten o'clock at night when the three returned to the judge's chambers.

"The court recognizes the importance of establishing paternity in the Megan Tanner case," the judge said. "The court recognizes that, at this stage of the pregnancy, there exists no way to determine the biological father's identity without obtaining DNA diagnosis. That it is crucial to determine paternity is heightened several-fold by the unusual circumstance that the mother is in a deep, most likely irreversible, coma. Establishing the father's identity would be of cardinal importance to the baby, even if she ended up adopted. In addition, the court accepts the argument that identifying the rapist may help prevent him from assaulting other helpless patients, even though it is somewhat speculative, at this point, to assume that the violator was indeed a serial rapist.

"The court finds it is impossible to fairly weigh the benefits from identifying paternity against the potential risks of the procedure. The court would like to commend Doctor Krim for her solid resolve to be her patient's advocate. Unfortunately, the baby's mother is incapable of voicing her opinion and is legally represented not by her caring physician but by her biological father acting as her proxy. Therefore, the court hereby instructs Doctor Anya Krim to perform the PUBS procedure on her patient Megan Tanner at Lincoln Hospital as soon as can be accomplished safely."

The street was empty when Anya left, but she heard the familiar wooden thump behind her.

"Doctor Krim, I know this was difficult for you," Tanner said, "as it was for me. I hope you and I can continue to work together."

Watch out what you're saying. No use telling him you hate him for forcing you to do a procedure you don't want to do. "Don't worry, Senator," she said, making great effort to eliminate emotion from her voice. "This changes nothing. I will continue to care for Megan as before."

"I'm glad. Once you do the procedure, we can both erase today's hearing from our memory."

Not me, Senator, she wanted to say. *I have this problem: everything I go through is forever encrypted into my memory cells with indelible ink.* "There's just one thing I don't get," she said. "I know how much you love Megan. Why would you take the risk?"

He looked her straight in the eyes. "One day you'll find out—when you have your own child."

CHAPTER 37

▼

One day ... when you have your own child.

Tanner was right. There was no way she could imagine what a parent would feel toward a child without being one.

Anya stood at Megan's bedside, squeezing her patient's flaccid hand against her own waist. Each time they met, Anya grew a little closer to Megan, closer than to many of her conscious patients with whom she'd had lengthy conversations. Sometimes, so many times, words got in the way.

Maybe, it occurred to her, it was actually a good thing she wasn't the parent, not even *a* parent. With so many people pulling from different directions, trying to pry in Megan's business, she was the only one with no ulterior motive; she was there for Megan.

Moment of truth: Is it really the baby I'm concerned about? Or am I more concerned with what would happen to me— to my *insides—if something went wrong?*

Megan must have just had a bath. Her long hair, now combed straight, smelled fresh. Her left arm rested on her pregnant belly. Her long, delicate fingers ended in perfectly manicured, polished nails.

I'm not afraid of you, Megan. I worry about the procedure, because I care so much about you. And your baby.

She wished Megan could wake up, if only for a minute or two, so Anya could make sure she understood what she was about to go through, knew the potential complications, and above all, agreed to have the procedure done.

She lined up the instruments she was about to use for the procedure atop a raised tray covered with a blue sterile towel.

The chief resident, Nina Russo, came in dragging an ultrasound machine.

"Couldn't get a single sono machine from L&D." Nina was still catching her breath. "They're too busy to give it up. They have two sets of triplets in preterm labor, a bleeding previa, and a breech. The house is a zoo. The residents laughed when I told them why I needed the machine."

"Let them laugh," Anya said quietly, viewing Megan's stomach, which she was about to paint with an iodine solution. "Where did you get the machine from?"

"It's the old GE from the ER. There was, like, no one to get permission from."

"You mean you stole it," Anya said.

Nina didn't respond. Anya knew her mind was wandering, as usual.

Anya squirted iodine solution on Megan's belly and covered the transducer of the ultrasound machine—the rectangular device that transmitted images from the patient through a cable into the machine, where they were visualized in real time on the monitor—with a sterile drape.

She started a meticulous scan of the baby. Both the head circumference and femur length measurements were in agreement: Megan was twenty-two weeks pregnant. The baby moved her arms and legs in the amniotic fluid like a scuba diver. The monitor showed a rapidly pumping four-chamber heart, a pair of lungs, a pair of kidneys, a head, and this time, a clear view of the female genitals.

"Where's the cord?" Nina asked, waking from her trance.

The more Anya saw of the baby's normal anatomy, the more apprehensive she became about the procedure. "There." Anya pointed at the screen. An umbilical cord, coiled around itself, connected the baby to the placenta, the baby's lifeline.

"Do you, like, see a clear pocket we could stick?"

Anya trekked the transducer across Meghan's belly. She found a deep pocket, at the far end of which she could see the umbilical cord attached to the placenta. But then the baby somersaulted, her rump landing in the space that was vacant seconds earlier.

"Okay, Megan Tanner II. Behave yourself, please," said Anya.

"We'll just have to, like, wait for her to flip," Nina said. "She needs to calm down. Too wiggly for this procedure."

"You're telling me? I'm the one who has to stick the needle."

"Let's put on some soft music. The amniotic fluid exaggerates the noise in the room, makes the fetus freak out."

"Really?" Anya suppressed a smile. She wondered when Nina had become an expert on uterine acoustics. Meanwhile, the baby started to curl herself into the fetal position, again leaving an open space in the amniotic cavity.

"Get back here, please," Anya told her resident, who had left the patient to find a "mood" CD. "Time to start, before she flips again."

Nina held the transducer steady over the belly. Anya put on a pair of sterile gloves and turned to her tray. The spinal needle was long and skinny. She connected it to a 20 cc syringe.

God help me.

Anya pierced the right lower quarter of the abdominal skin, drove the needle through it, and then through the wall of the uterus into the amniotic cavity. The needle neared the umbilical cord. Anya chose a spot where the cord connected to the placenta and stuck it with one small, decisive movement. The blood return in the syringe indicated she was in the right place. Anya withdrew the plunger slowly, up to the 5 cc level—the equivalent of a teaspoon. She thought for a moment and then drew another 3 cc and pulled the needle, still attached to the syringe, out of the body.

Anya disconnected the syringe from the needle and injected the blood into two purple-top test tubes containing heparin, a blood thinner, to prevent clotting.

Exhaling, she realized she had stopped breathing for the entire time the needle was in Megan's body. It was an old reflex she had developed in residency, a means to avoid even the slightest tremor during a procedure.

Nina used a moist towel to wipe off the iodine solution from the belly, readjusted the fetal heart monitor to the top of Megan's uterus, and increased the volume on the control board. A galloping heartbeat broke the tense silence. She applied a generous amount of ultrasound gel to the skin. With this much gel, they'd get a near-perfect picture of the baby, which was bouncing back and forth like a yo-yo.

Baby Tanner had survived the procedure.

Anya raced to the FBI DNA lab. The teaspoon of blood in each tube was sufficient to determine who the father was.

Taking extra care to hold the tubes steady and upright, she decided to make a stop at Labor and Delivery. Luckily, a new father had just been buzzed in and the doors flung open. She followed him, going past the door to the obstetricians' lounge on her right, astir with the nervous energy of doctors, residents, and medical students.

All the way in the back was the refrigeration room, where cord blood from newborn babies was stored before it got shipped out to the cord blood bank. She found a sealed specimen bag and wrote on the label ANYA KRIM and then added, "Please do not touch." She put the one tube of blood inside the bag, sealed the bag, and placed it inside the refrigerator. She secured the other in her upper coat pocket.

A minute later, she was on her way to the hospital garage.

CHAPTER 38

▼

Anya turned cold and clammy as she pushed open the door to the L2 level of the garage. The silence, the emptiness, the dim lighting: everything seemed eerie and threatening.

Ever since she'd been assaulted, she hated such places and always came to work early enough to make sure she could pick a spot as close to the guards as possible. But because of the court hearing, she couldn't find a free spot until she got to the second level. Her green Saab convertible was parked at the far end of the floor.

Don't panic!

Nothing was going to happen because she was alone in an empty garage. Or because in her pocket she happened to carry the highly contested piece of evidence the FBI was so eagerly awaiting.

But the feeling of doom had already set in. She recognized the familiar signs: the panic attack was already in progress. She was hyperventilating. Her breathing got faster and shallower. There'd be no one to call if anything happened to her. No one would hear her even if she screamed. She'd have to run up two flights of stairs to find the guards.

Get a hold of yourself, Anya. Take a deep breath. Forget everything. Focus on stomach breathing. That's it. Deep breath.

She needed to get out! She started to walk to her car as fast as she could, ignoring a hot flash that swept throughout her body.

Thank God. The car. In forty minutes, she'd be at the FBI lab in Quantico, where she could deliver the blood sample and be set free.

She used her right hand to fumble for the car keys, while her left hand held onto her upper coat pocket, securing the test tube in place.

She pulled on the door handle. Two large men stood close to her. Was she delusional? Cold sweat covered her. She looked again. They were still there. The place was empty only seconds ago. Where had they come from?

A bald man wearing sunglasses approached her first. He wore a gray T-shirt, which showed off robust muscles she'd only seen before on the heavy-duty weight lifters at Gold's Gym.

An elaborate tattoo of a dragon was on display across his biceps.

Was he the man who'd been to her office the other day, sitting in an examination room alone, pretending to be a patient's husband? God, he could've raped her right there and then! But he hadn't. They are going to rape her. Rape her again. Then kill her, pack her in the trunk and dump her in the Potomac River.

Her heart pounded so violently against her chest she was afraid they'd hear it.

"Dragon Man" grabbed her, clasping her arms, her chest, and her stomach with his left arm, while the right went for her mouth. He stank of sweat. The pressure of his arm on her chest and his hand against her mouth threatened to suffocate her.

The man's partner approached, a crop-haired giant, his arms dangling to his sides prepared for a knockout. An ugly keloid scar traversed his right cheek. A smaller one made a half turn on the same side of his neck, bypassing the jugular.

"You give us the tube of blood, Doctor, and we let you go," said Boxer.

So this is what they wanted. I should've known. Where did they follow me from?

"Maybe you should let go of her mouth so she can talk. We want the test tube, Doctor."

Dragon Man tightened his squeeze, pulling her body into his stomach. Only then did he lift his hand from of her mouth.

"I don't have any tube," she groaned.

"Give it to us if you want to drive out alive." The hand went back over her mouth.

"Be reasonable," Boxer said. "You know we're going nowhere without it."

"Search her."

Once again, a male beast invaded her. She felt Dragon Man reach into her coat pocket, felt him play with her gloves, her car keys. There was no test tube. He searched on the other side. That pocket was empty, too. She felt his hand slide against her thighs, feeling for the tubes inside the pockets of her hospital coat. He moaned with impatience.

"Give it up, bitch!"

She fought a wave of nausea.

Dragon Man felt in the upper pocket, squeezing her breast. His fat fingers reached behind her pen.

"I got it," he said to Boxer, showing the tube triumphantly.

"Great. I'll bring the car around."

Don't leave me alone with the beast.

She had a premonition that Dragon Man wasn't finished with her.

His right arm squeezed her windpipe. It felt like her cartilage was cracking. Blood rushed to her head.

She collapsed. Dragon Man bent with her, still holding her firmly.

I'm running out of oxygen. He's finishing me. I'll be dead before Boxer returns.

Dragon Man positioned a knife at her neck. She felt pain. A slow ooze of blood started from the wound.

A car screeched to her side, a black Bentley.

"Kill her and the boss is going to have *your* neck!" yelled Boxer. He sprang out of the car.

Dragon Man slid into the passenger seat.

The Bentley charged toward the exit and was soon out of sight.

Anya started to get up. Her neck hurt so badly she thought he might have broken it. She got into her convertible and locked the door even before she turned on the engine.

CHAPTER 39

— ▼ —

Anya drove aimlessly for a few minutes, incessantly checking the rearview mirror. No sign of the Bentley.

She couldn't go home. No doubt these people, whoever they were, had her place under twenty-four-hour surveillance. Though hot air blew straight in her face from the car's heater, she was still shivering.

What could she do? Whom should she turn to?

She thought of Caroline, but remembered her last visit. Caroline herself seemed to be in some kind of trouble; what comfort could she give?

Blood dripped on her pants. She examined her neck in the mirror. Dragon Man had missed the jugular by less than an inch. Images of the animal clasping her onto his rancid body came back to her.

She was on Dupont Circle. Dario.

Please, please be home, she prayed as she dialed his number on her cell. His recording came on.

"Dario, if you're there, please pick up. It's me."

"I'm glad you called." His voice was soothing.

"Thank God!"

"What happened? You sound awful."

"I was attacked. Would you let me come to your place now? I need to spend the night."

"Do you want me to come and get you?"

"No. You're so kind, and I'm such a jerk. I'll be there in ten minutes."

Dario had taken her in with joy, and while she told him what had happened, he cleaned the wound in her neck with iodine, dressed it with a piece of gauze and tape, and ran a bath for her.

When Anya undressed, she assessed the damage. A bruise on her right cheekbone. Another, uglier bruise on her left breast. Black and blue marks over her ribcage. Each of her ribs hurt. Breathing was painful, but there wasn't any palpable fracture.

She stepped into the water. Her aches eased, but there was a pounding headache in both temples.

The room filled up with steam. Dario had lit a couple of fragrant candles on the bathtub ledge. She inhaled the perfumed air. Lavender was her favorite scent. And he remembered.

She heard music from the living room. Massenet's *Meditation.*

A knock on the door. "May I come in?"

"I'm not sure."

"I just want to be in the same space as you."

Her instinct was to plunge into the water. What was wrong with her? Why would she hide her nakedness from Dario, the man she'd just run to for refuge? Her body lead-heavy, she sat up in the water. "Come in."

She could hardly see him through the steam. "I brought you a pair of my pajamas," he said, "and a robe." He sat on the side of the tub. "Feeling better?"

"I've a headache."

"I can make it go away," he said. She felt his strong fingers massaging her scalp, then move to her temples.

She closed her eyes.

His hands traveled down to the small of her neck, taking care not to touch her cut. The bleeding had stopped. Vertebra by vertebra, he didn't miss a spot. The headache disappeared.

He massaged her trapezius muscles, taut as violin strings, applying just enough energy to soften them without making them sore. His hands were loving. She felt his body behind hers.

Anya turned her head halfway toward Dario and raised her mouth. His kiss was gentle. Welcome.

She stood naked in front of him. He kissed her nipples democratically, one kiss for each. Then he wrapped her in a towel.

The bedroom was next door to the bathroom. They held hands and walked in. The room was dark, the only light provided by two candles on either sides of the bed. The bed itself was queen size, with all-white linen. The music had changed to a Brazilian piece, *Concerto De Aranjuez* by Villa Lobos.

He let her take his clothes off. Her towel fell. He embraced her gently, careful not to hurt her.

They snuggled in bed, covered by the white comforter and sheets. His lips traveled across her body. She closed her eyes. He was gentle, considerate.

He kissed her thighs. She wanted to receive everything from him. And she wanted to give all she had to him. She wasn't sure of the order of giving, but she was sure of one thing:

She loved this man.

When she felt his hardness, the feelings evaporated.

The python's going to bite me!

She sat up. A flash traveled through the back of her brain. She could hear the beast's laughter.

"Stop it! Now!"

"What?"

She rubbed her temples, willing the flash to disappear. "I can't do it, Dario. I'm so sorry. I thought I was ready. But I'm not."

Dario said nothing. He drew the sheet over him and held her hand.

God, what did I just do? Dario must hate me for making him feel like shit.

"I understand," he said. But she wasn't sure he did. "Don't worry, Anya. I told you I'm patient. I'll wait for you. I'll wait until you tell me that you're ready."

If that time ever comes, she thought.

CHAPTER 40

▼

Anya didn't see any Secret Service guards outside the lab door when she came in. Maybe the chief had changed the orders for around the clock surveillance until the First Lady's cycle was completed.

It's just me here. She bolted the ladies' locker room door behind her. The sight of the fresh red scab on her neck sent a chill through her spine. Moving away from the mirror, she willed herself to suspend any memory of the attack. She changed her street clothes for a pair of blue scrubs and paper booties, put her hair up in a bun and covered it with a cap. She was ready to scrub.

The lab was tranquil. She changed Caroline's Ricky Martin CD to Yevgeny Kissin's rendition of Rachmaninoff's second piano concerto. It was at least two hours before anyone else would show up. She hadn't seen Caroline and wondered if she'd worked at all since her ATM assault.

Normally, Anya would have trusted her embryologist to look at the embryos and give her a progress report. But given the high profile of the case, she preferred to do it herself. She had been sidetracked, pulled in so many different directions and involved in so many issues that had nothing to do with the First Lady's treatment, that she was determined to make up for it.

Reverently, she approached the First Lady's incubator. The Secret Service had switched the key lock on the incubator to a combination lock. Anya had made up a four-digit combination and was the only one who knew it. Caroline had made up her own code and was the only other person who had access to Janet's embryos.

Anya removed the metal tray with the two petri dishes. Each housed five embryos submerged in fluid. She sat down at the new Everest microscope, set up within a protective hood, and switched to high magnification.

The First Lady of the United States had ten magnificent embryos.

Anya could barely contain herself. Each embryo had between two and four cells, all round and symmetrical. Any one of them had the potential to turn into a baby.

Anya saved the image of each embryo. She could save the ten images onto a disk and send it via courier to Janet later. But she remembered her last visit at the White House: Janet's gloomy mood and Peggy Wheeler's suggestion she's better off not going back to Lincoln Hospital. Instead of messaging the photos, Anya decided to e-mail them. This way, Janet would see them when she woke up and return her allegiance to Lincoln.

Anya had the First Lady's private e-mail address memorized for urgent communications. Janet had told her not to share it and to erase any message as soon as the message was sent. She typed in Janet's address, inserted the ten images of the embryos as attachments, and pressed "send."

Embryo transfer was scheduled for tomorrow afternoon. Anya was going to suggest to the Cartwrights to transfer at least four embryos into Janet's womb.

Naturally, she'd choose the ones of superior quality. The remaining embryos would be frozen, to be thawed only when Janet Cartwright and her husband desired, maybe even after his presidency was over, since the embryos themselves would stay forever young.

Yes, she should definitely freeze some, unless—

Unless I use them on myself!

Anya continued to stare at the embryos.

Madness!

What happened last night was the strongest proof yet of her impotence. She loved Dario. He had taken her in when she needed to feel safe and protected, immersed her in warmth and affection, worked his way gently into intimacy—and she panicked!

She wasn't *normal*. Her PTSD was virulent. The monster had set in for good and made sure she wouldn't be able to have sex with the man she loved.

Staring at ten dots-of-dust-size potential babies, she knew that having babies the *other way*, through lovemaking, was not an option. Forever. And there was no way Dario was going to agree to sacrifice sex and settle for having kids in the dish instead. Giving up sex for love wasn't something any man was capable of doing for the rest of his life.

There was nothing she wanted more than to have her own baby to hold, to feed, to raise … to love.

Anya closed her eyes.

She could see the embryo transfer room. The lights were dimmed, and soft music was playing. She lay on the transfer stretcher, naked under the gown, her legs in the retractable stirrups. Free of her old inhibitions, peeled of her protective layers, she was lying there like any other patient. Caroline's smile was reassuring.

"We got real winners. Four handsome little suckers." She painlessly placed the speculum in Anya's vagina, took the catheter loaded with the embryos, and slipped it in.

Meditating to the music, Anya fell sound asleep.

Then the phone rang. She only let it ring once before picking up.

It's positive, Anya! You're pregnant!

Pregnant. What a wonderful word. Pregnant. And she had thought it was a word that would never be said to her.

It's three weeks later. The ultrasound shows a little heart racing, faster than hers, much faster. That little beep-beep-beep on the screen is not a patient's baby. It's hers. Finally.

She's been asleep for nine months. And she's in the delivery room, recognizing the familiar faces between contractions.

A live, beautiful baby is placed on her belly, for her, only for her to hold ... there's music in the background ... she isn't sure ... it gets stronger ... there's no mistake ... She'll ask Grandma to play it again. She loved it so much, maybe because it was a child singing in Russian:

Budjet gda budjet neva
Let there always be sunshine
Let there always be blue sky
Let there always be mama
Let there always be me—

A tap on her shoulder startled Anya. She hit the bridge of her nose against the microscope's eyepiece.

"Is anything wrong?"

Anya was caught off guard. How long had Caroline been standing there?

"I just came in," Caroline said, as if reading her mind.

"I wanted to get a sneak preview of the fruits of your labor," Anya said.

"*Our* labor." Fresh from her morning shower, Caroline looked gorgeous. There were no signs of black-and-blue marks on her face. The wounds on her neck were gone. Self-conscious, Anya's hand went to cover the cut on her neck. "I see you're taking pictures. Who're you sending them to, the First Lady?"

Janet realized that her e-mail to Janet was still up on the screen. Good God! She'd revealed Janet's e-mail address to her embryologist.

"And your vote?" Caroline asked, unfazed by Anya's panic.

"Two thumbs up. Good work."

"Thanks, but you know I don't create these embryos from nothing. It was up to Janet Cartwright and her man to provide us with sperm and eggs of decent quality. I didn't do anything different than I do on all the Smiths and Joneses I work with every single day."

"You're too modest. If the First Lady gets pregnant, she'll owe it mostly to you."

Caroline shrugged. "I'm delighted you got involved. Makes me feel better knowing that I'm not handling the First Lady's embryos on my own."

Anya chose not to respond. She eyed the large electronic clock that hung on the wall across from her. Barely six o'clock. An hour before Caroline would usually show up. What was *she* up to? But she had no right to question her embryologist's motives.

CHAPTER 41

▼

"What's taking them so long?"

"You've got to stop pacing. You're making me nauseated," Anya said. Dario had walked the twenty-foot-long conference room six times. Why was he so nervous about the results of Megan's paternity testing? His involvement in the case was tangential at most. Granted, he was the senator's therapist, and the results could impact his patient's state of mind. But other than that, his impatience seemed inappropriate.

Shortly after Caroline had walked into the lab, Detective Fitzpatrick of the FBI paged Anya, asking her to bring the extra blood sample she had put away in Labor and Delivery's fridge before the garage assault. Anya had no idea how the detective had found out about the backup sample. Nor did she fully understand what instinct had made her secure a backup in the first place.

She knew Dario had risked her resentment at being "babied" when he insisted on going with her to the FBI. But she was comforted by his company and didn't mind being pampered while the winds of adversity blew strongly in her face.

Now, four hours later, they waited for the verdict, seated in the small waiting area in front of the door to the DNA Analysis Unit I of the FBI's crime laboratory on the grounds of the Quantico Marine Corps Base. Dario's impatience was irritating her already raw nerves.

"I doubt you understand how involved this testing is," she said.

"I thought this was routine."

"You watch too much CSI."

"Me and the rest of the nation."

"Right," she said. "In less than an hour, you get the entire package— crime, investigation, resolution—neatly wrapped up. But in the real world, you're talking hours and hours of hard labor. Tedious. I did some testing in med school. I used to hate it."

"How does it work?"

"First you have to 'wash' DNA chemically or apply pressure to 'squeeze' the DNA from the cell."

He nodded. "I learned something about it from watching the OJ trial. Then you have to cut the DNA, right?"

"Right. The most reliable system is STRs, which stands for short tandem repeats. These are accordion-like sequences that occur between genes."

"Example?"

"Let's say these four DNA bases, GATA, keep repeating twelve times in one person. This STR will be read as 12."

"So this number of consecutive repeats can vary between people."

"You're a quick study," she said. "I'm impressed."

He bowed his head. "I thank you, ma'am. How do they read STRs?"

"They separate the DNA snippets according to their size by moving them through an electric field. The smaller ones travel faster. The fragments are then detected using fluorescent dye. They make each tiny piece of DNA much bigger, or amplified, and they have these kits that will run a bunch of them at the same time. The kit will count how many repeat snippets of the same kind that person has and will show it as a color graphic on the computer screen."

"Is this what the FBI uses?"

She nodded. "Have you heard of CODIS?"

Dario's eyes brightened. Anya wondered if forensics was a secret hobby of his. "Of course. CODIS is the FBI's fingerprint database of DNA profiles from convicted offenders, unsolved crime scene evidence, and missing persons. Do you think they used it on Megan's baby?"

"I'd be surprised if they didn't. STR technology is highly accurate. For CODIS, the FBI uses a standard set of thirteen specific STRs."

"We inherit the STRs from our parents, right?"

"Right." He continued to surprise her with the depth of his understanding. "Your STRs come from both parents."

"But how truly unique is this DNA ID? What's the chance that somewhere in the world, there's another person with the exact same DNA fingerprint?"

"One in a billion!" Anya said.

"Watching the OJ trial," Dario said, "you got the impression that there was a huge chance for an error. In fact, if I recall correctly, the defense claimed that five different DNA labs were all in error, right?"

"The possibilities for human error are definitely there. But it's still the best test to date. The closest thing we have is a good old fingerprint, which can be smudged or otherwise distorted."

"So, why even bother if a smart lawyer is more than likely to prove the test wrong?"

"Because there's nothing better out there. DNA fingerprinting's done a lot of good."

Dario's eyes brightened again. "Like the Innocence Project."

"So you know about that, too?"

"Sure. I heard Barry Scheck interviewed on NPR. He and this other guy, Peter Neufeld, have made postconviction exonerations their primary mission. In the United States, 242 were set free. Seventeen of them were on death row!"

"I didn't know there were so many of them," admitted Anya.

Dario was clearly intrigued. "They use it in the military, right?"

"Right, in place of the dog tag. Each new recruit must provide blood and saliva samples, and the stored samples can subsequently be used as a positive ID for the dead or the missing—"

Chief Examiner Darryl Fitzpatrick stuck his head in the conference room door. "We're ready for you, Doctor Krim."

They both jumped to their feet.

"Your friend may wait here," Fitzpatrick said. "Follow me, Doctor."

They crossed the open space between the FBI DNA Analysis Unit I and the reading room. "This is a crazy case, I'm telling you," Fitzpatrick said. "Is it weird taking care of a pregnant comatose patient?"

"Have you confirmed paternity?" Anya asked, in no mood to talk. "The suspense is dreadful."

"Let's not rush it. We need to examine the evidence carefully to make the correct diagnosis. Sounds familiar?" He smirked at her.

"Where are you taking me now?"

"To the reading room." They entered it. Fitzpatrick introduced an Asian woman in a white coat. "This is Doctor Huang Chin, our fingerprint analyzer."

"You're here for the Tanner case?" Chin asked.

"Yes. Doctor Krim is Megan's obstetrician."

Doctor Chin sat down at the computer screen and typed "Baby Tanner" on her keyboard.

A graphic with multiple peaks in different colors appeared on the screen.

"This is Baby Tanner's DNA fingerprint from the blood you provided us." Doctor Chin left Baby Tanner's fingerprint on the screen and used a second computer to type "Tanner Paternity." Four graphics appeared on a single screen.

"And these are the paternity studies done on all the suspects we've received blood from."

"You had *four* suspects?"

"We have a routine procedural of gathering suspects at the FBI," Fitzpatrick said.

"I hate routines," Anya burst out. "They're the enemy of good medicine."

"Great minds think alike. But when an unconscious girl is found pregnant in the hospital, my charge as the chief of forensics is to cover every possibility. We need to know who might have knocked her up and who could very well still be out there."

"But—"

"The hospital supplied us with a list of the ten people who have had exclusive rights to enter Megan's room since her accident two years ago."

Fitzpatrick took out a list from his coat pocket. "Five of them haven't been fingerprinted, four because they're females. We also ruled out the night orderly, James Pierce. He carries a gene for Wilson's disease, which can be passed on to his children. So he's voluntarily undergone a vasectomy." He sighed. "These are the men we were left with. Five." He indicated the paper in front of him. "Getting a blood sample from some of them was worse than pulling teeth, court order not withstanding. Take it from me: my father was a dentist." He read aloud: "Jose Gomez, also known as Pepe, the nighttime maintenance man; John White, daytime maintenance; the security man who calls himself Zaro. And then we have the senator's therapist, Doctor Dario D'Acosta; and, of course, Senator Nelson Tanner III."

A bolt of shock shot through Anya. *That explains Dario's nervousness. Why would he let her give him a crash course on fingerprinting and not bother telling her that he was one of the FBI's prime suspects? He must've been embarrassed. Still, that doesn't make him a rapist.*

"You look pale," Fitzpatrick said.

"Excuse me, Detective, but I'm not sure that I heard you correctly. Did you just say that you took blood from Doctor D'Acosta? Is he one of your suspects?"

"He was one of the five men who had visiting privileges. Why?"

"Doctor D'Acosta is the man you saw sitting with me at the conference room."

"I'm well aware of that."

If only he knew that last night we shared a bed!

Anya shook herself out of contemplation. "And Megan's father? Is he one of your suspects as well? You must be out of your mind."

"Why? Are you making a class statement here? Because if you are, not only are you prejudiced, you're also wrong."

"We've kept the samples anonymous. No one besides us two has access to the log book where the codes are listed," said Doctor Chin.

"Doctor Krim, you know how to read these DNA fingerprints, right?" asked Fitzpatrick.

"I hardly have a forensic background, Detective. But earlier in my career, I ran some DNA gels."

"Excellent. See, before I release the results to Detective Relman, I'd love to have an independent observer verify them, ideally not from the FBI. You'd do me a big favor if you read these for us. Now."

"What do you mean by 'read' them?"

"Be an independent interpreter of the results. You tell us which one of The five fingerprints is the best match for Baby Tanner's."

"You must be kidding. You want *me* to determine—"

"Guilt. That's correct. I want to see whether your choice is same as ours."

Her eyes wandered back and forth from the baby's DNA to The other five. There was only one fingerprint that had a striking similarity to the baby's. Number 3. Any first-year genetics student could have spotted it from a distance.

Anya neared the computer screen board and pointed to number 3's DNA.

"Bingo," said Fitzpatrick. "You've confirmed our suspicion. Now we can go public. You don't know how much we appreciate this, Doctor Krim. I needed to be 100 percent sure."

"And—"

"And what, Doctor?"

"Who *is* number 3?"

"You have to swear the name doesn't leave the room."

"Of course, Detective. You have my word."

It's not Dario. It can't be.

"I warn you, you may find the news disturbing. Are you sure that you're up for it?"

God.

"I'm ready. Spit it out, already."

"I'm sorry to tell you, but—"

"Just say it."

"Suspect number 3 is Senator Nelson Tanner III."

CHAPTER 42

▼

Caroline flashed her flirtatious smile as she walked past the two White House Security officers who had showed up at 6:30 AM. She made sure her pace was slow enough to let the fragrance she had just sprayed on herself intoxicate the two kids in uniform. One thing she could be certain of: she got them distracted enough not to wonder what business she had walking into the embryo lab at the break of dawn.

The lab was quiet, a sleepy embryo hotel. The dim lights were never switched on or off. Hundreds of fresh embryos rested in incubators.

Anya was still in Quantico, Caroline knew. She calculated it would take at least forty minutes to get back to the hospital. And the embryo lab might not be the first place she'd go anyway.

Still, she had to work expeditiously and be done and gone by the time Anya returned.

She approached the Safe Nest incubator that housed the First Lady's embryos and used her own combination to unlock it, feeling an amazing rush as she opened the door.

She was ready. With confident hands, Caroline removed the tray that carried two dishes—all the First Lady's embryos—and brought them carefully to the laminar flow hood, where a constant flow of CO_2 gas kept embryos alive and well. She then sat down at her favorite microscope. She put the first dish on the microscope's heated stage.

First you have to ID them, she reminded herself. She took out the cover slip of the petri dish and looked through the light.

Janet Cartwright

ss # ... 1709

She put the cover slip aside and peered through the microscope. A perfectly symmetrical four-cell embryo rested in the middle of the dish. *Grade I,* she thought. The best. Had she not known the patient's age, she would have predicted a high likelihood for a viable pregnancy.

Caroline took a Narita digital camera out of the drawer and connected it to the microscope. She zoomed in, refocused, and clicked four times, proceeding quickly, repeating the same routine on each embryo. Focus.

Zoom. Click. All the embryos were of excellent quality. This should make everything that was about to happen even more exciting than she'd expected.

She worked for no longer than ten minutes.

She needed to store the embryo photos on a flash drive before she proceeded with the rest of her job. In the meantime, she thought, she'd better return the embryos to the incubator.

Caroline removed the petri dishes from the heated stage, placed them on the metal tray, carried the tray to the incubator, shut the incubator door, and locked it.

Then she unhooked the camera from the microscope and went over to her computer station. She connected the camera wire to the computer, inserted a new flash drive, and clicked to download all the embryo images onto the flash drive, taking extra care to avoid inadvertent saving of the images on the hard drive. Using the Photoshop program, she created three pages with the best image of each embryo. Two pages displayed four embryos each, and the third showed the remaining two. In total, she had created a digital image of First Lady Cartwright's ten potential offspring.

She saved them onto her disk.

Caroline clicked "send as an attachment."

Your message hasn't been sent yet. Do you still want to send it?

She clicked yes.

She heard the door open.

Anya noticed an image of four eight-cell embryos disappear from the screen. She had dropped Dario off at his place. All she had told him after they left Quantico was that he was no longer a suspect. Dario shrugged. It was no surprise. The rest of the tense forty-minute ride they'd spent in silence, while Anya processed the disturbing news she'd just heard. She wished she could share the burden with Dario. He knew the senator better than she. Perhaps better than anybody. She wanted to find out if he felt the senator was capable of so dreadful an act. She was tired of having to handle one crisis after another alone. But she knew there was no other choice. She was the only one outside the FBI who knew Megan's paternity findings. The scientist in her battled her instincts. She was shown hard-core evidence— state-of-the-art DNA fingerprinting. Yet, there was a human being behind these mute blots, a loving father who'd give anything to see his daughter wake up from her coma. Tanner wouldn't have dragged her to court and forced her to draw blood from the baby's umbilical cord if he were the baby's father! No, it just couldn't be … it couldn't be that he'd done what the DNA accused him of doing! Science was wrong!

"What are you doing here so early?" she asked Caroline. Her purpose in coming to the lab was to make sure that things were going well on her other front, that Janet's embryos were developing normally and were ready to be transferred.

Caroline glared at her. "I could ask you the same question."

"Whose embryos were you looking at?"

"Nobody's. These are leftover embryos from a transfer a patient wanted us to discard. I took their picture for documentation." She removed the flash drive and put it in her pocket. "Why? You don't trust me?"

The answer came to Anya with a shock. No.

CHAPTER 43

▼

Anya didn't get a chance to look at the First Lady's embryos when she was summoned to the White House. She hoped there was more to this call than just an urgent need for TLC. With all that she had been through, the TLC reserve had drained out of her. For Janet. Or for anyone else. Except Megan.

Megan. The oblivious, innocent bystander to the events surrounding her. That poor, unblemished soul had only Anya for protection. Everyone else had an ulterior motive. An agenda. It wasn't even clear whether Megan could trust her own father.

Janet Cartwright got up from behind her desk at her East Wing study and walked toward Anya, stretching out both her hands to hers, squeezing them warmly. "I'm so sorry I had to drag you here again. I know you have a lot going on. But the president is really upset and wanted me to discuss it with you in person."

They sat next to each other on the sofa.

"What did the president want you to discuss?"

"He's upset about Tanner. So am I, but for different reasons."

It was stupid of her to think the FBI wouldn't tell the president of their findings. The FBI chief met every morning with the president, and no doubt the scandal was going to become public. He wouldn't want the president caught off guard. But what did they want from her?

"Why are you upset?" she asked Janet.

"Because I've grown fond of Nelson Tanner. When we were first briefed by my husband's predecessor, he told us to beware of him, a dangerous powerhouse, wheeler, and dealer, that kind of thing. But I got to know him. He's an honest broker, a straight shooter, and 100 percent loyal to the president. Which is more than I could say about almost anybody else on Capitol Hill."

"And how does he feel about this as the president?"

"He remembers the impeachment hearing Congress held for Clinton over the Monica affair. How destructive it was. How it had paralyzed

164

Washington. Even international affairs had to be put on hold. Now they're going to have expulsion hearings on Tanner that will last forever. And Robert is convinced that until the matter is closed, he won't be able to get Congress's attention."

This could ruin his chances for reelection, Anya wanted to add. But she spared Janet. She was just the messenger.

"For all it's worth, I wanted to tell you that I don't believe the FBI's findings," she said.

"Why? Do you think their DNA testing could be wrong? That would be great!"

"Unfortunately, I saw the evidence myself. I couldn't find an error. It's my intuition talking. The impression I have of Tanner doesn't jibe with the allegations."

"That makes two of us. I've been praying for him ever since we've heard from the FBI. But my husband has already moved on. He has to."

"What does he want of me?" Anya asked.

"Robert thinks that the only way to contain the damage from this case is if," Janet paused, "if the baby didn't make it."

Anya's entire body tensed. Her heart's quickened response rushed the blood to her head.

Think before you react. They want me to kill the baby. It's not just Feinberg anymore. The president of the United States wants the baby terminated.

"And how do *you* feel about it?"

"Uncomfortable," Janet lowered her gaze. "But it's not my call. Robert has the nation to worry about."

"The president is pro-life, isn't he? He's threatening to veto Congress on stem cells because he considers an embryo in the dish a human being with full rights. Megan's baby is alive, twenty-two weeks old. Her heart's pumping, her arms and legs are moving, she's sucking her thumb. And he wants me to kill her?"

"Not exactly."

"Janet, listen to me." They made eye contact. Anya weighed each word. "Don't bother going further. Please tell the president whichever way one chooses to terminate this baby's life, it would be, in effect, a partial-birth abortion, which President G. W. Bush had outlawed, and I won't be a party to it." She got up. "I have to go now, Janet. I need to make sure Megan's baby's safe."

CHAPTER 44

▼
─────────────────────────────

They were stopped in dead-end traffic on Route 270 North, heading to Frederick, Maryland. Anya stole a glance at Dario. *Thank you for not chastising me. For not telling me I'm an idiot for driving so far in rush hour in this desperate attempt to clear Tanner.*

"You know what I love about you?" he asked.

"What?"

He smiled. "The nonscientist part."

The traffic started moving. "I'm not sure what you mean."

"It's your *passion,* honey," he squeezed her thigh. "That's where our hearts connect."

She knew he was right. A warm feeling filled her at the core. She removed her hand from the steering wheel and placed it on top of his. "It's okay to tell me I'm crazy doing this. I know I am."

"Now, Cornelia, that's her name, right?"

"Yes. Cornelia Lynch."

"You think she can do *another* DNA test, a test that's *better* than the FBI's?" he asked. Maybe it was the psychologist in him that let him question her action so gently it didn't feel like he was criticizing her. She had never before met a man who could challenge her without scolding or scuffing.

"Honestly, I doubt it," she admitted. "But if anyone can do it, she'd be the one."

"Didn't she work once at the FBI?"

Anya concentrated on the road, both hands on the wheel. Her navigation system said they were only ten minutes away from LifeCodes. "Good memory," she said. "I'd mentioned it to you ages ago. She did her internship in forensic science at the FBI and landed a job there by the end of the year. But she couldn't stand her boss who was lesbo-phobic, so she left."

"And now—"

"Now she's a big cheese," Anya said. "Chief scientist in this private DNA lab. She's the person defense lawyers call on to prove the FBI wrong."

"So what you're asking her to do she's done before, right?"

"Yes, only in our case, we're not talking about proving a wrong conviction given many years ago when DNA testing was in its diapers. The STR system used by the FBI for Megan's case is rock solid."

"That's why I love you so much," he said. She felt his eyes on her. His voice was soft. He massaged the nape of her neck, sending electricity up her scalp. "You know the chances they're wrong are almost none, yet you feel so empathetic toward Tanner that you'd go this far, literally, for the remote possibility—"

Anya remembered that Dario was Tanner's therapist. That he, too, felt deeply for this man. Her feelings were more mixed than his, since she'd been bullied by the man she now sought to exculpate.

"It's not just what I feel for Tanner," she said. "I have to do whatever I can for Megan and her baby. As long as Tanner's the suspected father, the White House won't ease the pressure on me to terminate the pregnancy."

It took Anya a few minutes to fill Cornelia in. They were seated at her study, her desk piled with disorganized paperwork. Cornelia chewed gum, at times loudly. Her hair was cropped below her ears. She must have put on At least ten pounds since medical school reunion a couple of years ago. Cornelia checked her computer screen the whole time Anya was talking.

"Messy case," Cornelia commented when Anya finished. "And don't believe any word coming out of Fitzpatrick's mouth."

Anya wondered if Fitzpatrick was one of the people Cornelia had a conflict with when she worked at the FBI, or whether this was a newer rivalry evolving from the cases she'd been dealing with recently. "I'd love to discredit the FBI's conclusion," Anya said. "The problem is, I've seen it with my own eyes! It's the DNA evidence I'm trying to disprove, not Fitzpatrick!"

Cornelia typed something on her computer. Then she ogled Dario, "Don't tell me you thought it could've been your boyfriend." She turned to Anya and swiveled the computer screen in Anya's direction.

He's hot!
Definitely a keeper!

Anya felt her face flush. She smiled back at Cornelia. "Listen to me. Whether it's Fitzpatrick or someone else, the evidence against Tanner is strong."

"From what I hear, he's not the nicest man on the Hill."

Dario broke his silence. "I've gotten to know him closely. The man has a big heart."

"From what I hear, that's not the only thing he got that's big," Cornelia said.

Anya giggled. "Thank God. Now you're back to yourself." She shot an "I told you so" glance in Dario's direction. "Tanner may not be the nicest guy. Still, I don't buy the —"

"Incest theory, right? I agree that being a shark on Capitol Hill doesn't necessarily make you a sex offender."

"So," Anya said.

"So nothing," Cornelia shrugged and lit a cigarette. "What do you expect of me? Just because Fitzpatrick's an asshole doesn't mean I can prove him wrong. This STR system they use now is highly accurate."

"They've made errors before, haven't they?"

"Of course the FBI's made mistakes. Sent innocent people to the electric chair. This is what I've been making a living on—proving them wrong. It gives me great pleasure, and it more than pays the rent. But all the screw-ups in the past were with old methods, R(i)FL(i)ps, shmiplips. Now we're onto STRs. Bad news for my bank account. Believe me, a monkey can operate it. By the time they're done sorting thirteen different STRs, they've nailed the suspect good. We'd have to go to China or India—the only countries with more than a billion people—to maybe find someone else with an identical DNA."

"What about mitochondrial DNA?" Anya asked.

"How's that different?" Dario wondered.

Cornelia was delighted to elaborate. "There's DNA not only in the nucleus but also in this organelle called mitochondria. It comes only from the mother's egg. The father only contributes to the DNA from the nucleus."

"If it's only from the mom, how could testing for it change a paternity test?" Dario asked.

"Great question. Why don't we ask your girlfriend?"

"Mitochondrial DNA is like a *maternity* test," Anya said, "which may shed light on the paternity as well." Anya turned to Cornelia. "Here. I brought you the only sample I had." Anya handed her a small white envelope.

Cornelia took out a piece of white cloth stained with red. "What is it?"

"I cut it out from my lab coat, which was splattered with the baby's blood when they attacked me. Do you think you could lift some DNA from it?"

"Sure. We do it all the time." Anya took two tubes of blood from her bag. "Now don't tell me this is—"

"Blood from the Tanners. Yes. I kept an extra tube for each when I drew the bloods."

"This is how she was in med school," Cornelia told Dario. "Always one step ahead. That's why she's heading for the Nobel Prize and I'm stuck here, fingerprinting criminals."

Anya got up to leave. "You'll do it for me?"

Cornelia stood. "I'm glad you finally came to visit. It was so nice to meet you, Dario." Cornelia gave him a hug and a peck on his cheek. "Don't let her out of your sight. This woman's pure gold."

"You can stop here," Dario said when her Saab got to his street. "I'm a big boy. I can cross the street. I promise to look left, right, left," he grinned and turned around to hug her.

"Thank you for coming with me." She buried her head in his chest.

He squeezed her. "Thank *you*! I learnt a lot."

They kissed. She didn't want them to separate. When he reached for the handle, she stopped short of saying, "Don't go." "I just have a few quick things to do in the hospital. And then I'll come over."

"Just be careful driving," he said. "You haven't had much sleep."

She watched him step out of the car, his taste left on her lips.

CHAPTER 45

▼

Barely over a year since Robert had taken office, and they were already facing their first major domestic crisis, the First Lady thought, sitting at her desk in her East Wing office, watching Peggy Wheeler arrange the morning newspapers. If she had any illusions the crisis could be contained, the headlines that jumped off the pages snapped her back into reality. The media had gotten hold of the FBI's findings. Once the allegations against Tanner became public knowledge, neither Congress nor the president would have control over the consequences. Robert was in the midst of the Iran nuclear crisis and had asked her if she could write the response the White House spokesman would read to the press.

"The *New York Times:* Majority Whip Suspected of Incest.

"The *Washington Post:* Capitol Hill is Talking Expulsion.

"The *Chicago Herald:* Tanner's Paternity Beyond Doubt.

"The *Wall Street Journal:* Expulsion Hearings Expected to Hurt President's Agenda and Reelectability.

"Okay," Janet raised her hand. "I've read enough." Peggy withdrew her hand from *USA Today.*

"There may be a positive side," Peggy said.

She's promoted herself to White House strategist, Janet thought. "I refuse to take pleasure in someone else's misery. Enlighten me, please. How might the nation benefit from this?"

"It's a chance to get rid of Senator Tanner as chairperson of the Appropriations Subcommittee. The man's a liability, particularly now that he intends to vote in favor of the stem-cell bill. Republicans will be delighted if the president did the dirty work for them and asked him to resign. The president's better off replacing him with someone we can count on."

Janet wished she could fire Peggy immediately. But as a rooky First Lady, she'd learned the hard way how little room she'd actually had to maneuver. Peggy's job was secure for a long time, and Peggy knew it. First, because she was already the replacement for Larry Shafer, who'd been fired. Second, because firing of senior White House staff in the midst of a crisis was always perceived by the public as admission of failure. "I don't pull the rug from under a man who's about to fall," Janet said, her tone severe. "So you might as well not bring this up again. Understood?"

"Maybe we should hold off on this discussion until your IVF cycle is over," Peggy said.

"I can't stop everything because of my fertility treatment," Janet fought to contain her anger. "The president isn't going to make any move until the FBI concludes the investigation. For the time being, you should take notes for the press." Peggy reluctantly pulled a notepad and a pen out of her pocketbook and started to write. "The president regards Senator Tanner, as he always has, as a man of honor and personal integrity, a war hero," the First Lady dictated. "The president continues to have his full trust in the senator. We urge the media to refrain from reaching their own verdict. Premature allegations against the senator undermine our judicial system and demonstrate a lack of compassion toward the senator's personal tragedy."

"Blah, blah, blah," said Peggy Wheeler.

CHAPTER 46

▼

Isabelle, Dario's El Salvadorian housekeeper, opened the door. The minute she saw Anya, she burst out crying.

"What happened, Isabelle? Where's Doctor D'Acosta?"

Isabelle's weeping intensified. She couldn't talk. Anya patted her shoulders. "Try to calm down. What happened? Where is he?"

Isabelle suppressed a sob. "They ... a man called here. Said Doctor D'Acosta had an accident. A b-bbad accident. They ... they took him to hospital. They said he was bad. Real bad."

No! This couldn't be happening! Anya had dropped him off barely two hours ago. And he said he was going home and staying home. An accident? How could it be?

"Which hospital?" she asked Isabelle.

"Washington General."

Washington General was the city's best trauma center. The accident had to be serious. Shit! Anya's breathing grew rapid and shallow. She felt needle-pricks at her fingertips. *You're hyperventilating.* She took a deep breath. "I'll call you as soon as I know how he is," she told Isabelle.

"I pray for him, Doctora. I pray he live."

Anya released her arm from Isabelle's grasp. "I'll make sure he gets the best care. When I see him, I'll give him your love."

Washington General got a new trauma case every three minutes, Anya thought, sitting in the waiting room in front of the OR. Before she ran out of her car, she'd put on her white hospital coat, which got her through security. Gunshot wounds, knife assaults, drug ODs came here from all over the city. One out of three cases went to the OR. Anya figured she'd seen at least six, maybe seven, gurneys rushed through the doors.

Trying to distract herself counting gurneys only made things worse. Her thoughts honed in on Dario. Images of the worst trauma cases she'd taken care of came back: pieces of shattered skull cutting into a brain; crush injury to the chest, doctors fighting for an airway; massive tears of the spleen, doctors pumping blood into large-bore veins; extremities disembodied. In every single scene, she could see Dario's face, yellowing in pain.

She shook her head, trying to make the images disappear. *Please, tell me what's really going on so I don't keep guessing!*

A graying surgeon in green scrubs emerged. A light blue face mask still hung on his neck. He looked exhausted.

He read her name tag. "Doctor Krim, I'm Ted Greenhouse, the senior attending physician of the Blue Team. How are you related to Doctor D'Acosta, if I may ask?"

"He's my boyfriend," she said. *Just don't pull HIPPA on me now please,* Anya thought. HIPPA forbade doctors to give medical information to anyone without patient's written consent.

"Doctor D'Acosta is still in surgery. Several teams are operating on him simultaneously."

He's alive, thank God! From the doctor's stern face she could tell Dario was still critical. "What happened?"

"He was run over when he tried to cross the street. Judging from the nature of the injuries, he was hit twice by an SUV."

This wasn't just an accident! Someone was trying to kill him. They tried to kill Dario because of me!

"Twice?" she managed.

"Two separate sets of wheel tracks. A hit-and-run. We don't know the exact lag time from the injury until the EMTs got to him. All I know is that when my team first saw him in the ER, he was unconscious with a depressed skull fracture. Neurosurgery burr-holed him at the bedside almost immediately."

Burr holes! Goddamn murderers! Even if he survives, if they got his brain stem, he's gone! "I've got to see him, Doctor Greenhouse."

"He's still in surgery."

I have to see him while he's still alive. "You have an OR observation deck, don't you?"

"It's strictly for teaching, Doctor."

No way is he going to stop me from seeing Dario. She could see Grandma's hands, hardened from housework, seize her feisty young body and tell her, "No, Anuchka. You've got to play nice! Play nice and you'll get anything you want."

"I realize what I'm asking you is outside your standard policy," she said. "But you *have* to help me on this. If I wait to see him after surgery, I may never again see him alive again."

Doctor Greenhouse indicated a door behind them. "Let's go." She followed him up a winding staircase and entered the OR observation deck, a 360-degree rotunda arranged around a central, all-glass core, with the operating theater underneath in full view. Young men and women in short white coats—medical students, Anya assumed—were watching the case intently.

Anya peered down. A breathing tube and a stomach-draining tube emerged through small holes in the white bandages wrapped around Dario's head and midsection. Teams of surgeons, assistants, and scrub nurses were working on different parts of Dario's body. Three anesthesiologists labored at the head of the table, two of them manually squeezing blood units into an IV set connected to a central line, while a third watched the monitors, adjusting the respirator.

"We had to remove his spleen," said Doctor Greenhouse. "Shattered. Between blood and blood products, he must've gotten at least fifty units already. We also excised a small portion of his liver and sutured over it. The urologists sutured over the torn bladder."

It will be a miracle if he comes out alive, she thought. But then she remembered trauma cases she'd seen in her internship. Other patients whose bodies were broken up and torn to pieces. They'd survived. And Dario was at the nation's prime trauma center.

Hang in there. You're going to make it.

"So the belly is closed now?"

"Yes. The chest surgeons are inserting drains to evacuate all the blood around his lung. Most of his ribs have double fractures. His rib cage makes his breathing ineffective. The machine is blowing high air pressure to overcome the flail chest."

"The team at the foot of the table—orthopods?"

"Yes. They're pinning and plating every leg and every arm."

"So, those bastards tried to flatten his body like they were pressing a suit."

Doctor Greenhouse squeezed Anya's shoulders. "I'm sorry, Doctor Krim. This is really bad. I expect him to remain critical for a long time. But he may pull through."

"You don't have to baby me. I'd rather you be honest."

"He's a young, healthy man. In this place we've seen shattered bodies come back together like a thousand-piece puzzle. The $64,000 question: will his brain tolerate the insult, or has it already suffered irreversible damage? The next twenty-four hours will tell."

"My advice, though, Doctor Krim, is to prepare for the worst."

CHAPTER 47

▼

Cody's last encounter with Destiny lasted no more than a few seconds when she'd dropped off Baby Marshall's blood. All he remembered was the cloud of perfume she'd left behind.

He was seated on a chair next to Nicholson, going through files of "pet projects" when Destiny walked in. For the first time since Cody remembered, she wore a white lab coat. Underneath, she wore a simple, black, buttoned-down shirt and black slacks. He couldn't detect a drop of makeup.

Cody got up in a hurry. He was used to leaving the two to themselves. But Nicholson said, "Sit down. I want you to stay for this."

Destiny remained standing. "What is it, exactly, that he's staying to watch, a public lynching?"

"Please sit," Nicholson told her, pointing to the chair in front of his desk.

"I have work to do. Whatever it is you have to say, just say it." She sat down.

Cody felt Nicholson's knee start to shake under his desk, a familiar barometer of the boss's nerves. "So what's the holdup, for Christ's sake?" Nicholson asked.

Destiny sat back. "This isn't as simple as you think it is. She almost caught me in the act." Her face was sullen.

Nicholson had ordered him to stay, but didn't bother to fill him in. What were these two up to? And who was the woman Destiny was referring to? With a shock, he thought he knew.

"How did that happen?"

"She waltzed into the lab as I was getting the embryos together."

Embryos! I was right then! It's Anya they're talking about. He could almost hear the palpitations within his chest. *They better tell me soon. Nicholson's treating me like no more than a piece of furniture. And Destiny's totally ignoring me.*

"So, they're still there?" Nicholson asked. *He must be talking about the embryos. What has he concocted now, for God's sake? Whose embryos are they*

175

talking about? Cody processed different possible scenarios, none of which were good.

"They're still in the lab, safe and sound," Destiny waved her hand. "I just moved them to new dishes with new culture fluid." She knew how to take care of embryos.

"Good. Make sure you give *her* a chance to look at them before you take them from the lab," Nicholson's knee slowed. *Nicholson's plotting to steal embryos? He's out of his fucking mind!*

"Why? I was going to go back in a couple of hours, when I know she'd be seeing patients.

"You're not listening to me," Nicholson squeaked. "You've got to make sure she looks at the embryos one more time. Even if you have to go back in the middle of the night to get them."

Destiny's voice rose as well. "I don't get it. What are you trying to do? Are you trying to arrange for a last-rites session between Anya Krim and the embryos?"

Cody's heart quickened. It *was* Anya they were talking about all along. And the embryos had to be the president and First Lady's! Why had the boss decided to make him part of this? There was only one answer: Cody only found out about "stuff" when Nicholson was ready to put him to work. He would soon become guardian of the president's embryos, or even worse, ordered to alter the president's embryos. How stupid has he, Cody, been to admire this man?

"I can't believe I have to spell it out." Nicholson chastised Destiny like a high school teacher. "I want Krim's fingerprints to be found all over those dishes."

I have to stay calm. Play dumb. Pretend like I'm barely tuned in.

"You're trying to frame her. I get it. And why would you do that?"

What was Destiny's relationship with Anya?

Nicholson grinned. "Kill two birds with one stone. As close as we are to getting rid of Tanner, this woman, single-handedly, is trying to prove the FBI's wrong on the incest charges against him."

"And the other bird?" Destiny sighed.

"The other bird is *you*, my dear."

Destiny's voice went up again, "What do you mean?"

"With Krim's fingerprints all over the embryo dishes, you'd be off the hook."

Cody moved uncomfortably in his chair, trying to conceal his violent emotions. He had to find a way to tell Anya. Fast!

Destiny sprung up from her chair. "I'm not doing it."

Nicholson's eyebrows rose. His voice remained calm. "You're not doing what?"

"Setting her up like this."

"You're not making sense," Nicholson's voice cracked. "Destiny, listen!"

Destiny was almost at the door. "I'm going to do it *my* way. And I'm no longer Destiny. It's Caroline to you, as it is to Anya Krim. Anya Krim, my primary and direct boss. And my friend."

Cody had to gulp down the shocking revelation.

Destiny was already at the door when she stopped, hesitated for a moment, turned around, took out a scrap of paper, and tossed it on Nicholson's desk. "Janet Cartwright's e-mail address, as promised," she said.

Cody could see the boss's back slump, his shoulders droop. *This would be a good time to leave*, he thought. He got up and excused himself. Nicholson paid no attention to his words or his actions.

CHAPTER 48

▼

The woman who stooped over Dario was oblivious to Anya's presence. Mrs. D'Acosta barely resembled her picture. She looked old and disheveled. Deformed by arthritis, her shaking hand caressed Dario's bandaged head. Her other hand, swollen at the knuckle, rested gently on his right palm, the only exposed part of his body.

Anya touched her shoulder. "I'm Anya Krim, Mrs. D'Acosta."

His mother glanced up with grateful eyes. "You're his doctor friend? He never told me you were so pretty."

"How are you holding up?"

A burst of tears erupted. "He was such a careful man. They told me the van ran him over and then came back to hit him again. Anya, you *have* to tell me. Was he in some kind of trouble?"

His only trouble's me. "Dario's always played everything straight," Anya said. "You have my word. I don't know who ran him over. The police are investigating."

She didn't add that it was she the driver was after. Someone had tried to scare her by hurting the person closest to her. It was all her fault, and she didn't have the guts to tell his mom.

Mrs. D'Acosta stood. The two women embraced. "Please make sure they do *everything* in their power to keep my boy alive. He's all I've got." She kissed Dario's hand, kissed Anya's cheek, and left.

Anya sat on Dario's bed. Senator Tanner's continuing communication with Megan seemed to Anya much less insane. Even reading her the newspapers made sense. In case her brain *was* capable of understanding, Anya thought, she wouldn't be so behind. One day … one day—when she woke up …

One day, *when he wakes up* … She clutched Dario's hand, "I love you. I love you, Dario. And you're going to make it. I promise."

Did he tighten his grip voluntarily, or was his hand muscle reflexively contracting in response to her squeeze?

With the rhythmic, monotonous sighs of the respirator as a backdrop, Anya watched the ruins of her boyfriend, now reassembled and kept alive through artificial means. Guilt engulfed her. He never quite said it, but Anya knew Dario felt she was too emotionally caught up in her work and her patients. And that she'd never given their relationship priority. Now her priorities were much clearer.

Anya made a vow:

I promise I'll no longer seek Baby Marshall's adoption.

When you recover, I want to make love to you. I want to have a baby with you.

For a moment she imagined them together in bed. The pins, plates, and nails that held his skeleton together made a screeching noise that sent a chill through her spine.

CHAPTER 49

▼

"Urgent. For your eyes only."

Janet Cartwright stared at the computer screen.

Urgent? Who'd be sending an urgent e-mail to her private address, one so highly classified that fewer than a handful of people had it? Security had warned her time and again not to open any mail when she didn't know the sender.

Janet Cartwright was the sender's address. This was possible if someone hit "Reply" to an e-mail she'd sent earlier. At least she knew the sender had to be someone she had written to. But who?

She opened the e-mail:

Get ready. A second message will follow shortly, which will have a critical impact on your life. Make sure your room stays clear of any other person. Lock your doors, and don't let anyone in, not your press secretary or your husband.

Do not, I repeat, do not call the FBI, White House Security, or anyone else. I am following you closely. Don't try to trick me.

Stay tuned.

She felt cold, exposed. Instinctively, she tightened her robe. Was someone watching her? Who?

Her eyes wandered around the room, looking for hidden cameras. Nothing. She examined the computer screen, the speakers and the hard-drive box. Nothing.

She clicked on Microsoft Outlook inbox.

The screen filled up with a photo of ten perfect embryos.

Janet read:

Greetings from your embryos.

Yes, this digital image is a group photo of your own flesh and blood—the little embryos that you and your husband had Lincoln Hospital's IVF Lab custom-make for you.

For the time being, your children-to-be are safe and sound with me. Their conditions are identical to the ones at the Lincoln Hospital IVF lab.

In upcoming messages, I will inform you of the kind of actions you must take to bring your embryos home unharmed.

In the meantime, Janet, I trust you won't do anything rash. Any stupid move and I start eliminating them, one embryo at a time.

Make enough stupid moves, and you can kiss motherhood good-bye.

The Presidential Emergency Operations Center was a tube-like structure immediately beneath the East Wing. Janet was only familiar with it from the tour she'd been given by the Secret Service chief on her first day at the White House.

If the place was safe against a nuclear attack, Janet assumed it had a secure communications system. From there, she called her husband on the hot line.

"What happened?" The president came through the door, alone as she'd asked him. His arms enveloped her.

"Our embryos … our embryos were—" She couldn't finish the sentence. She felt her ovaries throbbing, but the pain was gone. Even the knot she'd felt in her womb was no longer there. Instead, there was a strange feeling of emptiness. A void.

"What happened to our embryos?"

Janet's hand was still massaging her pelvic area. "I got an e-mail from someone who claims he's kidnapped our embryos."

She could feel his "hazard" antennas go up. One of Robert's strengths was his capacity to hone in on any new crisis, even if it involved something he hadn't paid much attention to before. "This is a huge breach of security, honey, getting into your e-mail like this. It must've shaken you good. We have several computer safety officers as part of the Secret Service. I'll have them get on the job right aw—"

"Rob, listen to me, please! I'm worried this … person has got the East Wing under surveillance. It's not just my e-mail that's been invaded!"

He squeezed her shoulders. "Your imagination is going wild. The White House, East Wing included, is shielded from surveillance. But if it makes you feel safer, I can have them set you up here for a few days. Make you cozy and safe. We'll spend the nights here together, if you want."

Was he ignoring the rest of what she'd told him on purpose? "That would hardly get us our embryos back," she raged. "This person, whoever he is, sent me a photo of all ten of them. He says he's got them in his custody!"

"Believe me, honey. I care about our embryos as much as you do," he said. *I wish I believed that!* "I'm simply trying to be rational."

When aren't you rational? Maybe, just this one time, you'd be less of a president and more of a husband.

"This is how I see it. We have the embryos tucked away in a locked incubator at Lincoln Hospital. We have two Secret Service agents on guard outside the embryology lab. Why don't you call Doctor Krim and have her verify that our embryos are safe? In the meantime, they'll get you settled here while I calm the staff. They must be thinking we're getting ready for another terrorist attack."

Robert planted a kiss on her forehead and left in a hurry, back to his day job. Since the first day they were married, she'd never gotten his full attention. Long before he became president, he'd always had something else he was dealing with that took precedence. Now that he was president, she had to share him with the rest of the world. If her personal issues were belittled before, now they were dwarfed, miniaturized almost to nonexistence, compared to the global crises that never left Robert's agenda.

But what was she saying? That the embryo kidnapping was *her* personal issue? Wrong! *Their* embryos, *their* potential children, had been hijacked, and her husband had given her all of what, ten minutes? And what was the solution of the leader of the free world? Stick her in this bunker and have her call Anya.

Fine. She'll call Anya. But once Anya verified she no longer had the embryos, she'd get Robert wherever he'd be, make him use everything that's in his power to bring her babies home.

CHAPTER 50

▼

The vibrations of Anya's beeper woke her from the short nap she'd taken on the chair next to Dario's bed. Worn out, she fumbled for the beeper. Shit! The First Lady!

She crossed the hallway to a pay phone and dialed the number on the screen.

"Where have you been?" Janet's voice was shrill.

You have no right to scold me like this, Anya's half-awake brain thought, *even if you're the First Lady.* "I fell asleep at my boyfriend's bedside in the Intensive Care Unit."

The First Lady didn't ask why Dario was in intensive care. "Are you on a land phone?" She asked instead. Her tone was icy.

"I am," Anya responded. Land phone? What now?

"While you were sleeping, Doctor, my embryos were stolen. All ten of them. I thought they were safe and sound. Now they're gone."

Anya stood, too shocked to speak.

"Did you hear me?"

Anya rubbed her eyes. "I—"

"Wake up! Wake up and listen! My embryos. They're gone!"

Anya cupped the receiver's mouthpiece. "What do you mean, gone?"

"I got an e-mail that my embryos have been kidnapped."

"No, Janet. It can't be. I was in the lab," she checked her watch, "less than three hours ago. Your embryos were safe. I saw them myself."

She heard Janet sigh. "Did you lock them?"

"Of course. And I'm the only one who knows the combination."

"No one else knows it?"

Caroline had her own code. But mentioning it to Janet would make Caroline an immediate suspect.

"You're hesitating."

"I made up the combination. It's in my head. I haven't written it anywhere."

Janet didn't sound convinced. "Someone e-mailed me digital photos of what they claim are my embryos."

183

There hasn't been a single case where embryos had been maliciously removed from an IVF lab. Not once. This had to be a sham. She had to calm Janet. "Someone's trying to scare you. It's easy to reproduce a photograph of generic embryos. You can download them straight off the Internet. There are no identifying features. None whatsoever."

"I know. I know. I'm not stupid. I'm going to forward you what I got. Maybe you'd be able to tell if these could be my babies—" the First Lady choked on her words.

No longer the First Lady, just a vulnerable patient.

"Janet?"

"Do me a favor, even if you think the whole thing's a prank. Go to your lab, immediately, and make sure ... make sure they're still there."

"I'm on my way. I'll call you as soon as I'm with your embryos."

The relentless thumping of Anya's heart belied the words she had just uttered.

"My gut tells me this is real," Janet said. "I think my embryos are no longer in the custody of Lincoln Hospital."

"I'll call you soon."

"Call me at this number." She gave it. "I'm in the Presidential Emergency Operations Center."

CHAPTER 51

▼

Traffic was the last thing Anya needed. But there was nothing she could do to move faster. It was 8:30 in the morning.

She should have asked the First Lady to send a helicopter to Washington General.

What should've taken no longer than twenty minutes turned into a ninety-minute drive. By this time, the entire crew—three embryologists, four sperm technicians, and a secretary—would be in the lab. It was tempting to call someone to look in the First Lady's incubator. But Anya didn't think it wise.

She was jolted by the ringing of her phone.

"Anya?" A man's voice. What now?

"It's Alex Gordon. I have something to tell you. Are you driving?"

"Yes, why?"

"We'll talk when you get here."

"No, Alex. Tell me. I won't have any time to talk once I reach the hospital."

He hesitated.

"Alex?"

"It's ... it's about Baby Marshall. They found his ... remains in a garbage dump. I'm sorry I couldn't tell you this in person."

Tears started to trickle down her cheeks. *Remains. Garbage dump.* She shivered. Her vision blurred. "No ... thank you ... better off this way," she said and hung up.

Finally, the Lincoln Hospital exit.

Anya ran through the corridors of the Henley Building, slowing down as she neared the IVF lab.

The Secret Service agent saluted. "Good morning, Doctor Krim."

She read the name on his badge. "How long have you been out here, Blaine?"

"Since 7 AM sharp, ma'am."

"And you never left your post? Not even to go the men's room?"

"No, ma'am. In the Secret Service, we develop huge bladders. Last you a whole shift."

"Has anyone unusual entered the lab?"

"Absolutely not, ma'am, only technicians who are on my list. And, of course, I checked IDs on each one."

"Thank you, Blaine. Good job." Anya entered the lab.

The embryologists were in the midst of an egg harvest, so no one noticed her entry. Anya went straight to the incubator marked JC and unlocked it.

Two petri dishes, filled with fluid, sat atop the metal tray. So far so good. At her microscope station, Anya positioned the tray in the protected hood and placed the first dish on the microscope's heated stage.

It took her a few minutes to get the scope into focus. The fluid in the dish was clear. Maybe the embryos had settled deeper, she thought, and adjusted the focus. But there was only water for her to look at.

There was no embryo in that dish.

She switched to the second dish and then the third. All ten of them. Empty!

Someone had probably sat here, at her microscope, collected all ten embryos, and kidnapped them in one dish.

Janet Cartwright's embryos had been removed from the IVF lab.

CHAPTER 52

▼

"Can you believe how well the First Lady did? Ten good-looking embryos. Not bad for a forty-two-year-old, huh?" Caroline beamed.

Her exhilaration erupted into the office where Anya sat alone with the lights off, her head between her hands.

How do I break the news to her?

"I think you better sit down." She waved Caroline to sit in front of her desk. "When did you last see them?"

"Last night. Why?"

"Because they're gone."

"What do you mean, gone?" All Anya could read on Caroline's face was annoyance, the kind of expression she'd frequently wear, part of her discontent with authority. "You mean, like, they went out for a walk or something?"

"I wish it were funny," Anya said. "I've just come back from the lab. There are no embryos there."

Caroline was no longer smiling. "Maybe you checked the wrong incubator."

"Don't be ridiculous. There's only one incubator with the initials JC on it. And only one incubator that has a combination lock on it, installed by the Secret Service."

"Maybe you looked at the wrong dishes?"

"There are only two on the tray. They're still there. Plenty of fluid. And no embryos!"

"Anya, I know you've been trained in the lab." *Now don't patronize me. Go ahead with the "but."* "But you don't sit at a microscope day-in day-out. Sometimes it can get tricky. The embryos are tiny. You could just miss them. Plain and simple."

"I know." Anya leaned on her desk, summoning every bit of patience left in her. "Believe me. I went up and down on the scope. Tried all magnifications. Both dishes have clear fluid but not one embryo."

Caroline stretched her arm across the desk, her hand touching Anya's. "For whatever it's worth, I want you to know I'll try to help in any way

187

possible. For everybody's sake—you, me, the Cartwrights—I hope this is some kind of mistake. But would you mind if I went over and checked it out myself?"

"Of course not."

Caroline walked to the door. "It shouldn't take long. I'll call you when I'm done."

Anya remained sitting. The world was black.

There was a knock on the door.

"Who is it?" Anya asked.

"Tanner."

"Come in." Anya sprung up from her desk. The senator limped in. He was unusually stooped, his dress shirt badly wrinkled, his tie loosened. There were bags under his eyes, and his usual confident smile had vanished. He looked back through the open door.

"Someone else with you, Senator?" Anya asked.

"No," he said. "The woman who just walked out of your office. Who's she?"

"It's my embryologist. Caroline."

"She looks familiar," he said. "The name doesn't ring a bell. You said—s"

"Caroline," Anya said.

"Hmm—"

Whatever "hmm" meant.

Tanner limped to the chair in front of her desk. Anya walked closer to him but remained standing, eager to make this meeting short.

"I don't mean to intrude," he said, "but there's something I need to tell you. I haven't stopped thinking about the Embryonic Stem-Cell Bill. I've changed my mind. I'm going to support the bill—if they keep me as chairman."

She felt nothing. It meant nothing. All she managed to say was, "I'm glad, Senator. This is an important step in the right direction."

"I also came here to thank you," he added. "I know how you stood by me when the FBI presented the DNA evidence incriminating me. Hats off, Doctor. I haven't seen such courage since I walked the minefields in Vietnam."

Tanner's words only added pain to her open sore.

CHAPTER 53

▼

Reprotech, West Virginia

"Destiny did an excellent job," Cody told Nicholson. It was all he could come up with to break the uncomfortable silence between him and his boss.

For the last fifteen minutes, he had been sitting at his inverted microscope, examining the First Lady's embryos. "It's not an easy task to transport fresh embryos for such a distance," he added.

Cody felt the weight of responsibility on him. Over the last forty-eight hours, disdain and contempt had replaced any feeling of admiration he once had for his boss. Not having a good grip on Nicholson's sick and convoluted mind, Cody had no idea how the boss was going to use the embryos. Yet, while keeping him ignorant, Nicholson had still managed to make him, Cody, an accomplice to an outrageous crime against the First Couple of the United States.

"This was her swan song," Nicholson said.

"I beg your pardon?"

"This was Destiny's last job with us."

Last job? "Has she resigned?"

Nicholson chuckled. "I wouldn't put it this way. Let's just say she's no longer a team player."

He had to keep on working. Nicholson was crowding him now, standing right behind him. At least he didn't seem to know he knew what Cody was doing. Cody had unplugged the TV monitors ahead of time, making sure the boss couldn't visualize that he was trying to create new embryos from the First Couple's embryos, in case something happened to the originals.

Cody had no idea if it was going to work. He'd read of someone who'd removed a single cell from an eight-cell embryo and grew it in special solution, and the cell had multiplied and made a whole new embryo, identical to the one the cell came from. Overnight, Cody had prepared the special solution, an artificial zona, which mimicked the natural envelope that usually surrounded each embryo. This fluid was expected to allow a single cell to continue to divide.

Nicholson paced the lab. "What's taking you so long? Just take the damn pictures already."

"I need to clean them up and get rid of all the junk around them. Make them picture-perfect." Cody said.

Cody picked up two pipettes, his surgical tools. There was no way for Nicholson to tell he wasn't simply cleaning the embryos. For now, Cody blocked any thoughts of what could happen to him if the boss did find out.

I've got to distract him a few minutes longer.

"The embryos are gorgeous."

Stabilizing the embryo with the holding pipette, he used the other to puncture a hole in the embryo.

"Looks like you're doing major surgery," Nicholson said from uncomfortable proximity.

"Cosmetic," Cody said hurriedly. "Just cleaning them up." He finished with the first embryo. He had a single cell now in his pipette. He carefully moved it into a separate dish with the artificial zona.

"This one's ready to have its picture taken," Cody said. He turned on the monitor and took a series of shots. The digital images came out perfectly. He could detect the exact spot where his needle had stuck the wall. Right next to it, a single cell was missing. But it had been subtle enough to escape Nicholson's eye.

Cody took a deep breath.

"I see it's going to take a while," he heard his boss say. "I'm going back to my office. Have these photos ready when I get back. I need them for the next e-mail." He sighed. "And you don't have to be so meticulous, Coddington. I don't give a shit if any of these embryos survive."

CHAPTER 54

━━━━━━━━━━━━━━▼━━━━━━━━━━━━━━

"I think we should quit," Janet said.

"Quit what, honey," Rob asked.

"The progesterone injections. I want to stop taking them."

Robert had just filled the syringe with medicine in the bathroom. He had brought it downstairs to the Presidential Emergency Operations Center, where a makeshift suite had been arranged for them.

"You can't stop the injections now. They're—"

"Preparing the uterus for the embryos. For the embryos that are *not* coming, right?" She wanted to punch someone. Hard. Robert would be an excellent target.

Robert stood at the door. "That doesn't sound like you. You're not a quitter."

"You know why it seems so odd to you? Because I haven't been myself. For a long time! That's why!" She couldn't tell him about the emptiness in her womb. He wouldn't understand. "And yes I can quit. It's not *your* butt that's getting stuck with a needle every night like a pin cushion. Have you looked at it recently?" Reluctantly, he came closer, like a shy boy. Janet unbuckled her belt, pulled on her jeans down enough to expose her black-and-blue buttocks, full of hard knots from the oil the medicine was dissolved in.

His hand rubbed her gently.

"Ouch," she yelled, pulling her jeans back up.

"Sorry," he said, his voice conciliatory. "We'll get them back, honey. Trust me."

She sat at the end of the bed. "I wish I could. I trusted you before when you said these people were playing a trick on us, that they never removed them from Lincol—"

"I was wrong, and I admitted that. What else do you want?"

What *did* she want? It wasn't his fault the embryos were gone. Well, in a way: had he not been president, this wouldn't have happened. His presidency was part of the package he came in, like she came with her cancer *and* her advanced age. She glanced at him. They were together on the same bed, yet they were worlds apart. Alone. They both stood to lose their chance to have a baby. But for each of them, the loss meant something different.

"What do you want me to do, honey?" Rob asked.

She felt her eyes well with tears. "Bring our babies home. All of them."

CHAPTER 55

▼

Anya hastened through the corridor that led to Washington Hospital's ICU.

She had no idea in what state she'd find Dario. With one emergency chasing another, she'd not had a second to check his condition. Actually, it would be better for him to stay in coma a while longer. She wanted to spare him the agony she was going through. During the last twenty-four hours, when the pain of everything seemed too much to take, she'd imagined losing consciousness with him, escaping it all.

She paused at the ICU door. Dario was gone. There was no breathing machine next to his bed. Bed 3 was empty, new linen stretched on the mattress.

Be careful what you wish for. You might get it. Grandma's words resounded in her brain. *Didn't I just wish for him to stay unconscious? He's unconscious all right. Forever!*

Anya stood, keeping vigil.

I didn't have a chance to tell you I'd given up on the adoption. That I wanted us to have a child. Together.

Her eyes stayed dry. She had nothing left in her. She wasn't immune. Just numb.

"Are you looking for Doctor D'Acosta?" The unit nurse startled her from behind. "He was moved today to 5 Tower."

She took a minute to process what she'd just been told. "Oh, thank you. I was so worried."

I should be ashamed of myself.

"I know," the nurse said. "Around here, families freak out when they find an empty bed. And most of the time, they're right."

Something *was* really wrong with her, Anya decided, taking the stairs, two at a time. What happened to her eternal optimism?

Dario was alive. His leg in a cast, hanging in traction on a metal bar craned above his bed, he was breathing room air. The bandages around his face were gone. And he was grinning at her. Anya touched her lips to a small, nontraumatized island on his cheek.

"Thank God," she said.

"Did you have any doubt I'd make it?" he asked, his voice hoarse. "Someone was just trying to iron out a few wrinkles. They didn't read the label. Says dry cleaning only."

"Jokes, yet," she said.

"I'm worried about you. What a mess."

"You've already found out?"

"The first thing I saw on CNN when I woke up from the coma was a report on Senator Tanner's incest charges."

Anya shut the door behind her and walked back to Dario's bed. "You mean there's nothing about the president's stolen embryos?"

Dario glanced at her in amazement. "What do you mean, stolen? From your lab?"

"Yes," she said, "and I have no idea where they are or who could've done it."

"This is crazy," Dario said. "Why would anyone want the president's embryos?"

Anya shrugged. "Apparently the kidnappers have sent a note. The demands are to follow. Sounds like they want something from the president. No one knows what, though."

"I'm worried about what would happen to you."

She squeezed his hand gently. "Sweet of you. But this isn't about me."

Dario leaned forward. "I know all you care about is Tanner's acquittal and that the embryos will be found. But it's possible someone's incriminating you and planted evidence along the way to make it look like you stole the embryos."

His worry matched her own. "Is that what your unconscious brain concocted?"

"No, it's what my brain that just came back to life is telling me. You were the only one who had access to the embryos."

"Not true. Caroline had independent access. She was the embryologist in charge."

"Then doesn't it make sense that she could've stolen them?"

"Not really. I should give her the same level of trust I demand for myself."

"Is that how you really feel?"

She freed herself of his gaze. "I don't know anymore. I honestly don't know." Was she naïve? Maybe, but Caroline was her mainstay at the hospital, her friend, and without absolute proof, she would continue to rely on her.

CHAPTER 56

▼
_____

"HRT SAC Gary Givens at your service, Mrs. Cartwright." He strode into the Emergency Presidential Operations Center. She estimated him at 6'5", 250 pounds. His dark blue business suit was a tight fit to his triangular, athletic torso. Thick, blond, wavy hair crowned his prominent brow. A pair of sky blue eyes stared her with compassion.

Janet didn't expect him so soon. Last time she'd looked in the mirror, she had bags under her eyes. Her hair was messy. She had put on no makeup, and her face was lime white. Now she felt the blood rush to her face. "Good to have you on board, Commander." She wasn't free to express her real feelings: the amazing sense of relief. Givens and his team of close to 100 trained Special Agents had been dispatched to get her embryos back.

"We're waiting to hear from the kidnappers," Givens said. "We should know soon what kind of deadline we're dealing with. Right now we're trying to trace back their IP addresses."

"The problem is that no one, including you, Commander, has had the experience in dealing with this kind of crisis before."

"You're right, ma'am. This is a one-of-a-kind mission. Has your doctor told you how long we have? I mean do we know how much longer these embryos can survive outside the womb?"

Janet fought to keep a blank face. "Honestly, I was so upset at Doctor Krim when I got the e-mail that I didn't think to ask. But now it seems critical."

Janet dialed Anya's number from memory and put her on the speakerphone.

"I'm here with Gary Givens, the commander of the rescue team. How long do you expect my embryos to remain viable?"

Anya's voice was calm. "They can spend up to five days outside the womb. But since we don't know the conditions they're kept in, I can't guarantee their survival for any length of time. Your embryos are extremely delicate at this stage, and if anything in their immediate environment was thrown off balance, that could, unfortunately—"

Just say it. Damn it. I'm not as fragile as you think. "I know," Janet said. "It could kill them. The longer it takes to find them, the higher the chance we'd end up with nothing. We're working on a rescue mission right now. I'll keep you posted." She hung up.

Janet sat at the conference table, disengaged. Anya couldn't guarantee their survival. No one could. She felt guilty for feeling so numb. This wasn't normal. She didn't deserve to be a mother. And God was aware of it.

Givens established eye contact. "I'm so sorry, ma'am. I know how tough this is. I can't even imagine what it would feel like, with everything you've been through."

How sweet, she thought. A sensitive SWAT man. Did he have kids of his own? Was he married?

"You're very kind."

"I want you to know I have the full intention of bringing your embryos back. Please trust me."

She appraised him. Rugged, professional, stalwart, a weight lifter to judge from his physique. Surely a crack marksman.

She didn't trust him for a second.

CHAPTER 57

▼

The announcement on the morning news that a Senate committee was to meet today to discuss Tanner's expulsion reminded Anya, while she was driving to the hospital, that she'd not heard back from Cornelia regarding the results of Megan's baby's paternity studies. She dialed LifeCodes.

"How's lover boy?" Cornelia asked.

"Fine, thank you." She was in no mood to tell her what had happened to Dario. "Do you have any news for me?"

"No. No news at all. The sample was deficient."

"What do you mean by deficient?"

"It means I could've nailed you as the rapist."

Anya had little patience for humor. "Cornelia, I don't have much time. Do you have any results?"

"None whatsoever. The sample you gave me from your lab coat was contaminated by adult blood. Did *you* experience any bleeding when they attacked you?"

Damn! I should've expected that. "Yes. In my neck. Some of it probably dripped on my lapel. Sorry I didn't mention it before."

"That's why they pay me the big bucks." Cornelia sounded jovial. "At least we had a little reunion, and I got to meet Dario."

"Where does that leave Tanner?" Anya asked.

"Right where he was. There's nothing to shake the evidence against him."

"I know intuition has little to do with hard-core evidence, but I just can't sit idle and let an innocent man—"

"He ain't innocent, my dear. All emotions aside. DNA's spoken. Loud and clear. There's no court in the world that would clear him."

"I'm determined to prove he's innocent."

"Well, good luck. I've known you long enough to know that once you're obsessed with something, you go all the way."

Obsessed. On her short list of most hated words. "Will you help me?"

197

Cornelia's voice softened. "I hope you know I'd do *anything* to help. I *want* to help. But I'm useless to you if I can't do DNA testing. Unless you get a whole new blood sample from the baby, I'm stymied."

Anya's secretary had left today's mail on her desk. Letters of support from her patients had arrived every day since the crisis started. Today she got at least a dozen.

She skimmed through them. A large envelope contained an 8″ x 12″ digital photo showing the smiling faces of healthy triplets, two girls and a boy, less than a year old. Attached to it was a handwritten note:

Dear Dr. Krim,

Our mommy said that you might be a little sad these days. Don't be sad, Dr. Krim. Mommy wanted us to remind you how depressed she had been before she came to see you. How all other doctors she had seen had told her that she should give up, that she was too old to have a baby. And you cheered her up and gave her new hope.

Thank you, Dr. Krim, for not giving up on our mommy. Had it not been for you, we wouldn't have come to this world. So far, the world looks like lots of fun. We're in for a ride we definitely don't want to miss.

Thank you, Dr. Krim, for our lives.
With much love,
Gillian, Gregory, and Samantha

Nice, she thought, moved. She had given her patients not just her professional expertise, she had given them a piece of herself. And her love. And they loved her back.

The nurse popped her head through the door. "There are patients waiting. You're already behind schedule."

Anya donned her white coat and followed the nurse to the patient exam area. She'd had to cancel office hours several times in the last couple of days. There were so many distractions in her life she hardly had time to be a doctor anymore.

After she was finished with her fourth patient, she sat down on a stool, getting ready to do a uterine biopsy. Someone—a nurse?—knocked on the door.

"I'm in the middle of an exam," she called.

"I'm sorry, Doctor Krim, but this can't wait. He's in your office."
Shit. This is getting ridiculous. Who?

A man in a business suit. He showed her a badge.
"FBI, Doctor."
FBI! In my office? He's come to tell me the embryos were found dead.
"How ... how can I help you?"
"I have a warrant for your arrest," he said.
Arrest! Inconceivable! "On what charges?"
"Stealing the First Lady's embryos. You'll have to come with me."

CHAPTER 58

▼

The FBI detective apologized for slapping the handcuffs on her, citing regulations. At least he was sensitive enough to bring her out of the office through a back door instead of parading her in front of patients in the waiting room.

"Where are you taking me?" she asked when they got into an unmarked car.

"Central detention facility of the D.C. jail on D Street. When we get there, you're allowed one phone call. I suggest you make it to your lawyer."

A criminal lawyer was who she needed. And it better be a good one, too. They'd have to fight the FBI. Perhaps even the White House. Whom could she call? She didn't know whom to ask, where to begin.

The car was now in front of a huge complex of tan buildings. A heavy-set female correction officer, J. Clarence, her badge read, was there to greet Anya. *VIP prisoner,* Anya thought. *For sure I'm getting the Jacuzzi room with a water view on the concierge floor.*

"Take all your clothes off," Clarence said, after taking her through the metal detector and bringing her to the inmates' changing area. Anya removed her white coat and then her black slacks and her angora sweater with the white stripes. "E-ve-ry-thing," Clarence said when she saw Anya hesitate, "including underwear and bra. Throw them in this plastic bag. You'll wear this while you're here." Clarence smiled like a zookeeper. "In this bag you have one jumpsuit, two T-shirts, two pair of underwear, two sets of socks." Clarence produced one of each. "Hurry up. The doctor's waiting for us."

The doctor? Clarence was full of surprises. Anya dressed.

"You're the first doctor I get to check," the old, bespectacled physician told her. "Is that a good thing?" she wanted to ask. She let him take her history. Do the physical. Draw her blood. He was just doing his job. Like everybody else. No use to transfer anger.

Clarence didn't leave her side when she went to make a call from one of the dozen of phones attached to the wall in the large common room. "Your last name's ..."

"Krim," Anya said, dialing Dario's number from memory.

"For letters I to P, visitation days are Wednesday and Friday, 12 noon to 7:00 PM," Clarence told her. "Legal visits are permitted twenty-four hours a day, seven days a week."

"Who're you talking to?" Dario's voice came on the other end.

"My private warden."

"Correction officer, doctor," Clarence said.

"They arrested me for kidnapping the embryos."

"Jesus Christ! Where are you?"

"1901 D Street. Central detention facility."

"I'm coming right away."

"Don't you dare leave the hospital," she said. "What I need you to do now is to find me a good lawyer."

"I'll find you someone good. Don't worry! Do you need anything?"

"Yes. To get out of here. Sorry, Dario, but I have to hang up now."

"Here's your hygiene kit," Clarence said with professional pride as they walked to the inmate cells. "You got soap, toothpaste, toothbrush, deodorant, lotion, shampoo, and Tampax. Let's go, Doctor, you're not an only child here. There're 2,500 people in this facility."

"We're here," Clarence finally said when they got to an isolated cell. There was a toilet in the corner and a single iron bed with a thin, bare mattress. "Here's your bedroll," Clarence threw a package on the bed. "It's got a blanket, washcloth, towel, and sheets. Anything else you need, just holler."

"You have a visitor. Ten minutes. That's all you get," Clarence announced.

Anya was seated at the edge of the bed, fighting depression. But when she heard the screech of the wheelchair, she got up, her heart racing in the kind of joy she hadn't felt in a long time.

"Dario!" She practically tripped on his wheelchair, so small was the space, and then rested her bottom on the handle.

Clarence, disgusted, left the cell.

"I can't believe they put you in one of these," Dario said, indicating her army green jumpsuit.

"Givenchy. Eat your heart out. How did you get here?"

"There are still a few saints left in this town."

"You're not supposed to be out of the hospital yet. I want you to take care of yourself."

"Ay-ay, Doctor. Your word is my command. But before I leave, we need to figure out how to get you out."

"How're we doing with a lawyer?"

"I've called two. They're both in court, but their assistants promised they'd get them during the first break. They know it's urgent."

"You don't understand, Dario. This isn't about me. If they do manage to find the kidnappers, they won't know how to transport the embryos back safely."

"Right," Dario said. "I tried to call Caroline. She hasn't shown up at work, and I got the answering machine at her home." Dario lowered his voice. "Don't you find that suspicious?"

What Dario didn't realize was how much fertility doctors had to rely on their embryologists. And how, by now, after hundreds of cases they'd shared, Anya's trust in Caroline was difficult to shake. "I don't know. I've only seen her once since the kidnapping, right after the embryos disappeared. She seemed as shocked as I was. And she was very helpful."

"Isn't that the behavior you'd expect if she had anything to do with the removal of the embryos?"

"I've considered it. But it would be ridiculously obvious if the chief embryologist—the only other person, besides me, who had access to the First Couple's incubator—was the one to remove them."

"Still, she's scrammed. And you've been arrested. Who set you up?"

They both had the same question. "The First Lady's furious at me, but I just can't imagine her giving the order."

Dario nodded. "What about the FBI?"

"They didn't particularly appreciate how I've stood by Tanner. But what good does my arrest do them? They still have no idea who's behind this."

The jiggle of the keys. Door unlocked twice. Clarence was back. "Time's up."

"I'm working on your bail," Dario said. "They want a million dollars."

"Try Victor Sachs." She leaned toward him, wondering where the section dealing with grateful patients bailing their doctor out of prison was in the code book of medical ethics. Dario cupped her hands with his. She felt a crumpled piece of paper.

"I've already called his office. He's in Europe. They're trying to locate him."

"Great," Anya smiled. "I love you."

"Dear Dr. D'Acosta," Anya started reading as soon as Clarence locked the door behind her.

I don't have much time to write. My name is Dr. Jeremy Coddington, AKA Cody.

I hope you find a way to get this message to Anya.

The First Lady's embryos are held at Reprotech, a cloning facility in West Virginia, where I have been working for the last two years.

Please tell Anya I had no hand in the removal of the embryos. When I found out that my boss, Hugh Nicholson, had not only orchestrated the kidnapping but had also tried to plant evidence incriminating Anya in the abduction, I decided to write you.

At the moment, the embryos are alive in an incubator, which I keep under tight control for CO_2 pressure, PH, humidity and temperature.

Reprotech is located in an underground facility in West Virginia.

Time is running out. Please relay this information to Anya and the FBI ASAP. I'm sending you three attachments: a map of the area with the facility marked on it; floor plans of Reprotech that I've sketched; and two codes—the first, to get through Reprotech's door, and the second, to open the incubator with the First Lady's embryos.

Anya reread Cody's message. Dario didn't bring the attachments; she assumed the FBI had them. They'd follow Dario's directions, she assumed. Would they trust him enough to release her? Would she be able to help in the embryo rescue operation?

CHAPTER 59

▼

The Kit-Kat was finished, Janet realized, taking stock of the small fridge Peggy had filled for her. On to Crunch. She took two bars and slammed shut the fridge door.

She'd been trying to reach Robert all morning, but he was in a cabinet meeting. "We have Gary Givens on the case," he said before he left her, meaning their embryos. "He's the best HRT operative out there. I know he'll bring them back home safely."

With every minute that went by, the chances of seeing the embryos back alive became slimmer. Janet felt like Mother Goose, whose eggs were snatched from under her before she was done hatching. Janet knew she wasn't in reactive depression. It was worse: a total collapse of a building she had constructed. The only scaffolding that had held it together was her prospect of motherhood, and now that was gone.

Why, for God's sake, wasn't Anya answering her phone. Why was everyone too busy to talk to her? Maybe they were intentionally staying away. Robert's had Iran. Great excuse. What's Anya's excuse? She was Janet's doctor, wasn't she?

Finally, Givens arrived.

"Any news?"

"We've made some progress."

"Like what?"

Givens paused a minute.

More bad news. I can't take it.

"Actually, we've gotten information from your doctor."

"Anya! I've been trying to reach her. Where is she?"

"She's being held at D.C. Metro Detention."

Janet felt dizzy, pain spreading from the back of her head, threatening to split her skull in half. "You put my doctor in jail?"

"The FBI has linked her to the embryo kidnapping and got a court order for her arrest."

"Bunch of assholes." She lowered the volume but not the intensity in her voice. "Don't take it personally, Commander."

"I had nothing to do with this arrest, ma'am!"

"Fine. But why would a judge agree to arrest a fertility doctor for stealing embryos she'd created for a patient she'd been treating?"

Givens shifted in his chair. "The California precedent."

"Which case?"

"This fertility doctor from University of California—"

"Irvine stole patients' eggs and used them to treat other patients. I heard about it. But those doctors were criminals. My doctor is a saint. You've just arrested the most dedicated doctor I've ever had." *This is the woman who hugged me when I cried, who held my hand until I fell asleep before my procedure, who told me she'd stick with me until I had a baby.* "So what you're saying is they think my doctor stole the embryos of the First Couple of the United States—to do what with them? The FBI must've had some working hypothesis, no?"

Givens was silent.

"And wait a minute," Janet continued. "You said there's new information you got from Anya? About what? The embryos' whereabouts? The kidnappers? Isn't that enough to set her free?"

"The FBI's checking this inform—"

"There's no time to check! There's no time to go by the book. Can't you see, Commander? You're wasting precious hours." She choked on her words.

"I promise you, ma'am," Givens's blue eyes stared at her, "we're not waiting for anything. Right now I'm on my way to see if I can contact the kidnappers."

Janet got up as well. "I want you to set Doctor Krim free immediately."

Givens was back in his military mode. "For now, there's a bail—"

She felt blood rush to her cheeks. "I'm the First Lady of the United States. I'm ordering you, Commander, to release her now."

Givens knocked his heels together. "Ma'am, with all due respect, I can only take such an order from the president himself."

She felt her ears get warm with rage. "And what if he's indisposed of, at the moment?"

"Then it would just have to wait."

As Givens was about to leave the Emergency Presidential Operation Center, he was approached by an FBI messenger carrying a sealed envelope addressed to "Chief HRT Negotiator." Givens found an unoccupied room. He shut the door behind him and opened the letter.

Dear HRT Negotiator,
We are enjoying the company of our tiny VIP guests.

I will be meeting with you later today to discuss the conditions for their safe return. My next letter, due in 2 hours, will have your moving orders. You'll be taken to meet with me blindfolded.

Do not try to outsmart me, or you'll be returned to Quantico by UPS. And our precious guests will never be seen alive again.

Have a pleasant ride.

CHAPTER 60

▼

Blindfolded and disarmed, Givens guessed the ride lasted about an hour and a half. Just as he'd been trained to do at HRT, he gathered his information by maximizing his nonvisual senses. He counted the number of stops the SUV made, the number of sharp turns, the up and down inclines. He knew he'd be asked to provide this information at the debriefing.

Not one word was exchanged during the ride, allowing him time to strategize. He recalled what the guys from the Crisis Negotiation Unit had taught him in training. First, figure out the most realistic expectation: will the hostage taker give them up once they got the ransom? Was Nicholson some kind of a nutcase, taking on the president of the United States? And if he was, was that necessarily a bad thing? Perhaps they could fool him into believing the president was ready to make a deal? Second, don't underestimate the captors' intelligence, and never talk down to them. From the FBI check, Nicholson seemed like a sharp guy.

His main goal, Givens realized, was not to botch the case. He had to make sure that even if his encounter with Nicholson didn't get them any closer to a solution, it didn't make things worse. The SUV stopped. "We're here," the driver said.

Two men supported his arms and guided him out of the SUV. "Three steps ahead," one of them said. "One, two, three," he counted for him. Givens was trained to stay calm. He'd been in more dangerous situations before: at a religious fanatics' mercy or in the company of terrorists. "Stick to your mission. Remember everything depends on you now," was his mantra. But that never calmed his nerves. Hostage takers were unpredictable, their behavior erratic.

A cloning operation wasn't exactly a high-risk situation, Givens considered. What made this one unique were the stakes! The blackout he'd been subjected to left his mind clear as to his objectives. He had to establish that the embryos were indeed in their hands, he needed proof that they were still alive (though he had no idea what counted as proof when it came to embryos), and he had make them spell out the ransom. Givens knew he wouldn't be able to negotiate a deal immediately. The best he could hope for was a clear demand he could take back to the president.

His blindfold was removed. A door closed behind him. As the black blotches that clouded his vision started to dissipate, he scanned the room. He'd expected a real farm, but the mahogany-paneled office, meticulously organized bookshelves and desk, gave him the feeling it belonged to a midlevel executive or a university professor. The only clue to the unusual nature of the work done in this office was a small cage at the wall encasing what Givens guessed was a giant fruit fly.

"I trust you had a pleasant ride." The man behind the desk got up and walked toward him. "Hugh Nicholson." They shook hands. "Pleasure to meet you."

"Commander Gary Givens, sir."

The man had no muscle mass; his spine couldn't keep his gaunt body straight. The hair on his scalp was sparse and on his face prepubescent. His sunken eyes and prominent facial bones made Givens think that Nicholson wasn't well.

There wasn't even a trace of the image in Givens's head. No boots. No cowboy hat. No pistol. No Southern drag.

And this was the man threatening the president of the United States?

Nicholson walked back to his desk and collapsed into his chair. Givens sat on the sofa, his back taut. "Can I see the embryos, sir?"

Nicholson buzzed the intercom. "Cody, could you please come in? Our guest is looking for proof that we have the president's embryos."

Cody entered, holding what seemed like an accounting book. He looked just like his photos gathered by the FBI. Short, small frame, baby face. His head bowed, Cody seemed subservient to his boss. *Don Quixote and Sancho Panza*, Givens thought. Instead of windmills, Nicholson had chosen to fight the president and the First Lady.

"Do you want to see the entry I've made into our embryo storage log book?" Cody asked Givens.

"No no no," Nicholson said. "This isn't how we do business. Before our distinguished guest comes up with the ransom, he needs to set his eyes on the hostages. It's only fair." The boss blinked with virginal innocence.

"I can take him to the lab," Cody said hurriedly.

"You know perfectly what I mean, Cody. Bring them here."

"But—" So, Cody wasn't simply a Sancho Panza, Givens realized. He had his own convictions. He was protecting the embryos.

But Nicholson didn't relent. "Cody!" the tone was prolonged and threatening.

Cody left reluctantly. Givens tried to imagine what went on in Cody's mind. Raji Kumar, an embryologist at Lincoln Hospital's embryology lab, had given him a crash course, showing him how embryos were stored and identified. Cody could try to trick his boss, Givens figured, pour some fluid into fresh petri dishes, put the First Lady's initials on them, and pretend the embryos were there. But if Cody actually showed Givens the embryos, he'd be caught red-handed.

Cody returned with a tray bearing two petri dishes. The hostages! Until this moment, his mission seemed surreal. But now, as he heard Nicholson say, "Put them on the desk," reality hit. Seeing how exposed they were to room air, away from the protective environment of the incubator, he should speed up their return to the lab, he thought, and leaned over to check the ID engraved on each dish.

Janet Cartwright
ss # ... 1709

"Do you need to see them under the microscope?" Nicholson asked.

"That won't be necessary," Givens said. He'd given up his goal to confirm the embryos' viability. Secretly, he hoped Cody had left the embryos in the incubator. But Cody's expression surrendered nothing. "I'd rather you return them to the incubator in the lab."

"You're the one who asked to see them." Nicholson leaned back in his chair, hands behind his back, smiling. He had all the time in the world. Idiot! Givens felt his face grow hot. To Nicholson, this was one big game. And he was enjoying every minute of it. "Don't you worry. We'll put them back after you leave."

"I'd like you to return them right now."

"Ay-ay, Commander." Nicholson sat up, the smile never leaving his face. "Cody." He pointed to the tray.

Cody seemed happy to oblige. He shut the door behind him before Givens could figure out where they kept the embryos.

"So, how much do you want?" he asked Nicholson.

Nicholson giggled. "I should be insulted, Commander. What do you take us for? We're in possession of ten embryos. Each one is a unique mix of genes from the president and the First Lady. One of them could become America's First Child—and you want me to put a price tag on them? You should be ashamed. This isn't some merchandise we're talking about."

"What do you want, then?"

"The Embryonic Stem-Cell Bill. We want the president to vow he won't veto it."

I'll be damned! This man had gone to the trouble of kidnapping the best-guarded embryos in the nation in order to change the political process and legalize embryonic stem-cell therapy. Givens knew he was just the messenger, but even as a conduit, he had a hard time finding the right words to say.

"In what form do you want to hear from the president," Givens finally managed. "The vote isn't anytime soon."

"I know. A public statement that he'd not veto the bill will be acceptable. Tell your boss he has fifteen hours from now, sharp."

"And if he refuses?"

"His little guys will be destroyed."

Givens stood. "How ... how do I contact you?"

"Don't worry. We'll call you," Nicholson gave him a pat on the back. "Now hold it," he said before Givens had a chance to open the door. "We have to send you out exactly the way you came in." He took the black piece of cloth that rested on the console, covered Givens's eyes, and tied it behind his head.

"Say hail to the chief," Nicholson said, and he put his guest in the hands of his henchmen.

CHAPTER 61

———————————▼———————————

Janet had to beg the White House chief of staff to get Robert out of the meeting.

"What now?" Robert asked over the phone, clearly impatient.

"Did you know that they'd arrested Anya Krim?"

"No! On what charges?"

"For stealing our embryos."

For a moment there was silence. "This is ridiculous. Why didn't you tell me before?"

"I couldn't get through to you. They said you weren't to be interrupted." Did he know she was trying to reach him? Did he care?

"I'm sorry, honey. Don't worry. The FBI chief is with me in the Oval Office now."

"Thank God. Tell him to release Anya immediately. If he only knew how much I need her!"

"Will do," the president said.

CHAPTER 62

▼

"The rules of engagement are like no other operation any of you have been ever involved in," Givens had told his camouflage-wearing audience, a mix of HRT snipers and assaulters as well as agents from other units cleared to get them into the briefing room at Quantico. Standing next to a topographic map, he'd had just finished going over the plans to rescue the First Couple's embryos. Operation Fledgling had been okayed by the president after Givens had reported back from his meeting with Nicholson. "Agents are absolutely forbidden to open fire," he emphasized, "even when their lives are in danger, unless instructed to shoot by the TOC."

Not a sound was heard in the room. They all knew "TOC" meant him: Givens.

"Any questions?" Givens asked.

Silence.

"Good. Then let's go."

It was 4:30 PM when the Gulfstream G-5 executive jet touched down on the runway of Yeager Airport in Charleston, West Virginia. Givens had nine HRT operatives with him: eight snipers and an evidence technician. The latter was the closest to an embryologist that HRT could come up with on short notice. His job was to make sure the transfer of the embryos went safely.

Givens placed his troops into the two, smoked-window, black Suburbans and guided the drivers to the Reprotech facility, situated in an old WWII shelter, at the meeting of the Kanawha and Pocatalico Rivers.

With the eight snipers following him, each carrying their day and night rifles, Givens proceeded down toward the river bend. As they approached the water, they could see the gray one-story building that blended with its surroundings. Reprotech was in the underground level of this building. *This is where the maniac is hiding the embryos*, Givens thought. He assumed it was where he had been taken for his meeting with Nicholson.

With his men following, he chose the sniper stations, dropping his men off two at a time.

More than thirty minutes had passed since they established perimeter of the building. Givens received the second round of reporting from all four sniper stations, to which he had given the code name "Sahara." They saw nothing. *Surprise surprise.*

How long will it take headquarters to send the assault team? Givens wondered. He checked his watch. Eleven hours to the deadline given by Nicholson. Eleven hours from now, if his demands were not met, he'd toss the embryos in the garbage.

It got dark fast. The sun would set at 5:35 pm. Givens figured that by now, the snipers had switched to the 308 night guns topped with a telescopic scope. They'd don night goggles shortly. Night optics reduced effective range, but they were within 100 yards, which should be adequate.

"HR-1 to SI-1," he radioed. "Request permission to move to green."

"This is SI-1. Request denied. You stay at yellow. I repeat. Yellow. Sit tight on your hands until additional troops arrive."

Aware of how many ears were listening in on their conversation, Givens censored himself from giving headquarters a piece of his mind. "HR-1 to SI-1. When will that happen?"

"I'll tell you when they leave."

The embryos were not going to wait until the assaulters finished rehearsing, Givens fumed. You had to see the situation on the ground and keep modifying your plans. How else could you expect to win over a devious, conniving mind? With good routine?

It was up to him, he realized. Here in the trenches. Headquarters was only a hindrance.

"Get ready," he told the evidence tech. "You and I are going in."

Givens reviewed the map one last time. He had planned the breach on the jet coming here and had checked it on the ground as soon as they arrived.

Givens used the old WW II plans to determine his point of entry. You could enter the compound through a tunnel, accessed through a covered hole in the ground less than a hundred yards from the building.

"HR-1 to Sahara 1, 2, 3, and 4. We're going in. Stay where you are and provide cover."

He donned his night vision goggles. The opening to the tunnel was seventy five yards west of the building. The armor and Nomex suit, the flame-resistant coverall, made moving difficult. For Givens, this was trivial; he'd been through rigorous HRT training and operations, where he'd carried eighty pounds of equipment on his back through bad terrain. But he wasn't sure what training the evidence tech had. The tech's backpack was filled with embryo lab equipment. In addition, he hauled a metal canister filled to the top with liquid nitrogen, in case the embryos had already been frozen.

The metal lid covering the access to the shelter wasn't easy to find. Only the sounds of the river nightlife broke the silence.

Givens noticed a one-foot square covered with low grass, but looking bald compared to its surroundings. He bent down and found the handle. The lid gave easily.

With his gun in a ready position and the tech in tow, Givens descended the dilapidated stairs that led to the tunnel. The place smelled mildewed. Flashlights in hand, they rushed through the tunnel and came to a half-open metal door.

Givens had memorized the floor plans. They were now inside the Reprotech maze. To their left was the door to Nicholson's office. He pried it open. There was no one there. Papers were scattered on the floor. The desk was cleared, cabinet drawers open and empty. Random books remained on the bookshelves. The phone jack stood naked.

The bedrooms Nicholson and Cody must have slept in were across the corridor. The beds were unmade, as if their dwellers had left in a hurry. He felt the beds in what he figured out from Cody's description were the surrogate quarters. They were still warm.

A strong dog scent indicated to him that the next room was the animal cloning facility. All he found was a stack of empty cages. The next room was loaded with computers. It, too, was empty. This had to be the GIS room. At the end of the corridor was the embryo lab. Ten incubators were stacked up in twos. The tech checked each incubator. Not a single embryo was left behind. The linoleum floor showed track marks. From the wheels of liquid nitrogen embryo storage tanks, Givens assumed.

Nicholson must have used the two hours since he'd met with Givens to clear out. Givens wasn't surprised: Nicholson was clever. He knew that even with HRT's quick response, it would take time to organize.

Givens radioed headquarters not to dispatch the assault team as had been previously planned.

CHAPTER 63

▼

The White House, in its enormity, was claustrophobic. Sitting in the Emergency Operations Center, Janet Cartwright felt it closing in on her. Had she been an ordinary citizen, she'd have gone for a jog. Vent. Shake off the increasingly heavy cloud of anxiety. But early in her tenure, she had given up mundane pleasures such as shopping and lunching with her friends. It was no longer fun, not when everyone stared at you and Special Service agents stood at your side. Her true friends told her they couldn't wait for the term to be over. But if Robert got reelected, her prison sentence would be extended, making her isolation seem endless.

Robert. She thought of him sitting in the Oval Office, surrounded by advisers and cabinet members, never left alone. But his was another kind of loneliness. Not a single person around him was tuned in to his emotions, well-camouflaged under his presidential mantle. She remembered Anya's words: "Men and women travel in different orbits when it comes to fertility treatment. Never underestimate your husband's involvement or his angst. Even if it is *your* bottom that feels like a pin cushion and *your* pelvis that's sore; don't think men are lucky, that all they have to do is provide the sperm. He's suffering like you are."

Janet realized how self-centered she'd been. She hadn't considered Robert's feelings, nor had she given a thought to the tremendous burden on him as president. She *was* his soul mate, and she should have been more sensitive to his feelings, for he had no one else to rely on.

This hope to have a child together had given them a common goal, had given their marriage a purpose. What would happen to their relationship if the option of parenthood was gone?

Her contemplation was interrupted by Robert's soft squeeze of her shoulders.

"Hi, honey," she said and reached out for his hand. "Did you get Doctor Krim released?"

"Didn't have to. By the time the FBI chief made the call, someone had already come up with the bail."

215

"There shouldn't have been any bail to begin with," she said, wondering who the benefactor was.

"I agree. Believe me. I don't know what to get aggravated about first." He sounded depressed. She turned to face him. His face was ashen.

"What's wrong?"

"I've just spoken to Gary Givens. Nicholson contacted him when he got back empty-handed from the rescue operation."

"What did he say?"

"That I'd missed the chance to support Embryonic Stem-Cell Research. Nicholson had shortened the deadline after he'd found out the FBI had broken into the compound."

"Robert! What happened to the embryos?'

"He said he'd destroyed them."

"What do you mean, destroyed them?" Janet screamed. "How?"

"He … he said he'd dumped them in the garbage."

CHAPTER 64

▼

Up to the last minute of her incarceration, she had been treated as dangerous. Clarence even stayed in the cell when Anya changed her clothes.

But putting on her slacks, sweater, and lab coat made Anya feel better. She'd spent sixteen hours in this place, hours that she'd not been in touch with the First Lady. She was furious not only at the ridiculousness but at the inopportune timing. She needed to be out. She needed to help find the embryos.

Who had taken them? She knew her four-digit code wasn't impenetrable. But as much as she tried to think of a list of suspects, her mind came back to one person: Caroline. Anya remembered the ATM robbery story. She'd never bought it. She'd caught Caroline printing pictures of embryos. Were they the First Lady's? Was Caroline getting ready to steal them?

They'd had their differences over the years. Every so often, things would evolve into uncomfortable friction. Yet, Caroline ardently believed in her mission to benefit infertile couples. To Caroline, this was a calling. It was just this dedication that allowed Anya and Caroline to forge a good working relationship.

And Caroline seemed as shocked as Anya at the embryos' disappearance. If this was all a show, it was damn good acting. Still, where was Caroline now? What was she up to?

Clarence handed her the bag of her belongings: wallet, set of keys, and her BlackBerry. The woman's eyes didn't change from their accusatory stare, as if saying, "You rich chicks always get a rich dude to bail you out, but I know you're still guilty."

Anya felt little sense of freedom when she finally left the detention facility and breathed the muggy Washington air. With the embryos gone, relief was impossible.

Dario waited at the bottom of the steps. She had to reciprocate to his broad smile, even though inside, she felt her heart shift gears as it got ready to resume battle following an imposed cease-fire. Dario placed one crutch

217

on the cab he had waiting for them and leaned on the other. His right arm opened toward her. Her dry lips caressed his. They stood motionless for a minute or so and then she gently released herself from his hold.

"The embryos, Dario. Have they found them?"

"I don't know. According to CNN, the FBI's put a lid on any information regarding the rescue efforts. So your devoted servant, like the rest of the nation, is ignorant."

They got into the cab. "Lincoln Hospital," she said to the driver.

The driver turned around. "Which entrance, ma'am?"

"Center for Human Reproduction, please."

He gave her a second look through his rearview mirror. Given her white coat and her destination, he must have figured out who she was. By now, her photo had appeared in every newspaper in town.

"Did he really have to come up with a million dollars to bail me out?" she whispered in Dario's ear.

"Absolutely." Their hips touching, his mouth blowing words mixed with warm air, his scent delectable; she enjoyed the intimate intermezzo. The cab driver watched them in the mirror with curiosity.

"Please thank Victor Sachs for me, would you?"

"It wasn't Victor who put up the bail. He was out of town when I called."

"So, who was my savior? I don't know anyone else that rich."

"Someone who'd prefer to stay anonymous."

"Please!" She sat up in the seat. "You're not going to tell me? Dario, I'm exhausted and frustrated. I have no patience for this."

"Sorry, honey. I knew you'd be mad. But this person made me give my word. And I had to agree. I had no choice."

CHAPTER 65

▼

She had forty-eight new e-mail messages. Anya scrolled through them. Most were letters of support from patients. One got her immediate attention.

Check the liquid nitrogen tanks.

Check the tanks?

Was it possible that the First Lady's embryos had been returned, that someone had frozen them and placed them into liquid nitrogen?

If the First Lady's embryos were indeed frozen, there was a chance they'd survived! Anya's spirits took an unexpected lift. Yes, embryos could lose some of their viability in the freezing process, but still ...

Filled with newly found energy, she rushed down the long corridor that led to the cryo room. *Please, please,* she prayed, *I need some good news, for a change. We all do.* She imagined the call she'd place to the White House. *They're here. Janet. All ten of them. Safe and sound.*

She stopped at the door and took a deep breath. "Control. Maximum control," she recited to herself.

Anya stood in front of the three giant freezing tanks. She climbed up a step stool. The top of the first tank was at her shoulder level. She opened the cover, her eyes watering as vapor rushed out. Embryos were stored in individual plastic tubes anchored by metal canes to the rim of the canister. She started to panic. It would take hours to sort through the canes, hours she didn't have. She scanned the sea of canes that rose like masts above the fluid levels. Each had a patient's initials. She looked for JC, but couldn't find it.

Anya doubted that whoever had e-mailed her had intended her to go sort through the entire inventory of frozen embryos.

Maybe the other tanks were less densely populated. She closed the cover of the tank and moved to the next one. A similar sight came to view: a sea of embryo flagships, too many to count.

If the content of the third tank was the same, she wouldn't know how to proceed, Anya realized. Maybe this was the spare tank she had once heard Caroline mention, the one she'd leave empty in case of emergencies. Hope

219

rose. She was the closest she'd been in the last two days to seeing the First Lady's embryos again.

She opened the lid, averting her face against the vapor, and looked into the tank. A wave of nausea assailed her. She felt like she was going to fall off the stool.

A woman's head floated in a pool of liquid nitrogen. It was detached from the body. It had no neck.

The woman's face was severely bruised. She must have been beaten mercilessly before being decapitated.

But even with all of the bruising, there was no doubt who this person was.

Caroline.

CHAPTER 66

▼

"I received this package for you. It's been cleared by security," Peggy Wheeler said. "It's a DVD, and it came with a note."

Janet put on her reading glasses:

There is a glimmer of hope. Before I threw away the embryos, I plucked out a single cell from each of them and left each one in a special solution in the petri dish. To see what happened, watch the DVD.

Breathless, Janet inserted the DVD into the player at the side of her desk. A series of frames appeared on the screen, each containing digital images of embryos with a printed subtitle: Frame 1: A single plucked cell. Frame 2: Ten two-cell embryos. Frame 3: Ten embryos, each between six to eight cells.

"This is the second page of the message," Peggy said.

Anya read,

As you've just witnessed, my experiment has succeeded. I've managed to clone new embryos from your old ones. They have the exact DNA as their ancestors. The First Couple's own flesh and blood.

If you meet my demands, these embryos will be returned.

The most progressive First Lady in the history of this great nation has a chance to boldly set her foot on the unconquered terrain of a Brave New World by giving birth to her very own cloned child.

There is no new deadline. My demands should be met immediately. Any further delay will force me to destroy your children again.

CHAPTER 67

▼

The sight of Caroline's frozen head had not left Anya's brain from the moment she saw it till now, an hour later, she answered a summons from the White House.

Caroline was alive two days ago, when Anya had last seen her. The sight she'd just witnessed could be a result of an execution, a primitive form of punishment. Chills traversed her spine. Was Caroline decapitated after she'd been killed, or was she beheaded alive?

"Do you have any idea, Doctor Krim, why anyone would want to kill your embryologist?" FBI Chief Relman had asked her when she called him to report the death.

She wasn't sure what to make of his tone of voice. Annoyed was her first impression. One more complication he didn't need. Did Relman think Caroline was involved in the kidnapping? Did he think that Anya had called him to clear herself?

Now she asked herself the same question she'd been asked by Relman. Why *would* anyone want to kill Caroline? Was it because she had evidence about the kidnapping? Caroline had been terrorized before. What kind of secret life did she lead while working for Anya? What did she know that had to be so brutally silenced?

There was another possibility. What if it wasn't something Caroline had done or seen but something she'd *refused* to do that led to her murder?

And why did the killers take the risk required to bring the head to her lab at Lincoln and submerge it in liquid nitrogen? There could be only one reason: they were trying to terrify her.

Janet Cartwright skipped the pleasantries when Anya walked into her office.

"I don't know if I can take much more of this," she said. No longer the fighter Anya had known, her patient sat at her desk with her shoulders slouched, a look of despair in her face.

Janet made no mention of Caroline. "I need your expert opinion," she said. "The embryo kidnappers claim that they've cloned my embryos before they tossed them in the ... garbage." The First Lady's voice trailed off. "They sent me a DVD to prove it. I need you to tell me if they're legitimate."

Anya neared the screen. The DVD started to play. Her mind was elsewhere. *The head.* All she saw was the head.

"What do you think?" Janet asked, her eyes meeting Anya's.

She tried to delete Caroline's frozen face from her mind. "Could you replay it, please?"

Cartwright replayed the DVD.

Still the face. Anya blinked her eyes, willing the demon to disappear. "Sorry. I need to see it one more time," she said. "Frame by frame, please."

Embryos. That's all she saw. Just embryos. Janet must have expected a strong reaction from her. Yet, Anya found herself unable to react to the familiar image.

A woman had been just brutally murdered. A very talented, beautiful woman who'd worked for me. And it may have been connected to her having created these embryos for you.

"Do you believe them? Do you really think that they could've cloned my embryos?" Janet asked.

"Them" would be Cody. By saying yes, Anya would incriminate him in another illegal action. "It's possible, though not a simple feat by any means," she managed. "It would require a great deal of expertise. Less than a handful of embryologists are capable of taking a single cell from a human embryo and growing a new embryo from it. You'd need a special solution to be able to continue dividing. This solution has to closely mimic the embryonic wall."

"But it's possible, right?"

"Right."

"How would I know that these are actually mine?"

"Good question. Embryos don't carry name tags. They could be anyone's."

"You mean there's no way to know for sure?"

"Actually there is. We could do genetic fingerprinting. We'd have to test the DNA of the embryos against DNA from you and the president. It's complicated, but it can be done."

"Doctor Krim." The First Lady turned toward Anya. "I know you're under an FBI investigation. But I can't wait until it's done. I need to ask you right now: are you involved in any way? Do you know how to get to my embryos?"

The undertow finally hit shore. Anya knew it was coming. Until now, Janet Cartwright had steadfastly defended her. But as desperation had closed in, Janet's horizon getting darker by the minute, anger and blame had replaced the positive karma the two women had enjoyed.

Their doctor–patient relationship revolving around a single common goal had been breached.

And the gap was opening wider.

"I'm not involved," Anya said, the words sounding hollow. "I swear it."

CHAPTER 68

————————▼————————

*G*o ahead. Fire me. At this point, you'd only be doing me a favor, Anya thought as she walked toward the OB/Gyn administrative offices.

Terminate—or be terminated.

So much had happened since Feinberg's pronouncement. Their dual over Megan's baby's fate had taken place less than three days ago.

She had imagined the professor ecstatic when she got arrested. Behind bars, she was effectively neutralized. He didn't have to take action against her. But here she was, free again.

The professor stood up when she entered and took her tentative hand with both of his.

"You've had quite a week, haven't you?" he smiled, his one good eye gazing at her fondly.

What does he want of me now?

"What a mess you've had to deal with. First the embryo kidnapping. And now, Caroline's head in the freezing canister."

She wasn't sure how to read him. Feinberg never wasted time on niceties.

"I want to make my position clear," he said, sitting at the edge of the desk. "I thought you could use some support for a change."

Anya felt delirious. She didn't think *support* was in Feinberg's vocabulary.

"First, I never believed you had anything to do with the embryo kidnapping."

She suppressed an urge to pinch herself.

"Second, I've told the FBI and hospital administration that I deplore any attempt to connect you to the death of your embryologist. If anything, this could be an important lead to the embryo snatchers. If you want my opinion, I think Caroline had to be part of it, otherwise, she wouldn't have been executed."

Wow.

"Number three," he continued, "someone's trying to scare you, stop you from finding these embryos. But I know you don't get intimidated so easily." He grinned at her. "I want you to know I stand squarely behind you. Find those embryos. And let me know if there's anything I can do to help."

CHAPTER 69

───────────▼───────────

They had turned fugitives overnight, Cody realized, replaying their hasty escape from the Reprotech grounds in his mind. He was alone in his trailer, parked like the rest of Reprotech's Caravans on the mountainside off of Limestone Road in Keyser, West Virginia, when Nicholson summoned him.

He dreaded facing his boss. Nicholson had hired him as a cutting-edge scientist. They were going to change the world. Now, Nicholson had made him a renegade. In order to thwart Nicholson's dump of the First Lady's embryos, Cody had split them to make identical replicas, a cloning of sorts. What he had done, he knew, was risky.

Years ago, when scientists had announced they had grown embryos in the lab by splitting cells from other human embryos, they were denounced by ethicists, state leaders, and the pope. Now, not only had Cody repeated the procedure, he was hoping to get the new embryos to the First Lady in time for a transfer. The almost-certain repercussions were daunting.

But Cody was determined to proceed. In a strange way, he felt liberated. At this point, he had nothing to lose. Since there was little doubt that when the FBI caught them, there would be enough charges to put him in jail forever, he had at least managed to rescue the Cartwrights' DNA and maybe enable Anya help them have a child.

"Which surrogates are available for transfer?" Nicholson asked Cody as soon as they were face to face.

What had Nicholson concocted now?

"We don't have any embryos to transfer," Cody dared.

"Except for? Why do I have to do all the thinking around here?"

The crazed eyes. Cody had seen them before. The man was trapped in his determination to prove that the little boy stigmatized as a Fragile Y grew up to become a genius. In his own delusional mind, the boss must have believed that the split cloning of the president's embryos was actually *his* idea and seized the opportunity to continue his reproductive adventures.

"We don't have any embryos floating around, except for the First Lady's clones," Cody said. Nicholson had walked in on him while he was splitting the embryos. He'd forced him to admit what he was doing. Yet, instead of reprimanding him, Nicholson immediately saw the newly created embryos as an opportunity to increase the pressure on the president.

"You got it, my boy. Finally. Now, why was it so hard to figure out?"

Cody hoped his face didn't reflect his rage. "But didn't you give her forty-eight hours to comply?" he ventured.

"You doctors never get it. Cartwright isn't going to give in. Not at this point. The president will not be intimidated … he refuses to run the nation's affairs at gunpoint. Blah … blah … blah. Therefore, you and I aren't going to wait for the deadline."

"But—"

"Don't interrupt. That we have her embryos in a petri dish—no matter whether they're originals or exact replicas—hasn't yet struck her." He paused, reflecting. "How did we get sidetracked? Are all the surrogates ready?"

The lunatic hasn't forgotten.

Four surrogates remained. They were all on estrogen pills, ready to have embryos transferred to them any time they became available.

"Christina and Lori both have their periods," Cody said. "They've been cycling together."

"What about Mimi and Jocelyn?"

"They're ready." He felt a touch of shame.

"Fine. Any two wombs will do. I want you to transfer half of the president's cloned embryos into each surrogate. Then, when Mimi, or Jocelyn, or both, carry the First Lady's baby, we'll send an endearing video image—heartbeat and all—to Mama Janet. I bet you her priorities will change real fast."

CHAPTER 70

▼

Anya Krim scanned her office, the room where her patients put their lives in her hands. They'd hide little, strip down to their bare emotions, express their growing frustrations with childlessness, confess to marital strife and sexual dysfunction. And once they had entrusted her with their secrets, each visit was like seeing a friend.

"I trust you, Doctor Krim," they'd say. *I trust you.* Three words that filled her with pride and a huge sense of responsibility.

Would trust remain? Her patients read the papers. Many of them worked where the news of the embryos' abduction had originated: Congress, the White House, the hospital. To them, her absence would be an indication that the hospital was no longer backing her, that her colleagues and superiors wouldn't deny the allegations against her, and that she might have been involved in Caroline's murder or stolen the embryos.

Would she ever see patients again?

Her life was in danger, she knew. On the way to assassinate her, they'd assassinated her career.

She started to clean out her desk, dropping everything in the large cardboard box she had brought from Labor and Delivery. Shortly after she'd been arrested, the hospital administration announced she was not going to see patients until further notice. Her appointments were diverted to other doctors. And they needed to use her office.

Professor Feinberg had gone to James Earl Knox, the hospital CEO, to try to get her privileges back. But it was too late, he told Anya apologetically, when he called to tell her about his failure to reinstate her. The Board of Trustees had decided to strip Anya of all her privileges, save for two patients: the First Lady and Megan Tanner. They didn't want to attract more attention by changing the physician in charge of these two well-publicized cases. The hospital wanted to avoid any further scandals by any means.

Her desk was empty. Not one chart remained. Two Xerox machines ran nonstop in the back office, staff members copying her charts for patients who'd chosen to go elsewhere for their fertility care.

It was like a bloodletting. She felt lightheaded, dizzy, weak in her knees. Anya slumped into her chair. Her patients were the fuel that had kept her engine running. And not just running. Running on high.

Could a doctor continue to be a doctor without patients?

The mail alert rang. Reflexively, she clicked on <u>Get Mail.</u> There was one new message, from <u>cody@reprotech.com.</u> Cody? This was the first time since he'd left, two years ago, that she was hearing directly from him. All she could anticipate was more bad news. Her pulse accelerated.

Nicholson has mobilized his entire operation to Keyser, West Virginia. You can find it on the attached map.

I beg you to do whatever you can to get someone to rescue the president's cloned embryos.

Anya, I ask for nothing in return except to fly back with you. I'd rather stand trial than continue to work one more day for this maniac.

Hurry up, please.

Cody

CHAPTER 71

————————▼————————

Could he trick Nicholson just one time? This was Cody's only opportunity to rescue the president's embryos from his boss. At 3 o'clock in the morning, as he got ready in the makeshift embryo lab he had put together when they evacuated the Reprotech compound, Cody knew there'd be no second chance.

Confused and sleepy, the two young surrogates shivered as they entered the lab. Nicholson had pulled them out of their beds in the middle of the night.

"Put on these gowns," Nicholson ordered, handing each woman one. "Come on, you've done it before a million times."

"Mimi, you hop on the stretcher," Nicholson said. "Jocelyn, you lie down on the couch, put a pillow under your butt. Pull your gown up above your hips. Oh, please, we're not having a bashfulness attack now, are we?"

Cody took the dishes out of the incubator. Using his glass pipette, he arranged the embryos so that each dish held five, one dish per surrogate.

Nicholson hovered over him as the image of the first group of five came up on the screen.

"Good quality, right?" Nicholson asked.

"Excellent. Each has six to eight pristine cells."

"Can't tell the replica from the originals, huh?"

Cody sighed in relief. Nicholson couldn't tell the subtle difference. Good. "Correct. They're exactly like the originals, if not better."

"You're looking at the future, my boy."

Cody went over to the stretcher. "Relax your legs, Mimi, please. You'll feel my fingers first and then the speculum."

Mimi spread her legs, her face expressionless. Cody sensed Nicholson's camera behind his back. The man would document every step of the process.

"I'll do my best not to hurt you," Cody told Jocelyn. "It's more difficult on the couch, you know."

"I don't mind," she said.

He left the speculums open in both surrogates, hurried to the microscope, and loaded the first set of embryos onto a tiny catheter.

Cody moved directly in front of Jocelyn's perineum, blocking it from Nicholson's camera. He placed a petri dish with embryo culture fluid in front of him. Working quickly, he emptied the contents of his syringe, which the boss had just seen on the screen, into the Petri dish. After making sure the syringe was empty, he pulled on the plunger halfway and then inserted it through the cervix into the uterus. He moved his body away, while keeping his hands on the syringe, reopening the visual field to the camera. Once he could tell Nicholson was watching, he pushed he plunger and released the droplet of air into the uterus.

"I have the perfect clip for our First Couple." Nicholson was virtually dancing with excitement. "You never thought you'd be world-famous, right, Jocelyn?"

Cody loaded a new transfer catheter with the remaining five embryos and went over to the stretcher. Mimi squeezed his hand.

Because she was more exposed, he had to use a different technique. His body was too slight to block the perineum from the scrutiny of his boss. Cody inserted the syringe loaded, but only pretended he was pushing the plunger. Instead, he moved the whole syringe through the cervix and then out, taking extra care that the droplet containing the embryos was still visible.

Walking back from Mimi's stretcher to the microscope, now off-camera, he pressed gently on the plunger, releasing the droplet onto another petri dish.

Once Nicholson was gone, Cody was able to replace the two petri dishes with the embryos in the incubator. Yet he could hardly regard the incubator a safe haven.

CHAPTER 72

▼

Anya knew she was the only woman in the Quantico briefing room, where Gary Givens addressed a sea of agents in black Nomex suits. No woman has ever passed HRT's selection process, Givens told her. To them, she was an extinct species.

"Remember HRT's motto," Givens told his men, "*Severare Vitas.*"

She knew what it meant: to save life. This operation gave it an extrapolated meaning: it was a mission to save *potential* life.

Givens used his laser pointer to indicate Reprotech's current location on the blown-up aerial surveillance photos. The E-8 Joint Stars—the long-range, joint army–air force aerial surveillance aircraft—had located and tracked down Reprotech's caravans. The briefing was short.

"Reprotech is packed into in three trailer-caravans. Two are identical—both Concord Class C motor homes," Givens said. "The EW Wells mobile lab trailer is easy to recognize by the two tanks in the back. We assume one has CO_2 in it, and the other contains liquid nitrogen. The lab trailer is shorter than the others. The entrance door is through the back, next to the tanks. From communications surveillance, we gather that Nicholson has one of the Concords for himself, while the rest of his staff is crammed into the second. These lab units come with a foldout bed." *Cody's bed*, Anya thought. *He's embryo-sitting around the clock.* "Since the bed is set against the right wall, we assume that the incubator that houses the president's embryos is against the left wall."

"Doctor Anya Krim is joining us." He grinned. The whole room was astir. Anya felt blood rushing to her head against her will. *What's wrong with them? The nation's boldest warriors can't deal with a woman?*

"You heard right," Givens hushed his audience. "A *woman* will join this HRT mission. Doctor Krim has the most important role of all. She's the only person with the expertise to know how to transport the embryos back safely. You're expected to treat Doctor Krim with respect and dignity, as one of us."

As if she needed this intro.

"No shots will be fired," Givens concluded. "Nicholson will be brought home alive. We have no idea how much resistance we'll meet, if any."

CHAPTER 73

▼

The Bell 412 twin-engine chopper lifted off from Lincoln Hospital, an embryo incubator and an embryo freezing canister secured to its wall.

"I'm so glad you're here," Gary Givens shouted over the chopper's noise. "I've had nightmares about this mission."

You were not the only one, Commander.

"I had this awful dream that I got there with my men, and inside the incubators were piles and piles of dishes, and we didn't know where and how to look for the embryos."

"Ahha," was all Anya said. She didn't feel like talking, even though she recognized his kindness in choosing to fly with her and not with the rest of the men aboard the other, much bigger bird.

"How'll we know for sure these are the president's embryos?" Givens asked. "Embryos don't have name tags or carry photo ID."

His question lay at the core of what bothered her.

"Name tags no. ID—they kind of do, actually."

"What's a, kind of ID?"

"DNA," she said.

"What's in that tank?" He continued to probe.

"Liquid nitrogen."

"Is that what they use to freeze sperm in?"

"And embryos. I brought it in case the embryos have already been frozen, in which case we'll have to keep them that way."

"My best friend's widow has his sperm frozen," he said. "She lost him six months ago in Iraq. Before he was dispatched, he arranged for a sperm bank to keep his sperm. His wife's fighting his parents for custody of the sperm. She told me if she couldn't have his child, she'd rather stay childless. Forever."

Certain words cut through her. "I'm sorry about your friend," she said.

"Thanks. That's why I feel so passionate about our mission. I know what the First Lady must be going through."

"Ten minutes to Keyser," the pilot said.

Ten minutes! It was like someone had poured cold water on her. Ten minutes to landing. Maybe another ten, perhaps twenty minutes until they got to Reprotech. In half an hour, she'd find out if the embryos were still alive!

"This guy Cody, you know him, right?" Givens asked.

She nodded, not certain where he was going.

Anya wasn't in the mood to dissect Cody's personality or listen to any criticism. She could see Cody's image, sitting across from her on the bed in the labor floor call room, in tears. Her hand reached out to his. "It's going to be fine, Cody. The baby will make it." How many times did she lie when she said, "It's going to be fine"? She had to let her compassion prevail over her anger, knowing that as hard as he tried, he was incapable of doing a better job. At times, he botched deliveries so badly she wanted to strangle him. Cody was easy prey. The rest of them, resident and attending physicians, would have no problem hounding him. Tell him he was dangerous. Except for Anya. She remained his friend. While she, too, had grown increasingly more uncomfortable with his patient management, she'd always stop short of accusing him for fear that if *she* did it, he'd kill himself.

What should she say to him when they meet again? In residency, she'd have to weigh every sentence that came out of her mouth for fear he might be hurt. What was he, a fine porcelain doll always at risk of breaking to pieces if not handled with care? Obviously he'd done fine without her. They've been apart for two years, and he was still in one piece. She felt a pinch in her heart. All along, she'd thought, *Poor Cody, he had to flee so insecure was he; flee and quit OB. How could he manage without me?* Now she was about to face not only him but also the reality that he'd managed to survive without her.

"Five minutes," the pilot announced.

"I was wondering what kind of person it took to clone people," Givens said.

A complicated rescue operation ahead of him, why would Givens waste the few minutes he had left talking about Cody? "I don't know, Commander. I haven't seen him in two years," she said. Good question, she admitted. Cody—a human cloner? How did that happen? Things had been so hectic the last couple of days, she'd given little thoughts to Cody's cloning career. Was it Cody's idea to clone humans, or did Nicholson drag him into this against his will? She voted for the latter.

"Anyone who tries to clone a human being is an immoral abuser of science, and his actions should be outlawed." Givens said this with the conviction of a soldier who always followed the moral compass.

Anya nodded. "But Cody shouldn't be held responsible. There's no question he was intimidated into this by Nicholson. For as long as I've known him, he was never an initiator."

"You'll need to get into one of those," Givens said and fished out the body armor and the black Nomex suit they'd found for her. He turned his back to give her some privacy while continuing to communicate on the radio with the rest of his troops. Anya wiggled her body into the armor and then put on the Nomex suit. It felt too big.

"You feel that we should spare him, right?"

"Sorry, I didn't hear you, Commander. What did you say?"

The chopper started its descent. "This Cody guy. How important is it to keep him alive?"

Anya felt blood leave her face. She held onto the bar on the helicopter wall. So that's where he was going with the Cody questions. Givens saw her reaction and added, "It's not part of our plan to kill him. But if he holds onto the president's embryos, if we have to make the choice between taking him out or rescuing the embr—"

"That's not going to happen," she screamed. "Don't you realize he's the one who created these new embryos before Nicholson tossed the originals? And that he tipped us off as to Reprotech's whereabouts? Twice?"

There she was again, defending Cody.

"I hope you're right, Doctor. In my job, I have to be prepared for all options. And if I have to pick between sparing Cody and getting the president's embryos, you know where my loyalty lies."

His words didn't calm her at all. They were going in with the most hardened fighters in the nation. It wouldn't take much—one word, the slightest movement—for one of them to pull the trigger.

Gary got off the radio. "They're in place now, in Bradley fighter vehicles, waiting for instructions."

"You're not planning to spend the night?" Anya asked.

"That's just in case. No. We're planning on a brief mission, Doctor. We're aware of the time constraints."

No you aren't, she thought, *because I'm not. I have no idea, how long these embryos can live. In fact, there may not be any time left.*

The Bell 412 touched down at Yeager Airport. Four assaulters removed the incubator from the helicopter and loaded it onto the back of a Suburban. Anya took Givens's hand and jumped off the chopper. With Givens and Anya in front, seven assault team members squeezed into the backseats.

Anya's exhaustion had vanished. Where was Cody now? Did he have any clue they were so close? She felt like warning him to freeze in place and remain silent when they arrived. But that was not an option.

With Cody's life in peril, all critical thoughts had dissipated. She loved this man like a brother. She couldn't wait to see him. Hug him. Protect him.

The troops on the ground reported no movement. There was no sign that anyone was awake or that their arrival had been noticed.

Givens fiddled with the gun.

The Suburban stopped 200 yards from the trailers. The driver killed the lights and the engine. They all put on their night goggles and jumped out of the vehicle. Four assaulters carried the incubator out of the van. Another man took the liquid nitrogen tank from Anya's hand. Givens signaled them to follow him as he navigated toward the trailers.

"Stick with me," he said. Anya followed.

Anya couldn't tell the location of the snipers, even with her night vision goggles. She assumed this was good. *If I can't see them, no one else can.*

Givens approached the lab trailer from its back. Anya was immediately behind him, followed by the four assaulters who carried the incubator, another carrying the freezing canister, and three with their rifles ready. When they got to the trailer, the four assaulters put down the incubator without a sound, each taking his position as planned. The other three stayed with Givens and Anya. Givens removed the Glock 18 from his belt and pressed on the door handle. It opened noiselessly.

"Cody!" she cried. She sprung toward him, seated on his bed, before he had a chance to get up. His body felt sweaty. A sparse beard scratched her face when she kissed his cheek. "Thank God you're alive," she whispered in his ears. She held onto him. "Don't move yet. And don't say a word until I signal you it's safe to talk."

"Commander," she turned to Givens. "This is Cody." Her body language, her pleading expression, said the rest. *Please don't hurt him!*

Givens put the gun back in his belt and held out his hand. "Nice to meet you, Doctor. Now let's take the embryos and get the hell out of here!"

Anya sighed. The immediate danger to Cody was over. But then another worry took over. The embryos had been dragged from place to place. She wanted to ask Cody when he'd last looked at them, but decided against it. "Not so fast, Commander," she said. "I need to make sure they're still alive."

"Whatever you have to do, do it fast."

Anya got up. "Cody, could you show me the embryos? The air is stifling."

"Musty, I know." He got up. "Hardly ideal for embryos. The best I could do was to maintain control over the CO_2 pressure, humidity, and temperature within the incubator."

"I'm still worried, though," she said. "Even seconds of exposure to this bad air could kill them."

"The embryos are here." Cody pointed to one of two incubators stacked across from the bed. "I moved them from the dishes to test tubes filled with media fluid and sealed them. It's the only possible way for them to survive a flight."

"Great idea. I need to look at them before we leave," Anya said. Givens checked his watch. Cody looked. *What difference does it make if they're alive or not?* Anya asked herself, not sure if she had an answer. What would she do at this point if she found out all the embryos were dead? Still, she *had* to check them herself. She'd never relied on anyone else before. She opened the incubator, found the test tubes, and took them to the microscope.

Anya removed the seal from the first test tube, poured its contents into an open petri dish, and fished out the embryos with the pipette, willing her hand to stabilize. Two good-looking blastocysts, she sighed. Two normal-looking five-day-old embryos.

Four more tubes to go. Eight more embryos to find. Anya repeated the maneuver. The embryos' resilience was remarkable. All ten of them seemed normal.

Anya took a deep breath. A feeling of urgency took hold. She had to hurry and get these embryos to Janet. Janet's womb was their only safe haven.

CHAPTER 74

▼

The radio message that Nicholson had been captured alive was no cause for joy. What was wrong with her? The operation was a success, the embryos were rescued, and she was on her way to deliver them to the First Lady. Why did she feel no pleasure? Her anxiety soared the closer she got to the White House.

"It's going to get choppy," the pilot warned.

She watched the clouds get heavier. Soon it would rain. Strong winds destabilized the chopper. What were the chances that the embryos would come out alive?

Anya held onto one side of the embryo incubator and gazed at Cody. He looked exhausted, holding onto the incubator on his side. Human shock absorbers.

Torrential rain. Anya tightened her grip, but it didn't stop the incubator from rolling back and forth on its wheels between Cody and her.

"I don't know how the embryos can survive," she yelled above the engine's noise.

"We filled each test tube and doubly sealed it," Cody said.

Why was she forecasting doomsday? "Still," she said, "with these shifts, even the slightest fluid leak might make the embryos stick to the wall of the test tube and die of dehydration."

The Bell 412 touched down at Quantico. Givens jumped out of the front passenger seat and offered Anya a hand.

"What are we doing now?" she demanded.

"You and I and the embryos are moving to *Marine 1*, the president's helicopter. They'd never allow our helicopter flown by our pilot to land on the White House lawn."

"What about Doctor Coddington?"

"Coddington stays here for questioning."

"But—"

Givens held up his hand. "President's orders."

Anya looked back into the empty chopper. Cody had been taken away through the other door.

"You have to promise me that they'll treat him fairly."

"Chief Relman is still in charge. You'll have to talk to him."

They climbed into *Marine 1*. "What's taking so long?" Anya asked. "We should've been in the air already."

"We need security clearance for the incubator."

"Do they think I've hidden a bomb in there? These embryos will die if we don't take off immediately."

"They're bringing it up now, Doctor," he said.

"Careful," Anya said. "Keep it horizontal at all times."

Two Secret Service agents lifted the incubator into the president's helicopter. Anya strapped the incubator into place with seat belts. Within seconds, they were in the air.

"How long *will* they last?" Givens yelled.

"Don't know," Anya yelled back. "They're already over five days old."

"What are you going to do if the embryos are dead?"

"It's the end," she said. "If none of the embryos survive, the First Lady won't have an embryo transfer."

"Doctor Krim, I hate to play devil's advocate, but even if the embryos *were* alive—"

"Is it safe to transfer them since they've been cloned?"

"You read my mind."

His questions stung her where she'd already been hurting, bringing back her worst fears. "I don't know how safe it is. Or legitimate. This would be the first time that embryos cloned by cleavage in the lab were transferred to a human womb." *And,* she thought, *the first patient, the guinea pig, is none other than the president's wife.*

"But why, if this is a perfect duplicate of the original, should anything go wrong?"

"I wish I knew this reproduction was a perfect copy," she said. "What if Nicholson tampered with these embryos?"

"So, you'll have no idea if the DNA is normal when you put the embryos in the First Lady's uterus. For all we know, the First Lady could conceive a—" he hesitated.

"Go ahead. It's okay to say it."

"A grotesquely malformed child, right?"

The image of Baby Marshall coming out through the birth canal flashed through her mind, more and more anomalies revealed as labor progressed. "Right," she said.

The helicopter started its descent toward the landing site on the South Lawn of the White House.

CHAPTER 75

▼

A nagging thought kept intruding as Anya got ready to prepare the embryos for transfer: *This is an experiment.*

She remembered Feinberg's criticism of the embryo splitting done years ago at another D.C. hospital without approval of the institutional review board. Back then, they had stopped short of transferring the embryos and creating a child. Still, it led to a worldwide scandal.

Now she was about to complete the experiment Cody had started clandestinely. Transferring the embryos created this way was what they hadn't dared do in the previous case. The safety of the procedure was unknown. If the child were malformed, the repercussions would be personally and scientifically devastating.

But what choice did she have? She would discuss the problem with Janet. And then what? The First Lady would want to proceed. It was Anya's job, she recognized, to remain unaffected by her patient's emotional maelstrom. But was she really objective here? Could she really say to her patient, "I'm sorry, Janet, but this is too risky. Unapproved. And of unproven consequences. I can't let you do it."

But then, she thought, *if I refuse to go ahead with the transfer, even if Janet wants me to, am I really being my patient's advocate? Am I putting my patient first?*

At the microscope, she removed the seals from the test tubes and poured their contents into a petri dish. She focused the lens up and down. All ten embryos were there. All viable.

The embryos were technically ready for transfer. And the First Lady expected an embryo transfer today.

Still, Anya knew it was the wrong thing to do.

Janet Cartwright was already lying in bed, her buttocks propped up on two pillows.

"Peggy, do you mind if we have a few minutes alone?" Anya asked.

"Not at all." Peggy left the room, shutting the door behind her.

Anya took Janet's hand. It was cold. "Before we go on any further, I need to ask you to reconsider. You know you have the option of *not* proceeding and starting again."

"Then let me ask you this," Janet replied. "How sure are you that these embryos are as good as the originals? *Will* they result in a healthy baby?"

Anya took a deep breath. *It was good Janet came up with these thoughts on her own,* she thought. "There's no way to tell. They look excellent. But if you want to know more, we'd have to delay the transfer so I can do some genetic testing."

"Delay again? How long *this* time?" Janet sat up, her face turning crimson.

"Less than a day. By tomorrow morning, I could have the results and, if everything's okay, do the transfer then."

"I'm not happy about that."

Peggy Wheeler entered without knocking. "Excuse me for interrupting, but it's urgent."

"*We* are having our embryos transferred," Janet said. "And *we* don't wish to be interrupted."

Peggy didn't flinch. "FBI Chief Relman called. They haven't been able to get any information from Doctor Coddington. He won't say what he did to your embryos."

Anya felt guilty. She should have insisted it was essential for Cody to stay with her until the First Lady's treatment was done. What was she thinking?

"Why?" Janet asked.

"He refuses to speak without a lawyer."

Of course, Anya thought. *They're going to make him pay for everything Nicholson made him do.* "Doctor Coddington risked his life to rescue your embryos," she said. "Doctor Coddington should be given immunity for any questions pertaining to the embryos. The embryo transfer will be delayed until I hear what he has to tell the FBI."

"I'll let Chief Relman know," Peggy said and left the room.

"Can I test the embryos in the meantime?" Anya asked.

"I don't see why not," the First Lady said. "Now you're going to tell me you need my blood, right? You, and everyone else in this town." She smiled faintly.

"A cheek swab will do. We have to compare your DNA to that of the embryos. I'll have to move the embryos to Lincoln Hospital so we can biopsy them there."

"Do I need to sign anything?"

"A consent form."

"That will state that I know this procedure could kill my embryos, right?"

"Yes. Though chances are that the embryos will make it through."

"Where do I sign," Janet asked matter-of-factly.

"I'll have my office type up consent, and we'll both sign it. But I have to ask you one more time: are you sure you want to try, or would you rather go through IVF a second time and get transferred with your own, original em—"

"You can stop right here. There will be no second chance." Janet's voice cracked. "Robert's made it clear. Things are crazy enough already. Many of his political opponents have suggested that some of his domestic and even international actions had been taken for the sole purpose of sidetracking the public from obsessing about our fertility treatment. This could end up costing Robert his career. No. It wouldn't be fair to him if I draw the process out." She began to cry. "Can't you see, Anya? This is my last chance ever to have a child."

CHAPTER 76

▼

*H*e left late, after spending more than four hours at her bedside. He was sad she had to miss the cherry blossoms. When she was a child, he would take her to the Cherry Blossom Festival in West Potomac Park. They'd walk along the Tidal Basin, and he'd tell her how the Japanese government had sent twelve varieties of trees, 3,000 of them, aboard the S.S. Maru. They'd stop by the first Yoshimo tree, planted by the then First Lady, Mrs. Taft.

"I'm the luckiest girl in the world," Megan had said once.

"Really?" he asked, "Now why are you saying that?"

"Look at these cherry trees. There's nothing more beautiful. And we live here. And I'm the luckiest, because I have you for a daddy."

He'd choked up when she said it. He wanted to freeze the moment. But just the memories remained.

My Daddy has got a ladder
Its top reaches the sky . . .

So went one of her favorite songs. She adored her daddy. He could do no wrong.

Now, coming to the Tidal Basin from another grueling day at the Capitol, the walk was painful. For Nelson Tanner knew, as he passed through the rows of cherry blossoms, that even though Megan was only a few blocks away, she'd never walk alongside him again.

He brought her fresh white and pink orchids to inject some spring color into her hospital room. The best doctors in world hadn't been successful at waking her up. Maybe his love, ceaseless and full of hope, expressed in the beauty of these flowers, would penetrate her dormant brain and find a single cell that would finally respond.

He had spent several hours being grilled by the House Ways and Means Committee, where the young new chairman, Andy Geiger, was determined to make political capital on the heels of his expulsion.

Incest.

Tanner looked at his angel. If she only knew what his colleagues had slandered him with, smearing the purest of all loves!

But she would never know. He thanked God for that.

Only the night-light was on in her room. The private duty nurse dozed on the sofa. These were her safe hours to sleep, long after the patient's father was gone and past the nursing supervisor's rounds.

The heavy-set man who tiptoed in on soft sneakers wore blue scrubs. A hospital ID with a Polaroid photo of his "new" face was clipped onto his white coat pocket. His entry did not faze the nurse, who barely moved.

The man approached the bed. Her eyes shut, her chest moving evenly, Megan Tanner slept peacefully. Normal saline solution dripped slowly through an IV line.

His easiest job yet. No resistance. No witnesses. Piece of cake.

He removed a vial and disposable syringe from his coat pocket and then uncapped a 22-gauge needle and drew 2 ml of clear fluid out of the vial. He stuck the needle into the rubber portion of the IV tubing in Megan's arm and injected.

CHAPTER 77

▼

Still in the East Wing of the White House, Anya's pager went off. She picked up the nearest phone and dialed.

"This is Doctor Krim. I was paged."

"This is Cecile, from ante partum."

"Cecile?"

"One of the nurses on the floor. It's about your patient, Megan Tanner."

"She's only twenty-four weeks. What happened?"

"Her blood pressure dropped. The Code Blue team is in her room doing CPR. They managed to bring it up a bit. They called me to check on the baby."

Bad news. Very bad news. Medicine wasn't very good at resurrection.

"I brought in the electronic fetal monitor."

"Are you getting a heartbeat?"

"Yes. The baby's tachy, at 200 beats per minute, but there are some variable decelerations."

Megan's baby was in severe fetal distress. They couldn't let Megan die! And Megan's baby!

Sweat covered Anya's body. And then—the shivers. A feeling of doom … of helplessness … The tom-tom in her chest beat out of control.

She'd become so involved in her other case, she wasn't at Megan's bedside when she started to show signs of total collapse. Now she was twenty minutes, maybe half an hour away.

She was a bad doctor.

From the first day, Anya knew it would take a miracle to bring her patient back into consciousness. But the baby! The baby had a real chance! At twenty-four weeks, though, this baby could only survive in the womb as long as the blood from the mother kept pumping. Keep inside—or bring out? Anya didn't know.

"Make sure she's getting at least 200 cc of saline IV an hour."

"She's getting lots of fluid already, Doctor Krim."

"Call Nina Russo to manage her until I get there. Have you notified the family?"

"We have. They're on their way to the hospital.

"Do they realize how serious this is?"

"I told the senator we're doing CPR on his daughter. I assume he's aware we could lose her."

"You're not going to leave the First Lady waiting." Peggy Wheeler was at the door. Anya didn't realize she had been standing there when she answered her page.

"My patient's dying. I have to go. I've already told the First Lady it will take several hours until the genetics test is back."

She ran down the stairs until she got to the back entrance.

"May I help you, Doctor?" a friendly Special Service officer asked.

"I need to get to Lincoln Hospital. It's an emergency."

"No problem, Doctor. I have a Navigator here on standby." He opened the door to let her in and gave the driver instructions.

"God, don't let me screw this one up," she said out loud as the driver gunned the engine.

She dialed Lincoln Hospital. It took ten nerve-wracking rings for an operator to answer.

"Page Nina Russo. It's urgent." She was put on hold.

"Godammit."

It took Nina forever to answer the page. "I just saw Megan, Doctor Krim. I think the baby has "lates.""

"Lates," short for "late decelerations," were ominous drops in the baby's heartbeat, indicating acute lack of oxygen.

"You need to get Megan to L&D," Anya said.

"Done already. Had to fight with the Code Blue team. They were afraid to move her."

Timing was everything in obstetrical emergencies. Anya dreaded not having full control. The driver floored the gas pedal. Anya wondered how much he could see through the thick fog. He braked at a red light. Her phone rang.

Nina again. "For the last seven minutes, the baby's had lates."

Anya had expected things to get worse, but not this fast. If the fetal distress lasted much longer, the baby would suffer serious brain damage, or die.

"Set up for a c-section." It was the only choice. "I think I can be there in two, maybe three minutes. Don't wait for me. And make sure you call the NICU team."

In less than a minute, the driver was in front of Lincoln's main entrance. Anya opened the door and ran into the hospital.

CHAPTER 78

▼

The sight of at least a dozen people at work, trying to resuscitate a comatose woman pregnant with an immature baby, was ominous. Anya couldn't see Megan at all when she walked into Labor and Delivery's OR. Nina Russo was running the full code, standing on a step stool while pumping oxygen into an air bag, belting out her commands to the rest of the team. She squeezed the bag in synchrony with the rhythmic thumping on Megan's chest by a young intern.

"Has anyone figured out why she's deteriorating?" Anya asked.

Nina continued her pumping. "No. I had no ideas besides sending a tox screen."

Tox screen? "You think someone tried to poison her?" The thought of a criminal act hadn't crossed her mind. Who would've wanted to hurt this angel, in a coma for two years? Maybe it was the senator someone was trying to hurt? Could someone be taking aim at her, at Anya, by trying to kill her patient?

"Don't know. This case has been giving me nightmares since day one."

"Welcome to the club," Anya gowned and gloved.

Megan Tanner had a do not resuscitate order written in her chart. Both Anya and Nina were aware of its existence. Yet, there had been no mention of DNR since Anya walked in the room.

This Code Blue team didn't look like they were going to give up, even though they had been trying to revive the patient for at least forty minutes. The head nurse sat at a raised nightstand behind them, recording the code events and the drugs injected into Megan's IV or directly into her heart. Anya knew their dedication was fueled by the pregnancy. The goal was clear: keep the patient stable long enough to allow delivery of a viable baby.

"Stop cardiac massage for a moment," Anya told the intern. "Let's see what she does on her own."

She checked the monitor. The unassisted heart rate was at sixty. But soon, the rhythm became fast and irregular.

"V-fib," said Nina. She looked at Anya. "What do you think, Doctor Krim?"

Nina was asking whether to call the code off when the v-fib went to a straight line.

"Zap her," Anya said.

"Everyone's hands off the bed," Nina said. The nurse poured contact gel over the two metallic surfaces of the defibrillator handles. A code tech turned up the voltage dial.

The nurse applied the electrodes to Megan's exposed chest. "Clear!" She pressed the button on the handle. Megan's arms and legs jerked.

The heart didn't respond.

"Again," said Anya.

If they managed to get a response, she'd deliver the baby. Otherwise, why bother? This was the toughest dilemma Anya had ever faced. The baby was barely on the verge of viability. How much was this fragile, uncertain life further compromised by the poor blood flow to the placenta during the past hour or so from a mother in a state of shock? If this baby came out alive, she'd very likely be handicapped.

Another electroshock. Another.

But what if she were wrong? What if Megan's baby came out alive and grew up to be the normal grandchild Senator Tanner so passionately wanted?

Anya eyed the monitor. Megan's heart muscle started to contract spontaneously. Anya knew this wouldn't last long.

"Sinus rhythm," she heard Nina say.

"Let's deliver this baby now," Anya said. Kara, her favorite scrub nurse, moved next to the surgical tray table. The circulating nurse wrung a sterile iodine solution over Megan's pregnant belly, painting it brown.

Anya took the scalpel from Kara. In a single, decisive stroke, she made a straight up-and-down incision from just below the belly button to the pubic bone. There was no fat under the skin. The fascia and peritoneum were both paper-thin. Nina had scrubbed in and was cauterizing little bleeders as Anya continued her way down.

The pregnant uterus was now in full view. Anya felt for the baby's positioning in order to determine where she should cut.

The baby lay across the belly. "She moved to transverse lie," Anya told Nina. "Second knife." Kara placed the scalpel against Anya's palm. Anya cut through the uterine muscle. Nina clamped all bleeders. Anya punctured the amniotic membrane; Nina suctioned the amniotic fluid.

The baby was curled up within her mother's cradle. Anya picked her up with her left hand. Nina double-clamped the cord and divided it.

"Control the bleeders," Anya said to Nina, handing the baby to the NICU nurse. The NICU team started resuscitation immediately in the open crib. From the operating table, Anya glanced at the team at work. She hadn't expected Alex Gordon to be there. Déjà vu. A painful reminder of Baby Marshall's delivery. Only Megan's baby was more compromised, having left the womb so much earlier. A micro-preemie. Birth weight could not have been more than one pound. Anya saw Alex try to slip the tiniest plastic tube into the baby's windpipe. This was no simple feat. But the sight of the nurse squeezing an air bag told her he must've managed to get it in.

"How many weeks?" Alex asked Anya.

"Twenty four, maybe a few days less," Anya said.

The baby stayed limp and pale. She didn't whimper.

"One-minute APGAR 0," the NICU nurse announced. No signs of life yet.

While they continued to work at the crib, Anya returned to the operating field.

It wasn't my fault that Megan collapsed.

Who am I kidding? The responsibility is all mine. Feinberg was right all along. OB is a full-time commitment. If you don't spend day and night in the trenches, living and sleeping OB, you get rusty. Look at my OB record.

She was Megan's obstetrician. She hadn't been at her bedside for a good twelve hours. Could she have overlooked something, because she had been so preoccupied with the First Lady's embryos?

Nina had already delivered the placenta and handed it to Kara to be sent over to pathology.

Anya snapped out of her self-torture. "I need two red-top tubes, Kara. And give me the bucket back for one minute."

Anya unclamped the umbilical cord, which was attached to the placenta, and squeezed the blood out of it, filling up the two tubes.

"Kara, take these and guard them with your life," Anya said. The memory of what happened the last time she took blood from the baby sent a chill through her spine.

The operating field was dry. Nina started to throw a heavy suture on a large needle to close the womb. They continued to close the uterus in silence.

"Five-minute APGAR is ... 0," the NICU nurse said.

The members of the NICU team looked at Anya and Nina. They were all digesting the news.

Megan's baby was born dead.

Anya walked over to the crib. Alex Gordon pulled down his face mask, looking drained and checkmated.

"Thank you for trying to save the baby," Anya said. "I feel like you stayed an extra long time for me. Sorry I had to put you through this."

"Don't be ridiculous. This is what I do for a living." He feigned a smile. "You couldn't help it."

"It was my decision to do the emergency c-section."

"Give yourself a break. What were you supposed to do? Not deliver a dying mother? Let the baby die in the womb? How should *I* feel? I do CPR on micro-preemies several times a week. And I lose most of them. And the ones I do manage to pull through often end up so handicapped, you wonder if they'd been better off dead."

"Which is exactly where my mind is right now."

Alex held both her arms. "Anya, look at me. Promise me you'll stop torturing yourself. We've both just lost a patient—"

No I can't! I can't detach myself like this! Stay cold and uninvolved. This feels like I've just lost my closest family members. They are my family. "I lost two," she said, the barely heard words camouflaging the turbulence within her. "Mother and child."

Nina hugged her shoulders. Her round, blotched face was sweaty, her goggles fogged. They both tore off their blood-soaked paper gowns and threw them in the trashcan with the gloves, shoe covers, and masks.

"Anya, why don't I go out first? I'll find a private room where you can speak with the family."

"Fine." Anya could barely speak.

"Are you going to show him the baby?"

"I was planning on it. What do you think?"

"I agree. He needs to see her to know that it's over."

The nurse wrapped the baby in a blanket and handed her to Anya. "She weighs 550 grams," Nina said.

A fresh white sheet covered Megan Tanner's body. Her angelic face was peaceful, unchanged by death.

CHAPTER 79

▼

Nelson Tanner kissed his daughter on the forehead for the last time. With a shaky left hand, he caressed the waves of her hair. Cradled in his right arm was the bundle that Anya had handed him: his lifeless granddaughter. He wiped away tears.

Megan and her baby were the first patients Anya had ever lost. When doctors lose a patient, they're expected to console the family, support them in their bereavement … be strong. Yet, she felt she wasn't capable of objectivity. Anya had grown attached to Megan. With not one word exchanged, they'd forged a bond. And the baby … the excitement of watching her heart gallop on ultrasounds, her hands and feet swim in the amniotic sea, sucking her thumb, huddled safely in the womb—how could she not have cared?

"Wrongful deaths. This is what these are," Tanner said, his eyes wandering between Megan and the baby in his arms. "A child and a grandchild shouldn't die before their elders."

Wrongful deaths. The legal term malpractice lawyers loved to use and doctors dreaded to hear. *He's blaming me for their deaths. And he's right. When I'd agreed to take Megan on as a patient, I made an obligation. To her father. And to her muted mind.*

"I'm sorry I failed you," Anya said

"Please don't blame yourself. I wouldn't have had anyone else take care of them. Megan and her baby were privileged to have had you as their doctor."

CHAPTER 80

▼

Anya sank into the old leather chair at the doctor's lounge on Labor and Delivery. Her scrub pants were soaked with Megan's blood.

Megan's blood, mixed with her baby's.

Anya took the two test tubes from her pocket and examined them. They were filled with Megan's baby's cord blood, the only remaining evidence that could shed light on the baby's paternity.

She checked her BlackBerry and dialed a number.

"What are you doing calling me at five o'clock in the morning?" Cornelia Lynch's voice was fuzzy with sleep.

"Sorry."

"Call me back at nine in the office," Cornelia hung up.

She pressed re-dial. "I'm really sorry, Cornelia, but this can't wait," Anya said. "I have the Tanner baby's cord blood. Two full tubes. I want you to fingerprint it right away. It's urgent."

Her intensity got through. "Bring the tubes to Life Codes," Cornelia said.

"I'll meet you there."

CHAPTER 81

▼

*D*NA *would solve the mystery. Finally and decisively. But what was the point of finding out who the father was— posthumously?* Anya asked herself while driving back from Life Codes. What difference was it going to make? The answer could prove more harmful than helpful, inflict even more pain on Megan's bereaved parents.

Once again, she'd managed to pull an "Anya," she figured. If she hadn't taken the blood, Cornelia would've stayed asleep. The Tanners would've gone through their grieving process peacefully. But no. She had to take what was already a complicated situation and make it worse. Yes, she was talented that way.

DNA held the keys to both cases. In Megan's case, DNA fingerprinting was going to prove who the father was, and at the same time, clear all other suspects. And DNA evidence was needed to prove that after Nicholson's manipulations, the president and the First Lady could claim the embryos as theirs.

As she was driving to Life Codes, the First Lady's embryos were transported from the White House to Lincoln Hospital's embryo lab, where Anya had instructed her new embryologist, Raji Kumar, to proceed with a biopsy on each one.

Two huge worries competed for her attention. First, survival. Even in the best of hands, the delicate surgery to remove a few cells from an embryo might kill the embryo. Second, the test could be wrong. This was the first time paternity was determined not on a blood sample or DNA extracted from skin … hair … saliva—but on cells removed from an embryo! Even the most experienced eyes and the most sophisticated computer software could miss a single "typo" in the genetic code—a single extra letter added or one deleted.

As she hurried up the stairs, Anya realized how high the stakes had become. Her heart accelerated with every step she took. What if Nicholson had inserted a bad gene into the embryos? Muscular dystrophy? Huntington's? A cancer gene? If Nicholson had experimented with these embryos, there was no way to find out. Neither Cornelia, nor anyone else could help her, not if they didn't know what to look for. All she could do was check for ID. And pray.

Even if there was no error in ID-ing the embryos—not in her lab and not on Cornelia's end—nine months from now, the baby born to the president and the First Lady could have a major disease. A malformation. Malforma*tions*!

Baby Marshall! God! Was the tragedy recurring?

She almost ran to the lab, as if it would matter if she got there two seconds earlier. Two men in White House Secret Service uniforms blocked her way.

"Excuse me, Doctor. Where do you think you're going?"

"I'm Doctor Krim." She flashed her ID. "I need to get in—"

"Hold it." One of them blocked the entrance. "I need to see if you're on the list."

"I am. I need to get in fast."

"Cool it, lady. I only take orders from the president of the United States." He reached to his coat pocket and took out a piece of paper. "Let me see, now. And you are …"

"Doctor Krim. Doctor Anya Krim," she yelled.

"Yes, I have you here. You're all clear." He moved out of the way.

Anya unlocked the lab and entered.

CHAPTER 82

▼
————————————————

She found a note on her desk.

Dear Dr. Krim,

I finished my work. The biopsies went well. I personally brought the test tubes to the DNA lab. He will be working on it all night and have the results for us in 6–8 hours.

Sorry I couldn't wait for you, but my wife is working the night shift and I am the babysitter. Also please check your e-mail.

Good luck with everything,
Raji

Anya entered her username and password.

Dr. Krim,

In case you want to see the embryos yourself, I placed them on a single tray inside incubator number 7, door 3. The dishes are each marked JC and have the First Lady's last four ss digits. Last time I saw them they were all alive.

Good luck again,
Raji

The First Lady's embryos were probably safer this time around, mingling with embryos of ordinary taxpayers, Anya thought. She found the First Lady's embryos, carefully removed the tray, and took small, steady steps back to Raji's area.

There, she focused on the first dish. A beautiful, viable, day-five embryo lay in its center. The hole created for the biopsy must have already closed.

Anya took a deep breath. One dish at a time. All ten embryos were viable, each ready to swim into the womb, drop anchor, start a new life.

Thank God! They were all alive. After everything that they'd been through, that she'd been through, she should've been jumping up and down in joy. But celebration was premature. She had to suspend everything until she heard back from Cornelia.

CHAPTER 83

———————▼———————

Cornelia called Anya while she was still at the embryo lab. "I need you here ASAP. It's urgent. You got me into this mess. Now you better help me get out of it."

"Urgencies. Emergencies. You're turning into an expert," Dario said. He had offered to join her when she called to tell him the embryos were still alive.

Traffic was stop and go on Route 270. Anya turned to Dario. "There's one thing you haven't told me yet."

"Only one?" he grinned.

"You never told me who bailed me out." She could tell he was hesitant. "Pleaaase!"

Dario shrugged. "I guess there's little point in keeping it secret much longer. You were bailed out by Professor Feinberg."

Barely avoiding rear-ending the car in front of her, Anya slammed on the brakes. "Feinberg? Impossible!"

He raised his hand like a Boy Scout. "I swear to God."

Anya replayed her last meeting with Feinberg. She was surprised by his kindness then. This was overwhelming proof of his caring. "Why did he make you swear to secrecy."

"Anonymous almsgiving is a Jewish tradition. Giving is for the sake of giving, not for glorifying the giver. Also, he thought he'd lose his edge as your mentor if you thought he was a 'softy.'"

She had misread Feinberg all along. She remembered a saying he had quoted once during her residency training, when his criticism brought her to tears: "Spare the rod and spoil the child."

"Forget what I said in the past about him feeling threatened by you," Dario said. "I was wrong. Only when you got arrested did I find out how much this man adored you. He'd worried about you as if you were his daughter."

Ten minutes later, they stood with Cornelia in Life Codes' reading room. Anya stared at the four DNA fingerprints hanging on the computer screen.

"Why four?" she asked.

"I'll tell you as we go along," Cornelia said. "All you need to know for now is that the DNA on the extreme left, marked 1, is the baby's."

Anya studied the baby's DNA and then the other three color graphics. She was sure one of them was the senator's but had no idea who the other two were.

"What do you think?"

"They're all so similar," Anya said.

"Similar or identical?"

"Number 2 is similar, not identical."

"Agreed!" Cornelia exclaimed. "What about number 3?"

"Very close, again, but not identical. Number 2 is different from number 3. They share different parts of DNA with the baby and none with each other."

"Right. So what would you call numbers 2 and 3?"

"I'm waiting for you to tell me."

"No, I mean. How might 2 and 3 *relate* to number 1, the baby?"

"Parents?" asked Anya.

"Yes! Yes!" Cornelia cried, raising both fisted hands. "This is the genetic likeness we see when a mom and a dad have a *natural* child. Now, to Final Jeopardy—"

"For God's sake, give up the game."

"You were right on all fronts," said Cornelia. "Number 2 is Senator Nelson Tanner and number 3 is his wife, Mrs. Gladys Tanner."

"Then why does their DNA so closely resemble the baby's? They're the *grandparents*, not the *parents*, right? Unless—"

"Unless Tanner slept with his daughter and *is* indeed the baby's pa and not grandpa, right?"

"You'd still have to explain Mrs. Tanner's DNA," Anya said. "Why would *her* DNA be so close?"

"That's why the case is so confusing. It would've only made sense if Mrs. Tanner could produce sperm."

"Now, number 4," Anya said, her eyes wandering back and forth between the graphics. "Number 4 looks very much like the baby's."

Cornelia smiled. "What do you mean, very much?"

Anya studied the blot carefully. "It's identical to the baby's."

"Bingo!" Cornelia beamed. "Identical is right. So …"

"So number 4 is another DNA sample from the baby?"

"No. In fact, number 4 is a sample from Megan Tanner herself," Cornelia said.

Megan's blood.

"Now, do you see why this is the craziest paternity mystery I've ever had to crack? If this is Megan's blood, her DNA should be similar to her baby's, but not identical. The baby's DNA should be a mix between her mother *and* her father."

"Unless," said Anya.

"Unless there *is* no father, and that seems to be the case," Cornelia grew serious. "I'm sorry, but I just don't get it."

Anya did. "The evidence is staring right at you! The baby wasn't the result of incest between Tanner and his daughter. This baby had to have been cloned from Megan's DNA."

CHAPTER 84

▼

──────────────────────────────

"Cloned!

"Megan's baby—a clone? *Megan's* clone? How crazy is that?" Dario asked as they left Life Codes.

Anya estimated it would take a half hour to drive from Frederick, Maryland, to the Tanner's house in Alexandria. Enough time to digest the news. "I had never thought I'd see a human being successfully cloned," she marveled. "Not in *my* life time."

"Isn't cloning a human close to impossible?"

"Absolutely. You need to make an identical template of *3 billion* DNA base pairs—the letters that make up all the genes in our body—without making a single error. That's like typing a 3-billion letter document without a typo. Hard to believe. Yet the evidence was staring at us at Life Code. DNA always has the last word."

"I still remember," Dario said, "how many failed attempts at cloning sheep Ian Wilmut had to go through before he created Dolly. But if a sheep had a difficult personality, something wrong with its social skills, or ADHD, would anyone have noticed?"

Anya smiled. "The psychologist's take on cloning."

"What did you expect?" he grinned at her. "In a human, you're almost guaranteed that a spelling mistake will translate into a defect in the cloned human—either as a growing child or as an adult. By the way, didn't you just do an ultrasound on Megan's baby a few days ago?"

"Yes."

"And everything was perfect, right?"

"Perfect is a loaded word. What I was able to determine was that the baby had an intact brain, two eyes, a four-chambered heart, two lungs, two kidneys, a liver, a normal-looking GI tract, five digits on her hands and feet—"

"So, you could've predicted the child was going to be fine, right?"

"To a point." But *did* she know Megan's baby was going to turn out normal? How many genetic errors might go undetected by ultrasound? What about diseases that only show up later in life? Huntington's disease, myotonic dystrophy, neurofibromatosis, noonan, marfan, osteogenesis imperfecta; the list went on and on. Each could be the result of a single spelling error. And none would've been realized until after birth, in many cases long after birth.

Misspelled DNA!

The attack in the garage flashed through Anya's mind. Someone had sent these two men to get Megan's baby's blood. Why? What was so critical that they'd almost killed her for that? All of a sudden, she understood. Maybe … maybe the very same people who'd cloned the baby were looking for her blood to test for errors … and maybe … yes, maybe they found an error, perhaps more than one, enough for them to decide they had to make sure the baby would never come out alive.

The more she thought about it, the surer she became. But who was behind the attack on her?

She thought she knew.

CHAPTER 85

▼

"What do I tell Gladys Tanner?" Anya asked. They both sat in Anya's Saab in front of Tanners' house at the end of the cul-de-sac. "There are no other cars in the driveway. She must be alone."

"This has to be so tough for her," Dario said, "with the allegations of incest against the senator. I bet you even their close friends are afraid to show their faces."

"You think the senator's back?"

"No. They took him for another round of interrogation at the FBI. He called me just before we left D.C. and asked me to meet him at the house, so I guess he'll be here shortly."

"I had a premonition that nothing good was going to come from Cornelia's refingerprinting. I doubt the Tanners will find solace in how their granddaughter was conceived." Anya turned to face him. "I need your help. What could I tell her? 'I'm so sorry, ma'am, for your losses. And by the way, we just found out the baby was Megan's clone'?"

She let him draw her into his chest. "I think you should go in by yourself. Mrs. Tanner will appreciate it. And I know you'll find the right words. I'll join you as soon as Tanner shows up."

They hugged. Anya got out of the car and approached the door.

The butler greeted her and took her coat. Anya had to take a second look at the woman who stood behind him. She knew it was Gladys Tanner—radically changed. Gladys stood erect. She wore a simple black velvet skirt and jacket, a white orchid pinned onto its lapel. She had no makeup or jewelry.

She approached with open arms. "Thank you for coming, Doctor Krim," she said. "You don't know how much it means to me." The two women embraced.

They went into the living room and sat on the sofa. Their eyes connected.

"I never thanked you enough for having taken care of my daughter, Doctor."

"Please, call me Anya."

"Anya. I know how much you cared about Megan. And her baby. Too bad there was nothing you could do once she started deteriorating." *Did she know I wasn't at the bedside when Megan collapsed?* "It was all in the hands of God. You're just his emissary."

Gladys was being kind. And accepting. Anya wished she herself had learned to accept death as part of life. She wished she were a believer. Faith would have helped her through losing Megan and her baby as it did her mom. But even had she been religious, she doubted she'd ever feel like she was God's messenger.

"I'm glad you're the first one here," Gladys said. "I feel closer to her now." A tear erupted from the corner of her eye. "I loved Megan, more than anyone in the whole world," she went on. "More than myself."

"I know," Anya said.

"My husband managed to suggest he alone cared about my daughter. That he had the monopoly on Megan's love."

And even though I resented his attitude as chauvinistic and self-centered, unconsciously I still gave into it. "It's quite common that the parents compete for their child's love," Anya said. This wasn't just competition. It was a hostile takeover.

"I know. His focus on our daughter testified to how lifeless our marriage had been."

Gladys had more to say. "If Megan had occupied 90 percent of Nelson's attention, after the accident, it became 100 percent. You've seen her room at the hospital. The shrine. Fresh flowers. Reading her the headlines."

Tanner had made Megan's room off-limits to his wife. This wasn't only inconsiderate and selfish. They could have dealt with their loss together, instead of separate and alone, fighting each other over who'd loved Megan more. "Did you feel as if you'd been cheated?" Anya asked.

"His presence filled up every ounce of air surrounding her. And I was driven out. How I felt didn't matter. My love for Megan had no outlet."

Anya guessed that for the last two years, not once was Gladys able to sit down with her husband and share her emotions. How awful it must have been to have to deal with it alone. "You didn't think that she'd wake up from her coma, did you?" she asked.

"I'd done my own research. I listened to the doctors. I knew she wasn't going to wake up. But Nelson, he went on fantasizing. He thought that by refusing to accept reality he could will her brain cells to regenerate. And in the process of losing my daughter, I realized I was losing my husband as well. Megan, while she was still alive, was the glue that kept us together."

"Have you two gotten closer since the allegations against your husband?"

Anya regretted her question. She felt like she had crossed a line, abused their newly formed bond and invaded a private territory. But Gladys didn't seem to mind. Her eyes were dry now and her voice confident.

"The way things were going, I would be without a daughter *or* a husband. So, the only solution I had was to find a way to re-create this magical child."

No!

Nelson Tanner and Dario came into the room. Limping, Tanner made his way to the chair across from the two women and sank into it. His hair disheveled, slouched in his chair, the man looked broken.

"Please don't let us interrupt you," he said. There was no indication he'd heard what Gladys had just said.

"Are you okay, Nelson? Do you want something to drink?" Gladys asked.

"I'm fine," he sighed. "We're both fine. Just go on with what you were saying, please."

"I was about to tell Anya something I haven't told anyone before. Including you. It could be very disturbing. Maybe I should wait."

So, what Gladys had just said, "to re-create this magical child," wasn't fantasy, Anya thought.

"No, Gladys. Go on. Nothing could faze me at this point."

Gladys nervously played with her hair. "You remember when they launched the Megan Tanner Pavilion at Lincoln Hospital. You hosted the reception. I was upset that night. I went to the ladies' room, bawling. This young, gorgeous woman offered to help fix my mascara."

Someone I know? "Was she a hospital employee?" Anya asked.

"Caroline. She said she worked in the embryo lab."

My Caroline! Anya thought. All she could see was Caroline's floating head in the freezing canister.

"She was sweet to me. I hadn't been treated with such kindness in a very long time. So I opened up to her. I told her I was Megan's mom and that my husband was going to leave me."

Tanner remained quiet. Anya tried to shake the image of Caroline's head. "So she offered her help?" Anya asked.

Gladys nodded. "It took her a minute. And then she said she had an idea. She told me she knew someone who could clone Megan. That she could be impregnated with her clone, an exact genetic replica of my daughter."

Tanner didn't say a word, but his face clearly showed he was caught off guard.

"And you agreed to have Megan cloned?" she asked Gladys.

"It took a lot of convincing. I hung onto this option as a last resort. I met with Caroline several times. I read up on cloning. And then I thought, I have nothing to lose."

Anya's sympathy stopped right there. What was Gladys saying? She had nothing to lose, so she just went ahead and had her daughter cloned without telling her husband? "What happened next?" Anya asked.

"We made arrangements with Reprotech for Caroline to perform the procedure. Caroline took two tiny pieces of skin from Megan's belly button. She hand-delivered Megan's skin to Reprotech the same night."

My embryologist. At my hospital, goddammit! "She didn't remove any eggs?" she asked, feeling her blood boil. That would top it off, if Caroline did that on Anya's watch.

"No. No. They took eggs out of two Reprotech surrogates stimulated with fertility drugs, then transferred the DNA from Megan's skin cells into the eggs."

No wonder I could never figure Caroline out. She had a double life. "And Caroline drove back to D.C. with the embryos?"

"Yes. Of the almost fifty eggs we started out with, two embryos continued to grow. Now, the embryo transfer—that was much more of an operation. I helped Caroline spread my daughter's legs apart, even held the flashlight for her, as she injected the embryos into Megan's womb. I asked how sure she was that the baby would come out normal."

"And how did she answer?' Anya asked.

"She said something like, 'We've checked and double-checked for errors. Everything came out fine. I expect the baby to be normal, unless—" She never completed the sentence.

Unless. That was the word Anya had used with Dario.

Unless? Unless she wasn't the only one who'd realized that Megan's cloned baby would probably end up abnormal. The attack in the garage flashed through her brain once more. Her attackers had to be sent by Nicholson. He knew how precious that blood was, how much information could be gleamed from it. Who would've wanted it if not the person who'd cloned Megan? She could picture Cody running a check on the DNA of the baby's blood. And then what?

What if Cody found out there were spelling errors in the baby? What would have Nicholson done with that information? What if his Reprotech's poster child, born to the conservative U.S. Senate leader Nelson Tanner III's daughter, was going to come out damaged? He'd have to do something, something extreme. Anything to make sure the baby wasn't born alive. And what was the surest way? To slip something into Megan's IV so that the already comatose girl would drift into death—and take her unborn baby with her.

"Your daughter and her fetus have been murdered," Anya wanted to scream. "Killed in cold blood by the same person you hired to clone her."

"Yes, it was me who got Megan cloned," Gladys said. "Until now, Nelson had no knowledge of what I did. I didn't want him to know how she got pregnant. But now that we've lost both my daughter and her baby, I have nothing left to lose. At least I can save his honor." Gladys Tanner took a sip of water, very much at peace. "Nelson, forgive me for the heartache I've caused. I did it out of love."

CHAPTER 86

▼

As the Secret Service van that drove her approached the White House gates, every muscle in Anya's body got tighter.

Genetics had spoken. The verdict was clear. The embryos were a perfect match. She could slow her breathing and get ready to face the First Lady. Two embryos had normal chromosomes.

Normal.

Yes, but! But the embryos she was about to transfer were the result of embryo splitting. Human cloning. For the first time ever.

No wonder she was nervous. She took a deep breath and got out of the car. She was ready now.

The First Lady was ready, too.

The lights in the bedroom were dimmed.

Moki Cartwright, the "First Dog," lay down on the king-size bed next to his mistress. Janet was once again propped up on two pillows. President Robert Cartwright sat at his wife's bedside, holding her hand.

You better not screw up.

Nervousness returned. Anya knew what she had to do was to perform the embryo transfer flawlessly. She had to stay connected to her core.

It was time. She exposed the First Lady's pubic area, gently inserted the speculum, and started to clean the cervix with sterile wet swabs.

Anya unhooked the door of the mobile incubator, removed the top of the petri dish, and with a catheter, pulled a tiny droplet of fluid followed by an air bubble. She sank her catheter tip in the water again and fished out the two embryos. Examining the catheter against the light, the two air bubbles flanking the middle droplet were safety buttresses against an accidental spill.

The president put on some music. "All is fair in love," boomed Stevie Wonder's voice into the quiet room.

Anya inserted the catheter through the cervix with ease and pressed the plunger of the syringe.

Please God, after all that they've been through, make it work.

Epilogue

Anya walked into the alcove off the East Wing bedroom. The First Lady, her back military-straight with tension, sat on the exam table in a patient gown, her fists clenched on her knees. Her face was bloodless. When she saw Anya, she forced a smile.

Silence.

The First Lady expects bad news.

Since she called her patient with the news of the positive pregnancy test, Anya kept a balance between encouragement and restraint. "Looks good so far," she said; the repeat blood tests indicated the appropriate rise. But with every call she would add, "A word of caution: the numbers mean very little, unless we see a heartbeat at seven weeks."

Today was seven weeks.

The president came into the room and stood next to his wife, facing the ultrasound screen.

"Let's get right to it," Anya said. She turned the room lights off, leaving only the dim fluorescents on above the sink.

She heard the First Lady take a deep breath as she assumed the position, her feet in stirrups. Anya squirted sonographic jelly on the probe and gently inserted it.

The screen faced Anya, away from the Cartwrights' view. All that Anya could see at first were Janet's ovaries, abundant with fluid-filled cysts where eggs had previously nested. She found the uterus and turned her probe slightly to focus on the uterine cavity. Then she identified the pregnancy sac.

Anya magnified the picture to maximum and swung around the screen. Janet sat part way up. Robert took her hand.

"We have a heartbeat. It's viable," Anya said, using an arrow on the screen to point to the tiny beating heart.

Viable. This wasn't the time to warn Janet and Robert that even after a heartbeat was seen, there was still a risk of losing the pregnancy.

She took a measurement. "The baby is 1 centimeter long. Normal for seven weeks."

Normal. She knew they had to hear that. And true, there was nothing to indicate at this point that the pregnancy wasn't going to be fine. Yet Anya knew she'd be worried if the baby was going to progress normally for the rest of the pregnancy and even after the baby was born.

Genetics was fickle.

"Congratulations," she said to the First Couple, who hugged each other over the exam table. Janet's tears wet Robert's light blue dress shirt.

She turned to Anya. "Thank you for sticking with me, for not giving up on me even when your career was on the line. And your life."

Robert grinned. "This will be only the second time in American history that a baby is born at the White House," he said.

Janet turned to her husband. "Right. Except First Lady Frances Cleveland was only twenty-nine when she delivered Esther. I'll be forty-three when I give birth to my first—and last—child."

Dario opened the door and pulled her into his chest. She squeezed him tightly, closed her eyes, and relaxed. She was back. He was back. Finally. She didn't want to move. Then she opened her eyes and looked up at the chiseled cheekbones. The thick lips parted in a beautiful smile. She reached up to them. Her thin lips got lost in his.

"I need to take a shower," she said.

"There's a fresh towel in the bathroom," he said, releasing her slowly from his embrace. "I'll get the wine ready."

Anya stepped out of her clothes the way she did as a teenager, all in one, underpants wrapped up with her pants and pantyhose, her bra lost somewhere in her inside-out top. She left her clothes on the floor and stepped into the shower.

Slow down. He'll still be there when you come out.

She rubbed liquid soap against her body. Then she shampooed her hair. When she stepped back under the shower, she closed her eyes, letting the water wash off the soap from her entire body, head to toe. The stream massaged her aching muscles.

Anya opened her eyes and looked at the shower floor. Everything she'd been through felt washed off. All she could think of was the man waiting for her.

She turned off the shower and stepped out, drying herself in the towel. She used a hand towel to wipe the steamed mirror.

Not bad, not bad at all, thought the world's worst self-critic, looking at herself in the mirror. Her belly was flat. She had hardly eaten during the last week. Any baby fat she might have had was gone.

She put on his bathrobe.

Dario waited for her at his bedroom door, holding two glasses of wine. The only lights in the room came from scented candles he'd lit around the bed. A Chopin nocturne played in the background.

He gave her a glass. They crossed arms and sipped. Then they both put down the wine glasses and kissed.

You're ready, her body signaled within the bathrobe. Am I too ready? Is this too early?

Stop worrying. Relax. There's no such thing as being too ready.

I want to give him everything I have.

When their lovemaking was over, Anya closed her eyes. She wrapped herself around the man who made her so happy.

"Thank you," she said.

"I love it when girls thank me after sex."

"You know what I mean. Thank you for being my friend *and* my lover."

"My pleasure," he said.

9 781440 183874